Brenna Lyons

LAST CHANCE
FOR LOVE

Kegin Series #1

FIREBORN PUBLISHING

COPYRIGHT STATEMENT

Last Chance for Love
In Her Ladyship's Service
Graham: Training the Earth-Born Lord
Earth-Born Lord
© 2004/2008/2017 by Brenna Lyons
Print ISBN: 978-1-946004-83-3
Print Publication: March 2017

Cover Artist: Brenna Lyons
Photo Credit: 123rf
Editor: Kathryn Lively
Logo copyright © 2014 by Fireborn Publishing and
Allison Cassatta
Licensed material is being used for illustrative
purposes only. Any person depicted in the licensed
material is a model.

DEDICATION

Shadoe, who kicked me into gear to get this submitted.

Nora, for saying the magic word "diary," which sparked Pyter's tale.

My husband, Rob, for giving me a love of science fiction that has never faded.

Rob and my kids, for putting up with my mood swings when my characters are noisy. (And, Mik was very noisy.)

Sean and Lisa, for teaching me how much fun it is to revisit old friends in my worlds, over and over again.

All my readers and my "pros," for telling me that "those with a gift are bound to serve." In other words, I am not allowed to give up.

GLOSSARY OF KEEN TERMS

USED IN THE BOOK

NOTE: Keen is a lyrical language, and minor changes in pitch and inflection denote a slightly different word in the language. The Keen calendar follows.

Ack- that, this

Ami tol.- I love you.

Assurances- the presentation of a bloodied blade to an injured woman, offering proof that the guilty party has faced his punishment at your hand

Auguren- a disinfectant used in the paste with Felgren to sterilize skin and equipment, poisonous when ingested

Ba- the band they wear for gateway travel

Ban- big

Ben- back

Braek- barbarian

Bree- baby

Burgel- a small blue flower that blooms late in winter/early in spring as the last of the snow recedes

Chidan- beloved

Choc- a soft brown color

Cimmeg- a heavy spice like cinnamon and vanilla mixed that strengthens the blood and aids in healing

Clo- clothing, garments

Cultay- curious

Diten- tradition

Dolgen- a yellow/orange scrubby plant which yields a powerful aphrodisiac; sucre sweet, it can be ingested in a tea; for the most powerful and immediate potency, it is mixed in oil and applied to genitalia

Duten- duty

Eir- an evergreen tree that gives a thick sugary sap which is edible and used for bottling fruits

Emi bead- a soft (consistency of amber) clear emerald green stone usually shaped into beads and used for decoration

Felgren- a light choc plant with antibiotic properties; can be ingested in a tea, used in a paste with Auguren to sterilize skin and equipment, and burned to create acidic fumes to ward off dangerous animals and enemies

Ferdil- Merciful

Fion- Keen queen of the gods; Goddess of love, balance, and mercy

Fion's Children/Daughters- The matriarchal priestess race wiped out by the Lengar in Ti 10-452

Frelang- freedom

Gan- get

Garigol- a powerful sedative and muscle relaxant derived from the leaves of the tree of the same name; causes confusion and lethargy followed by sleep in higher doses; Jaglin crave it and will attack to steal stores of it, so it is stored in air-tight containers

Ge- go

Geela- a cliff-diving, carrion eating bird with gray and black feathers

Gelgrin- a confection made of Eir sap, lizor berries, implin, and cream

Gi- servant

Gola- a plant that resembles mistletoe; its pink berries produce a poison that induces miscarriage and kills if left untreated; used to treat mother's sickness, it is treated with Triclum; a pernicious bush

Har- hurt

Hi- prince, Your/His Highness

Hir- princess, Your/Her Highness

Hol- help

Hottel- a horse-like creature (female pony-size and male Clydesdale size)

Hypocil- a metal pen-shaped device that injects medications through the dermis without an open site or risk of infection

Implin- a Kegin fruit akin to a Bosc pear; the core is a strong stimulant; the main ingredient in lover's repast

Iri- golden flowers that grow on vines as thick as a man's wrist; makes a soothing topical drug for use on rashes, minor burns and abrasions

Jaglin- large jaguar-like cats with thick black fur, dotted with gray spots as cubs

Kit- breeding cattle, which are used for food

Kittle- a small, furry domestic animal like a cross between a kitten and a rabbit

Laes- Lady, noblewoman

Lamor fish that tastes like salmon but has blue-tinged meat

Le- leave

Len- God of the underworld, vows broken, trickery, and havoc

Li- Lord, nobleman

Lio- little

Lizor- a fragrant purple flower whose berries make a calming tea, the stems make a powerful sedative to relax the mind and body, lizor is also used in forming a healing circle

Lover's Repast- the traditional cake of new lovers and new mothers; Cimmeg and Implin cakes with warmed sucre sap served on the side

Ma- my

Mae- me/I

Maiden Bride- a tradition whereby a male may have the night before the contract signing with a bride believed virginal; if she proves virginal, by the blood on the sheets, her husband owes her father 500 gold coin at signing; if not, her father owes her husband that amount

Mag- Keen king of the gods; God of justice, law, and vows unbroken

Magden- the race ruled by Ro Ti in the days before unification *Mot-* bomb

Magetra- Magistrate

Mu- too, much, many

Muklin- a plant akin to an Earth mushroom...small ones, the size of Portobello are stuffed and baked...larger ones are diced and fried or breaded and baked

Na- us, we

Ni- never, no

Nuglin- a noose-like hunting tool with a locking device, designed for capturing large carnivores like jaglin

Oct- out

Olum- a drug like an opiate that relaxes muscles, relieves pain, and suppresses the drive to vomit

Ort- order, request

Portrain- a boar-like creature found in the lower foothills of several mountain ranges

Regit Lus- (SEE Trial Moon)

Ri- king, Your/His Majesty

Rig- queen, Your/Her Majesty

Sa- safe

Schaen- a male harem that, in ancient times, was kept for the use of royal females; named for the Schen.

Schen the insatiable sex drive of a pregnant Keen woman

Schente- a harem of sterilized women kept for the use of royal men

Silin- silk-like fabric that most women's clothing and royal bedding are made from

Sivrah- the Keen equivalent to Romany gypsy; they are often migrant field hands, living in traveling family communities, a matriarchal society; they rarely interact with the Keen, save the landowners; they are mistrusted, most of all, because they have the strongest genetic base on Kegin but do not subscribe to the breeding measures or technology, in general

Stei- stop

Stride- a measure of distance; the distance the average war-buck can travel at a loping stride (half-speed) in the space of five minutes

Sucre- a thick sugar syrup from Eir trees

Ti- conqueror, king who takes his land by force

Tie- take

Trial Moon- an ancient custom by which a Keen man may demand a contract by a woman he has had sex with, if certain conditions are met

Triclum- the drug used to treat gola poison

Tu- there

Walla- a deep green wild herb that will act as a contraceptive when taken in a tea or used as a paste

Wariken- a large gray or deep choc furred beast which runs wild in packs in mountain areas; can be trained as a hunting beast or companion though always a bit wild

Zura- a gray bush; used in protection oils for blessing and healing circles; makes a tonic when mixed with Garigol that eases painful breathing

KEEN CALENDAR

A year on Kegin is roughly equivalent to an Earth year. Days are twenty Earth-hours long, but the year is separated into twelve months consisting of thirty-seven days each. I formatted the calendar as if the Keen year started in January, like an Earth year. In reality, the Keen year begins in Endl. The end of winter and beginning of spring is a time of rebirth, and so it is the start of the Keen New Year.

Pri- January
Ite- February
Endl- March
Wos- April
Zor- May
Fim- June
Jad- July
Caj- August
Wend- September
Abrin- October
Veril- November
Iric- December

SECTION ⊕NE:
Jole

Cross-Mate

CHAPTER ⊕NE

Caj 29ᵗʰ, Ri 25-2986

Jole Hi, prince of the Keen Republic and heir apparent, stared out across the hills surrounding his retreat home. It was the home of his childhood, the home he'd shared with his mother, until his father had taken him by virtue of their contract. Now, it would be the home of his marriage.

The lizors were in full bloom, and the fragrant purple flowers blanketed the landscape. Normally, Jole found that comforting. The flower had been his mother's favorite, and the finest cosmeticists had fashioned a scent for her from it. The scent was haunting, a distant memory of home and family, of the mother he hadn't seen for twenty years.

Today, Jole found the scent of lizors terrifying. It meant that summer was nearly over, his twenty-eighth summer.

The day he had trained for since birth had arrived. His bride would be brought to him soon. It was a day Jole had looked forward to since he was five, and the announcement had been made that she'd been born. It was a day he had dreaded since he was fifteen, and he'd learned how hopeless the match was.

He sighed. She'd hate him for taking her from her home and family, as each cross-mate had hated her husband. She would never share his bed. None of them had ever done so.

It had to be different this time, and not simply because she was to be *his* cross-mate. Bio-fertilization produced less viable embryos than true mating. The female children, typically thought to be the stronger sex, did not survive the Keen mechanical implantation process. A mate, who could have three or even five children over their years together, was unlikely to carry more than one child. The lack of mate-touch and the stress of their imprisonment made pregnancy a difficult process for them.

The project would fail and their civilization be lost if he couldn't convince his cross-mate to accept him. Worse, he would have to watch his mate suffer. If he could make her happy, any cost would be worth it.

His mother— "Jenneane," he whispered the Human name forbidden by Kell Ri.

Jenneane had taught him what she felt would help him most. Jole knew the language his mate would speak. He knew her culture and her pride. Knowing her son would face his own test with a cross-mate, Jenneane had educated him in all the ways Kell had failed with her.

Pyter bowed as he entered the study. "She will be here soon, Highness."

Jole nodded, gritting his teeth at the thought that Pyter was assigned to him again. The last thing he needed was one of his father's most loyal supporters underfoot now, but he had no choice in the matter.

"What can you tell me about her, Pyter?" The chief of security would have monopolized gateway time to study the new cross-mate, looking for potential problems in handling.

"She is a small woman." Pyter's tone was snide.

"It makes no difference. Kell's woman was only half his size and presented him with two sons."

"True," he conceded.

"What else?"

"She has hair like golden iri flowers and eyes like mature lizors."

Jole smiled. He had always wanted a cross-mate with eyes that were undeniably not the eyes of a Keen woman. "Perfect. Have you done what I ordered?"

"Yes, Highness. This has never been tried before. The men are not happy. It balks all the traditions."

"I know. Perhaps that is why we have always failed."

Pyter shook his head. "We fail, because they are barbarians. We had no choice but to seed among them, to use their strengths. Perhaps if we took them younger and raised them here—"

"Enough! You will never refer to my cross-mate as a barbarian." Jole relaxed the tension in his jaw.

They weren't barbarians. They had a fine culture, not as old or advanced as that of Kegin, but it was culture. Despite what Pyter had taught him at his father's command, Jole knew they had culture.

Moreover... "And you know full well that the laws of sanction do not allow for taking children, even children of our seed, before their twentieth year. Be mindful, Pyter. Such talk is treason."

He bowed, his cheeks a vivid red at the reminder. "Many pardons, Highness." A red light blinked on his belt. "It is time."

Jole nodded and followed Pyter to the gateway chamber. The technicians were busy pulling boxes away from the gateway. The crew chief bowed deeply, and Jole waved to him to continue with his work.

He looked at the boxes in amazement. The most prized possessions of his cross-mate were being hastily passed through the gateway.

It had never been done this way before. Cross-mates were typically presented to their husbands with no possessions but the clothes on their bodies. Thus, they'd failed, again and again.

The women faced exile. Exile with nothing of their former lives was cruel. Even if Kell Ri was right and she was a barbarian, the possessions were her own.

A yellow light blinked on over the gateway, and several boxes came through in the hands of soldiers. Jole prayed they hadn't missed any of her most prized possessions. What was left now could not be retrieved later.

A woman's scream echoed through the gateway.

Pyter restrained him as Jole surged toward his mate. They had orders. They were not to harm her. Jole hadn't wanted her to be traumatized this way. Pyter tightened his hold at her second scream.

"No! Let me go, you bastard." Her voice warbled through the gateway, taking on a musical quality, despite her anger.

Jole ached to take away her pain and fear. No wonder they hated their husbands.

"Still, Highness," Pyter breathed. "She'll be in your arms in a moment."

Jole nodded, his gaze riveted to the gateway.

A soldier stepped through with one final box. His cheek was an angry red, where he had been struck with formidable force.

Jole stilled in amazement. *My cross-mate did that?*

The moments ticked away. A third scream ripped through the room...then silence.

The captain stepped through, just as the light turned green. He marched to Jole with the woman cradled in his arms and offered her to her husband. The captain didn't look at her. She wasn't his to gaze upon. It was an honor for him to be allowed to touch her at all.

Jole stroked at her cheek with shaking fingers. This was his cross-mate, the woman he had waited twenty-three years for.

He furrowed his brow. She was still and silent in the captain's arms. "What have you done to her?" Jole demanded.

The captain blanched, sweat breaking out on his upper lip. "She fought the band like a jaglin, Highness. It was necessary to render her unconscious. It was the only way to—"

Jole silenced him with a glare, fighting the urge to strike him. If he did, the captain might drop his mate. Instead, he took her from the man's arms. "If she has been harmed, in any way, it means your life."

The captain bowed and moved away.

Jole carried her to her room while Pyter gave commands to relocate the gateway.

That would be Pyter's greatest fear, that she would try to escape with no knowledge of how the gateway worked or its limitations. It would mean her death, a very painful way to die, at that.

He laid her on the bed he'd had prepared for her. Jole pulled the quilt over her bare legs to her hips then touched her cheek again.

Her lizor eyes were closed to him, but he stroked her iri gold hair, a cap of curls the length of his own. She was soft. Her skin and hair were like silin, like the sheets and dresses prepared for her.

Jole switched to his long-disused English, a language he'd ordered Pyter to practice with him in preparation for this day. He'd muttered to himself for more than a year, making translations of everything he thought and uttered in Keen, even checking the electronic scans of Earth media when his vid-like memory of his mother's voice and language failed him.

His mate deserved at least a few people who could understand her; she deserved the answers his mother hadn't been given. He'd made a decision to speak only her language in her presence, unless he had a reason to speak Keen...and then he would explain it to her. It was better that way; it was the best he could do for her.

"I am sorry, love. It was not supposed to be this way. I wanted to explain to you. I wanted to be there for you when you came through the gateway. I will do my best to make you happy. You have my vow."

Pyter cleared his throat. "Highness, the men are ready to arrange her possessions."

Jole furrowed his brow, matching Pyter's Keen with his English, knowing the guard had learned it sometime before Jole's eighth birthday. "What is my mate's name, Pyter?"

"Highness, it is not usually—"

"Her name," he demanded.

"She is called Susan Braeden, Highness."

He smiled sadly. "Welcome to Kegin, Susan Braeden."

* * * *

August 24ᵗʰ, 2002

Susan rubbed her cheek on the silken material under her. She must have fallen asleep with her robe thrown over the bed. She tried to grab it and toss it away, but it seemed to be stuck on something.

Grumbling a curse, she opened her eyes to the sight of a man sitting cross-legged on the bed next to her. Susan scrambled away from him, pushing herself into the white wood of the headboard.

White? She scanned her eyes over her surroundings fearfully. Susan could pick out shelves of her books, pictures, belongings...but this wasn't her apartment.

Susan assessed the man on the bed. It was impossible to accurately guess his height while he was seated, but she guessed he was over six feet tall. He looked strong, muscular, like he would be a dangerous man in a fight. His eyes were a vibrant green, and his hair was a mass of black waves that brushed the middle of his neck in back. He made no move to touch her or even to speak to her.

"Where am I?" she ventured.

He sighed. "You are on Kegin. This is your new home, Susan Braeden." His voice was lyrical and lightly accented, as if he wasn't accustomed to speaking English.

"On? You mean in." *Obviously not accustomed to English.* "Where is Kegin?"

He lowered his eyes. "On," he corrected her. "Kegin is a world several galaxies from your Earth."

Susan stifled a laugh. The man was crazy.

She eased off the bed and backed toward the door, trying to make sense of what had happened to her through the pounding in her skull.

The man stood but made no effort to follow her, watching her progress with sad eyes. He wasn't trying to stop her. Something about that move was frightening. Did he think she had nowhere to go?

Her heart racing, Susan turned the handle and pulled the door open to run. She whirled around, ready to bolt, but two men in black uniforms blocked her way.

A memory of two men in similar uniforms attacking her in her bed flashed through her mind. A thunder roll of pain accompanied it, and Susan screamed in a mixture of fear and agony.

Strong arms encircled her, and cool fingers ran through her hair. "Shhh. I am sorry, love. I know you are hurt and confused. If you allow me, I will ease your pain."

Susan pushed him away, shaking and backing toward the armoire against the far wall. He didn't try to hold her when she pulled away, but he closed the door and followed her slowly, his hands up in a calming gesture.

She reached behind her for the rough walking stick she'd seen placed on top of the armoire. Her father's stick was heavy and formed of hard wood. Her hand closed around it, and she swung it in an arc aimed at his head.

The man could have stopped her. He didn't. Susan faltered in confusion, her swing losing its force as she met his eyes. She felt a momentary qualm. He could stop her. Why wasn't he stopping her? He *should* stop her.

A hand darted over her shoulder, and the weapon was ripped from her grip, a slight little twist forcing her fingers open.

Susan swung around to face the new arrival. He'd come from nowhere, a full head taller than the first man, with piercing black eyes, narrowed in fury. He stood over her with the walking stick in his hand, hefting it as if considering using it against her.

"Stei ack! Jole Hi! Ni har, Braek!"

Susan stumbled back. She had no idea what he'd said, but it wasn't friendly.

She startled as the first man's hands closed

9

on her shoulders, steadying her. His hands kneaded at her muscles, and Susan felt the strength in him. He was an important man, not a man to be crossed. The black-eyed man had crossed him.

"You will address Susan Braeden with respect and in her own language, Pyter. I only forgive your outburst, because she did not understand your insult."

"She would have killed you," Pyter protested in a thick accent.

"No. She would not. She pulled back. I would have had little more damage than the soldier she struck." He reached out and plucked the walking stick from Pyter's hands.

He guided Susan back to the bed. Once she was seated, he squatted to her eye level. He took her hand gently and placed the walking stick in it, closing her fist around the wood. "If this will make you feel at ease, take it."

Susan met his green eyes. He waited patiently for her answer. She looked at the stick in confusion. She'd tried to take his head off with it, and he handed it back. He was more concerned with her comfort than his safety?

She held the stick to her chest. "Thank you. It means..."

He nodded. "Anything that will put you at ease." He stared at her, waiting for something more but not pressuring her in any way.

"Who—" She shook her head, the lump in her throat and the pounding in her skull making it difficult to discuss anything with him.

The man nodded. "I am called Jole Hi."

"Joel Hi."

She knew her pronunciation wasn't perfect, but Jole looked pleased.

Pyter's eyes widened, and he moved his mouth as if to speak but didn't.

"You pronounce it like my mother did," Jole explained. "Thank you."

Susan nodded uncertainly.

"Jole will be fine. Only my people call me Hi."

"Susan."

He cocked his head at her in what she'd lay bets was confusion.

"Only people who don't know me call me Braeden. It's—tedious."

Jole laughed lightly. "Susan. You must be hungry. Will you come to morning meal?"

She blushed and smoothed her nightshirt over her thighs. "I need to dress."

Susan glanced at Jole. His eyes were darkened and intense. She sucked in her breath. Something about that look frightened her.

Jole nodded. He rose slowly and pushed open a door near the bed, most likely the door Pyter had come through. "You can wash here. If you like, I can have servants attend to you."

She shook her head. "I prefer to do it myself."

He nodded again and turned to open the armoire. Jole turned his head to Pyter, and Susan shuddered at the fury in his expression.

"Hir clo? Ma ort?" Jole demanded.

Pyter furrowed his brow. "Diten. Ni tie clo."

Jole looked skyward and sighed. "I am sorry, Susan. My people didn't understand. I wanted them to bring all your most precious

11

possessions. Our—our traditions say that you should come here with nothing but the clothes you wear. I have only the clothing made for you. My people brought none of yours."

Susan rubbed at the ache settling into her forehead. "I—anything is better than nothing, Joel."

He nodded and pulled out a silky purple dress. He laid it on the bed next to her. "We will leave while you dress. I will wait in the corridor to escort you to the meal."

Jole squatted before her again, staring at her as if he expected something. She nodded, blinking back tears. Susan needed answers, but her head ached so badly that she could barely think.

Jole's eyes narrowed. He touched her cheek, and she ducked away. Jole clasped her head between his hands, and his fingers found a lump on the back of her skull. Susan cried out in pain as he brushed over it, and the throbbing in her head intensified.

"Joel!" She pushed back her fear and tightened her grip on the walking stick. She didn't want to hurt him.

He pulled her closer to him, cradling her face against his shoulder. Jole's voice rumbled out next to her ear. "Let me help you. Please, Susan."

His grip was suddenly gentle, almost non-existent. Jole started to massage her scalp in delicious little circles.

Susan was shocked by her reaction to him. The intimacy of his touch and his voice sent an ache for him curling down her body to her core.

She pushed at his chest weakly, more a caress over the hard muscles under her cheek than a serious attempt at escape.

His scent was a sharp, spicy musk that made her dizzy. Being in his arms was far more inviting than she was comfortable with. Susan relaxed against his body, reveling in his warmth surrounding her.

"Yes," she murmured.

She didn't know Jole. Susan didn't know where she was or how long he intended to keep her here. Still, she wanted him to help her. At the very least, she didn't want Jole to stop what he was doing. She gasped as his hands dropped slightly and he leaned around her, wrapping her further in his larger body.

His lips touched the lump. A shock wave not unlike the splash ice cold water washed over her. His mouth lingered, and his warmth seeped into her...followed by a wave of pleasure, traveling from the point of contact out to her tips of her fingers and toes.

His fingers massaged her scalp, under her hair and to her temples. Jole eased her head back and planted his lips on her forehead.

Susan groaned at the cold wash seeping through her, knowing that the warmth and pleasure would follow in its wake. When it came, she went weak and pliant in his hands. She brushed her leg against his hip, opening her knees to invite him closer, closing her eyes as he dropped to his knees, his hips settling between her thighs. Her fingers went slack, and the walking stick hit the rug with a dull thud.

His hands moved to the tense muscles of her neck and shoulders, and his lips followed.

Her entire body was pulsing for him. The alternating cold and hot fired her nerves and sent erotic visions of Jole pushing her knees further out and placing his lips on her wet, aching slit through her.

Susan opened her eyes as Jole pulled back.

His eyes had darkened to a Hunter green ring around dilated pupils. His breathing was ragged, and his hand shook against her cheek. His lips hovered inches above hers. Susan licked her dry upper lip, and he locked on the movement.

The sexual tension between them seemed to thicken into a cloud she could smell and taste. Susan inhaled it, greedy for more.

Jole wanted her. The thought thrilled her far more than she would have liked. She wanted his lips to explore all of her. She wanted to feel the press of his body.

Jole nodded. "Is the pain less?" he asked quietly.

"Yes. Yes, it is. Thank you."

"I would gladly take away all your pain. I will take as much as you let me. Remember that."

She nodded, still trapped in the power of his gaze.

He smiled and pushed away from her, leaving a chill at her chest, where his nearness had been warming her moments before.

"Dress for the meal. We will discuss all of this once you have eaten." Jole stood and walked to the door with Pyter at his back. As the door closed, he smiled at her.

Susan stared at the closed door in confusion. She took several deep breaths, missing his scent already.

Her mind cleared slowly, and she tried to piece together what had happened to her. Her cheeks flooded with heat at the memory of her reactions.

She would have had sex with him if he'd asked. Given a few more minutes, she would've asked to have sex with him. She still wanted him.

Susan fisted her hands and pressed them against the ache still blooming inside her. What was wrong with her?

CHAPTER TWO

Pyter shook his head angrily. He switched back to Keen for his rebuke. "She would have taken you," he groused. "Why didn't you consummate?"

Jole sighed. "She was confused, in pain. Susan would regret the decision when she came to her senses. I have no doubts that she is, even now, embarrassed by her reaction to me. I will not take her that way, Pyter. When I take her, she will be willing."

"She *was* willing," he argued from between clenched teeth.

"Not in her heart. Not yet. There will be no regrets when I lay claim to her. She doesn't even know what's happened yet."

"You realize that may turn her from you."

"All the worse, if I had taken her that way. I want her to know the depth of my feelings for her, Pyter. She will know it."

"As you wish, Highness. It's just—"

"I will not fail. I cannot fail."

Pyter nodded and bowed his head. They stood in silence and waited for the lady's arrival.

The door opened behind them, and Susan stepped into the corridor. Her golden curls were tamed into a cap around her head and brushed against her neck. Jole longed to touch them again. Her deep purple eyes were made brighter by the dress he'd chosen for her and the blush that seemed to cover her entire body, releasing more of her maddening scent.

She glanced at him shyly, trying to pull the neckline of the dress closer over the cleavage it was cut to showcase for him. Jole surveyed the outfit, his breathing going labored in response. The dress was cut low between her breasts, and cap sleeves covered her upper arms. The skirt ended at the top of her knees, covering more than her sleeping garment had but not by much. Her long legs ended in bare feet now that she had removed the little socks she'd worn to bed.

Jole took her hand and kissed it, placing it on his arm. Susan seemed unsure, but a glance at Pyter convinced her that accepting his company might be a good idea.

It wasn't that Pyter was issuing any silent threats. Rather he stared straight ahead, his stance rigid. It was not his place to look at Susan unless he was being addressed directly by her. Pyter was not one to balk at the traditions.

His face was a mask of harsh lines. Jole could barely remember a time when Pyter smiled. There were hazy half-remembrances from his childhood with Jenneane, but over the years, Jole had ceased to question whether the images were real or a portion of a dream.

Pyter led the way down the hall toward the main stairs, acting as Susan's personal guard until another was assigned.

Jole squeezed Susan's hand. "You look stunning," he assured her.

"I couldn't find shoes." Her voice was uncertain.

"The leatherworker has been sent for. Boots

are more difficult to fit than clothing."

"And underwear?" Her blush deepened.

Pyter grumbled a curse in Keen. "You won't be needing such things," he informed her in English.

All color drained from Susan's face. She glanced at Pyter fearfully and started to pull her hand from Jole's arm.

Jole placed his hand over hers again. "I will send for the clothier immediately. Anything within her power to make is yours."

Susan nodded and squeezed his arm. She looked to Pyter and sank closer to Jole's side. "Thank you again," she whispered to him.

"If such a simple thing will put you at ease, it is yours."

Susan stepped down onto the polished stone stairs. "I take it going home is out of the question." Her voice was surprisingly calm.

Jole sighed. "We have only a brief period of alignment. It is not possible."

She looked away, her gaze settling on the portrait of Fion mounted on a war-buck that hung in the entry hall. "Then I'm trapped here."

"In time, I hope you will not see it that way. I promise we will discuss this later. For now, will you eat please?"

"Yes. I'll eat."

Susan ate with a fervor that made Jole wonder at her social standing in her own world. She was beyond trim. Susan was what Jole would classify as thin. She would have to gain weight before she carried a child.

At the end of the meal, she met with the

leatherworker, a slight man who kept his eyes respectfully down as he fit her for the boots he would deliver at the end of the week.

Back at her room, Jole dismissed Pyter and closed the door behind them.

Susan looked up from her seat at the edge of the mattress, staring at the door, swallowing some strong emotion, most likely fear. "Why did you send him away?"

"Do you prefer Pyter's company?"

Her emotions shifted so quickly, it was difficult to name a single one before it was gone. Jole could almost read the implications in her mind. Susan was afraid of Pyter, but she was also afraid to be alone with Jole.

He knelt before her, taking her hands in his. Susan pulled away, moving further onto the bed, curling her legs under her, nervous as a young hottel.

Jole sighed. "Susan, you must understand. I will never do anything against your will. I want you to be happy here, at ease."

Susan took a shaky breath. "Why am I here, Joel? What do you want from me?"

"You were born to be my bride."

She paled, swallowing with some difficulty.

"If you can come to love me, I should very much like to have you as my bride."

Her breathing went ragged and her eyes wide. "Why me?" Her voice shook.

Jole fought the urge to touch her again; fearing that Susan would bolt. "Your chemistry is right. You are the one for me."

"I don't—"

He put up a hand, stilling her questions. "Let me explain. The people of Kegin are an ancient race. Our recorded history dates back hundreds of thousands of years.

"We are at an evolutionary stasis. We have been for millennia. That is not a good thing. Our DNA has stopped mutating. It is no longer pliable. It fractures rather than change. As the degeneration becomes worse, our people face extinction.

"When the problem was discovered, scientists started a breeding program to save as many of the traits being lost as they could." He didn't add that most of that breeding was used to benefit the royal family. Jole was sure that would push Susan too far.

"When all means at our disposal failed to correct this, our ancestors tried something desperate. For centuries, we used the gateway to sample alien cultures, to find a seed race. We found humans.

"The human race is a close, but not perfect, match for us. In fact, few are close enough to attempt splicing, at all. Perhaps...one in a few thousand sampled. By chance, we lucked upon one in the first few dozen we sampled. The Council of Worlds gave their blessings for limited use of the gateway to save our people.

"We tried to involve the humans as little as possible. At first, we used the short window of true alignment every five years to collect DNA samples from humans rendered unconscious with a harmless drug. We spliced that DNA with our own mechanically. We even combined the

DNA of two human subjects with the idea of creating human babies raised on Kegin in our culture. The babies, both cross-bred and human mix, were implanted in Keen females."

She took a calming breath. "Why didn't you stick to it?"

"You are familiar with the problems your people face with rH or ABO incompatibility in pregnancy?"

Susan nodded. "When a child's blood contains proteins the mother's blood lacks, her blood attacks. It gets worse with every child carried."

Jole sighed. "That is human to human protein. Humans are not a perfect match for us, and the proteins in question are not even Keen proteins but an alien source. The babies are rejected, usually to the loss of both mother and child. A Keen woman cannot carry even a child of mixed race."

"So, you need me to carry your test tube babies?" Susan scowled at the thought, and her fist pressed to her stomach, though she didn't seem to consciously note it.

Jole blushed. "No. We need our own children. Implanted children are all male. Even though zygotes of both sexes form, only the males survive mechanical implantation."

Susan sucked in her breath and backed further away. "You've done this before."

"Not me. Please let me explain."

She nodded, but she was shaking.

He sighed. He was frightening her. Jole hadn't wanted to frighten her. *Of course, it*

21

frightens her. Any sane woman would be terrified by being yanked from her world and faced with this.

"When attempts to reproduce on Kegin failed, the scientists of the time used existing samples to splice new cross-bred zygotes. They used the gateway window to implant zygotes in carefully-chosen human women. The human women were able to carry the cross-bred babies with few problems."

"And?" she prodded.

"The offspring were male. The first males were brought through the gateway at maturity. They could naturally impregnate Keen women with only minor mechanical assistance, but the results were disastrous. We still lost every child and more than half the women who were implanted. It was impossible for a Keen woman to carry children for the cross-bred males."

"Kegin.....Keen women can't carry a child with any human protein at all?" Susan asked.

"No. They can't. But a cross-bred male is a close enough match to reproduce with human women...at times and produce both male and female children. But, there is a problem. Many of the traits necessary to a cross-mate are lost in the mating that produces the second generation female. The women are no longer close enough for direct reproduction with a Keen male. In order for those women to carry a child for us, it must be spliced and implanted."

"A male?" she guessed.

He nodded.

"What happened?"

Jole sighed. "We were at an impasse for a full generation or more, searching frantically for another seed race that we were unlikely to find, watching our seed children become more human with their matings. Then purely by chance, a first generation cross-bred male encountered at second-generation re-bred female and produced a third-generation re-bred female."

Susan nodded, her eyes momentarily far away. "And those third-generation females have the right chemistry to carry children for you?"

"Yes. Nearly all of them are Keen enough... Each window, we implanted more human women with first generation males, in close proximity to those already cross-bred, hoping more of them would find each other. You are a strong re-bred. You had a first generation father and a second generation mother." Jole cleared his throat. "You cannot reproduce with a human male and produce viable offspring."

"I can't reproduce at all," she offered bitterly. "I don't cycle. Not even drugs can correct that."

Jole smiled. "Not with a human male," he assured her. "But, the doctors on Earth wouldn't know that. Would they?"

Susan swallowed hard. Disbelief and shock warred in her face. "I'm not the first, am I?"

"To be brought through the gateway? No."

"Then why do you need me? What went wrong?"

"The women wouldn't accept their mates. Since a Keen man will not take a mate by force, many have not reproduced at all. Those that did reproduce only agreed to do so mechanically."

"The offspring were male." Susan grimaced.

He nodded. "Since they couldn't have children here, two agreed to pass through the gateway and try to mate with a third generation re-bred there."

She nodded, motioning him to continue.

Jole dropped his gaze in respect for those brave souls. "They died."

"What? Why?" Tears brimmed in her wide eyes.

"Raised on Kegin, they had not developed a resistance to Earth's natural radiation and contaminants. A person raised here cannot survive long there."

Susan shook her head. "So, you brought me here to mate with a Keen man."

"Not quite. I am a re-bred. My mother was a third generation Earth-born re-bred like you are. My father was a fourth generation Kegin-born re-bred. I'm more Keen than any re-bred ever produced but I'm not a pure Keen male any more than you are a pure human female."

Susan bit at her lower lip. "Your mother was brought here like I was?"

"My mother was taken from Earth much as you were, but she was brought here with nothing and treated—" He shook his head. "I'm not surprised she refused Kell Ri in her bed."

"You can never have children if I don't mate with you?"

"No. I can't. Not natural children. Not daughters."

"And you allow me leeway the others don't approve of, so I won't refuse you?"

Jole ran his fingers over her cheek. Susan jumped, but she didn't push him away.

"I do it, because it is the right thing to do. I will never force you. I will never treat you the way my mother was treated. I hope you can come to love me. If you cannot, there is no hope for me or for Kegin."

"I don't understand."

"Our daughters would be able to carry children for Keen men. They would have their choices of any men they wished for mate. The human ability to adapt and change would save our world, as they produced daughters and so on."

"If it's so important, why don't you just take what you need?"

He caressed her cheek again, heartened by the fact that she didn't startle to his touch. "We don't. It's...not our way."

If it were, the Council of Worlds would have disallowed their bid to seed from the beginning. Even the law of Conquest from the Warlord era had endangered their bid for this program, and the very thought of that practice was distasteful to the modern Keen male.

Susan's eyes pleaded silently, a sure sign that she was still unsettled. "It's my choice then?"

"Of course. If you refuse me, I must accept your decision." Jole prayed fervently that it would never come to that.

"How much time will you give me to decide?"

"As much as you need. I only ask that you get to know me while you decide."

Her eyes narrowed. "How?"

"Take meals with me. Talk to me. Take walks in the countryside with me." Jole held his breath for an agonizing moment then forced it out again. He could request all of that, but she could refuse him just as easily.

Her eyes lit. "Walks? I'm not a prisoner."

"No, you're not. As soon as you have boots, we can arrange time outdoors." He sobered. "But, you must go with me or with a guard. It is not safe for you alone."

Susan nodded. "I understand."

It was obvious that she didn't, but she was calmer than he'd hoped.

Jole touched her cheek, sorry that he had to leave her when he had made so much progress. "I must go now. I have to deal with the captain who brought you through the gateway."

She furrowed her brow. "Deal with him? Why?"

"He injured you." Jole stood and straightened his tunic.

"What will you do?"

"He— Such an offense means his life." Perhaps it was better to let her see what lengths he would go to for her. It might sway Susan toward him, if she understood what she meant to him.

Susan paled and grasped his wrist in shaking hands. "You can't."

He studied her expression, his head spinning. What was this reaction? Certainly nothing he'd anticipated. "What would you have me do?"

She stuttered out something he didn't catch. "He was acting on your orders."

"He was *ordered* not to harm you. You are my mate, my bride."

"Please Joel. Don't you have a lesser punishment? Demotion? Work? A like injury? You can't kill him." Her voice went shrill.

"He means that much to you?" The idea of the captain having her heart so effortlessly hurt. For a fleeting moment, he considered killing the soldier for that offense alone.

"Not him. Anyone." Susan shook her head, tears escaping her lizor eyes to make tracks down her face. "In the culture I was raised in, we prize human life. Being put to death is for heinous crimes. You cannot do this. I— I won't allow it, Joel." An edge not unlike the blue laser edge of his sword made that last cutting, an order....no doubt with some consequences, if he dared balk her.

Jole smiled. He didn't want to balk her. *And my people think humans are barbarians?* He squatted to her eye level again and cupped her cheek in his hand, wiping her tears away with his thumb. "Very well. Would demoting him to lieutenant and reassigning him to lesser duties suit you?"

Her grip on his wrist loosened. "Yes. That punishment would fit the crime."

"For your peace of mind, it will be done." He kissed her forehead, lingering at the feeling of her skin under his lips.

Susan closed her eyes, looking weary. "Thank you."

"Sleep now. I will come for you at midday meal."

She nodded and curled into a ball at the head of the bed.

Jole smiled as he pulled a quilt over her. He returned to the corridor and closed her door, nodding to the guards on his way past. Perhaps there was a chance for them after all.

He entered his study, his smile fading.

The captain knelt on the floor, stripped to his trousers and boots. His hands were shackled behind his back and his head was bowed. He waited for his death silently. No one would dare take the retribution from Jole's hands.

Pyter handed him the ceremonial sword, and Jole fingered the edge. He didn't switch the laser cauter on. Instead, he considered the prisoner.

"What is your name, captain?" he asked in Keen, knowing the Captain would have little or no knowledge of his mate's language.

He looked up with frightened eyes. "Bell, Highness."

"You injured my bride. For that, there must be punishment."

"I understand, Highness. My life is yours."

Jole sat the sword on his desk. "And if I choose not to end it? What would you give me in return?"

Pyter clamped a hand on his shoulder and whispered a harsh warning in Jole's ear. "Highness, you cannot do this. He has injured a royal cross-mate."

"Stand down, Pyter. Bell, what would you give me in return, if I spared your life?"

He shook his head. "My life is yours. Whatever you would have me do."

"Very well. You owe your continued existence to the sensibilities of my bride. It seems, in her culture, you would not be put to death for your crime. By her wish alone, you are now a lieutenant. Your duties are to my bride's safety. Any injury done her in your care will be repeated back on you. Do you accept this punishment, or would you rather the one I promised you last night?"

"I am at your service, Highness. I will give my life to protect your bride."

Jole nodded. *Bell will give his life, because he knows he lives on borrowed time won him by the woman he serves. There can be no stronger incentive than that.* Jole motioned to the soldiers standing guard. "Free him. Feed him, and get him his new uniform. I expect him at his post by this evening."

He left the room and headed to the library with a smile on his face. This was what his mother meant. She'd told him often about the sense of goodwill humans were capable of displaying. It felt wonderful to spare Bell's life, when he knew he had the power to end it. It felt even better to make Susan happy, to put her at ease.

Jenneane had made it a condition of her mechanical implantations that her first son would be raised by her to the age of eight. Those years were the happiest of Jole's life, a fact that angered Kell.

Mik had always been Kell's favorite. Five

years younger than Jole, Mik had been taken from Jenneane almost at birth to be raised in Kell's manner. It was no wonder that Mik and Jole rarely saw eye to eye. Mik would have killed Bell without a thought of Susan's distress.

CHAPTER THREE

Wend 16th, Ri 25-2986

Susan ran a hand down the front of the poet shirt that brushed her thighs, feeling the snug pants beneath through the thin material.

Jole's clothier was becoming quite adept at recreating the human fashions Susan sketched and described to her. Bessa tended to make everything skin tight, unless Susan made it very clear that it was supposed to hang loose, but with the give of the fabrics she used, even those clothes were butter soft and comfortable. Bessa had balked at what Susan wanted at first, but Jole had proven true to his word.

Susan smiled at the fine array of pants and shirts in the armoire. She wore the dresses Jole's people made for her when she had dinner with him, but dressing for dinner was more her treat to him...and to herself than a standing order of some sort. Jole had requested it, and Susan was happy to oblige.

Bessa made almost everything Susan asked for, everything that she had hoped for in clothing when she was still on Earth but could never hope to afford on her medical secretary salary, at least while she was still in college for her nursing degree. Jole was particularly taken with the knock-offs of Earth designer dresses Susan had requested, when she substituted them at dinner.

Bessa had even managed to fashion Earth-style underwear, though bras seemed beyond her understanding. Keen clothing was designed with bodices that did the job for them.

Maybe a halter top? That was a possibility to consider for the next time she spoke to the clothier.

Susan smiled. Jole had been wonderful. She had been on Kegin for three of their weeks, eight twenty-hour days. Though it was obvious that Jole wanted her desperately, he respected her need for time.

The morning the array of boots and shoes arrived, he'd taken her on her first tour of his estate. When Susan showed an interest in the flowers they called lizors, Jole had tucked one behind her ear. Fresh cuttings of them had graced her room and their table ever since.

Though she feared horses, Susan found that she loved her rides with Jole on hottels. The horse-like animals stood her chest height at the shoulder with humps at the shoulder and hip that formed a natural saddle. Their fur was as thick and long as the fur of the Persian cat she'd owned as a child. Her favorite was a white mare with brown markings named Chidan. To put her at ease, Jole often rode a mare instead of his war-buck, a male hottel that stood as tall as a Clydesdale.

Jole was as solicitous and kind as she could have ever hoped for in a husband. He spent every moment he could with her. When she asked for time alone, he obliged her. He taught her Keen games, and she taught him Earth games. He read the books they'd brought from her library and discussed American and

European literature with her. Jole wanted to know everything, every nuance of her life, her dreams, and her wishes. Then he slowly made as many as he could come true for her.

As the days passed, Susan found it more and more difficult to come up with reasons not to go to bed with Jole. He touched her often, light, loving touches that were far from sexual. He kissed her cheek or forehead whenever he left her, and every touch left her aching for more.

The only time they'd come close to more was when Susan rose to brush a kiss over his lips as they left the stables just days ago. Jole had stopped and met her eyes, lowering his face to nuzzle her lips. He hadn't pressed for more, and neither had she. Susan had wished that he would ask for more, but he simply brushed his lips over hers, again and again, his scent surrounding her, firing her nerves until she thought she would go crazy. He'd pulled back, flushed and smiling, to lead her back to the house.

There was only one reason Susan hadn't slept with Jole yet. When she did, there would be no birth control. Susan found it strange that she'd longed for the children she couldn't have without major medical interventions, since the doctors on Earth decided that she would never cycle, but she was skittish of the idea, now that the opportunity to have them had arisen and become a reality.

Still, she had seen Jole with the cook's baby. He would make a wonderful father, and he seemed to want children as much as she did. Her reasons for holding back were disappearing daily.

Susan glanced at the sun ascending over the hilltop and furrowed her brow. Jole was never this late. She headed for the door.

Lieutenant Bell would escort her to Jole if she asked. He'd ordered as much, told his servants and soldiers that he was always available, if she wanted to see him.

Susan was suddenly very anxious to see Jole, to invite more of the intimacy he kept burying.

Bell shot a nervous look around as she stepped into the corridor. His English was weak, and he struggled for words.

"Your room, Lady. Please. Hi.....father here."

"Kell Ri?"

He nodded. "Room, please, Lady."

Susan nodded and turned for the door. Jole didn't want his father near her. She didn't know how Jole's mother had been treated, but she knew Jole didn't want her treated the same way.

She clasped the door handle, turning it, deep in thought. Bell cried out a warning in Keen, and she turned, her heart pounding, looking for signs of danger.

The man was in front of her, pushing her back into her room and blocking everything but the span of his chest from her sight. Somewhere behind him, Bell kept shouting.

Why wasn't he doing something? She knew their laws. No man was to touch her, unless it was an emergency of some sort. No man was to look at her unless she was in direct conversation with him and only then by her invitation to meet her eyes. Why wasn't Bell enforcing that?

Susan ducked her head around the man, finding Bell's terrified face. "Bell," she screamed. She searched for the words she wanted in her limited Keen. "Bell, hol. Gan Joel!" *Please God, let that have been an order to get Jole for me.*

The man glared at Bell over his shoulder, as if he just realized that the soldier stood protesting behind him. "Gi, le na," he growled.

Susan backed off another step in shock. That much, she could translate. *Servant, leave us.*

"Ge o mae har, Gi. Ma ort."

What was that? Ma... That was my, I think.

Bell gave her a pained look and stalked off. Susan clamped her hand over her mouth in disbelief, trying to hold in a sob. He was supposed to protect her. Why was he leaving her with this madman?

The man swung the door shut and turned his hard eyes back to her. This wasn't Kell Ri. He was too young, younger than Jole, she was sure.

While she was still locked in shock and indecision, he moved. He clamped his hand around her chin, digging his fingertips in when she tried to pull away from him. He forced her chin up, meeting her eyes.

Susan shuddered at the cold regard in his black eyes. She was on her own with a man who was obviously crazy. Susan pulled back her fist and aimed for the solar plexus, praying the anatomy was roughly the same. The man grunted and released her, but he didn't go down as she'd hoped he would.

She wasted no time. Susan launched over the bed and pulled down the walking stick, but he had it locked in his hand between them before she could use it.

He grumbled what she assumed was a series of curses in Keen. He surveyed her outfit, a scowl turning his lips down further. "Lio Braek."

There was no translation she could make for that remark, though it sounded like a threat.

He cupped her breast and squeezed painfully. Susan tried to knock his hand away, but he pushed her back into the wall, using the walking stick they both held, his eyes fierce.

Susan ground her teeth. She reasoned her experience into the situation. Face, solar plexus, and instep had all failed her in the past. He'd see a neck shot coming. Susan brought her knee up into his groin as hard as she could.

He stiffened, his hand tightening as his eyes narrowed. Susan counted the seconds, praying that his stillness meant the move had been effective. If it hadn't, he was going to hurt her much worse. She could see the promise of that in his eyes. At six, he fell back, one hand still holding the walking stick while the other moved to cup his injured genitalia.

Susan pushed back on the stick, launching around him as he stumbled back, weaved forward again and landed on his knees on the carpet. She was three steps into the corridor when she ran headlong into a man's chest. She stifled a scream as she looked up at— *Jole!* Susan threw herself into his arms.

* * * *

Jole stood before his father, and Kell ranted. Overall, this was not a new scene for them to play out.

"You disappoint me, Jole."

That's news? "In what way, Father?"

"You have had your mate under your roof for three weeks. You've not mated or even seriously pursued mating with her. I've been told that you've passed over moments when she was willing to mate."

"She wasn't willing, Father. She was injured and confused. In time, I hope she will be truly willing."

"By plying her with gifts?" He scowled. "You let her dress like a man and treat her..."

Jole sighed. *I don't treat her like a barbarian. That was Kell's problem.* "Father, you failed with Jenneane." He used the forbidden name, watching Kell grimace in response. "She was left with nothing of herself. Had you ever talked to her, you might have learned how little it would have taken to convince her to accept you."

"Talk? In that guttural gibberish they call a language? You jest. She would never learn Keen for me. Why should I have learned her language?"

Because you dragged her from her home to live in your world. It was the least you could have done for her. "I did learn it from Jenneane. It was one of the few things you couldn't force her to sacrifice. They have law, poetry, art. They care for their fellows. Jenneane never learned more than a few precious words of Keen." *Enough to refuse you and little more.* "Susan is learning it. I heard her crooning to the cook's baby in our language yesterday."

Kell shook his head in disgust. "Why do you persist in calling those women by their Barbarian names?"

"Because they have them. They have identities they treasure."

"Barbarian trash that should be left on their polluted planet."

"I have high hopes for Susan. She has adjusted well, and I believe she will ultimately accept me as her mate."

"Your time is limited, Jole."

"In what way?"

"Mik has petitioned the Council. If she does not carry your child by mid-winter, Mik will have a chance to convince her to his bed."

Jole bit back pure fury. "No. He has his own—"

"The one who should have been his has died. It will be fifteen years before another bride matures and can be brought through the gateway."

"Susan is mine." *She will always be mine, and I will not give her up without a fight.*

"Then lay claim to her before the Council lets Mik take her from you."

Jole's protest was cut off by the sound of a scuffle outside the door. He heard a panicked man screaming his name. Jole pulled the door open to find Bell pinned to the floor by both of his father's guards.

"Your brother, Highness. Prince Mik is at the Princess's room."

Jole vaulted over the struggling men and raced for the stairs, leaving his father behind. He turned the corner into her corridor in time to see Susan shoot from her room. She was running blind, in a panic and heedless of her direction. Jole steadied her as she crashed into him. She looked up at him, and he saw her fear clearly. Susan fell into his arms with a sob. For a long moment, Jole simply held her.

He raised his head at a crash from her room. A scream of rage erupted and gained steam. Jole swept Susan to his back and drew his dagger as Mik stumbled into the corridor.

His brother was red-faced, and his eyes were hot in the promise of malice. Several locks of his black hair fell across his forehead, in contrast to his normal polished style. He advanced on Jole with his hand on the hilt of his weapon. "Stand aside, brother. I have unfinished business with that little barbarian."

Jole felt the heat rise in his cheeks. He was thankful Susan didn't know more Keen. "You will never call my bride that again. Susan is *my* bride, Mik."

A cold grin took over Mik's face. "Only for four more months. When you fail to tame her, she is mine." He ducked his head to the side as if trying to meet Susan's eyes.

Jole blocked whatever view Mik might have by shifting his arm.

"I'm pleased with my examination, though you permit her too many clothes. When she is mine, she will be naked in my bed."

"She will never be yours." *Even if I have to fight the Council troops for her.* "Leave my house, Mik."

His brother bowed his head with a leer that told of his plans for Susan if he had his chance. "As you wish, brother."

Mik walked back toward the main stairs, giving Jole's blade a wide berth, as Jole turned to keep himself between his bride and his brother. When he disappeared from sight, Jole sheathed his dagger and gathered Susan into his arms.

He led her to her room and settled her on the bed, cringing at her cold skin and shaking. The stick she'd swung at him the first day lay broken on the floor. Susan was crying, and she had her arms crossed over her chest. Her blouse was misshapen, as if—

Jole shouted a curse after his brother and slammed the door. He turned back to Susan, at a loss to undo the damage Mik had undoubtedly inflicted on her. Physically, he could heal her, but these wounds were not entirely physical. He could see angry red marks rising on her face. Her chest was probably worse.

He sank to his knees before her and reverted to English. "I'm sorry. He'll never come near you again, if I live to stop him."

Susan nodded. "Who was he? Why did Bell let him...?"

Jole grimaced. "I'm ashamed to admit that he's my brother."

40

"Delightful family you have there, Joel." She was trying to make light of the attack, but she was failing miserably. "What did I do to deserve this?"

"He wants you for himself."

"No. I won't. I can't. Joel, you can't let him." She held to his tunic, and her eyes pleaded with him.

Jole wiped the tears from her cheek. "I—"

He couldn't promise her that now. If Jole failed to win her heart soon, Mik would have leave to manhandle her again. Jole could fight, but there was little chance that he would win against the Council troops, Mik's troops, *and* his father's. Jole had no doubts that Kell would side with Mik.

Susan shook her head. "My choice, Joel. You told me I had a choice."

"Mik cares little for your choice." He fingered her ruined blouse. "You can see how little he cares." Would that sway the Council? Jole wasn't sure that it would.

"There has to be a way."

Jole closed his eyes. If he pushed her, he would lose her, because she would not submit. If he didn't push her, he would lose her, because she wouldn't submit in time.

"Joel? There has to be. Please, tell me there is," she whispered, her voice tear-choked.

"There is." *Fion, forgive me. I don't want to do this.*

"Tell me. Please. Whatever it is, it has to be better than Mik."

He met her eyes. "If you carry my child

41

before mid-winter, he cannot touch you."

Susan stared at him in shock. "If I—"

"My natural child," he qualified. "I have to claim you as true mate or lose you. I don't want to do this to you, Susan."

She took a deep breath, rose and started pacing the room, chewing on the edge of her thumb lightly. "If we're expecting, he can't ever touch me again?"

"According to what Kell told me."

He held his breath. Susan didn't answer for several long moments. She paced the length of her room, over and over. Jole prayed she wasn't considering running. If he allowed that, the Council would give her to Mik. If he didn't, she'd hate him.

She stopped and sank to the bed in front of him again, nodding. "All right then."

Jole stared, at a loss. "I don't understand."

Susan leaned toward him and brushed her lips over his. "How long is it until mid-winter?"

He found it hard to think. "Four months. Susan, you're not—"

She silenced him with another kiss, a more purposeful kiss that scattered his thoughts. "I was considering it already, but I won't deny that your brother was the deciding vote. I was actually coming to you when he—"

Jole cupped her head, laying little tasting kisses on her lips to keep her from saying what Mik did. Susan reacted with unrestrained passion, her mouth tangling with his. His cock ached as it did every time they touched.

He pulled back slowly. "I don't want you to

come to me just to avoid Mik. If I have to find another way—"

"You do want me, don't you?" Her hands brushed over his chest and her mouth met his urgently.

He groaned into her mouth then parted from her. "Yes." Jole moved his mouth to the rising bruises on her face, healing them with his magic. *Oh, how I want you.*

Susan threw her head back, baring her throat to him, holding his head to her for his healing. Jole hardened as she wrapped her legs around him and drew him closer. He explored her throat and face, laying kisses between bursts of healing, drawing in lungfuls of her aphrodisiac musk.

She drew his hand to her abdomen. "You want a baby?"

"Yes." He loosened the tie on her blouse. "Do you?"

"I always have," she assured him.

"Are you sure?" He wanted a true mating, a mating for life. If she felt pressured in any way, Susan might not give him that.

Susan nodded, her eyes glittering. She loosened his belt and dropped it to the floor. "We only have four months, Joel. Let's not waste time."

"And after you carry my child and you're safe from Mik?"

She raised her arms to help him, as he peeled her blouse off over her head. Jole closed his eyes to the sight of the damage Mik had done to her. He ran his lips over the bruises, and she arched to him, asking mutely for his healing...or perhaps for more.

Jole lifted her and settled her on her back on the bed. "After you carry my child?" he repeated. Would she be a bride to him after that? Would she only give him a child to escape Mik and then lock herself away from him? She could refuse more.

Susan darkened, and the blush ran down her chest. "Will you want me for more, Joel?"

"As much as you'll grant me." He healed another of the bruises Mik left.

She ran her fingers through his hair and cradled his head to her breast. "Will your lips always feel this good on my body?" she whispered.

Jole furrowed his brow. "My healing is pleasurable to you?"

"Very."

He smiled. The healing magic had never been enjoyed before. He suspected it had something to do with the human genes in her. "Were you excited by it when I healed you your first morning here?" It would certainly explain her reaction to him, if she had.

Susan's lilting little laugh surrounded him. "Enough that I considered bumping my knee or something equally ridiculous to get you to do it again."

"In that case—" Jole closed his mouth over one rosy nipple and concentrated on his healing, though there was no bruise to heal.

Her body bowed up beneath him. Her fingers brushed the back of his neck and kneaded the muscles of his shoulders. Her body wept musk from her pleasure points, a potent call that made him dizzy in need.

Jole moved to her other breast, running his tongue around the rigid peak and teasing her with more. "Tell me what it feels like for you," he requested. He closed his mouth on the peek, taunting her.

She shuddered, and a mew of delight escaped her lips. "Cold. A single moment of ice followed by the heat of your mouth and a pulse of energy."

He concentrated his healing again, and she cried out, her hands tightening on his shoulders. Susan tried to draw him closer, but Jole held back, enjoying this form of love play and the effect it had on her.

"What kind of energy?" he prodded.

Susan reached down and caressed the length of him through his trousers. Jole panted, hardening further beneath her fingers. He had never climaxed without making it into a woman before, but Susan had him close to that.

"That kind," she whispered, pulling the buttons on his trousers from their holes.

Her hand closed around him, and Jole bent to her waiting nipple. His hands were busy undoing her trousers while his mouth nuzzled at her breast. Susan stroked him slowly, keeping time with his attentions. Jole dragged off his tunic, knowing that he would disgrace himself by spending in her hand, if he didn't do something else very soon.

She lost contact with him as he moved to

pull her boots and trousers off, but she contented herself with sitting up to massage his shoulders. Positioned to do that, she ran her lips over his chest muscles.

Jole's breathing was harsh in his own ears, and his blood rushed like river rapids in his veins, loud and fast. His schente, the women assigned to please him over the years, sterilized for their own protection, had never shown him such intimacy. They'd taught him about pleasing a woman when he'd asked, eager to keep their positions in the royal household by making him happy. But they were there to fulfill his desires. They were there to be used, as he cared to use them.

He smiled. "Will your lips always feel this wonderful on my body?"

Susan smiled up at him, a playful smile not unlike the one he'd seen when she rolled in the lizor flowers. Oh, how he'd wanted to take her in their fragrant depths.

"They can feel better," she offered.

Jole worked at deciphering that, to no avail. "In what way?"

She motioned for him to kneel further up and pulled his trousers down to his knees. Jole lifted one leg, sure that she wanted to remove them.

He dropped his weight back down, almost losing his balance as her lips closed around the head of him and drew his cock deep into her mouth. Jole sank back to his heels, and Susan followed him down.

Jole groaned and settled one hand on her

shoulder and the other in her hair. She started moving his length in and out. He watched, spellbound, as he disappeared into the heat of her and reappeared, over and over. Never had one of those provided for him taken such care in pleasuring him.

He wondered if this exquisite torture was something only humans knew of or if the Keen women did this for men they cared for. Jole had never deluded himself that any of those women cared for him, though more than a few enjoyed sex with him.

His body tensed, so close to release that Jole could barely refrain from giving in to the urge to complete in the depths she offered him. He couldn't let her continue. He was too close to allow any more.

"Susan, if you want to be carrying my child, you can't do this," he breathed, half-hoping that she would ignore his warning and take him over. What he wouldn't give to know what such a climax felt like.

She released him slowly, blushing as she flicked a glance at his eyes. "You're right. I got...carried away."

He lifted her to her knees before him, pulling her to his aching body. "You would have sought completion for me?" he asked, stunned that it had been her intent, that she wasn't ignorant to what she'd been doing to him.

Her cheeks darkened. "You don't? On Kegin, you don't?"

"Not that I know of, but once we know you're carrying my child, would you do that for me?"

Susan met his eyes. "Yes. If you'd like to experience it, I'd like to do that for you."

If I'd like to? Gods, I would give anything to experience that. "Susan." His voice was rough in his need. "We have time to explore every possibility you know or I do. But for now, I have to feel you around me."

Her fingertips moved down his chest to circle the hair at the base of his erection. He pulsed in response, and her eyes darkened as she watched it.

"Why are you waiting?" She didn't smile as she said it.

Jole lifted her gently, cupping his hands under her thighs and planting himself just inside her. "Tell me, Susan." He wouldn't take her, until she asked him. That was their way, their tradition. He shook in his restraint, anticipating her answer.

Susan settled her hands on his shoulders. She looked between their bodies to where they were loosely joined. "Make love to me, Joel."

Jole shivered, glad that Susan had never changed the way she said his name after finding out that he liked it. The long-unused Earth pronunciation in Susan's sex-charged voice made him crazy in need for her. His name rolled off her tongue like a caress direct to the base of his raging erection.

He lowered her over him slowly, filling her as her body stretched to accommodate him.

His heart ached as he did. Susan had asked him to make love to her. Not to mate or to have sex with her or even to give her a child. *Make love to me, Joel.* He raised his hips to join with her fully, determined to do that. He'd never made love to a woman before, but he had no doubts that he would find the way with Susan.

She shifted against him, matching his movements as he climbed steadily, thrusting faster and harder into her. Susan threw her head back, baring her chest to his ravenous mouth and gasping for him as he suckled at her body. She buried her face in his shoulder as her channel started contracting around him, little whimpering sounds of pleasure vibrating through him.

Susan was ready for him, still lost in the high her climax provided for her. Jole pulled her hips to him as he cried out his release and emptied into her in long spasms that shook him to his core. His cock swelled further, locking her body to him.

She cried out in surprise and pain, pulling back against his grip. Jole furrowed his brow as he locked her hips firmly to him. What was she doing? Moving at joining would be excruciating. Susan swung frightened eyes to him, silently pleading with him, but for what, Jole had no idea.

The door swung open, and Pyter's fury melted into a mixture of surprise and amusement.

Jole pulled Susan to his chest, shielding as much of her body from his chief of security as he could. He glared at the older man. "Get out," he barked. "Get out, before I take your head."

Jole said it in English, so Susan would know

49

what was said. Her embarrassment deserved that much from him.

Pyter nodded and disappeared behind the door with a self-satisfied look. Jole felt his stomach clench. Of course Pyter was happy. There was surely a handsome reward in store for him being the first to report back that Jole had claimed his bride as true mate.

He ran his hands in soothing arcs over Susan's back, wincing at her sobs. "Please, tell me what's wrong," he begged of her. Was she upset at Pyter barging in on them, or did something in his lovemaking disturb or injure her? Pulling away at the moment of joining could do considerable damage.

Susan raised her tear-stained cheeks to him. "What did you do?" she whispered, her lip trembling.

Jole groaned. "The swelling? It only hurts if you try to move. It will subside in a few minutes." *And then I can gauge if there was damage done. Gods, I hope there was no damage done.* "I should have warned you." He ran the backs of his fingers along her cheek. "Human men don't do that at climax, do they?"

She shook her head. "My father didn't— My mother never—"

"He was a first generation cross-bred and much more human than I am or you are."

"No, but I felt—" Susan pulled his hand to her abdomen, at a loss to put her fears into words. "When you stretched me—"

Jole nodded in understanding, smiling in spite of her upset. She'd never been stimulated by a Keen male. Human men didn't complete the fertility cycle she required.

"My body enticed yours to release an egg," he explained slowly. "That is what happens in Keen mating. That is one of the reasons you cannot reproduce with a human male."

His amusement fled, as she burst into tears.

"Susan..... Did I hurt you? Please...tell me what's wrong."

She nestled her cheek to him. "I'm not— Humans don't—"

Understanding came slowly. Humans didn't feel the release of an egg. Humans had some other way of stimulating that release. Susan wasn't prepared to relinquish her identity as human. "How is it with humans, Susan?"

"Human women release an egg once a month. If the man's sperm is there at the right time and the fertilized egg catches at the uterine walls, she carries a baby."

Jole nodded. His heart took up a choppy rhythm. He knew she had been with human men. Was the difference too much for her? "Can you... Will you consent to mate with me again?"

Susan sighed as he became more flaccid, releasing the band of tissue at the gates to her womb.

"If I don't move, it won't hurt?" she asked.

"You have my word. I'll take you as slowly and gently as I can. Please say you'll let me try again."

She laughed nervously. "Can we eat first?"

Jole smiled. "That and much more. Allow me to pamper you until after dinner?"

Susan nodded, and Jole folded her into his body. She couldn't refuse him now that he'd learned the joys of being with her.

CHAPTER FOUR

Susan blushed deeply and sank closer to Jole, as the people in the dining room cheered their arrival. Jole wrapped his arms around her and barked several commands in Keen.

She could only pick out a few words in the rush—stop, no, leave. He used the terms Hi and Hir. She knew Hi was what his servants called Jole, and Hir was what some of them called her, those who weren't calling her Braek. She still had no clue what any of those terms meant. Susan was determined to learn more of his language. She hated being left out of discussions.

He brushed a kiss to her forehead and switched back to English. "It's embarrassing, I know. If it helps, think of Mik cursing when he hears the news."

Susan nodded and managed a strained smile. "It makes me feel better that they won't be cheering for him." She sobered.

"Four months, love."

"How often can a—can a Keen woman drop an egg? What are the odds of pregnancy at any given drop?"

Jole sighed. "The numbers I know are meaningless."

"Why?"

"No re-bred woman has ever mated on Kegin. Even though first generation cross-bred males have reproduced with second generation females, they did it in the human way. I have no idea how often they mated or how successful they were, and we're not doing this the human way. I'm a fifth generation re-bred and you're a third generation."

She shook her head. "I was afraid of that."

Jole glanced over her shoulder and guided her to the table, as food was brought to them.

Susan gasped at the huge portions set before her. She looked at the serving woman in confusion and floundered for words in Keen.

"Gilan—Gi, mu ban?" She looked to Jole for confirmation, and he nodded. Susan had asked the question correctly. Her usage was choppy, but she had asked why her portions were so big.

Gilan was the woman's name, a servant not much older than Jole, who made a note of Susan's likes and dislikes and instructed the cook accordingly. Gi, she'd learned, was a generic word for any servant. On Kegin, it was considered poor form to question or order a servant who was not of your personal staff without using the term.

Gilan chuckled and bowed her head. She patted Susan's stomach lightly. "Hir, ban bree." Gilan bowed to Jole, and he smiled in encouragement. She exited to the kitchen doorway to survey what foods Susan took the greatest liking to.

Susan looked to Jole in disbelief and gestured to her plate. "Ban bree? Are they insane? This won't give me a big baby. This will give them a portly Susan."

He tried to hold in his laughter, turning a

deep crimson in the effort. "Eat as much as you like and no more. Look at it this way. Our children mean new life to them."

She sighed. "What do Hi and Hir mean?"

He shrugged. "Terms of respect."

"Joel, I know you better than this."

He darkened, avoiding her eyes. "Eat dinner with me in my rooms, and I'll explain. I promise."

Susan nodded, feeling a thrill of delight. She'd never seen Jole's rooms. They met in her rooms or elsewhere on the property but never in his rooms.

It was several more bites before she thought of her other question. "All right. At least tell me what Braek means."

Jole's eyes widened, and he slammed his fork down on his plate, darkening again in what she as sure wasn't amusement. The room went dead still. Susan looked at the stunned faces, breathless in shock. Gilan paled and pressed her hand to her throat as if she was about to swoon.

"Who said that to you?" he demanded.

She blushed. "I take it that one isn't a term of respect. Well, that makes a lot of sense."

"Why? Who said it?"

Susan pushed her food around her plate and shrugged. "Several people. My first day here, Pyter said it. You did say he insulted me, didn't you?" She had forgotten.

"Who else?"

"Your brother."

Jole's jaw clenched. "And?"

"I don't know, Joel. It doesn't matter."

He came to kneel beside her and turned her

face to his. "It does," he whispered. "They have no right..... If anyone says that to you again, I want you to tell me immediately. Please. I won't stand for it. I can't."

Susan nodded and touched his cheek. "I'm not really hungry, Joel."

He lifted her hand and kissed it. "I'll have fruit and cheese sent to your room. Why don't you rest until dinner?"

"I think I will. It's been a long, hard day."

* * * *

Jole paced his study, willing the anger welling in him to subside. He'd issued the order as soon as Susan was settled in her room with the tray he'd ordered for her to nibble on.

The servant who'd had taken so markedly to Susan, Gilan, had added pastries and sugared sweets above what he asked for her. Jole had nodded his thanks as she'd left them. He doubted Susan would eat much, but the enticement of her favorite desserts couldn't hurt.

Pyter strode through the door and bowed deeply. "They are assembled, Highness."

Jole nodded and marched through the outer office, through the entry hall, and into the ballroom. Pyter had assembled the entire household, including the night captains, who stood before him bleary-eyed and half-dressed, dragged from their beds. Jole faced them, more ready to take his blade to a man or men than he'd ever been.

"My bride is now my mate."

There was a murmur of surprise and delight from those who had been sleeping in preparation for their shifts.

"Had my bride not been deemed worthy of your respect before now, which I would take personal offense to—" Jole shot them a hard look in warning. "She will soon be your salvation."

Nervous glances shot back and forth between the assembled servants and guards.

"From her womb will come the daughters that will save Kegin. She is your princess by virtue of our mating. She will be your queen, when I accede to the throne."

Several of his people dropped their heads, red-faced. Jole made note of them despite knowing that Pyter would be keeping track of the situation for him.

"From this moment on, any person who shows disrespect to my bride, in any way, will face death for it. Any person who dares call her 'barbarian' will taste my blade, before the word echoes."

A soft choking sound came from the rear of the room. Jole stopped, searching for its source without fruit for his labors. He met Pyter's eyes, calmed by the almost imperceptible nod from the older man.

"I will issue no further warnings. I expect you all understand me perfectly. Captains, you will inform your troops what was said here today."

Pyter sighed as the servants and guards left the room. "It will be difficult to get them to accept her as princess. You know that."

"No one will show her disrespect as long as I live to stop them."

The rest of the afternoon passed in preparation. Jole spoke to the cook and ordered a dinner of delicacies to be served in his rooms. Then he sent a group of maids to his bride with her presentation dress and orders to only help her as much as she was comfortable with.

That completed, Jole retired to his own preparations. He bathed and dressed. His ceremonial uniform wasn't the most comfortable piece of clothing he owned, but he would give Susan her answer in style. She deserved no less.

* * * *

Susan woke to the vision of several servants standing over her. An older red-haired woman bowed and stepped forward. Her English was better than most of the servants, much better than Bell's.

"We come to prepare you, Lady—for meal with Hi."

"Prepare?"

"You bath and dress." She waved her hand at a long, silky red gown with gold and purple flowers. "This, Lady—for Hi?"

Susan nodded. "All right." Jole didn't typically choose her clothes for her, but for dinner in his room, she supposed he wanted a special night.

The red-haired woman turned and ordered two of the others away to draw a bath. She offered Susan her hand. "We help, Lady? Great honor prepare Lady for Hi."

Susan looked at the group of giggling women in growing apprehension. "All of you? No."

She nodded. "Lady allow Barri to help?"

"Are you Barri?"

She bowed her head in response.

"Yes. You may help, Barri." At least, Barri spoke some English, and it seemed that Susan would offend them if she refused all help.

Her smile widened. She gave more orders, and the other women bowed and went out into the corridor, closing the door behind them.

Barri motioned up and down Susan's body. "Help undress Lady or wait at bath?"

Susan blushed. "Wait at the bath. I'll be in in a few minutes."

Barri laughed and touched Susan's face. "Like Neane Hir." Her eyes glistened with tears.

Susan followed her into the bathroom, shaking her head in confusion. "Jenneane? You knew Jole's mother?" No wonder she spoke English so well.

Barri nodded happily. "She teach your words." She suddenly seemed sad. "Barri prepare Neane Hir much nights, but she never want Kell Ri."

Susan noticed that the bath was close to full and started dragging off her clothes. "If she didn't want Kell Ri, why was she prepared for him?" She couldn't imagine Jenneane willingly spending any time with Kell, if he was anything like Mik.

"He order, Lady." She scowled. "He order

Neane Hir prepare for him each night. Then he treat her—"

"How, Barri? What did Kell do?" She could take a wild guess, based on Mik's actions.

"Treat her like *kit*." Barri shook her head. "Animal meant for breeding, animal meat for eating."

Susan blanched. She considered Mik's treatment of her. What he was doing wasn't sexual. He was evaluating her as breeding stock. "Livestock."

"Lady?"

She waved off the question. "Kell Ri handled—touched Jenneane, when she didn't want him?"

Barri's jaw tightened and she nodded stiffly. "Neane Hir deal to have doctor babies, if Kell Ri stay away."

Susan pulled off the last of her clothes and sank into the tub full of floral-scented bubbles. "You knew Joel as a baby?" She smiled at the thought.

Barri laughed, picking up a cloth to wash Susan's back. "Him— I birth."

"You're a midwife?"

Barri's smile faltered.

"You help mothers have babies, when the time comes?"

Her smile returned. "Yes. I birth Jole Hi. Jole good baby, good boy. Hurt Neane Hir when Kell Ri take Hi from her." She paused in her washing and sighed.

"Kell took Joel from his mother?"

"Boys Kell Ri—own. Take Mik Hi from birth

bed. Neane Hir deal to keep Jole Hi—" She furrowed her brow and raised eight fingers. "Keep years. Then Kell Ri take him. Kill Neane Hir to lose son."

Susan took a deep, shuddering breath. "Keen men own their children?"

"Yes, Lady."

Susan suddenly didn't feel like taking a bath anymore. She sat silently, as Barri helped her bathe and styled her hair, taming her curls and adding fragrant baby lizors in a crown around her face.

When the red gown had been tied in bows down the back, Susan looked at her reflection in the mirror. The gown was ankle-length but with a slit almost to the apex of her thigh on the left. It was cut deep between her breasts, almost to her navel, and pushed her breasts up and in to enhance the effect. The ties down her back left a latticework of open spaces from her shoulders to her waist. The gown was worn, as all Keen clothing typically was, without underclothes.

She looked at Barri uncertainly. The men were forbidden to look at her, but this was expecting too much of them. "I walk through the halls this way?"

Barri laughed heartily. "No, Lady." She draped a matching floor-length red silk cloak over Susan's shoulders and tied it at the neck and waist. "Other men do not look at Hi woman."

Susan nodded and followed Barri to the door. Outside, the other women waited under the watchful eye of Bell. He turned without acknowledging Susan's presence and led Susan, surrounded by the group of women, to the stairs and up to the third floor. Bell met the eyes of every man they passed and held their gazes until they turned away. Obviously, the punishment for presuming to look at her now was even more severe than it was any other time.

Barri and a younger woman, who could be her daughter save her dark curls, opened a set of heavy, engraved wooden doors. Susan gasped at the room beyond.

A huge four-poster bed, hung with something that looked like red velvet and gold cord, took up a full quarter of the room. There were four immense cabinets along one wall.

Susan's bare feet sank into the cream-colored carpet as she walked through the room. One door led to a library with a stone fireplace and leather chairs. A second led to a bath bigger than she imagined a palace would have. It was done in wood and white marble with a tub big enough for a multitude of people, set on a wood dais beneath a glass wall that looked out over the fields of lizors.

Barri called for her, and Susan turned away, shaking her head. Flame lamps with sweet-smelling oils were lit on several surfaces in the bedroom, casting a warm glow over the room.

Barri removed her cloak and smiled warmly. "You make Barri very happy, Lady."

"How? What have I done?"

"You prepared for Hi like Barri prepare Neane, but you want Hi. Hi a good man. He make you good husband."

Susan smiled weakly and nodded. Yes, she

wanted Jole, but she wasn't sure she was comfortable with the arrangements of marriages on Kegin.

Barri opened the final door for her, and Susan stepped through. She found herself on a wide terrace with a waist-high wall. A table for two was set with covered platters of food. Beyond that, Jole stood with his back to her, his hands clasped behind his back, gazing out over the landscape.

Barri bowed deeply. "Hir, Jole Hi."

Jole turned with a smile on his face.

Susan took in his outfit. It was a military uniform not unlike the ones his soldiers wore, but Jole's jacket was red with gold braid at the shoulders. He scanned his eyes over her then favored her with a hungry look that made Susan gasp and her body throb for him.

He crossed to her, waving the woman behind her away. "Barri, le na."

Barri chuckled and shook her head, scurrying away. Susan dissected that. Jole rarely called a servant or guard by name. Until now, only Pyter and Bell were favored. Barri must mean a lot to him, but that made sense. She'd been close to his mother and close to him as a child.

Jole stepped to her, half-raised his hand to touch her arm then scowled and rolled his shoulder under his uniform jacket. He kissed her cheek, and his smile returned. "You're beautiful." His voice was a wisp of heat that stroked her ear and traveled the length of her body.

Susan smiled. "You look dashing and

handsome and...completely uncomfortable."

He laughed heartily and pulled at his collar, popping the top button free and sighing in relief. "I was never good at hiding it, I suppose."

"What is this uniform? Are you a general or something?"

His smile faded. "Let's eat while the food is hot, and I'll tell you."

She slid into the seat he offered. Susan looked at him expectantly, but Jole motioned to the food. She removed the lid, then speared a forkful of the food on her plate, something that looked and smelled much like a stuffed mushroom.

"You're avoiding the subject," she accused.

Jole pulled at the stiff collar of his uniform jacket again, opening another button to reveal the tunic beneath. "Yes, I am."

Susan swallowed the morsel in her mouth. She raised her goblet and looked at him over the rim. "What does Hi mean, Joel?" She sampled the vintage.

He met her eyes, looking truly uncertain for the first time in weeks. "It means your Highness.... Prince, with the upward inflection."

Susan choked on the mouthful of wine. Of everything she'd expected him to say, this wasn't even on the list. "You're a prince? Like the son of a king? Heir apparent? That sort of thing?"

He nodded. "Precisely. All of that sort of thing. All of the cross-mates brought through the gateway have been brought for members of the royal family."

"So, Ri means king?"

"More or less. Your majesty, king."

"And Hir?"

"Princess. My mother was Hir, even though Kell was King, because she chose not to be his true mate."

"I can't blame her."

Jole's expression said that he completely agreed with the sentiment.

"What about me?" she continued.

"What about you?"

"Well, we...uh... I am your—"

He nodded. "You're my true mate. When I am Jole Ri, you will be Susan Rig."

"Queen?"

He nodded, smiling weakly.

"Oh, no. I did not sign on for this. I don't know how to be a queen. I was working in an office a month ago. In case you don't know what that means, it means I was the one everyone dumped on, Joel. I'm not good at being the boss."

"There's nothing to it. You entertain guests, run the household, give me babies..." His eyes glittered.

"You've had almost a month, Joel," she stormed at him. "It never occurred to you to let me in on this? You could have said, 'Oh, by the way, Susan, I happen to be a prince.'"

"This upsets you?"

Susan hesitated. She knew he was important the first day. She'd felt it in him when he'd touched her and when he'd handled Pyter for her. Why was she making a big deal about it now?

Because, I'm terrified. He's a prince, and he

will own me and own our children. And he never told me any of it.

Jole sighed and took her hand, rubbing his thumb over the hollow of her palm slowly. "You are upset. You've been upset since you came to my rooms. Why?"

She sighed. "Is it true that our children will belong to you? That I have no rights?"

His face darkened. "No! I can grant you any rights I deem appropriate. I want to raise our children together."

"Grant me rights? Can you revoke them?"

"I would never do that to you." His voice was full of something that sounded remarkably like horror.

"That means you can. Do all Keen women have to endure this, or is it because I was brought through the gateway?"

Jole blushed deeply. "Our daughters would have all the rights of a Kegin-born woman."

"Which are?"

"Freedom to choose a husband, inherit and own property, the guardianship of their children..... All the things you have, except they won't be presented to husbands with the choice of mating or not. They will meet men socially and choose only those men they want. The men will then have to contract with me for them." He paused. "They will have to agree to our daughters' terms for marriage. If a husband breaks the contract, she can dissolve the marriage and take the penalty stated in the contract.

"Their contracts would have such

stipulations as the children being hers alone in a split. I would not allow a contract that didn't protect their rights, and men will be generous in the rights they defer to our daughters and the penalties they offer to win their hands. Men will want to treat them well."

"Did your parents have a contract?" Tears stung her eyes, and she tried to blink them away. She knew they did, but she wanted to see how Jole would answer.

He grimaced. "Yes. Jenneane allowed for two successful mechanical implantations to the production of viable sons. Kell took guardianship of Mik immediately."

"And she had you until you were eight."

Jole nodded slowly. "I don't know why she allowed it at all. I never did."

"Her contract stated that Kell Ri was forbidden to touch her or force her to be prepared for him, ever again. I don't know what his penalty was, but I would assume it was full custody of you for your lifetime."

Jole paled. "Who told you that?"

"Barri."

"Kell—" He swallowed hard and shook his head.

"He ordered Jenneane prepared for him every night. He manhandled her and treated her like *kit*. I assume that means livestock or cattle of some sort."

Jole nodded miserably. "I saw how he treated her later, after he had to be mindful of the penalty. I thought that was reason enough for her not to go to his bed."

"Well, he was worse than that before she agreed to have children. Probably like Mik was—"

She swallowed the rest of that statement as Jole's jaw clenched and his eyes lit in fury.

"He will never lay hands on you again," Jole promised. "I will die first."

Susan took a deep breath. "Joel, I think we need a contract."

He stared at her for several tense heartbeats before he answered. "You're afraid I'll take away your rights after we have children."

The pain in his eyes made her blanch. "If you die, will Kell Ri and Mik still allow me the rights you granted me, without a contract? If it's not written and notarized...or whatever you do here to make it legal?"

Jole rubbed at his forehead. "You're right. You'll only be free of them if it's in writing.....and if we've produced a child. Without that step, I have no legal right to grant you anything." He looked at her fearfully. "The contract will take time, and I cannot legally sign it until you carry a child. We have little time to produce a child. Will you trust me that long?"

Susan furrowed her brow. "You mean, will I still work on a baby before there is a contract?"

He nodded and waited patiently for her answer.

"Yes, Joel. You've given me your word. We don't have time to waste bickering over things like this."

"Do you trust me?"

"Yes. I do."

His smile spread. "Then eat. I've been hungry

for you all day."

Susan blushed. Her hand moved down the deep neckline of the dress, and Jole's eyes followed, his gaze heating. Susan cracked a smile as she deliberately caressed her breast. He leaned forward, his attention riveted to the movement.

"Joel? Could this meal be reheated?" She issued the invitation, stroking her breast again, her nipple standing out against the thin layer of material that covered it. Susan dropped her head back, arching her back to push her breasts toward him.

Jole moved so quickly that she barely realized he'd reacted before the length of her body was pressed to him. His hands cupped her bottom, drawing her to the hard ridge behind his trousers, his mouth closing over hers.

Susan parted her lips, admitting the tongue that was questing with barely leashed passion. She slid her leg through the slit of the skirt and hooked it around his thigh to fit her body against his hardening cock.

His legs shifted against her, the only indication she had that the sense of movement wasn't caused by dizziness alone. Susan moaned, as he followed her down onto the bed. He pulled back to take her breast into his mouth through the insubstantial silk of her gown.

"I thought you wanted to take me slowly," she teased, her taste buds tingling as she drew in his alluring scent.

His laughter rumbled through her body. "You incite me to passion and ask me to rein it in?

Very well, my love."

Jole was slow and thorough. His mouth and hands wrecked havoc on her through the silk. He swept the skirt back at the slit, uncovering her from the top of her pubic curls to her ankles, and stroked his fingers inside her.

Susan bit her lip at the spike of pain. She was tender from her reaction last time.

His eyes darkened in concern. "You're in pain."

She nodded, though it wasn't a question. "When I moved this morning—" She didn't want to make him stop. Her body was in a riot for him, her heart pounding, the blood rushing in her ears, but this couldn't work.

He feathered a kiss over her lips then moved to replace his fingers with his mouth. Susan sucked in her breath, as his tongue darted inside her.

"Joel!" She was on the verge of tears. She hadn't realized how sore she'd be. There was no way she could finish this.

The shock of ice inside her hit her first. Susan threw her arms out, and her entire body went taut and unresponsive. She cried out, as the warmth followed. The pulse of pleasure shot through her, and Susan climaxed, screaming Jole's name as he provided another jolt of ice to her.

His mouth moved higher. His tongue flicked at her clit, sending a slice of pleasure through her that overlapped with the pulse of the same from his last healing jolt.

He kissed her clit, the constant pressure

allowing her body to come down slightly from the mind-numbing ebb and flow rocking through her. The jolt of ice came unexpectedly, pushing her body over endurance again. Susan sobbed, and he smiled up at her from between her thighs.

Jole started removing his clothes, kneeling nude between her parted legs in moments. Her body was still contracting, when he started pushing slowly into her. Susan braced her hands on the smooth skin of his chest, her fingers tangling with the pendant he wore, and Jole stilled.

His eyes were wide and unsure. "Do you want me to stop?"

Susan moaned as her muscles stretched around him only to grip him again rhythmically. She shook her head. Unable to form a verbal response, she tipped her hips to urge him further.

Jole gathered her shaking hands in his and pressed them to the bed near her head, lending the delicious sensation of his weight over her. He took her by bits, deeper with each forward thrust until he was seated in her fully. A harsh cry escaped his lips, and he muttered a phrase in Keen.

"Ami tol."

He met her eyes as he slid in and out of her still-spasming depths. Susan stopped counting the peaks and valleys he drove her to after her body reached that third crest. She existed only in the haze of climax that seemed never to end. Jole chuckled as she met his eyes, pleading silently for him to join her.

His laugh choked off as he tensed over her, and the warm wash of his release filled her. He swelled, stretching her further as he locked his come inside her to find— She stilled as her body erupted in a series of tiny shocks, releasing an egg for Jole. It wasn't frightening, now that she knew what was happening. Susan rather enjoyed the feeling.

She brushed her fingers through his hair, drawing his mouth down to hers; opening to him as he lay locked inside her. Susan had never felt anything so erotic. He was part of her for these precious moments.

When his body released its hold on her, Jole looked down at her. "It didn't hurt?" he asked.

Susan shook her head. "I think making a baby with you is going to be the highlight of my life."

"Good. Then maybe you'll allow me to bring you back here after we eat."

* * * *

Jole glanced across the table at Susan. She was beautiful, sensual, and more than he'd dared dream for in a mate. When they'd come back to the balcony to eat, he'd decided to forego his uniform in favor of a pair of silin lounging pants and a bare chest that drew Susan's eyes often.

He stroked his hand over the length of his cock straining against the silin. Just being close to Susan made him want her again. He smiled at the memory of how she'd come for him. No woman had ever had such a startling reaction to his touch.

The presentation dress was a perfect complement to her beauty, but next time, he would remove it. He wanted to see her body again. He wanted to claim her skin-to-skin. He had mated with her twice, and they had yet to remove all the clothes from each of them simultaneously.

Susan smiled at him over her goblet of wine. "Do I need to ask what you're thinking?"

He circled his fingers around the hand in her lap and pulled it to the bulge in his. "I'm thinking of you."

She blushed, stroking him. "I like the way your mind works."

"Are you done eating?"

She smiled a sly smile. "If you mean food, the answer is yes." Her hand became more purposeful. "If you mean for you—"

Jole gathered her into his arms and carried her back to the bedroom. He stood Susan on her feet next to the bed and reached a hand to undo the ties at the back of her gown.

Susan stiffened in his arms as someone knocked lightly at the door.

He shielded her with his body. "Yes?" he called out.

Barri stepped into the room, her head bowed. There was a smile curving her lips. "*The others and I will attend to our other duties, since it seems you will remain occupied for some time.*"

Jole attempted a stern look that failed utterly. Only Barri would dare say something so outrageous to him, and he loved her dearly for it. "*Go on then,*" he instructed her.

Barri switched to her broken English. "Lady, you call when time go to your room."

Susan jerked her head up to his. Jole sucked in his breath. Her expression fluctuated between dismay and something sad or desperate. Tears pooled at the join of lid and lashes.

He waved Barri away. "*Leave us.*"

What had gone wrong? He could never anticipate what would upset Susan next. Jole touched her cheek, and Susan dropped her gaze.

"Susan, what's wrong?"

She didn't meet his eyes. "Nothing. I just keep forgetting that this is Kegin, and Kegin has its own rules."

"No. Tell me. I won't have you unhappy."

Susan wiped her eyes and squared her shoulders, as if she was preparing to pick up a weapon and stride into battle. "I suppose mates on Kegin don't share a bed for more than sex. I can live with that. It's nice to have personal space, and we're both accustomed to it."

Jole furrowed his brow. "You want to share a room with me?"

Susan looked away to the closed door to the corridor. "If it isn't done, don't make an exception for me, or your people will hate us both for it."

He cupped her chin back to him, stung by her acceptance of the perceived truth as much as he was stunned by the fact that she wanted such

74

a thing. "You want to make me a legend, don't you?" Jole whispered.

"I don't—"

"You let me touch you and heal you your first day on Kegin. You agreed to take meals with me, walk with me, and learn Keen." He kissed her gently, pouring every tender gift she gave him back to her in words and touch. "You agreed to be true mate to me beyond simply producing children. You let me make love to you in my bed." Jole kissed her again, more passionately.

"No cross-mate has ever done any of that, Susan. Now, you would agree— No, you *ask* to live with me, to share my bed for more than producing a child. Even some Keen couples never agree to that in contract. Women almost always demand their own space that their husbands may never enter." His kiss was less restrained, more fevered as he considered what she wanted of him. How could she think he would refuse such a gift?

"Please, tell me I've interpreted what you want correctly," Jole begged her.

He nuzzled her jaw line and pressed his lips to the soft spot behind her ear. Susan dropped her head back, melting into his embrace.

"Is that really your wish, Susan?"

She sighed, her hands tracing the lines of his chest. "Do you really want me here?"

Jole moved his hands to the ties on her gown again. "Say the word, and I will have the entire floor converted for us. We'll punch through doorways into the neighboring rooms to make you a dressing room and a nursery." He swirled his tongue over the spot behind her ear. "I'll have to share your room for a month or more, while they work."

Susan groaned. She met his eyes, her color high and a hint of a secret in her expression. "I'd like to negotiate two points." She was breathless, excited.

"Which are?"

"I get to decorate the nursery."

"Agreed. And?"

"We will have another small bedroom with a bath set up on the other side of the nursery."

Jole stilled. Was that to be her personal sanctuary to escape him? "For what reason?" he asked nervously.

"I want Barri as my midwife and nanny. After all, you keep talking about more than one child. Even a princess needs help sometimes, and a nanny needs a room of her own near the nursery."

"You could have any doctor you want," he offered, untying the first three ties in quick succession, kissing at her pulse point. He collected her rising musk on his tongue, enflaming himself, sending himself into a mating frenzy.

"I trust Barri."

He felt Susan working free the tie on his lounging pants. Her face nestled to his chest, seeking out the well of his musk above one male nipple, speeding her frenzy, though he knew she didn't understand the aphrodisiac qualities yet.

He nodded, his breathing ragged. He undid the next two ties, and the gown started to slide from her shoulders. Jole kissed the smooth skin beneath.

"Barri is yours," he breathed into her.

"And the room for her?"

"Yes. Anything you wish."

Susan kissed at his chest, releasing his pants, so they slid to his ankles. "One last thing, Joel."

"Anything." He pulled her dress down her chest and caressed her hips as he worked it further off. It landed in a pool around her ankles.

"What does 'ami tol' mean?"

His erection pulsed at the words on her lips. Jole kissed her, kicking away his pants and lifting her out of her dress. "It means I love you. Maybe you'll say it for me one day." *Oh Fion, what I wouldn't give for that.*

Susan blushed, and he felt her pulse speed beneath his fingertips. "Ami tol," she whispered, brushing her lips over his. "I do love you, Joel."

CHAPTER FIVE

Iric 19th, Ri 25-2986

Jole sighed and wrapped his body further around Susan's. She was spooned to his chest, playing with the jewel on the necklace he'd given her, his mother's necklace.

The necklace had come from Earth on Jenneane's body when she'd been taken through the gateway. Even when everything else had been taken from her, by tradition, she'd been permitted to keep the jewel of her homeland.

Susan was upset again. It wasn't just her nervous fiddling with the necklace that told him she was unsettled. Her heart rate was quick, and her muscles were tense. She hadn't been sleeping well lately. As every month passed without a baby, she became more withdrawn.

He kissed her shoulder. "Susan, please tell me what's wrong."

"You know what's wrong." Her voice held more sadness than he had heard since her first morning on Kegin. Hopelessness. She was giving up.

"We still have a month, Susan."

Her shoulders shook as she started crying. "It won't work, Joel."

"It will." *It has to. I won't lose her to Mik. I won't let Mik touch her.*

She turned to face him. Susan started to speak then buried her face in his chest and sobbed harder.

"It will work. It has to. If we have to inseminate this time and try again when there's no pressure— That's all this is. Pressure to succeed is holding us back. Even Barri says so."

Susan stared at him, hope lighting her eyes. "Will that work? Will it be enough for the Council?"

Jole hesitated. "I don't know. They want us to produce daughters."

She nodded, the light dying that quickly. "We're sunk."

"We have thirty-seven days left. It's not like it is for humans. We don't have only four or five fertile days in that month. You release an egg—"

"I'm not," she wailed. Susan bit her lip and waited for his answer.

"Not what?"

"Releasing eggs. I—I h-haven't been," she hitched out.

"For how long?"

"Weeks. I thought there might be some sort of cycle to it, but Barri said that's not right."

"If you're not releasing eggs, you're pregnant." He felt a laugh bubbling up.

"I can't be." She choked back a sob. Susan rubbed her forehead roughly.

"Why not?"

"No signs. Barri said the signs start immediately." He could hear the frustration in her voice.

"Why didn't you tell me?" Jole pulled her to his chest. "We could see a doctor. Something can be done." *How much of our precious time did we waste?*

"I don't know. I was afraid."

"Afraid of what?" She wasn't making sense. If she was afraid of something, why didn't she come to him? He'd asked her to...many times.

"What if I can't— What if something is wrong with me, like the doctors on Earth said?" Tears spilled down her cheeks, and she ran a shaking hand through her hair.

"Then Mik won't want you."

Susan looked at him in confusion. "You want children, Joel." Even face to face with her, he barely heard her.

"I want you. I'd like children with you, but I want you. That makes a big difference. I want you, Susan. Only you."

"What if—"

"What if you're pregnant and you're getting yourself upset for no good reason? That's not good for you, and it's not good for the baby."

She shook her head. "No signs, remember? Barri said immediately."

Jole nodded. The signs were immediate, as soon as the fertilized sac implanted in the womb.

Susan rubbed her temples and winced.

Jole watched the move in dawning understanding. "Did Barri tell you what to look for?"

She furrowed her brow. "Signs of pregnancy, Joel. What idiot doesn't know the signs of pregnancy?"

He waved his hand for her to continue, praying that his suspicions were founded.

Susan rolled her eyes. "Men! Morning sickness, sore breasts, dizziness, exhaustion, frequent urination, mood swings— Any of this ring a bell for you?"

Jole bit his cheek to keep from laughing out loud. That would never do. "Are you cold?"

"It's winter, and we get drafts from the windows. Of course, I'm cold." She pressed her hand to her forehead.

"Headache?"

She nodded. He cupped her head to his lips and took away her pain.

Susan sighed in relief. "Thank you."

"I've healed several headaches recently," he commented more to himself than her.

"Stress," she dismissed the comment.

Jole kneaded his hands in her shoulders, finding the knots of muscles. *How blind have I been?*

Susan went boneless in his hands, as he started to massage them out for her.

No wonder she's been so tense. No wonder she hasn't been sleeping well.

One more test— "Please, don't be so depressed, Susan."

She buried her face in his chest. "Of course, I'm depressed. I'm defective and I only have one more month to do this or—" She sobbed.

Jole wanted to laugh and whoop in joy, but he found himself holding her, soothing her. "Shhh. I'm sorry, love. I should have told you when I realized."

"Realized what?"

"You're pregnant. You're worrying for no good reason." He massaged a knot from her shoulder and moved his hand down her spine to find

81

another.

"I can't be," she huffed.

"Human signs, Susan."

She looked up at him in disbelief.

"You were looking for human signs."

"But—"

He shook his head. "Feeling cold, even in a warm room, depression, weeping, headaches and muscle aches. Those are Keen signs."

Susan glanced at her abdomen in amazement, pressing her hand to it. "I'm— I really am..."

"Pregnant. The signs will get worse, in time. I'll spend a good bit of time easing them for you, as the pregnancy progresses. Breast tenderness will be a sign of imminent delivery. If you are nauseated and dizzy, you really are sick and need to see a doctor."

Jole cupped her chin back up to him. "Now, how long has it been since you have dropped an egg?"

"I don't— I'm sorry, Joel. I really don't know."

He kissed her forehead. "It's all right. Stay here, while I get Barri. If you've been pregnant this long, she'll feel your cap."

"Cap?"

"A cover your body produces to protect the infant until birth. After the breast tenderness, the cap will expel, as you dilate."

She nodded slowly, and Jole kissed her forehead as he slid from the bed. He covered her with a quilt then pulled a second from the cabinet and added it with a smile.

He kept smiling as he pulled on his lounging

pants and a tunic. *My child! Mik can never take her now.*

Jole descended the stairs to the kitchen two at a time, nodding to several guards on his way. The servants were having breakfast, and they scurried to stand when Jole entered the room.

He turned to the counter and poured a glass of juice to hide his grin. *"My bride and I wish to enjoy a breakfast in bed. Eggs, steak, pastry, fruit, and milk.....in half an hour."*

"As you wish, Highness," the cook replied immediately. She scurried to the cold storage to get meat for the meal.

"Barri, I'll need you to come with me. My bride wishes to discuss work on the auxiliary rooms on our floor. If you're about done anyway?"

"Yes, Highness."

He stifled a laugh. Barri only called him that for show. He was Jole to her, as she would never be Gi to him. He nodded and headed for the stairs with the juice for Susan in his hand.

Barri fell in beside him, as they passed the second floor. *"Tell me, Jole,"* she whispered.

"My bride wishes to discuss an addition to the nursery."

"What addition? I thought her plans for furnishings and decoration were final."

Jole shrugged as he reached for the door handle. Barri scowled at him as she had when he was a boy acting innocent after some misdeed. She knew him so well. He pulled open the door and followed her into the dim bedroom.

Susan lay, curled beneath the quilts, her eyes closed and looking much more at peace than she had when he'd left. Barri moved to her side and gasped at Susan's puffy, tear-streaked cheeks.

She turned on Jole, poking one finger in the center of his chest. Her voice came out in a harsh whisper so as not to disturb Susan. "*Why is she crying? What is wrong?*"

He laughed lightly. "*She had a headache, Barri.*"

She furrowed her brow.

"*She's cold. She's weeping. Her muscles are—*"

He signaled her for silence as Barri stifled a squeal of delight into her fist.

She smacked Jole on the upper arm. "*It took you long enough,*" she accused.

He sobered. "*You didn't tell her what she was looking for. Susan was looking for human signs of pregnancy. She was afraid to tell me when she stopped releasing eggs.*"

Barri's eyes widened. "*How long has she been hiding this from you?*"

"*Even she isn't sure. She was so upset, Barri. She was terrified that—*" He sighed.

Barri squeezed his hand in comfort. "*I can estimate. May I examine her?*"

"*That's why I came for you.*"

She smiled and moved to the bed. Barri touched Susan's shoulder and switched to English. "Lady, wake."

Susan yawned and nodded. Jole winced. He should have seen the signs. He knew what he was looking for. Barri had trained him for this day, practically from his birth.

"I check baby, Lady?"

Susan nodded grimly and rolled to her back. She pulled her knees up, as Jole sat beside her and took her hand. He decided that the position must be universal. Barri nodded her approval and lifted the quilts to Susan's hips. Susan looked to the far wall then closed her eyes; Jole smoothed her hair, at a loss to offer comfort.

"Relax, Lady. No hurt."

Jole watched long enough to see the older woman's hand disappear inside his bride before examining the intense expression on Barri's face.

She furrowed her brow as she eased her hand out. "Baby fine," she pronounced. She prodded at Susan's lower abdomen and shook her head.

Jole scowled at her. "How far, Barri?"

Barri shook her head again. "Strange. Big baby."

"Barri," he barked, in no mood for cryptic answers.

"Cap thick. More than one month, less than three. Baby bigger. Definitely three month or more."

Susan squeezed his hand. "I don't understand. Is it because I'm an Earth-born re-bred?"

"No. Neane Hir no have cap like that. First baby like this I see. No happen before." She shrugged and sent Jole a worried frown.

Jole nodded. "We'll have to consult a doctor."

Susan shook her head. "I want Barri."

"You'll have her, but first we have to make sure you're both all right."

Susan nodded in exhaustion. Jole grimaced. Between the aches and worry, it was no wonder she was sleeping poorly.

"*Call Doctor Peri,*" he instructed Barri. "*Tell him that we will be at his office in two hours, but do not tell him why. He will clear a space for us.*"

* * * *

Susan stared at Dr. Peri fearfully.

Jole squeezed her hand. "*It's all right,*" he soothed her.

Peri's eyes widened.

Jole scowled at him and switched to Keen. "Remember who you serve, and get to work," he ordered.

Peri nodded and addressed Jole. "Tell your mate to put up her knees for the exam."

Susan sighed and pulled her knees back, until her heels rested in the indentations on the table. Jole hid his surprise. She understood more of the Keen language every day.

Peri paled considerably and bowed to Susan with a mumbled apology. He conducted the same exam Barri had and exhibited the same lost expression. After a moment, he pulled the sheet back down and headed for a piece of heavy equipment on wheels.

"What is that?" Jole demanded.

Peri blanched. "It is safe, Highness. It allows me to see the womb and the baby within."

Susan nodded. "*Sonogram,*" she pronounced in English.

Peri and Jole both questioned her silently.

She waved them off. "*Later*," she promised Jole.

Peri stripped the sheet off of her entirely. Susan blushed, crossing her free arm over her breasts, and Jole shot the doctor a stern look. He didn't care for this man seeing his bride, under the best of circumstances, but stripping her naked seemed extreme.

Taking the warning to heart, Peri draped the sheet over Susan's shoulders and chest, offering his apologies again. She sank to the table, her breathing easing, grasping at Jole's hand, as Peri readied the machine.

Jole watched in amazement, as the doctor put a bag of warming gel over her hips and abdomen. He lowered the screen pad attached to the machine into the cushion of the bag. Peri worked quickly, adjusting dials and looking at unusual colored shapes on the screen.

The doctor startled and looked at them with wide eyes.

Jole felt the last of his patience slip away. "What is it?" he demanded.

The doctor bowed to Susan reverently before turning to Jole. "The princess conceived in the vicinity of seven weeks ago, Highness."

"That long?" He kissed her hand. "No wonder she's so large."

Peri laughed heartily. "She is large, because she carries two of your heirs, Highness."

Jole sucked in his breath. "How? The cap secures the cervix immediately."

"Immediately upon implantation. I imagine

you had sex several times within two days' time?"

Jole nodded with a sly smile. Until Susan's depression became severe, it had not been unusual for them to make love two or three times in a day. One night, they were insatiable. Jole had woken Susan well past middle-night and she'd returned the favor before dawn. They'd made love three times the day before and twice the day after. Jole's smile widened. That was a little less than two months ago, he'd wager.

Peri continued with his explanation, though Jole hardly needed it. "You fertilized an egg, had sex again, fertilized a second egg before the first implanted and formed the cap. The second egg implanted as well."

"This has happened before?"

"Very rarely. Most couples are not so— dedicated."

Susan looked from one to the other in confusion. She hadn't been able to keep up with their rapid conversation. "*What's wrong, Joel?*"

He kissed her passionately despite the doctor's presence. Peri had proof enough of their sexual exploits to guess that they were not strangers to each other. "*You carry two,*" he told her happily.

"*Twins?*"

Jole searched for the word but came up with a blank. "*Two babies.*"

Her smile widened. "*Twins. The word is twins, Joel.*"

He laughed. "*Twins.*"

* * * *

Susan fell asleep on the trip back to the house. Jole sparred verbally with Pyter, his heart soaring all the while. The older man was furious that Jole wouldn't tell him the reason for the visit to Peri...or the diagnosis.

"It's nothing serious," Jole informed him for the third time.

Pyter set his jaw angrily. "If the princess requires medical care of some sort—"

"My bride is just fine, Pyter. She is simply fatigued. She requires nothing more than rest, food, and occasional exercise."

Pyter nodded but his face darkened. Jole hid his smile behind his hand. Someone might get the bonus for being the first to report the details of their lives, but this time, it wouldn't be Pyter.

Jole carried Susan into the house and up the main staircase, jerking his head at Barri to accompany him to their room. Barri could barely contain herself. When Susan was tucked under the quilts, she pulled at Jole's arm.

"Tell me, Jole. What is the news?"

His smile burst out again, and he kissed her cheek. "Two babies, Barri. She's giving me two instead of one."

Her amazement was replaced by a sly smile. "You have been keeping occupied, haven't you?"

"I love her and I love being with her."

"Then you shouldn't stop. It's beneficial to her pregnancy and delivery. Up until her birth signals begin, you should take her sexually any time she is willing, and her schen will make her very willing."

89

Jole hardened at the thought of the Keen female's sex drive during pregnancy. He wondered if Susan might share that drive. None of the other cross-mates had, but he held out hope that Susan would. It seemed Barri thought she would, too. Barri glanced at the evidence of his agreement, and his cheeks burned in embarrassment.

She raised an eyebrow, adopting her most clinical voice. "Good. I have counseled you in the other things she requires. Plenty of meat and cheese, fruit and milk. A detriment in any one of them—"

He nodded. "Her headache and muscle cramps would become unbearable."

"All the more so with two babies. The toxins will accumulate faster. Be always mindful of her needs. She may not realize how dire they are, until she is in pain. See that you remember it."

A knock on the door interrupted them.

Jole furrowed his brow, glancing to Susan then the door, his senses on alert for danger. Who would interrupt them this way? "Who is it?" he called out.

"Gilan, Highness."

He moved to the door in confusion. What was Gilan doing here? He opened the door half a foot. "What is it, Gilan?"

"Your father will call to see you soon, Highness."

Ice settled in his stomach. Kell Ri visiting now could only mean bad news. "How soon?"

Gilan shook her head. "He travels from his office in the capitol."

"Three hours. Thank you, Gilan. Tell the cook to prepare for him. She knows his tastes."

She nodded and disappeared down the stairs.

Jole considered the possibilities, pacing the length of the double doors. He turned back to Barri slowly. "I'll be back in less than two hours. I have to bring the magistrate out, so she will be protected."

"What can I do?"

"Stay with Susan. I'll send a squad of men to guard you while I am gone."

"Pyter?"

He hesitated. "No. I don't trust him. He'll come with me."

Barri shook her head. "He serves *you*, Jole."

"And informs my father of every move I make."

"Just because he was the one assigned to take you from Neane—"

Jole fisted his hands, willing his jaw to relax. "He served my father well."

"He'll serve you better. He hated what he had to do. You couldn't see the anguish in his face, Jole."

"I find it hard to imagine."

She shook her head. "Go, but come back quickly."

He didn't even take the time to kiss Barri goodbye. Stopping only to order a squad under Bell's command to the royal chamber and the house shut tight as if for a siege, Jole raced to the vehicle and off toward town.

Jole considered Pyter, as they made their

way to the magistrate. Pyter reported to Kell, and he was infuriating at times. Still, he seemed to have Jole's best interests at heart. Moreover, Barri trusted him, though he couldn't understand her reasons at times.

He vaguely remembered his early days with his mother. They'd been happy days, full of love and laughter, before the strict rules and cold loneliness of life with Kell Ri. He'd trusted Pyter then. The big man had been everything to him, the father he'd wished Kell Ri would be but never had.

Pyter had played with Jole and given him treats snuck from the kitchens. Pyter had taught him to fight and hunt. He'd treated Jenneane with respect such as Kell never would. Jole would have given anything to be the low-born son of Pyter rather than the son of an indifferent king.

Jole closed his eyes, remembering the last time he saw Jenneane.

* * * *

They were celebrating his birthday. He made a wish on his candles, as his mother instructed. It was a wish he would never have fulfilled. It was a simple wish, a wish for a trip to the Garesh Mountains with his mother.

Pyter came to the doorway, looking grim.

Jole tried to cheer him. He offered Pyter a slice of the cake.

The room went still.

"It is time, Princess."

Those words would haunt Jole for years. They haunted him still, in dark, unguarded moments like this.

Jenneane shook her head, tears shining in her eyes. "No," she protested. "I have the night."

"The sun is down, and the day is ended. Kell Ri demands his son, by virtue of the contract. If you refuse, you will breach the trust."

She paled and scrambled to remove the necklace from around her neck, pushing the cascade of auburn hair aside impatiently. She reached out to place it in Jole's hand, but Pyter brushed her hand away.

"Please, Pyter. This one thing."

Jole stared at her in shock. His mother was a princess of Kegin. He had never seen her beg.

"Kell Ri will not permit him to have it. You know that."

Jenneane started sobbing. She knelt before Jole and kissed his cheek. "He must, Pyter. I ask so little of him."

"It is not in the contract. He will not bend. He never bends."

She looked up, lost and hopeless, her green eyes over-bright. Her hand wavered, the necklace cradled in her palm.

Finally, Pyter took it from her and tucked it in his pouch. "When he is a man, I will see that he gets this. You have my vow."

She nodded her thanks to Pyter and placed Jole's hand in his. "Protect him for me, Pyter." Jenneane turned her face away, no doubt ashamed to be begging favors of him again.

"As much as Kell Ri will allow." He led Jole away.

Jenneane didn't watch them go. Barri sank to the floor beside her and cradled the princess to her chest, while she cried. Jenneane let Barri comfort her, curling her bare feet under her like a child.

Jole looked up at Pyter as they left the house and headed toward the transports. The bodyguard's face was set in harsh lines, and he looked straight ahead.

"I'm going to my father's house?"

Pyter sighed. "To live, Highness."

Jole nodded in confusion. He'd known he had to live in his father's house when he reached a certain age. "When will I see my mother again?"

"You will not."

Jole stopped, trying to yank his hand from Pyter's grasp. "Why not?" he demanded.

Pyter's voice was bitter and cold. "It was not in the contract."

"My father has seen me every holiday of my life. Was that in the contract?"

"No, but your mother trusted that—" He shook his head and motioned to a transport waiting for them, the soldiers standing at attention for him. "We must go. Your father waits for you."

Jole didn't need Pyter to finish his statement. Jenneane had bent on the agreed terms, believing Kell would extend her the same courtesy. Kell would not extend her that kindness.

He tried again to free his hand, but Pyter's grip was like iron. "No," Jole shouted. "I made no agreement. I won't go."

"Until you are grown, you are at your father's command, Jole."

"No." Jole started kicking and beating at Pyter, screaming for his mother to come to him, to take him back into her home.

Pyter immobilized him, locking Jole to his chest. "You see those soldiers," he whispered. "You are their prince. If you wish your father's approval, you will remember that and act your role."

Jole stilled, suddenly unsure of his course. He would need Kell's permission to see his mother again.

"It is an act, Jole. Only an act. You know who you truly are. Your mother taught you well what you must be, and I've taught you what you must pretend to be."

Jole nodded, and Pyter dropped him to his feet. Pyter reached for his hand, but Jole straightened his spine and walked to the transport with Pyter a step behind.

* * * *

That was the last time Pyter had ever called him 'Jole.'

Over the years, Pyter had been a constant figure in Jole's life. He'd been the one ordered to tell Jole, when his mother died shortly after his twelfth birthday. He'd been the one ordered to tell Jole, whenever his father gave commands Jole would balk at.

Pyter was also the one who'd come to Jole's

rooms when he'd turned twenty and had taken him aside to give him a long-forgotten memento his mother had entrusted to Pyter. Jole had worn that necklace under his uniform or tunic, next to his heart, from that day until the day he'd entrusted it to Susan. Jenneane would have been happy to know that his bride now wore it, as proud as she would be to know that her teachings had allowed Jole to find peace with his mate.

CHAPTER SIX

Susan snapped awake to a hand over her mouth.

Barri's face was inches from her own. "Must be silent, Lady." Her voice was a whisper. "You understand?"

She nodded, and Barri eased her hand away.

"What?" she mouthed. She heard shouts and crashes from far corners of the house, but none of it made sense to her.

"Mik is here. Hi men hold him, but Mik has many men."

"Joel?" She fought to stay calm.

"Still in town. Gone half hour. Not sure how much longer."

Susan nodded and slid off the bed, pulling her boots on. She collected her coat, gloves, and cap, then pulled them on. The echoes of fighting and men shouting got louder, and she looked to the heavy wood doors.

Barri followed, as Susan went to the terrace door and peeked out. She stepped out onto the snow-covered perch.

Barri grasped her arm, wide-eyed, panicked. "What you doing?"

"Just looking." Susan startled at a cry of pain from the stairs. "For now. I hope that was one of Mik's."

She crept further onto the terrace and looked around. Susan could barely make out the backs of several vehicles near the front of the house but no men. The terrace ran along the rear uphill portion of the house.

Susan assured herself that the latticework that reached the two and a half stories to the ground was still in place. She had pointed the structure out to Jole weeks ago and commented that someone could use it to break in. She sighed in relief that he had stalled the work until the snow melted.

That lattice might just be her salvation. Jungle gyms and gymnastics had been years ago, but Susan was confident that she could make it down that way, if she had to. It had to be strong enough to support her weight if it supported iri vines all summer. She nodded to Barri as she slipped back inside.

The servant's eyes narrowed. "What you do?"

"Planned my escape...if I need to."

Barri sighed and shook her head. Whatever protest she was about to make was lost in the sound of Bell's shouted commands and the metallic ring of steel on steel. Mik may be crazy enough to have them use projectile weapons on the lower floors, but he wouldn't risk that near the royal chamber, any more than Bell would typically unholster that type of weapon in this area.

She looked to Susan with a pained expression. "They break through. You right."

Susan shivered. "Only if they breach the doors," she promised.

She didn't add that she had no idea what she'd do if she made it down the latticework. She could hide in the stable, she supposed. It was on the same side of the house. It wasn't heated, but she could bury herself in the feed on the upper levels to conserve heat.

A male scream sent Susan back several steps. She grimaced at Bell's curse at the man who'd downed him. There was a brief silence, and Susan held her breath.

"*We know you're in there, Princess. Don't make us break down the door.*" His Keen was smooth and slow, so that she would be sure to catch every word he spoke.

Susan looked to Barri hopelessly but didn't respond.

The man outside the door switched to deeply accented English. His tone announced that he found using her language disgusting. "Open door or we break."

Susan fastened her coat and nodded to Barri, pulling on her gloves and turning to the terrace door. Something hit the doors, and she winced as she heard wood splinter. "Battering ram," she grumbled as she slipped out onto the terrace. Behind her, the door suffered a new assault. The doors wouldn't hold long.

Barri stepped out behind her and stifled a scream into her fist as Susan threw her leg over the wall. "*No, Princess. You cannot do this,*" she begged in Keen.

Susan smiled weakly. "Don't Keen girls climb trees?"

"*Not usually.*" She looked down at the drop, then closed her eyes. "*Please, don't do this.*"

"Don't worry, Barri. Human and Earth-born re-bred girls do this all the time. Don't watch if it disturbs you."

Liar! Okay, the only major difference is the relative height.

Susan reached out toward the latticework. There was an eight-inch gap between her fingers and the edge. She swore fluently in both languages. "I'll have to make the jump."

Barri grabbed her wrist. "*No. I cannot allow that.*"

Wood splintering steeled Susan's resolve. "Hold my arm and let go when I tell you to."

Barri glanced over her shoulder and nodded, extending her arms, as Susan leaned further out.

Her gloved fingers curled into the lattice. It wasn't a great hold, and Susan knew she couldn't confide her next move to Barri. Better to let her think the hold was solid. "Let go," she ordered in a low voice.

Barri released Susan's arm with a groan of anticipated pain. As Susan expected, her grip wasn't strong enough to support her weight, but the direction of her fall drove her into the lattice. Susan grunted, fisting her hands on the slats and swinging her legs up to grip the toes of her boots in the lower openings. She brushed her cheek on the rough wood but didn't draw blood.

Susan sighed. She looked up at Barri and smiled. Barri seemed unconvinced. She shook fiercely and sank her weight onto the top of the wall.

She descended the lattice easily and offered Barri another smile. That time, the woman nodded and waved her away.

Susan ran for the stable. She was winded

halfway there and stopped to catch her breath, knowing that she had to be hidden before Mik's soldiers broke through onto the terrace.

She glanced back at the house as she rested...and startled at the sight of Gilan's face in one of the kitchen windows. For a moment, they stared at each other, Susan's breath curling before her face in the arctic chill of winter on Kegin.

Susan glanced at the stable and back to the window with a pang of regret. There was no way for her to protect the others in the house.

How angry would Mik be when she wasn't in the royal chamber? Would he hurt her people? She waved to Gilan with a shaky hand and turned away, walking as quickly as she could to the stable. There was nothing she could do but see that Jole avenged any harm Mik did to them. The best thing she could do was hide and hope Jole and Pyter could settle this when they returned.

She looked back in surprise as Gilan's voice reached her through the glass.

"Mik Hi! Hir oct tu!"

"Oh no." That was easy enough to translate. Gilan had told Mik she was outside the window. How could she? Susan must have misheard. She shook her head in dumb shock.

Gilan's face disappeared, pushed aside. Mik's took its place. There was no mistake. Gilan was a traitor. Susan turned and ran. It was no longer a matter of hiding. She had to get away. There were dangerous creatures in the woods, but they were probably less dangerous than Mik.

Susan pushed the stable doors open and rushed inside. She was winded again and her ribs ached beneath her hand. She picked out Chidan in the dim light. The mare accepted her bridle, and Susan launched onto her back.

A man appeared in the doorway. She locked her knees to the hottel's sides and leaned forward with a battle cry. Startled, Chidan shot around Mik's soldier and out onto the hillside. The soldier landed unceremoniously in a heap on the frozen ground.

She reined in for a quick turn and gave Chidan her head toward the woods. The hottel laid on speed, and Susan's hat was whipped off by the wind. Susan heard a sharp report and ducked reflexively. Chidan stumbled, and she was thrown over the mare's head.

The reins were ripped out of her fingers as the animal landed and Susan flew. She landed in a snow bank. The force knocked the air out of her, and Susan struggled as the shock of snow being forced down her neck and boots made her try to suck in air.

A soldier hovered over her, as she coughed weakly, ordering her not to move in a panicked voice. It wasn't in concern for her. He trained his rifle on her as if she would fight him. Susan was caught between the urge to sob and the urge to laugh and had air enough to do neither. Her body felt leaden, and she ached from her head to her wet, frozen feet.

Mik shoved the soldier aside and ran his hands over her. Susan tried to push him away, but he deflected her hands easily. She sank back into the snow. She couldn't fight him yet.

Mik turned on his soldier, landing a punch that knocked him flat. "*You idiot! You could've killed her,*" he roared. Before the downed man could react, Mik grabbed the rifle from his hand and fired a round through his head.

Susan managed a weak scream as his blood sprayed her. She wiped at it with her snow-covered gloves.

Mik dropped the rifle over the soldier's still form and turned to her with wide eyes. "*Be still. It is simply what we do for our mates, what my brother should have done for you,*" he explained. Mik peeled off her ruined gloves and coat, wrapping her in his own.

He pulled her up into his arms, and Susan closed her eyes. She could tell when they neared the house by Barri's screaming. Susan couldn't seem to figure out if it was simply fading away with the distance or being drowned out by the rushing in her ears.

* * * *

Jole startled as Syl ran down the front stairs and waved down the vehicle. Pyter uttered several curses; he swerved to miss the girl, then braked hard. The engine whined at the change and stuttered in protest.

Her screamed entreaties were a jumble that made no sense. Syl was shaking...hitching words between tears. Barri's daughter was a levelheaded young woman. Jole had never seen her so scattered.

He jumped from the vehicle as Syl launched into Pyter's hands and stuttered out the beginnings of a story. Jole sprinted up the porch stairs and into the house.

The entry hall and ballroom had been converted into a field hospital and a morgue. Barri was busy tending to Bell, though it was a better than even chance that her efforts would be in vain. Jole couldn't heal wounds this severe. His healing magic was for minor aches and injuries. Bell grimaced as she tied off the last of the stitches with little or no pain relief. This man had given his all as he'd promised he would.

Jole knelt next to him. "What happened?"

Bell groaned and turned his face away. "I failed you, Highness. I failed the Princess. There were too many and they were let in."

"Let in? By who?"

Barri layered a salve on the stitches and prepared to bind the wound. "It was Gilan, Jole. She let in your brother and his men. Then she turned your bride over to them when Susan would have escaped."

Jole looked at her in disbelief. "Escaped?"

"She climbed down the latticework outside your rooms and ran for the stables. She meant only to hide until you could return for her, but Gilan saw her and called for Mik."

Jole dropped his head to his hands. His eyes locked onto a bundle by Barri's knee. He picked it up with shaking hands and surveyed the bloodstains on Susan's coat and gloves. "Barri?" he asked.

"The blood is not hers. She made it onto a hottel, the one you gave her."

He nodded. Susan loved Chidan; the mare was one of their most gentle.

"One of Mik's men shot it from under her."

Jole snapped his head up, fisting the clothing in his hands in fear and rage.

Barri didn't seem to notice. She pulled the bandage tight on Bell's shoulder. "At least he killed the man for it. The blood is of the soldier who shot at her."

"Susan?"

Barri met his eyes. "Considering the situation, she landed softly, in a bank of snow. She tried fighting Mik off, but she was too worn to stop him from taking her away."

"Was she injured?"

"I don't know, Jole. His men kept me trapped until he was gone."

Pyter stormed in the door with the magistrate at his heels. He paled as he scanned his eyes over the destruction.

"Pyter?" Jole reminded him.

He nodded and locked eyes with Jole. "Communications have been cut. Drive wires on the transports have all been cut. They've been gone for almost an hour."

Jole nodded. "Do we have any able-bodied men left?"

Calls went up from three men in the entry hall. One struggled to his feet and bowed unsteadily. "I cannot fight, but I can work. What would you have me do?"

"Repair the communications and then the

vehicles. Pyter, contact Kell."

Pyter looked at him in concern. "Why?"

"If he doesn't help me, I'll kill him too."

* * * *

Susan planted the heel of her hand to her aching head. Even that movement hurt.

"Ah. She's awake. Good morning, love."

She opened her eyes. Mik sat in a chair pulled next to the bed, smiling at her over a goblet of wine.

Susan grimaced as she tried to move. Her muscles burned in protest. Mik's smile spread. He found her pain funny?

"You hurt."

He certainly seemed amused by it. She looked away.

"I know you understand Keen. Perhaps I should simply heal you. You'd like to be in less pain, wouldn't you?"

"Don't touch me."

"That's better. Talking to me is a good first step. You're right. I won't touch you without your permission, but you'll ask for me soon enough."

"Like your mother asked for Kell Ri? I wouldn't place wagers on it."

"Do you want to know why you'll ask for me?"

Susan roamed her gaze over the room, ignoring him as best she could. Two doors, a minimum of furniture, and no visible windows.

"Come now. I'm sure you're cultay."

"Cultay?" She'd never heard the word before, but she cursed herself for asking. Asking what words she didn't know in Keen were had become a habit.

"Want to know," he explained patiently.

"*Curious*," she noted in English. That was a habit, too. Susan was accustomed to telling Jole and Barri the words in English to correspond to Keen.

Mik leaned forward, locking his hand on her face and dragging her eyes back to his. "Cul-tay," he growled at her. "You will speak Keen. If you ask for something in your Braek language, you will not get it."

Susan smiled sweetly and dusted off her blue-collar American roots. "*Fuck off,*" she suggested in English.

Mik let go of her chin and smacked her across the face so hard that her head swiveled back and pinpoints of pain exploded in her skull. Susan blinked, trying to clear her vision.

Mik's face was contorted with rage. For a split second, she wondered if he knew enough English to translate what she'd said to him. He leaned over her, close enough that she could smell the wine on his breath. His hair fell across his forehead over bloodshot eyes. Susan shrank from him on the bed, and he nodded and pushed back from her.

"You will not speak any language but Keen to me. Do you understand me?"

Susan nodded.

"In Keen," he crooned.

"Yes. I understood."

Mik took his seat, and his smile returned. "Now, I'm sure you're curious."

"I'm not," she whispered. She'd never ask Mik to touch her, and she didn't want to hear his plans for making her resort to that.

"I'll tell you anyway, just so you know the rules. You know the first one." He shot her a hard look, waiting for her to play along.

Susan rubbed her cheek then forced her hand back to her side. "Only Keen."

"Very good. Eventually, you will give me everything you gave my brother, but we will start slowly. You'll let me heal you."

"No." From what Jole said, Mik couldn't know what she felt when Jole used the healing magic, but that made no difference. It was too intimate, and no cross-mate had allowed it. She wouldn't agree to that. "No. You won't touch me."

His eyes narrowed. "In the end, I will."

Susan bit back the urge to give him a bruise to match hers. "Everything you do digs your grave deeper."

Mik laughed. "Because he succeeded in giving you a child? No. As long as you are in my hands, the Council doesn't dare take you by force."

"Joel will—"

"He has no chance. My brother never excelled at cut-throat tactics." He rolled the goblet between his fingers, watching her for a reaction to that. "Now, I am sure that my brother has had to ease your pregnancy signs. Eventually, you'll ask me to do the same, even if it is while you deliver his babies."

"Jenneane lived without it. I can too."

"That may be. I'll wait and see. You'll eat with me."

"I'd rather starve."

"I won't starve you. You do have babies to grow. If you eat with me, you will eat everything you need to do that well and comfortably. If not, I will provide you with pastry and a vitamin drink that will provide the nutrients you and the babies need without helping with your pregnancy signs."

Susan tried to make sense of what he was saying. "You'll use my concern for my babies against me."

"Eventually your concern would convince you, but you'll think you have a few weeks for that. You'll break sooner."

"Why?"

"My mother only lasted her pregnancy without healing, because her servants fed her correctly. I anticipate your need to feed the pain away will come before your willingness to let me heal it away."

Susan grumbled a complaint. Mik laughed and sipped his wine. That part of the plan could conceivably work.

"What are your other rules?" she asked.

"You'll get tired of your clothes when they're dirty enough. You can wear what I give you or wear nothing at all."

Susan swallowed a sour wave at the thought of that option. "You have this all figured out," she noted sarcastically.

"You don't think I do." He raised an eyebrow

in surprise.

She shrugged.

"You're right. I have planned for every eventuality."

"Go on." She might as well know the worst of it now.

"You'll spend time with me. I'll make this simple. The more time you spend with me, the more comfortable your life will be. Since I will be here for meals anyway— Spend an additional two hours a day with me, and you will have an extra quilt to offset the cold you'll feel. Spend an extra four with me, and I'll arrange for fresh air and sunshine."

Susan considered the possibilities of getting out of this room.

"With guards and myself, of course," he qualified.

Mik shot her a hungry look that made her skin crawl and her stomach rebel.

"Agree to let me sleep in your bed, and you'll be treated like a queen. Just to lay next to you, I would give you almost anything."

"And?" She resisted the urge to push further from him on the bed.

"You won't agree to more than that yet. Once your babies are born, they belong to my brother, and he is welcome to them. If you ever want to see them again, you and I will negotiate a contract. In order to see your children to Jole, you will give me my own children, true mate children—along with everything else I've asked for."

She closed her eyes against the wave of

nausea that picture set off. There was no way she would ever agree to that. She'd know Jole was raising their babies without her rather than give Mik what he wanted.

"I'll leave you to think about it. I assume you won't eat with me this morning?"

"No. I won't."

"I thought not. Very well. There is a tray of pastry and beverage on the table."

He had been gone for more than five minutes before Susan moved from the bed. She went to the bathroom first. After she relieved herself and washed her face and hands, she checked the cabinets and drawers. There was nothing she could use as a weapon or even to hurt herself.

Susan searched the bedroom. Her boots and socks were nowhere to be found. She'd lost her hat while she was on Chidan, and Mik had left her coat and gloves behind. Even if she could escape the house, she would freeze.

She groaned at the clothes Mik had for her. They were at least four inches shorter than the dresses Jole had made for her, making her wonder if they had been patterned for someone else. There was no way she would wear one of those, but she had to figure out something soon. Her clothing already carried a pungent odor thanks to her run, her ride on Chidan, and her romp in the snow.

Susan sat at the table and picked up a pastry that resembled a bear claw and was stuffed with a nut paste filling of some sort. She devoured it in four large bites and drank a full glass of the vitamin drink, a rather tasty concoction that reminded her of orange Kool-Aid. Susan was on her third pastry, one filled with cream icing, before she wondered at her voracious appetite. Mik said it was morning. She hadn't eaten in at least a day. She shrugged and reached for a fourth.

She considered Mik's plan. Susan would never contract with him or ask him to share her bed. She'd never let him heal her. Those things were well within her control.

Eventually, she would have to break down and take meals with him. Even if the pain was bearable, she couldn't short-change her babies if she could help it. Susan was hopeful that eating with him would be the only way she would have to fold until— She prayed Jole would get her back before she was big enough to need clothes aside from what she wore.

A smile lit her face. Mik wasn't counting on good old-fashioned Yankee ingenuity. *Never fuck with a Girl Scout.* He wasn't playing with an amateur. Susan liked roughing it. In fact, he was about to get an education.

CHAPTER SEVEN

By the time Mik arrived for lunch, Susan was satisfied with the results of her labor. She couldn't take out stains, but her clothing smelled much better. She would have to wash her clothes directly after one meal in order for them to be ready for the next meal or bed.

Ordinarily, she wouldn't worry about clothing that was still damp, but the blouse she had on was opaque when it was wet. Susan played with the idea of altering one of Mik's dresses to make an undershirt out of the bodice, but without scissors or a knife, even taking out seams was problematic. She settled for keeping a towel handy to wrap around her chest, in case anyone came in before the blouse was sufficiently dry. No one did. Susan was starting to think she'd break of boredom before anything else.

Susan sat at the table with a glass of the vitamin drink when Mik came in. Two soldiers ducked around him, one picking up the tray from the table and the other placing a new tray in its place. Mik raised an eyebrow at the fact that she was sitting at the table. Susan raised her glass to him in mute challenge. The soldiers left without a word, and the door closed.

Mik scowled as he sat across from her. "I suppose you're proud of yourself."

Susan shrugged. "I've learned to live with a lot less than you have. On Earth, we are taught to be resourceful. We're—" *Damn, no word for pioneer.* "We explore. When my babies are big enough, I'll concede defeat. By then, the clothes you have for me will be too small. I trust the—" *Maternity?* "Clothing for a pregnant woman will be suited."

"In what way?"

He took a bite of a native fish called lamor. It tasted quite a bit like salmon but had a blue tinge to the meat. It was one of her favorites. He smiled and motioned to her plate.

Susan set her vitamin drink on the table and crossed her arms over her chest. She tried to ignore her watering mouth and growling stomach. Gilan had done her work well. The servant had nearly four months of trial and error to report to Mik what she liked best. The table was full of her favorites.

She adopted a bored look, which wasn't far from the truth of the matter. "Those clothes are too short for me. They weren't made for me."

"I want to see your legs. You have very shapely legs—or so I believe. It is so hard to tell when you dress like a man."

"Fine. I'll just work something else out. I've been trained to work with what I have on hand."

Mik's eyes narrowed. "We'll see. Why don't you eat?"

"I'd rather starve than face you across a plate of food. It's enough to make me lose my appetite."

Mik stood and walked around her. His hands caressed her shoulders, and she stiffened.

"Get your hands off of me," she growled at

him.

Susan sucked in her breath as one of his hands left her shoulder and the edge of a blade returned. He pulled the fabric away from her shoulder and ripped through it with his knife.

He leaned his face close to her cheek. "Don't move. I don't want to cut you." His free hand locked around her shoulder, and he brushed his lips over her cheek.

She tried to pull her face away, but the point of the knife pressed into her back just far enough to fire her nerves. Susan stilled, her breathing coming in harsh gasps. He kissed her cheek again.

"Don't," she breathed.

Mik's laughter carried the sweet smell of the lamor fish to her. Her stomach rebelled.

"That's better." He moved and placed his lips on her other cheek, nuzzling the bruise he'd left. "Let me heal you."

"No. Never."

The knife moved, ripping a long line from one shoulder to the other of her blouse. Mik's lips found the skin of her back where the fabric gapped.

"Eat with me?" he crooned.

Susan bit her lip, refusing to let him hear the sob she was hiding inside. *No smart retorts. Not now...with that knife to your back.* "I'm not ready."

His fingers brushed inside the tear he made, and she closed her eyes.

"Will you reconsider? It's a small thing to ask. You gave my brother that much. You got to know him."

"Joel treats me with respect. He's never pulled a knife on me or made demands I wasn't ready and willing to meet."

Mik fisted his hand in the fabric and ripped the back out of her blouse with a single pull. "Let's see if you can work with that, love."

His hand moved over her back slowly. His voice was a whisper against her ear. "You know, women were provided for our use, women who couldn't carry children. Jole and I shared quite a few."

He was silent for a moment, and his lips touched her spine. Susan started to pull away, but his knife pressed into her shoulder again. She swallowed a scream of frustration.

Mik kissed the back of her neck. "They told me often that I was the better lover. You should consider that."

He moved away and took his seat. Mik sheathed his knife. Susan dropped her gaze, willing herself not to rock back and forth or cry, though she couldn't stop shivering.

"If you're sure you won't share this meal with me, I think I'll eat in my room. Go to the bathroom while the servants clear. I won't have them see you like this."

Susan ran for the other room, holding back tears as she slammed the door. She sobbed in the realization there was no lock. She slid down the door, shaking, and pulled her knees to her chest while the food was cleared away.

Mik came to the door before he left. "I ask very little. Your food is on the table. I trust you'll be dressed appropriately for the next meal."

As the outer door closed, Susan let the tears fall. It only took a few minutes for fury to overcome her fear and shock. She pushed to her feet and stormed out to the clothes cabinet. One of his accursed dresses in hand, Susan sat cross-legged on the bed.

She pulled at the seam between the bodice and the skirt, but it wouldn't rip. Susan fingered the pendant on her necklace while she pondered her problem. She pulled the necklace up to look at it. It was a simple rose quartz crystal from Earth that had belonged to Jole's mother. It was a thin column, and thin was what she needed.

Susan pulled off the necklace and used it to snag a thread in the seam. She used her teeth to break the thread, then started using the crystal to unravel the seam. It would take hours, but she would have a shirt.

She looked at the necklace in concern. Mik would take it if he saw it, and she couldn't hide it under the low-cut bodice like she could under her blouse. There were no pockets in her trousers and no boots to hide it in. Susan scrambled off the bed and pushed it as far under the mattress as she could reach before going back to her work.

When the seam was halfway out, she brought the tray to the bed and smiled as she ate a pastry that was reminiscent of a cream cheese croissant. "Dressed appropriately? When Hell freezes over." She offered that sentiment in English.

Susan shivered. She wrapped the quilt

around her shoulders as she worked. *Hell might freeze over—or at least, I might.* Mik was right about one thing. The pregnancy symptoms were getting worse.

* * * *

Susan pretended to be asleep while the servants cleared her lunch tray and set up dinner. Her stomach complained at her treatment of late. She didn't want to get out of bed. Facing Mik was one thing. Facing Mik over a plate full of steak and whatever other tortures Gilan had arranged for her was more than she could stand.

"Come to the table."

"I don't feel well." That wasn't a lie. She needed Jole.

You need to eat. Oh, shut up!

"I could heal you." It was a statement of fact, without emotion or embellishment.

"No." *Anything but that.*

"Then come eat with me. The food will make you feel better. Do you really think my brother wants this sacrifice from you? He'd want you to take away your pain and feed his babies."

Susan closed her eyes tighter and rubbed her aching neck. Jole would want that, but it went beyond that. She had to seem immovable. She wouldn't give up after only two meals—less than a day. "No."

"Come to the table." His voice was harsher, now.

"I told you—"

"You will join me, whether you choose to eat or not."

Susan groaned and pulled the quilt over her head. She couldn't face that food again. She stiffened, as Mik pulled the quilt back to just above her waist.

He made a sound of approval, his fingers tracing the line of ties down her back. "Sensible choice. I will give you another simple choice. Walk to the table, or I will carry you."

"I don't feel well," she whispered, her voice hoarse and weak.

Mik ran the palm of his hand around her ribs until it rested above her navel and below her breasts. His voice was husky in arousal. "I'd like to carry you. I'd like to feel you in my arms."

Susan launched off of the bed, tangling in the quilt and landing awkwardly on her knees on the floor. She pushed to her feet, turning back to him and smoothing the bodice over the waistline of her trousers.

Mik's smile disappeared as he surveyed her outfit. "What have you done?" he demanded.

"You ripped my shirt. I ripped your gown to make a new one. It was a fair trade."

He shook his head in obvious annoyance. "Do I have to cut those damned trousers off of you to get you to dress properly?"

Susan took a step back, and his smile returned. He'd enjoy that. Mik liked keeping her afraid of what he'd do next.

She shrugged. "You'll just make me hate you more if you do, and it won't matter. There are half a dozen things in this room I can fashion into another pair."

She kept a straight face as his eyes hardened. It was a white lie. She could fashion a pair of makeshift pants, but it wasn't nearly as easy as she was making it sound. Mik stretched out on the bed and ran his eyes over her with a hungry look. Susan forced her feet to the floor, on the verge of taking another automatic step back.

"I can see why my brother allowed this form of dress. Would you like to stay in bed this meal?"

"Not if you're staying there."

Mik unfurled from the bed and walked to her. "Name your price. I can be very generous. For the price of a kiss, I would leave now and allow you your fill of the foods you need. One kiss."

"Only an idiot presses for more, when I won't give at a lesser level."

"Only a fool denies me the things I can easily take."

"You can't," she stormed. "Joel said—"

Mik's hands closed on her arms. Susan saw him coming and set her lips in a thin line as he pressed his mouth to hers. She counted the seconds, trying to ignore his attempts to entice her to accept his advances. It wasn't that Mik didn't know how to convince a woman, but he chose the wrong woman to convince. He pushed away, fury in every inch of his darkened face.

"I could make you accept me."

"Not willingly. Not ever."

He brushed his fingertips over her nipple through the bodice. When Susan tried to pull away, he pushed her back into the cabinet behind her and continued his exploration of her. She reached toward his belt for a weapon. Mik smiled. He'd stopped wearing his knife. Susan started to knee him, and Mik crushed her against the cabinet with his body, capturing her hands when she tried to punch him.

His face was inches from hers. "There is always something more than what I am asking of you, and compliance will be very pleasant."

"You're breaking the rules of your people. You can't take me by force."

"I won't have to. I'll simply raise the wager of every interaction, until you decide the cost is too high for you to continue the game. When you do, you'll learn how enjoyable it is to accept me, and you will be more likely to accept my terms in the future.

"We'll start with a kiss. The wager has been raised. Between your failure to eat with me and your failure to let me heal you, you will eventually decide the cost is too high to continue your refusal. When you do, you will kiss me before you collect that which you seek."

He removed his hands from her wrists and cupped her closer to his body; caressing her back and buttocks as he pulled her away from the cabinet. Susan stiffened and looked away as his erection pressed into her hip. Mik's expression clearly showed that he didn't understand her complete lack of arousal with him. He eased his hands from her and let her distance herself from him.

"Will you eat with me?" His voice was uncertain this time.

"No."

"Very well. I'll leave you for the night then...unless you'd prefer to sit and talk a while to win a second quilt for your bed."

"No. I'll be fine."

Mik nodded and motioned her away from the cabinet. Susan moved, retreating to the bathroom door. He opened the cabinet and pulled out three cloaks and the matching presentation gowns.

"Just so you don't get the idea of pulling them apart and using them for their warmth," he commented with a strained smile.

Susan nodded. She hadn't considered that yet, but it might have been her next move.

Mik left, and the two soldiers removed the tray of food, replacing it with the tray of pastry and vitamin drink. Susan felt sick at the sight of it. She never realized how tired of sweets a person could become when they were all you had. She rubbed her forehead, grimacing at the blinding headache gaining steam.

Susan bit back tears. She should have given in while the stakes were low. Now, he was raising them to break her faster. Her stomach turned at the thought of letting Mik kiss her. If it meant not letting that happen, she'd almost consider letting him heal her and hiding her response, if there was a response to hide...but he said any choice she made. That would mean letting him kiss her and letting him heal her. This just kept getting worse.

Mik appeared in the doorway, looking at her as if he expected her to change her mind and invite him back into her room. The rebellion in her stomach reached a crescendo, and she stumbled into the bathroom.

His voice came through the closed door. "You have two days. Then the wager is raised again. Consider your position carefully."

"I will," she replied weakly, sinking down next to the toilet. She didn't throw up, though she supposed there wasn't much left to lose five hours after her last meal.

She rose, shaking, and turned on the shower as hot as she could bear. Susan stepped in fully clothed. Normally, she'd wash her clothing separate from her body, but she was beyond caring. The need to wash away the feel of Mik's hands and lips on her over the last day was intense. She couldn't let him touch her again. Whatever she had to do to stop that, she would do.

* * * *

"You didn't eat." Mik's voice cut through the fog in her mind like slivers of glass tearing through flesh, with as much pain and unwelcome appearance.

Susan pressed her hands to her temples, sweating and shaking. She shivered, cold even completely wrapped in the quilt like a sleeping bag. It wasn't large enough to make into a proper cocoon, though she doubted that would take away the feeling of being encased in ice.

"Come to the table."

She pulled herself out of the bed, her knees rubbery beneath her. Susan dropped into her chair at the table, avoiding Mik's eyes and the sight of food. If she could ignore the smell of it, she might stay sane for another day.

"Let's see. This morning we have eggs, fruit, milk, and—now that's odd. Why would Gilan add lamor again?"

Susan closed her eyes. Jole had fed her bits of lamor fish from the evening before the first morning she woke in his bed. Then he'd made love to her. He'd ordered her lamor countless times in their months together. It was her favorite, and both Jole and Gilan knew that.

"Why would Gilan add lamor?" he repeated, clearly demanding an answer this time.

"She thinks you can break me, if the payoff is good enough." She opened her eyes and let her gaze drift to the fish fillet.

"Lamor is a common fish." He sneered at that, as if something common was beneath him.

"I like it." It couldn't hurt to admit that. He'd know how determined she was, if he knew her favorites couldn't break her. Susan leaned her forehead into her hands and massaged her scalp.

"It's much worse today, isn't it? Carrying two babies must make the progression more severe. You can't think clearly, can you?"

Susan didn't answer. She was too busy trying to recite times tables while she kept massaging her scalp. *Seven times eight is fifty-*

six. Eight times eight...

"The toxins are building up in your system, but you can get rid of them before they do you damage. All you have to do is eat."

Eight times eight is... She looked up at the plate, and her mouth watered. Susan picked up the fork and stared at it. It would be so easy to give in. The pain would recede until she could think again. If only he'd made that argument last night instead of raising the stakes, she could take the out now. *Sixty-four. Eight times nine is...seventy-two.*

Mik was at her shoulder. "That's right, love. You do want to eat, don't you?"

Eight times ten is eighty. "You know I do."

"Good. Why don't you?"

Eight times eleven is eighty-eight. Eight times twelve is... "You know why." She looked at her reflection in the slight bowl of the fork then away as she saw Mik's satisfaction in his reflection. *Ninety-six. This isn't good enough. The capitol of Pennsylvania is Harrisburg.*

"My price? It's a small thing, meaningless."

Area forty-six thousand square miles. "No. It's not."

"Are you saying it would mean something more than defeat to you?"

Population twelve million. "No, but it would to you." *Population density 263 people per square mile.*

"Yes, it would." He shifted, and his lips brushed over hers. "Kiss me. Just one kiss."

Mik brushed his lips over hers again, and Susan struck. She grasped a handful of his hair in her left hand and planted the fork under his jaw with her right.

"This won't kill you, but it will hurt and leave a scar. If you touch me again— If you *ever* touch me again, I will do my best to kill you. Do you understand me?"

"Little Braek." His eyes glowed in the promise of violence.

"What is a Braek?" she demanded.

"An uncivilized animal."

"Good. Remember this image. The next time you see me like this, you won't survive." Her hands shook. If she killed him, Kell Ri would kill her. If he touched her again, she wasn't sure she'd care.

Mik grabbed for her hand, and the fork cut into his skin as he yanked it away. For a moment, she sat staring at the blood welling up in the cuts and running down the line of his jaw to his throat. Susan opened her hands, letting the fork fall away and releasing his hair. Mik pushed her away, and she wrapped her arms around her chest, meeting the fury in his eyes.

He scooped up the fork and threw it on the tray. Mik took the tray to the door and shoved it into the hands of a wide-eyed soldier. He barked a command at the man that Susan didn't recognize. When Mik returned to her side, he had a pair of shackles with a short bar between them in his hands.

His eyes were cold and flat. "If you need to relieve yourself, do it now."

Susan nodded and ambled to the bathroom. Mik was waiting for her outside the door. He pulled her to the bed by her upper arm and motioned to the mattress. She laid down as he instructed and extended her arms through the slats without him asking.

The shackles locked in place; he sat down beside her. "I could do you damage in return. I won't. You have one day. If you do not offer that kiss freely and make it worth my trouble, I will raise the wager again." He pulled the quilt over her and left without further comment.

Susan bit back a sob. It had been a stupid move, a desperate move. She knew that almost as much as she knew she could never give in, now. Susan had to start using her head, but how could she use her head when it felt like her brain was a time bomb, and the ticking was getting louder by the second?

* * * *

Susan didn't bother to open her eyes, as the shackles were removed.

"Clean yourself." The voice wasn't male.

She cracked her eyes open and groaned at the sight of Gilan. "Traitor," she croaked out.

"I said to clean yourself. Prince Mik will be here for lunch soon."

"I don't want any."

"You're being stubborn for no good reason. All you have to do is eat with him."

Susan moved her stiff arms down to her stomach and started rubbing away the soreness at her wrists. "And allow his filthy hands on me," she added.

"Would that be so terrible? I've had them both."

Susan scowled at her, her stomach turning at the idea of Jole in bed with this snake.

"Oh, yes. I volunteered to be schente and become one of the women for their use. It is a good thing for a woman with no prospects. You spend a year or two kept in comfort, while the young princes find their pleasure—and sometimes yours, until they tire of you and seek new lovers to hold their interest. Then you are rewarded with a lifetime position in royal service.

"I've had them both many times, and I must tell you that Prince Mik far outperforms his brother. When I was in the palace, I would switch with the other girls to find myself in Mik's bed whenever I could."

Susan snorted. "They switched with you. That should tell you something. So far, I've been unimpressed with Mik." She fought back nausea when she tried to move.

"If you tell Prince Mik that, he will kill you."

"Good. I'd rather be dead than have his hands on me again."

"Clean yourself."

Susan rolled to her feet and met Gilan's eyes. "Maybe I should take Mik up on his offer. I could make my own special deal. The head of Gilan on a platter in exchange for one evening sleeping in my room. Think it's worth that much to him to brag that he slept under the same quilts as I did, Gilan? Do you think you're worth that much to him?

"You were worth my guilt, when I had to leave you in his hands, before I knew you betrayed me. You were worth my vow once, that I'd have Joel revenge you if Mik hurt you. Are you worth that much to anyone, now that you're not worth it to me?"

Gilan stepped back as Susan lurched around her and into the bathroom. Susan may have to take Mik's crap, but she'd be damned if she'd take Gilan's. She fumed her way through a basic bathroom routine.

The scene in the bedroom confused her at first. Gilan stood transfixed, staring at something in the palm of her hand. The servant turned suddenly, and her hand closed on a flash of rose quartz.

Susan's fury cut through the pain in her head. She made it to Gilan before the other woman could move and grabbed her by the throat. "Drop it on the bed and get out," she roared.

Gilan's wide eyes narrowed as the door swung in.

The soldiers entered the room. "Let go of the servant," one of them ordered.

"When she returns what she has stolen."

He handed his weapons to the second soldier and stormed toward her. "I said to let her go. I will use force if necessary."

"The last man who injured me ate his own weapon at Mik's hand."

He looked to his partner as if seeking instruction. The other soldier waved him on.

"Let her go," the second man instructed in a

calmer voice than his underling.

"When she returns the necklace, I'll set her free."

The soldier attempted to remove her hands, and Susan kneed him solidly in the groin. As he went down, the second soldier huffed. He dropped his weapons and his friend's in the corridor and stalked her direction. One arm closed around her ribs and the other struck her once at the elbows to break her grip. He pinned her arms to her body before she could reason out a counterattack.

"Get out," he ordered Gilan.

Gilan nodded gratefully, still gasping for air, then ran, clutching the necklace to her chest. Susan watched her go, fighting back tears.

"Are you finished?" the soldier asked patiently.

She dropped her chin to her chest and nodded.

He placed her on the bed and dragged his partner up by the arm. The door closed behind them.

Susan allowed her tears to fall, curling to her side without pulling the quilt over herself. It was all she had left of Jole, and it was gone. Why hadn't she found a more secure place to hide it? She stifled her tears as the door opened again. It would be Mik this time.

"Does the pendant mean that much to you?" His voice was unreadable.

"It's not mine." It was technically a lie. Jole gave the necklace to her.

"Whose is it then?"

"It belongs to Joel. You would be wise if you returned it to him."

"Why would my brother have something like this?"

"That's right. You never met your mother, did you? You don't have any memories of her to hold dear." She was being snide. Susan had no idea if Mik's mother would mean anything to him. Maybe he didn't miss not having her, since he never knew her.

"This belonged to *her*?" His voice was a choked whisper at that.

"She gave it to Joel."

Mik took a long, deep breath. She didn't look at him. Telling him where the necklace came from was a long shot, but she hoped Mik wouldn't want to cross that line with Jole.

"I'll see that he gets it back."

Susan didn't answer. She'd rather have it, but it was the best she could do.

"Will you eat with me?"

"No."

There was a moment of silence before the tray clinked onto the table. "You've skipped two meals. Don't skip another. The guards will be in to bind you in an hour. I don't..." Mik sighed. He left without waiting for her response.

Susan forced herself up and managed two glasses of the vitamin drink. She took one bite of a cream-filled pastry before deciding that it wouldn't sit well in her stomach. Susan used the bathroom and lay on the bed, waiting for the soldiers to bind her hands again.

CHAPTER EIGHT

Jole looked up at Pyter in confusion. "What did you just say?"

"A package for you, Highness." The small, thick envelope rested in his hands.

"Who brought it?"

"One of your brother's men. He is being questioned."

Jole took a calming breath. Mik had all but disappeared with Susan. He wasn't at his home or his normal retreat home. So far, none of the properties Jole had checked showed any sign that Mik had used them recently.

Kell claimed he was helping in the search, but Jole wasn't taking the chance that his father was telling him the truth. There were too many years and too much history between them to trust Susan to his father.

The only communication from Mik so far had been a single notice to the Council, stating that he would care for Susan while she was his guest. Predictably, the Council was unwilling to interfere in Mik's plans.

He snatched the envelope from Pyter and ripped it open with shaking fingers. Jole groaned as the pendant slid into his hand and sat heavily on the stairs leading to the outer office. "Where did he come from? What direction?"

"North."

"I want to question him."

"Highness—"

"Now, Pyter," he demanded. "I will not beg you as my mother begged you. He's had her for three days. I must know if this man knows anything that can help me find her."

"As you wish. I'll have him brought here."

Jole watched Pyter walk away, his heart aching. He placed the pendant around his neck reverently, leaving it outside his tunic for the first time since he'd received it.

There was a reason for this. There was a reason Mik sent this to him. Susan would never give the pendant up willingly.

He scrubbed his hand over the stubble on his cheeks. Even if Mik were taking excellent care of her, Susan would be hurting. Jole grimaced at telling her that she was the first cross-mate to accept the healing magic. She'd never let Mik help her now.

The doors to the far corridor opened, and Jole rose to his feet. The prisoner came in, half-dragged by two soldiers. Pyter dismissed them and closed the doors behind them.

The messenger knelt on the floor, much as Bell had when he'd waited for his execution, but this man had been beaten severely in hopes of extracting information. The man looked at Jole fearfully.

"Where is my bride?"

"I don't know, Highness. I swear, I don't."

"Where and when were you given that package? Who gave it to you?"

"Your brother. In Lind, this afternoon."

Lind. Mik was only an hour away in Lind not more than three hours earlier. "What did you do to find yourself in poor graces with Mik?"

The man shrugged hopelessly.

Jole nodded. "Then he hopes I'll spare you as innocent in this matter." He shook his head in exhaustion. Where was Mik coming from if he was that close? He wouldn't leave Susan for long. "Where did you meet him?" Jole asked.

"The Jumping Lamor."

"An inn?" *What game was this? Mik wouldn't visit a common inn if his life depended on it.*

"Yes, Highness."

"In the common room?"

"No, he had rooms there."

Gods! It couldn't be that simple. "How many traveled with him?"

The man shrugged. "I saw only a woman. She was a servant, I believe, a bed maid or schente."

Jole felt a sick swirl in his stomach. "Young and golden-haired?"

He shook his head. "Your own age and dark haired."

Jole sighed in relief and looked at Pyter. "Have him put in a cell and have his wounds tended to. Tell the men that we leave in half an hour."

"How many?"

"Leave a small complement here. The rest travel with us."

"And me?"

Jole fingered the pendant. "She never gave up, did she? My mother tried to renegotiate until the day she died. What do you know, Pyter?"

He blanched. "Yes, but all she had to offer

was true mating to a daughter. You know she couldn't—"

"You'll come with me, Pyter. Promise me you'll protect Susan as you always did my mother and me. That's enough for me."

"You have my vow, Highness."

Jole nodded and retreated to his room. He hadn't slept in the bed since Susan was taken, and he looked it. The nights of catnaps in the chairs in his library or office had left him pale, with dark circles under his eyes, and rumpled. Jole hadn't bothered to bathe or shave, afraid to miss that one moment when he would learn where Mik was hiding her.

He shaved and showered. Then he put on his uniform.....with his dagger and the laser-edged sword. He'd meet his brother as a warrior, and Mik would regret taking Susan from him.

Jole surveyed the six dozen troops filing into the transports to follow him. Four dozen were his own men, called in as excess from his three estates on this continent. The other two were his father's; sent to him on the condition that Jole wouldn't kill Mik unless he was left with no choice.

He settled into his transport next to Pyter, looking to the disappearing sun in frustration. It would be dark by the time they reached the inn in Lind. Either way, there was little chance of a battle tonight.

* * * *

135

Susan could taste the lamor. *I'm hallucinating. Oh, but what an enjoyable hallucination.*

Something touched her lips, and she recoiled. *No!* There was food in her mouth. She spit it out and locked her jaws together, as more food touched her lips. She pulled at the shackles, feeling them bite into her wrists. She tried to roll away, but a hand cupped around her hip, stilling her escape.

"Eat. You must eat."

Mik's hand touched her shoulder, and Susan cried out in agony. Every muscle hurt. Her skin hurt. Her hair hurt. She'd always thought people who said that were exaggerating, but it was possible. His hand curled in her hair, and his lips touched her forehead. Susan brought her legs up, kicking him solidly if blindly.

"Your system can't handle this," he pleaded with her. "Eat or let me heal you."

Susan looked at him blearily. She couldn't give in to him now. There was too much at stake. "No. I know your price." Her voice was rough. It hurt to talk to him.

"Forget my price! You've gone too far." He sounded panicked. "Eat. Please eat."

"No." She threw her head aside and spit the food Mik popped into her mouth while she spoke back into his face.

A warm cloth bathed her face. "Please, Susan. You must eat."

She looked at him in confusion, but Mik was an indistinct blur. Mik and Kell didn't believe in calling cross-mates by their human names. Jole told her that, didn't he?

"Please eat, Susan. I want nothing more from you."

"No." He couldn't mean it. It was a trick. It had to be a trick. "Not for you."

The shackles were unlocked, and she pulled her arms to her chest.

"Drink then." His voice was low and soothing. "You need something. If you won't eat, drink."

Susan didn't answer. A cup touched her lips, and she gulped down several mouthfuls of the liquid inside. *Milk!* Susan took it in her hands and kept drinking.

Mik sighed. "It won't be enough to reverse this, but it will keep you from getting worse for a few hours. Please eat."

Susan stared at the empty cup and sobbed. "No."

Mik took the cup and refilled it, pressing it to her lips again. "Then drink more."

* * * *

Jole fingered the hilt of his dagger. Pyter had demanded to enter Mik's rooms at the inn first. Whether it was to keep Jole safe, to shield Mik from Jole, or to keep Jole from seeing what Mik might have done to Susan was a mystery to him.

Pyter called out to him, and Jole stormed into the room. He headed for the bed with a strangled cry, but the woman bound and gagged wasn't Susan. Pyter restrained him, when Jole would have killed Gilan with his bare hands.

"Susan," he whispered to Jole. "Remember your bride. You can't get information from her if she's dead."

Jole nodded, and Pyter released his grip. Jole ripped the tape from her mouth and smirked in satisfaction as Gilan winced and licked her lips.

"Haven't the tables turned?" Jole drawled at her. "The traitor placed in my hands to deal with by the master she served so well."

Gilan swallowed and nodded.

Pyter grasped her chin and tipped it up to examine the bruises around her throat. "Mik did this to you?"

She shook her head and glanced at Jole before meeting Pyter's eyes. "Not that. Just..." She looked to her bound hands.

"Who do we have to thank for it then?" Jole asked, smiling. "I'll have to reward him for his loyalty and good sense."

Gilan looked to Pyter as if asking for his help. "Princess Susan," she admitted.

Jole's smile disappeared. "Why? What did you do to her?"

"I took her pendant from her room."

Jole turned away, fisting his hands. She took the pendant from Susan. That was how Mik got it from her.

Pyter placed a hand on his shoulder and started talking. "Why were you left here?"

She paused. "To lead you to her."

"So Prince Mik can use the Princess against us?" Pyter asked in a voice dripping with sarcasm.

Her voice dropped to a whisper. "No. To take her back. She'll die before she submits to him. He knows that now."

Jole spun back to the bed, and Pyter placed a hand on his chest to stop him.

"What has he done to her?" Jole demanded.

Gilan met his eyes fully for the first time. "He tried to break her, but he broke first."

Pyter nodded. "Why leave you like this? So you couldn't run from your punishment?"

She shook her head. "It's my punishment from Prince Mik, for turning her over to him. It would have been better for each of them if I hadn't helped him capture her."

"Why the shackles?"

Gilan looked away. "He said— This is how he ends up treating someone he loves."

Jole swallowed a cry of pure rage and turned away. "We're going tonight. Unbind her and let the captains know that we're not staying here. The servant is going with us. If this is a trap, she dies by my dagger."

Pyter bowed and reached for the key left for them. "Yes, Highness. With pleasure."

* * * *

Jole and his men came at the house in force, but it proved unnecessary. The soldiers at the door opened for them and bowed to him. They were taken into custody, as Jole surveyed the wreckage around him.

He had forgotten these ruins. They hadn't

been used in two generations. From the dust on the surfaces, he guessed that there was no household staff save Gilan. Some of the furniture had crumbled, and there were broken windows with snow sifting around the wood patches. It was cold, much colder than Susan should have to be.

Gilan lead them up and out into one of the wings. They passed many open rooms; some ruins like the entry hall had been and some clean and in use by soldiers who surrendered themselves into his hands. It was warmer here, but not as warm as the rooms at his retreat home.

Jole nodded, as two soldiers set their weapons on the floor and backed from the last door on the corridor. "That is the room?" he asked Gilan.

"Yes, Highness. It is the Princess's room."

Jole pulled Pyter away from the door and drew his dagger. "No. I'll do this. If Mik is in there, he will not survive."

Pyter nodded and pushed Gilan toward Mik's soldiers, motioning their own men to handle the prisoners while he prepared to guard Jole's back.

There was no sign of Mik, but the unruly mop of gold curls on the bed was undoubtedly Susan. Jole muttered a string of harsh curses as he sheathed his dagger and crossed the room in three jumps.

She was curled into a ball and shivering despite the fact that her room was the warmest he had encountered and the two quilts that covered her. Her skin was cold, but she was sweating. The smell of toxins was strong. He pulled the quilts back to look at her.

Susan wore a bodice ripped from a gown in place of the blouse she'd worn when she was taken. Jole sobbed at the sight of the cuts and bruises on her wrists. Susan had been shackled. He cradled one hand to his mouth to heal her, but Susan moaned and her muscles bunched in protest to his touch.

Jole had more pressing problems. He cradled her head and pressed his lips to her forehead. Her pregnancy signs had reached dangerous levels, and he tasted the sour toxins on her skin. At the first burst of his healing, Susan's entire body started to seize.

Pyter rushed to the other side of the bed, banking the quilts around her to keep Susan from hurting herself. "Again," he shouted. "You must help her back."

Jole nodded and concentrated another burst.

Susan screamed and started flailing. She grasped the hilt of Jole's dagger and started to pull it free. "No! Told you— I told you I'd kill you." The words were uttered in a hoarse voice and broken Keen.

Pyter grasped her wrist. "She doesn't know it's you. Toss it away while you work."

Jole nodded. He pried the dagger from her hand and dropped it on the floor then sent his sword after it. He grimaced as he saw Pyter examining a deep bruise on her cheek.

What went on here?

Pyter started to pull her wrists over her head, and Susan screamed, sobbing at the move.

He shook his head and lowered them to her sides, holding them to the bed while Jole worked.

Jole let out his breath slowly and cupped her face. He administered another burst. Pyter dropped his upper body on her legs, halting her attempts at kicking.

She sobbed hopelessly. "Don't touch me again," she whispered. "Rather die."

Jole stifled a sob and called on his healing again. Susan relaxed in his hands. He started massaging her muscles, healing the painful knots and forcing the toxins out.

A commotion outside the door sent Pyter that direction. He returned with a tray of food, and Jole sent him a look of surprise.

"Mik ordered it," Pyter informed him. "She'll eat with you."

Jole groaned. "Why did I tell her?"

"Tell her what?"

"That other cross-mates refused to eat with the men they were brought to."

Pyter winced. "You couldn't know, and Mik could have allowed her to eat alone. If he was trying to force her to eat with him, he was trying to break her."

Susan opened her eyes, though they were still unfocused. "Didn't break. I'll never— Remember that."

Jole nodded. "Susan, it's me. You have to eat now."

She shook her head. "Know your price. No deal."

He looked at Pyter hopelessly. "She doesn't know me."

Pyter nodded. "She's trying to sweat out the toxins you released from her tissues. Help her."

"How?"

"A hot shower and milk from the tray."

Jole nodded and carried her to the bathroom. He stripped off her clothing and his own. Susan didn't seem to realize what he was doing. Jole was thankful for that. If she didn't realize, she wouldn't fight what he had to do. He stepped under the hot spray Pyter started for them and started washing the slick from her skin with a cloth.

Pyter handed in a cup of milk, pressing it to her lips. "Drink this, Princess," he ordered.

She sipped at it then grasped the cup and drank deeply.

Gods, she was starved. Jole looked to Pyter. "Get a pitcher of milk."

The older man nodded and headed away. Susan finished the cup and cradled it to her chest. Jole pulled her wrists to his mouth one at a time and healed the damage. Susan sighed against his chest and nestled closer to him. He started to heal the bruise on her face, and she screamed, pushing away from him.

Jole pulled her to his chest, and crooned to her, promising not to touch the bruise again. Susan shuddered and settled into his arms as Pyter bolted back into the room with the pitcher of milk and wild eyes. He retrieved the cup from the tub, returning it to her full again.

It was two more cups of milk and several rounds of his healing before Susan seemed to comprehend what was going on around her. She met Pyter's eyes and gasped, covering herself. Pyter bowed to her and left the room, allowing her privacy.

Susan ran her fingers over Jole's cheek and furrowed her brow. "I'm dreaming. I'm *hallucinating,*" she started in Keen and slipped the English word in. Susan stiffened and looked at him fearfully.

Jole kissed her forehead, reining in the need question that look. "*I'm no dream. Can you eat?*" Perhaps using English would soothe her.

She curled to his chest. "With you? Yes." As if in confirmation, her stomach grumbled.

Jole stood her against the wall, bracing her up with his body as he dried them both. He wrapped her in a towel and carried her back to the bedroom, nodding to Pyter on the way.

Pyter motioned to the bed. "I had the sheets changed to rid it of the smell of toxins."

Jole wrapped Susan in a fresh quilt. He fed her half of the food from the tray before she nodded off to sleep. Pyter motioned to a carafe of milk on ice, then removed the tray of food. Jole pulled the second quilt over both of them and wrapped her in his arms.

CHAPTER NINE

Susan smiled at the memory of her dreams. She had been back in Jole's arms. He'd kissed her, and there had been food. He'd healed her.

She shifted beneath the quilt and froze. Her clothes were gone. Susan opened her eyes slowly. She stifled a sob at the sight of the room she'd been trapped in with Mik. An arm crossed over her hip, and a man spooned up behind her.

Susan screamed in anguish. *I didn't— Oh God, tell me I couldn't have done this.* She remembered Mik trying to feed her. She'd hurt so badly, she couldn't think. Susan had wanted that food. She drank the milk like she was dying for it. She'd wanted the pain to end. *What did I agree to?*

She started crying as the arms wrapped around her. She should have given in earlier, when the price was just sharing a meal with him.

"Susan, please calm down."

She turned toward the voice in disbelief. Jole's face was frantic. His eyes were wide and he ran his fingers over her cheek.

"What is it? Please, Susan."

"Joel?"

He nodded, and she wrapped her arms around his shoulders and sank into his chest. She couldn't seem to stop shaking.

His arms tightened around her. "What did he do to you?" he breathed.

"Not now. Please, not now."

Jole kissed her forehead, healing the nagging headache she'd almost ceased to notice over the days without his healing.

"When you're ready," he assured her.

A knock sounded at the door, and Susan shrank closer to him.

Jole massaged her back. "It will be Pyter," he assured her. "Come in," he shouted toward the door.

As promised, Pyter ducked in the door, looking strained. "Is the Princess all right? Do you need anything?"

Susan bit back tears. Pyter asked his question in English. Jole spoke to her in English. She'd forgotten how wonderful it sounded to hear her native language.

"Food and milk," Jole requested.

"Princess?"

She took a deep breath. "*Clo.*" She blushed and started again. "Clothes. Please Pyter, not—" Susan looked toward the cabinet Mik stored the gowns in.

"I took the liberty of having your own things cleaned, though I found a man's shirt for you," Pyter offered.

"Not Mik's."

"No, Princess. One of our men. You have my word."

She nodded.

Jole stroked her back beneath the quilts. "Thank you, Pyter." His voice rumbled against her ear, and he kissed her hair.

Pyter left the room to arrange for their food, and Susan looked up at Jole, at a loss for words.

He brushed his fingers over her cheek. "Please, let me remove this now." He swallowed hard and met her eyes.

Susan touched the bruise on her cheek, then nodded.

Jole moved slowly, cupping her face up to his as he healed the bruise. Susan closed her eyes in the accompanying washes of pleasure that followed each pulse of ice and fire. She shivered, her nerves jumping at the feeling of his mouth on her. When the bruise was healed, he planted a gentle kiss on her lips and sighed.

Susan ran her hands over Jole's chest. "Is he—" She wasn't sure which answer she hoped for, alive so Jole wouldn't have to live with killing his brother or dead and no more danger to anyone.

"Mik?"

She nodded.

"I'll ask Pyter when he comes back. I was more concerned with you. The only reason I would have taken a moment for him would have been if Mik stood in my way."

"Are you going to kill him?"

"I promised my father I wouldn't, unless he forced me to. It may be kinder to kill him. Making him wait fifteen years for a mate is cruel, but I did promise."

"I've been wondering about that."

"About what?" He started healing the smaller bruises along her jaw line.

Susan sighed and tipped her head for him. "You mentioned rH incompatibility. Do you know how humans treat it?"

Jole pulled back and met her eyes in confusion. "Treat? There's a *treatment*?"

"Your scientists didn't scan human scientific developments over the years, did they?"

He shook his head.

"They thought human science was inferior to their own and didn't bother checking?"

He blushed. "There's really a treatment?"

"Yes. It's called Rhogam. It will help a mother carry a child, and another shot after delivery erases residual traces so she can deliver as many incompatible babies as she wants with the shots every time."

"If this technology works, Mik could choose any woman on Kegin to be his mate and carry his children."

"Better. Keen women could carry cross-bred implanted babies and speed up the process."

"They'd all be male."

"Yes, but they could mate with Keen women."

Jole sucked in his breath. "We have to get dressed."

"Why?"

"I have people to talk to. We only have a window of gateway scanning Earth electronic media for two more months. We have to start now."

* * * *

Jole surveyed the faces of the scientists gathered behind Susan's shoulders. She'd requested a scan gateway with an English keyboard and had been pulling up information at an incredible rate of speed for more than two hours. Her ability to read English allowed her to separate useful information from fluff almost immediately, and she marked positions for the scientists to use later.

The medical men were rapt, as she explained in detail how the process would work. Jole resisted the urge to remind them that they were not permitted to stare so intently at her. She was, after all, addressing them directly, and their interest was in her knowledge and not her beauty.

"Because *Rhogam* is a *gamma globulin*, which you gentlemen say you already understand, with *rH antibodies*, we'll need two groups of women. The first group of women will have to be implanted, on the agreement that their babies will be *aborted* before permanent damage is done to the mothers."

Dr. Peri stepped in. "What is that word? Ab—abor..."

Jole sighed. "Those first babies must be mechanically taken before they can survive—sacrificed."

"No. We can't do that."

Several of the other doctors and scientists grumbled their agreement, but three waited to hear the rest of Susan's plan.

Susan's hands froze on the keys. She turned her pale face to Peri. Even though Jole had removed the toxins and eased her pregnancy signs, her ordeal still showed in her pallor and her uncharacteristic reserve.

"How many babies and mothers have you sacrificed in pure trial and error?" she asked. "I'm talking about a limited number of babies lost to save an entire race, doctor. Don't judge me as a barbarian."

Jole winced at her use of the word. Mik had undoubtedly given her an education in what Braek meant.

"I have an *ulterior* motive. I find the entire idea of stealing cross-mates from their beds barbarian. If this works, I will expect you to stop doing that entirely."

Peri nodded and bowed to her.

Susan resumed her explanation without acknowledging him. "Now, since you said babies typically miscarry no earlier than six months, and mothers are lost at or near delivery, I'd say sacrificing at somewhere between four and five months should produce high enough levels of sensitized antibodies to create the serum for the next group.

"For that group, I would suggest a test group of at least twenty women. Test their blood levels, but I would suggest administering the first injection somewhere around the third month, perhaps earlier if the levels seem to warrant it. You'll have to continue monitoring their levels throughout the pregnancy. Since this is more severe than rH incompatibility, we can't know that one injection will last the entire pregnancy. Either way, the women should have another shot after delivery.

"Assuming a healthy crop of babies and your ability to synthesize biologicals once you analyze the composition, a larger group of women can be inseminated. Also, I would suggest enticing some of the test group to attempt more than one mechanical pregnancy to test the results over multiple pregnancies. I'll leave that up to you."

She met Jole's eyes. "And, if the women can carry a simple cross-bred, a woman should be able to mate fully with a fifth generation re-bred."

Jole kissed her. "I hope this works."

"It should, and the monitoring should eliminate the loss of mothers."

They left the scientists to discuss the possibilities and ate a hearty lunch. Jole winced at the joy she expressed at even the simple fare the soldiers had managed to prepare for them on short notice. Pyter had arranged for a few townswomen from Lind to cook their meals until they left, but the women had only just arrived.

"Why didn't you eat?" he asked quietly.

Susan pushed her food around her plate and glanced his way, her fingers finding the pendant over her breasts. "Everything was on his terms. If I ate with him, I ate properly. If not, I got pastry and a vitamin drink. I don't think I'll be able to face pastry and a drink like that for years." She managed a weak smile. "If he hadn't started raising the stakes, I would have folded, but the more he pushed, the harder it was to fold."

"Raising the stakes?" He remembered the term from one of her Earth books. It meant increasing the wager in gambling, but how did that apply here? "How?"

She blushed and fixed her gaze on the plate. "When I wouldn't break, it went from simply eating with him to eating with him and kissing him to get the food I needed." She met his eyes, holding back tears. "I couldn't— He planned to raise the stakes again today. I don't know what he planned, but—"

He took her hand, rubbing his thumb over her knuckles. "You would have had to give in before that happened. You couldn't risk what came next."

She nodded miserably. "If it was just eating with him, I would have broken yesterday. As he raised the stakes, I couldn't. I just couldn't convince myself to stomach what he wanted."

"What were his other terms?"

"If I agreed to spend time with him, I would have extra quilts, time outdoors, and other comforts based on how many hours I would agree to spend with him. If I let him sleep in my room—" She paled at the thought.

"When you woke this morning?" he asked. Jole felt a sick certainty sinking into his heart. She hadn't agreed to anything. She hadn't broken, in any way. He was sure of it.

Susan closed her eyes. "I know how bad it got. Mik was begging me to eat, trying to force it into my mouth. I kept spitting it back at him. I wanted that food so badly it hurt. I couldn't think straight. I thought you were a dream. So, when I woke up in that room, in that bed, naked with a man—"

He groaned and kissed her hand. "I'm sorry. I should have realized you wouldn't want to stay there and taken you to another room. It was warm and close, and I was an idiot."

She shook her head. "You couldn't know."

"What else did he do?"

"I was only permitted to speak Keen."

Jole nodded. Susan only spoke Keen to them when they arrived and slipped into it this morning, speaking it even when Jole spoke English to her. He remembered the fearful look when she'd slipped an English word in while they were in the shower.

"You were afraid to speak anything else," he noted, bracing for her explanation.

"When I spoke English to balk him—" Susan ran her fingers over the cheek where he'd healed the bruise, the bruise she wouldn't let him heal the night before.

"He struck you?"

She nodded slowly.

Jole tried to stamp down his fury. "What else did he do? Why were you wearing the bodice instead of your blouse?"

Susan stood abruptly and headed down the corridor at little less than a run, her arms crossed over her chest. Jole vaulted after her, stunned by her reaction.

She stopped, shaking. "I don't want to go to that room. When can we go home?"

Jole stepped up behind her but he didn't touch her, afraid that she would bolt again. "Tomorrow. We can switch rooms with Pyter, if it helps."

"It does." She turned and met his eyes, pulling back tears. Susan moved from foot to foot nervously. "I can't, Joel. Please don't ask me to do this yet."

He nodded and put out his arms in invitation. Susan stepped to him and pressed her cheek to his chest, allowing him to hold her.

Jole took a shaky breath and lifted her gently into his arms. "You need rest. We'll go see Pyter."

Jole carried her to the office he was using and found Pyter. Yet again proving how perceptive he was, the older man had another room prepared for them before Jole asked. He'd also contacted Barri and ordered a squad of soldiers to escort her to them with clothing for Susan and her medical bag, just in case Susan required her aid.

Jole stayed with her until Susan was asleep then searched out Pyter again. "I need to see Mik, but I'll need you there."

Pyter nodded. "May I suggest that I disarm you, until he is returned to his cell?"

He cringed at the word. Mik was in a cell, a common, cold holding cell. He hadn't been placed there. Jole would have ordered him held under arrest in a suite of rooms. Mik was waiting for his jailers when they arrived the previous night, sitting on a cot with his fists resting in his lap and staring blankly at a bare wall.

Mik's actions confused Jole, and the soldiers who had been questioned offered little insight into his brother's behavior. Every time Mik left Susan's room, he'd been more dispirited. The final time, he'd been completely distracted. That was when Mik called for Gilan and left the house for the day. Every move after that seemed designed to lead him to his death.

The guards informed Jole that, even now, his

brother stared at the walls and seemed to bide his time until Jole sent for him with a blade in hand. Mik hadn't eaten since he'd locked himself away. He hadn't shaved or bathed. If Mik slept at all, it went unnoticed.

Jole nodded. "I promised my father that I wouldn't kill him unless I had to, but I may be pressed to live up to that vow. I will strike him, Pyter. I have at least one score to settle with him that will stand for no less than that."

Pyter took his weapons on the way out of the room. When he returned, he was leading Mik by the upper arm. Pyter stepped back with his hand on the hilt of his dagger.

Mik didn't look at Jole. He didn't kneel, but he waited for whatever punishment was coming calmly as if he were any common soldier. Mik probably expected a ritual death. Jole realized that any death he gave Mik would be painful. Perhaps Pyter should have left his weapons. If he did kill Mik, it would be with his bare hands.

Jole walked to him without a word and punched Mik hard across the cheek. Mik fell back to the wall then steadied himself and stepped forward, offering his cheek for another blow.

Jole rubbed his knuckles. "That was for striking her," he growled.

Mik nodded, and Jole returned to the desk. When Mik didn't speak in his own defense, Jole raised an eyebrow at Pyter.

"You could have run from me, Mik. Why didn't you?"

"Where would I go? There is nothing for me

on Kegin, and even if the gateway was open for transport, Earth means death. All I could do was lead you in and try to keep her alive for you."

Mik was begging me to eat, trying to force it into my mouth. Susan's words danced in his mind. Mik really was trying to keep her alive.

"Why did you do this?" Jole asked.

"Fifteen years, Jole. I should have had my bride in five, when she was twenty-two, but those barbarians killed her. They used her and they killed her. I need— I can't wait that long. I've waited so long for her, and now, when the end is in sight—"

Jole nodded grimly. The loss of his cross-mate was a crushing blow for Mik. "Why take Susan?"

"You had children by her. She can tell you that I planned to give them to you." Mik sighed. "I thought— We've had the same women before, and they always said I was the better lover—"

Jole groaned. "They told me the same, Mik. They were paid to make us happy...in any way we desired."

Mik looked as if Jole had struck him a gut shot. He rubbed at his chest, at a nameless ache. Had the fact that the women had lied to either or both of them shaken him so badly? Had Mik really felt superior, based on the word of the schente?

It was a game, asking the woman if his brother was better between the sheets. Jole never took it to heart. In moments of passion, it fired his imagination, but when the women left his bed for their quarters afterward, reality was always waiting.

The schente were for their use, gone before they could become attached to a particular woman, never to be asked for specifically or she would be gone immediately, never to stay past the few moments after he was sated. If he became aroused again, another would be sent to him, never the same woman twice in a night. Most of all, if a schente displeased either of the brothers, she would be dismissed. What else would a schente say but what she thought he wanted to hear? Had Mik never reasoned that?

Jole rubbed at a tight spot in his neck. "You honestly thought if you convinced Susan to accept you, she'd prefer you to me?"

He nodded. "It's more than that, isn't it? The reason she refused me?"

"Yes. It is. How did you plan to get her to agree? I know about raising the wagers for a kiss."

Pyter shot Mik a look of disgust.

"Did you think she'd be so impressed that she'd let you continue?" Jole asked.

Mik blushed. "Maybe, as she became more practiced with me." He looked away as Jole tensed.

"But you knew it might fail. What was your plan if it failed?"

"If she wanted to see her children by you, she'd have to agree to be true mate to me. Once I had her and she knew I was better, she'd want to stay with me."

"You thought that would work?" Jole asked incredulously. How naïve was Mik?

"Until I saw our mother's pendant, I did. She never gave in, even for you. I knew then that Susan never would for her children."

Jole rubbed his neck again then his temple, feeling a sick headache coming on. "Why did you shackle her?"

Mik groaned and scrubbed his hands over his face. "She tried to kill me. She was at her breaking point. She wanted to eat so badly, and the pregnancy signs were so severe— I kissed her, just a gentle invitation."

Jole found it hard to breathe. Mik touched her. He had no right to touch her.

"I wanted her to accept me. I wanted it more than anything I've ever wanted in my life, Jole."

"What did she do? When you kissed her, what did she do?"

Mik raised his chin.

Pyter stepped forward to examine the bruise and three shallow cuts. "A fork?" he asked as he stepped back.

Mik nodded. "I don't know why she didn't do worse. She didn't fight me...when I disarmed her or when I shackled her. She simply told me that the next time I dared— I was angry. Not that she tried to kill me. She tried to kill you too."

Jole sighed. "Because she refused your advances."

"Yes. Because of that. Every bad move I made was because of that," he noted bitterly. "It hurt when she turned me away. I hadn't expected it to hurt so much."

"What happened to her blouse?"

Mik paled and took a step back. "I—ah..." He

closed his eyes, as if he was in pain. "She turned me away," he whispered.

Jole fisted his hand. "What did you do?"

"I cut and ripped it to make it unwearable."

Pyter moved to intercept Jole as he pounced on his brother. "Your vow," he breathed. "Remember your vow."

"On her?" Jole raged. "You took your blade to her?" No wonder Susan was so traumatized by the mention of it.

Mik winced. "I held her and used the threat of my blade, yes. I didn't cut her, Jole. I could never—"

"What were you thinking?"

"I wasn't," he moaned. "She refused me. Everything that came out of her mouth was in support of you and a refusal of me. Over and over, everything I asked of her. For those few precious moments she would fight nothing physically. She still refused me verbally, of course. Even with my dagger at her back, she refused me."

Pyter pushed him back, as Jole started forward again.

"Physically? What did you force on her? Tell me. If I find you've lied to me, I will kill you."

Mik backed off another step, and Pyter tightened his grip, reminding Jole of the damned vow that kept Mik's blood off of his blade.

"I climbed into her bed to convince her to leave it for a meal. I threatened to cut every piece of clothing you allowed her from her body."

"With your blade to her back, Mik. What did you do to her with your blade to her back?" he forced through clenched teeth.

"I kissed her cheek and her bare back. I enjoyed the feel of her skin under my hand and my lips."

Jole fisted his hands, and Mik swallowed a lump in his throat.

Mik nodded. "She tried to pull away from me, but I used the threat of my blade to still her. She continued to ask me to stop even when she stopped ordering me to."

Jole dropped his head. She'd begged him to stop, but he wouldn't retreat. "And?" he asked weakly.

"Later, when she refused me again, I pinned her to the wall to—" Mik sank to his knees with a tortured look. "All I wanted was a sign that she wouldn't always despise me. Anything, Jole. One kind word would have been enough.

"I couldn't excite her. Everything I did made her hate me more, made her frightened. I made her cry. She tried to explain that she valued the respect and patience you showed her, but I didn't listen. How could you be near her and not touch her? How could you control the need?"

"Did you take her?" Jole held his breath while he waited for Mik's answer. If Mik had, his vow was meaningless. Jole would kill him for that.

Mik shook his head. "No. I had to touch her." He looked at his shaking hands and fisted them in his lap. "When I realized she hated what other women had enjoyed— I didn't understand. I *don't* understand."

Jole groaned. "I don't know why she wants to

save your worthless skin. I want to kill you. Were it not for the vow I made our father and the fact that you didn't take her unwilling, I would kill you. You deserve no better."

Mik gaped at him, conflicting emotions warring on his unshaven face. "She wants to save me?"

No, not really. She wants an end to cross-mates being dragged from Earth. I want to save you. She is making me happy. "Yes."

"Why?"

"Susan understands your frustration, and in her culture, even something as loathsome as you is worth pity. She's been working with our scientists and doctors all morning. If her plan works, you could have a Keen woman as true mate and children by her in less than the five years you believed you had to wait."

"How?"

"There has been a human answer for forty years. We haven't checked to see if they ever solved their own incompatibility problems. They did, and Susan was familiar with the treatment they use. She was training to be one of their healers when she was brought to me."

Mik laughed nervously. "They are our salvation, after all."

Jole nodded. "Yes, they are."

* * * *

Jole removed his clothes and slid into bed next to Susan. It was still an hour until dinner.

Barri would want to examine Susan before that. Until then, he needed to feel the warmth of her next to his body.

Susan turned to him, opening her eyes for just a moment as if to assure herself that it was Jole in her bed and not Mik.

I climbed in her bed.

Jole pulled her to him, and Susan laid a kiss on his chest. Her hand slid from his hip to circle his length. He sucked in his breath and cupped her closer to him. Susan tipped her head up to kiss him and pressed her body to his.

He explored her mouth, becoming more fevered and less controlled with each passing minute. Some place in the back of his mind protested it. After Mik's treatment, he should be slow—patient as she'd told Mik she valued. Still, Jole pulled her mouth to him and stroked her body restlessly.

Susan guided him to her, and Jole claimed her in a single movement. Slow became a forgotten memory. She wrapped her legs around him and urged Jole on.

Her fingertips gripped his hips to her. "Please Joel," she breathed.

Jole locked his hips to her and speeded his movements. She started to make little gasping sounds and tightened her grip on him.

"That's right, Susan. Hold me."

He lowered his lips to the pulse point at her throat and concentrated a burst of healing. Susan shattered, contracting around him as she cried out his name. Jole's body was of control as he followed her over. He sank his face to her neck as he swelled within her.

Jole bit back tears. Susan came to him. She took him, here and now.

Susan touched his cheek. "What is it?"

"You let me touch you."

"I don't understand. You're my husband." Her confusion wounded him.

"After Mik—"

She turned her face away, her chest hitching. "I know the difference between the two of you, Joel."

He sighed. "I know you do. It's just— I promised to keep you safe. I promised he'd never lay hands on you again. He should never have touched you."

"It's not your fault. I don't blame you."

"The things he did—"

"When I'm ready, I'll tell you everything. I promise I will."

Jole brushed his hand through her curls and kissed her forehead. "You don't have to."

Susan met his gaze solidly. "Don't have to what?"

"Tell me."

She paled.

"I—had a long talk with my brother."

"He told you?"

Jole nodded.

"Everything?"

"If he didn't, I've promised to kill him."

Susan groaned and buried her face in his chest.

"Susan, please talk to me. What have I done wrong?"

"I'm not ready for this, Joel."

"You have all the time in the world. If you don't want to talk, we don't have to. There are no surprises now."

"You don't really believe that, do you?"

"Mik said—"

"I don't mean what he did. I mean what— What he did affected me, hurt me."

"Of course. The bruises and the trauma—"

"And the memories."

He stilled. "With me?" *Please Gods, not that.*

"No." Susan sighed. "Not the way you mean."

"Then what?"

"Remember the way I reacted in the kitchen?"

Jole nodded.

"Something as simple as that Joel. I don't want you to think it's you." She touched his cheek. "You've done nothing wrong. It's no reflection on you. It's—"

"It's all right. Tell me what you need, and I'll do it. If you need held, I'll hold you. If you need space, you'll have it."

Susan ran her hands through his hair and guided his mouth down to hers. "For now, I need this."

A knock on the door interrupted their moment and Jole pulled the quilts up over them, growling the intruder in.

Barri smiled and nodded to Susan. "*Jole must have learned his lessons about the dangers of pregnancy well,*" she noted. "*If your schen has returned, the toxins were successfully removed from your system.*"

Jole startled. "*Schen? But cross-mates don't experience schen,*" he argued. Oh, but he had dreamed that she would, hadn't he? Was he really that lucky?

The schen was the increased sexual drive of a pregnant Keen woman. Even when a cross-mate agreed to mechanical implantation, she never— *Mechanical! Could the difference be in true mating versus mechanically implanting children?*

Barri laughed heartily. "*You don't believe that, do you? Of course, they experienced the schen. They simply never had a man near that they wanted to explore their fantasies with.*"

"*So, they suffered.*"

Susan smiled weakly, slipping into Keen with them smoothly. "*That surprises you?*"

Jole shook his head. "*No. Not really.*"

CHAPTER TEN

Fim 23rd, Ri 25-2987

Susan groaned as she felt the cap slide free into the toilet. She slowed her breathing. "Okay. Let's be calm. I'm not having contractions, yet. I can probably make it through the evening before this gets serious."

She sighed. Kell Ri had drafted them into hosting the harvest feast for a hundred or so of his closest friends. He wanted to show off his very pregnant daughter-in-law and toast the future. Susan understood the importance of instilling hope, but the past four hours of making small talk while Keen nobles touched her beach ball belly had left her longing for a bed in a dark room. Now, to top it all off, her stubborn children were making an unexpected appearance, four weeks ahead of schedule.

Susan knew she had problems when her chest seemed to swell into the bodice of her gown and even brushing her arm against it became excruciating. She'd thought about asking Jole and Barri what they meant when they said delivery would be imminent, but Kell Ri would probably have trooped the entire assembly through their bedroom, if she was ordered to bed.

She straightened her gown over her stomach and made her way back down the corridor toward the ballroom. Just two more hours and Susan could bid the guests goodnight and get

166

Jole to help her back to bed. Until then, she could put her feet up, claiming the sore back that wasn't a lie.

The pain came suddenly, ripping through her and knocking Susan to her knees. She panted in breaths, unable to find her center and breathe deeply. Susan gripped her gloved hand on the spindle of the staircase, waiting to pull herself up when the pain receded, but it seemed endless.

"Princess," a voice shouted.

She looked up at Pyter hopelessly, thanking nameless gods under her breath as he sprinted the length of the corridor to her. At this point, she didn't care if the god aiding her was human or Keen, as long as she was in favor. Barri or Jole would be a better sight, but even Pyter was acceptable. She rubbed her stomach and grimaced as a fresh wash of pain hit her.

He knelt beside her and cupped a hand over her abdomen. Pyter uttered several harsh curses in Keen.

She slipped into his language. "You've got that right. Get...Joel." She panted out the last request.

"Has your cap passed?" he asked urgently.

Susan nodded. "Just now."

Pyter cursed again and scooped her into his arms. "Your breasts have been sore?"

The pain intensified. Susan managed a shaky nod. "Get Joel," she whimpered.

"How long?"

"I don't— While I was dressing, I guess. Please, Pyter."

His eyes burned in fury. "That was hours

ago."

Pyter started walking. Susan was still trying to form an answer when he turned up the staircase.

She looked at him in confusion. "Joel—"

"You will be cared for first."

He took her directly to bed and called out for Barri and her daughter, Syl. The two women came at a run, and Pyter started issuing orders.

"Syl, collect Prince Jole immediately. Barri, undress her while I get your bag."

Syl took one look at Susan and ran for the stairs.

Barri turned to Pyter. "How far is she?"

"She's lost her cap."

Barri's eyes widened. "Go. Get my bag and the bag from the cabinet."

She started pulling off Susan's clothes before he was out the door. With the minimum of dress Keen women wore, undressing her took barely more than a minute. Barri was pulling the quilt over Susan when Pyter breezed back in with her bag and dropped it on the foot of the bed. The bag of sterile towels and blankets landed next to it.

Pyter looked at Susan in concern as the pain intensified again. He knelt by her bedside and bowed his head. "Princess, until His Highness arrives, may I ease your pain?"

Susan blanched. She wouldn't accept healing from anyone but Jole. "Only Joel," she panted out.

Barri glanced up from the sterilizing gel she was rubbing into her hands. "Pyter means only to massage your nerve bundle. Jole will thank him for his help."

She nodded. "I'd appreciate that, Pyter."

He gestured for her to turn to her side and applied pressure to a spot near the small of her back. He chuckled as she sighed in relief. The pain didn't disappear, but it became manageable.

"This could have been nearly painless, if you had told the Prince immediately," Pyter chided her.

"I know."

"Why didn't you?"

Susan groaned. "Joel has enough problems with his father. Kell Ri and his guests—"

"Can be damned," Pyter interrupted her, the humor banished from his voice. "Do you feel better?"

She nodded. "How did you learn this?"

Pyter hesitated. "Barri taught me—to help Princess Jenneane."

"When she had Joel and Mik?"

"Only Jole. Kell Ri was there when Mik was born."

"And he wouldn't allow it," she guessed.

Barri laughed harshly. "If he couldn't touch her, no man would, even if it would ease his son into the world."

Jole rushed into the room, shedding his cloak and uniform jacket onto the floor. He nodded to Pyter on his way around the bed, and the older man applied more pressure, then moved away.

Jole ran his hand over her abdomen and

kissed her shoulder lightly. "Thank you, Pyter."

"The least I could do, Highness." His voice was a whisper.

Jole's lips touched the spot Pyter had been using and the pain receded to a dull ache as the calming chill raced over her nerves. Susan closed her eyes as her muscles unknotted.

Barri moved to the foot of the bed. "Jole, I must see how far she is."

He eased Susan to her back and kissed her forehead. She sighed as his healing touch washed through her mind. Jole nudged his hand under her closer knee, and Susan pulled them up in response.

Jole moved his attention to the swell of her abdomen, and the last of the pain disappeared. "That's right," he crooned to her. "If your muscles are lax, you will simply open for delivery."

She opened her eyes to the sight of Jole's dark head bent over her, laying kisses over his children. Susan ran her fingers through his hair. Was this what a Keen birth was? Painless? Calm and full of love? She laughed lightly.

Jole looked up in confusion. "What is it?"

"If the whole delivery is like this, I'll give you as many children as you want."

"Next time, maybe you'll tell me earlier, so the whole thing really can be like this."

"If I agree, will you forgive me?"

Jole's smile disappeared as Kell Ri's voice boomed out from the corridor.

"Where are they? Why have they deserted our guests this way?"

Syl tried to calm him. "The Princess has

reached her time, Majesty. Please be calm."

"Move aside."

"But Majesty—"

Susan met Jole's eyes. "No. I won't have him in here."

Barri shook her head. "She's tensing, Jole."

A wave of pain crested in her, and Susan groaned and arched her back.

"Pyter, escort my father to the stairs. He can see the babies when Susan has recovered," Jole barked out, taking her hand in his.

Pyter bowed and slipped out the door, while Jole set about relaxing the tension out of Susan's body again. She settled back into the pillows, feeling weightless.

"How is she?" Jole asked.

Barri smiled. "That's perfect. The baby's head is stretching her open the last that she needs."

Syl slipped into the room and nodded her assurances that Pyter had taken care of Kell Ri.

"Already?" Jole complained. He shot Susan a hurt look. "Why didn't you tell me? I would have shared this with you."

Susan blushed. "I didn't know what you meant by imminent. I thought we had hours. I wasn't in pain."

Jole raised an eyebrow.

"Well, not *debilitating* pain," she amended.

"You shouldn't have had to suffer *any* pain." As if to prove his point, Jole brushed his lips over her abdomen and sent a cool spike of healing through her.

Susan moaned. "Is it wrong to get aroused by this?"

Jole sent her a wicked grin. "You won't be ready to pay off for a little while."

Barri laughed lightly. "Only the most loving of couples experience that phenomenon."

Susan sucked in her breath. "Barri?"

Jole took her hand and helped her relax her muscles. "What is it?"

Barri scowled. "Calm her. She's tensing again."

"What is that?" Susan asked. "It feels like—" She darkened.

Barri nodded. "The baby has entered the birth canal. She is stimulating you, as Jole would at completion."

Susan managed a weak laugh. "It's a little early for a little sister."

"You will not release another egg for more than a year, even when Jole stimulates you."

"Why?"

"To allow you to nurse and rebuild your stores without having to support another new life."

Jole moved his lips to the bundle of nerves at the back of her neck. "Does waiting distress you?" he teased.

Susan sank further into his embrace. "No. Yes, it does. I don't know. I like being pregnant."

Jole stimulated the nerve bundle.

She sighed. "I definitely like this, and I like feeling my egg release for you."

Jole groaned into her neck. "I can't wait for you to release an egg for me."

Barri chuckled at them again. "I can tell I will be needed often. That is a good thing. Ah.

Syl, ready the towels please."

Syl laid a towel under Susan's thighs and Barri eased the baby out. Susan watched in awe. There was no pushing, no discomfort. The knife in Barri's hand glowed with a laser edge. She cut the cord, cauterizing both ends instantly. Syl wrapped the baby in a towel, slick in a coating of its amniot.

No blood, either. No tearing.

"It's a girl," Syl crowed.

Jole laughed heartily and kissed Susan. "A girl. We did it."

Susan groaned as she felt the stimulation again. This time, it wasn't the comfortable excitement. It hurt. "Not yet," she informed him, pressing her head back into the pillow.

Barri and Jole exchanged frowns.

Barri waved Syl away. "Place the babe near her mother and tell Pyter to send news down to the festivities."

Susan cried out as a spike of pain assaulted her. "Barri," she pleaded.

Barri's eyes were hard, as she examined Susan again. "Keep her muscles lax, Jole. She will try to tense with the pain."

Jole tried the bundles of nerves at her neck and abdomen, but the healing wasn't having its usual effect. Susan shifted restlessly in his arms.

"What is this?" he asked, sounding desperate.

"The baby faces the wrong direction. I must turn it. It will hurt her, but if I don't, we could lose them both."

"*Breech,*" Susan supplied automatically.

"Common with *twins*."

A cheer went up from downstairs that seemed to shake the house.

Jole continued to use his healing, but the pain wasn't abating. Barri tried to manipulate the baby, and Susan screamed in response.

Pyter launched back into the room. "Barri?" he asked in a low voice.

She nodded. "We need you. You know what to do."

He surged toward the bed, falling to his knees on the bed beside her. Pyter reached one hand under her body, finding the knot of nerves he'd used earlier. Susan sobbed as he planted his other hand over her ribs and squeezed together. She tried to arch away from his grip, but Jole held her shoulders to the bed. Susan rolled her head back and vented an ear-splitting scream.

Jole whispered to her. "I'm sorry, love. This is the only way. A few minutes. Only a few minutes."

"Done," Barri decreed. "Release her, Pyter."

Susan collapsed in Jole's arms, sobbing as the pressure disappeared. She glanced at Pyter through her tears. He eased off the bed and knelt with his shoulders slumped and eyes down, as if he expected to be punished for what he did.

Susan touched Jole's face. "Joel, please."

Jole ran his lips along her ear. "Shhh. I won't hurt him." He stimulated the nerve bundle at the back of her neck again, bringing relief. "Stand, Pyter. Make sure my father keeps his distance. Thank you for your help, for the lives of my bride and child."

Pyter nodded; he stood and bowed deeply. "It was the least I could do...Jole." He turned and strode away before either of them could form a response.

Susan felt a lump in her throat. Jole owed Pyter a great debt for Pyter's service. Jole had admitted it by thanking him for her life. It seemed Pyter made his wish known. He could have anything within Jole's power to give him in return for his service. He asked for the right to call him Jole instead of Highness, to return to the days before he took Jole from Jenneane at Kell's command. If it upset Jole, he didn't show it. Susan doubted that it did.

Susan sighed as she felt the stimulation again. It was the comfortable excitement this time.

"Good," Barri urged her. "Relax into the birth."

Susan nodded, feeling boneless in the release of pain. She felt Barri hand off the baby to Syl but didn't open her eyes. The room was oddly silent.

"Blood?" Jole whispered.

"A small tear," Barri assured him. "The turning is always difficult."

Susan felt sleep pulling her down. Why was it so quiet? She forced her eyes open. "What's wrong?" she asked in a thick voice. "Is the baby okay?"

Jole kissed her head. "He's fine, love. They're both just fine. Sleep while they do. Our babies will be hungry in an hour or two."

Susan sank into sleep. A boy. How could anyone mourn a new baby? When Hugam allowed successful babies, no one would mourn a re-bred male birth.

* * * *

Jole reached over Susan's sleeping form and ran his finger along his son's cheek. The boy turned to suck at his fingertip, and Jole chuckled. He grinned at his sleeping daughter. *My bride and my children.*

Finding no milk forthcoming, his son started to fuss. Jole scooped his hands under the baby and cuddled him to his bare chest, hoping to give Susan a few more precious moments of sleep. His son had other ideas. The boy sent up a furious wail.

Susan opened her eyes and smiled at the sight of Jole trying to calm the baby in his arms. She moved tenderly to sitting and took the baby from him. Susan crooned to him in a mixture of English and Keen, then offered him her breast.

Jole smiled, laying a kiss on his son's head. "They're both so beautiful."

Susan wound the fingers of her free hand through his. "You're not upset that we didn't have two daughters?" she asked.

"Why should I be?"

"There were no cheers for him. I noticed."

Jole leaned over and kissed the breast that fed his son...then her lips. "Prejudiced fools," he assured her. "When the first Kegin-born re-bred babies arrive, they'll know better."

Susan nodded, though he could see her nervousness. It was a discussion they'd had many times in the months since she'd returned home. If her plan failed, the gateway would continue to be used. It would be the only way to secure a bride for their son. Worse, Mik would have another Earth woman and no more control for his years of waiting.

The sacrificed babies from the first group of women had been taken only days ago. Susan had wanted to be there for the other women, knowing that their loss would be profound despite the fact that they were promised places in carrying the first round of cross-bred babies to term. Jole had refused her. Susan was too close to term for an upset like that. The stress of it may have been what called their babies early to begin with, though Susan warned him that twins often came early, for no reason but lack of space in the womb.

Jole brushed the black curls on his son's head. "They need names. Now is the time that a Keen mother typically names her children."

Susan looked at him in confusion. "But, on Kegin—"

"Do you honestly think my father would have chosen names like Jole and Mik? They are Earth names, my mother's father and brother. What names would you like?"

"My father is named Joseph."

Jole smiled. "I like it. And our daughter?"

Susan hesitated and met his eyes. "Would you mind if we named her Jenneane?"

Jole found it hard to form a response. "For my mother?"

Susan bit her lip and nodded nervously.

"I'd be honored. She'd be honored."

* * * *

Susan smiled down at Jenneane. After Joseph finished eating, Barri and Syl had cleaned the linens and dressed her in a purple silin nursing gown to prepare for Kell Ri's interference. Jenneane startled as the pounding came on the door, then sighed and resumed her feeding.

Barri opened the door for Kell, bowing deeply as he pushed past her.

His eyes opened in surprise, and a scowl settled on his face. He motioned to Susan and Jenneane angrily. "What is this? Why aren't you dressed?"

Jole looked up from Joseph, eyeing his lounging pants and her nursing gown as he did. "Why should we be?"

"For the presentation, of course. You can hardly present my granddaughter to the nobles dressed in your lounging pants."

"There will be no presentation tonight."

"The nobles are here, Jole. They expect to see the young princess."

"My children are newly born. The nobles will have to wait for the presentation according to tradition. In a month's time, when they are older and Susan has recovered, we will have her formal coronation as my Princess and presentation of my heirs."

For a moment, the two men faced off. Susan watched the muscle twitching in the back of Kell's jaw nervously.

Kell nodded. "I would hold my granddaughter."

Susan smiled. "She's eating, but you can hold Joseph." She nodded to her husband and son.

Kell bristled. He huffed out his chest and darkened. Susan edged closer to Jole, at a loss for what she might have said wrong.

"I have no interest in holding that child. I wish to hold my granddaughter—when she has feasted on your milk, of course." He executed a stiff bow of his head.

Susan blanched, her mouth moving but too shocked to find the words to express her outrage.

Jole placed a hand to her cheek and turned to Kell. "Get out." His voice was low and dangerous, a tone Susan hadn't heard since Jole confronted Mik outside her room.

"Jole," Kell began, his voice one demanding understanding rather than an order.

"Out," Jole ordered. "I will not allow you to upset Susan, and I will not allow you to ignore my son in favor of my daughter. Get out."

When Kell didn't move, Jole handed Joseph to Syl and rose from the bed, stalking the room to his father. He guided the open-mouthed leader by a grip on Kell's elbow. "I said leave, and I meant it."

Jenneane released her grip on Susan's

nipple and let out a thin cry that announced her discomfort.

Susan raised her to her shoulder and patted her back, crooning to her in English to annoy Kell Ri. "*It's okay. It's just gas, baby.*" She smiled at the sound of Jenneane's resounding burp and transferred her to the other nipple. Barri secured the flap over the first.

Kell pulled away from Jole and looked back at them in surprise, just as Jenneane took the other nipple in her mouth and started to eat with a sigh of contentment. He stood transfixed as Susan stroked the baby's cheek. Jole tried to grasp Kell's arm again, but Kell shook off his hold.

He motioned to Susan. "What did she do?" Kell demanded.

Jole shrugged. "Ask Susan."

Kell stared at his son as if he were a mad hottel.

"In Keen. She will understand. She has answered you in our language already, if you recall."

He nodded and turned his gaze back to her. "What did you do?"

"*Burped* the baby."

Kell raised an eyebrow and scowled.

Susan chuckled. "The baby swallowed air as she ate. The air in her stomach is painful. It hurts. So, you help the baby bring the air up to bring relief. It's called *burping* a baby."

Kell managed a weak smile. "Would Jole's mother have known about this—*burping*?"

"I'm sure she would. Most human babies—"

She nodded and looked back to Jenneane.

Kell sighed and spoke to Jole quietly. "Perhaps Mik would have been better left with your mother for his nursing year. We never knew." He bowed his head to Susan and left without another word.

Jole watched his father's departing back in open-mouthed amazement. "I never would have believed it."

"Believed what?" Susan asked.

"He complimented my mother."

CHAPTER ELEVEN

Jad 23ʳᵈ, Ri 25-2987

Jole smiled as Susan fussed with her dress. "You look wonderful," he assured her.

Susan scowled as she smoothed her coronation gown. "I don't understand. Why is this gown so—" She growled her frustration.

Jole ran his fingers over one nipple, which puckered in invitation through the silin of the bodice. Susan batted his hand away. She *was* out of sorts.

"What's the problem, love?"

"Daily gowns, presentation gowns, and party gowns are all light, almost indecently light. Why does a coronation gown have to be yards of fabric and layers and frills?" She brushed at a stubborn length of lace ruffle at the top of the skirt in annoyance.

Jole laughed. "Tradition. Once, all gowns were like this one." He released the ties for the nursing panel over one swollen breast and tasted her perfect body as the fabric fell away. "We've become much more civilized in our tastes in the intervening millennia, but a coronation still falls to tradition."

Susan groaned and cradled his head to her. "How long does the fast extend?" she asked breathlessly.

He smiled as he untied the other flap and licked the nipple straining into the cool air coming through the open terrace door. "The presentation of my heirs marks the end of the fast, if you feel ready for more."

Susan gripped his shoulders, as Jole traced her nipple again. "I've wanted more for most of the month, Joel. If we have to wait until after the presentation ceremony, you better stop."

Jole led her back toward the bed, sinking to the edge and dragging his trousers down his thighs in anticipation. It had been a long month. She laid her head back, as he took her breast in his mouth and sucked hard once, tasting just a hint of the sweet milk that fed his children so well.

"Joel," she moaned.

He had waited so long to hear his name from her lips in invitation again. Jole dragged the layers of dress up to her hips and ripped the insubstantial layer of her underwear away. He sank his fingers into the warmth of her, feeling the fresh wash of her personal lubricant add to the welcoming wetness already waiting his touch. Jole pulled her forward until Susan straddled his thighs.

"Tell me," he breathed, playing his fingers in her.

Susan gripped his shoulders. "Make love to me, Joel."

Jole guided her down, shuddering as Susan's body gripped his length. "I will always make love to you."

Susan wasted no time, raising her knees to the edge of the bed beside his hips. She pushed her body up to drop around him again. She was relentless; riding him while Jole fought for some semblance of control.

He hooked her ankles around his hips and stood, making his way to the vanity in her dressing room in five torturous, shorter-than-average steps thanks to his trousers. Jole settled her on the edge, capturing her mouth as he drove into her over and over.

"Joel," Susan gasped, her eyes wide.

Jole slowed, cupping his fingers around one exposed breast. "Am I hurting you?"

"No. Don't stop, Joel. Please don't stop. I want you."

He nodded. "Then hold on. I want you spread out around me." He started pounding again, as Susan tightened her grip, losing himself in his bride as he'd longed to do for so long.

Susan's lips curled into a little, feminine smile. "You just wanted to be in charge," she teased.

Jole nipped at her lips and down to her throat. "I want you to scream for me. If I had let you continue on the path you were on, I would have climaxed without waiting for you." As it was, he wasn't sure that he would outlast her. Jole closed his eyes, concentrating on holding back his release.

"What if I don't scream?"

Jole snapped his eyes open. Susan's eyes glittered in mischief, and he grinned.

He pushed further into her, feeling her body tighten in preparation for release. "I'm very determined. You will scream for me, if we are late to the coronation to accommodate that wish."

Her hand cupped his balls; raking her nails

under them and making him shudder. "I can see how determined you are, Joel." Her voice was like silin.

Jole's body tensed in pure need. He leaned Susan back, baring her breasts to hastily applied jolts of healing. She bowed up, forcing her nipple further into his mouth as she screamed his name.

Her body contracted around him, pushing Jole over the edge. He roared out a month's worth of release and sank his face to her shoulder, his member locked within her. Susan gasped, her hands fisting in his hair, guiding his mouth to hers, kissing him hungrily.

Susan smiled. "You cheated," she accused.

"You're lodging a formal complaint?"

"Would Kell Ri do anything about it?"

Jole laughed heartily. "No. You challenged me, and I prevailed."

"I challenged you? You stated the challenge."

"Okay. You accepted the challenge, and I still prevailed. To the victor—"

"Not for long," she warned.

"And what does that mean?"

Susan's eyes glittered. "Like this dress, not all of your traditions are civilized."

"For instance?"

"There are things we can do that don't require me to be fully recovered, but the tradition of the fast denies you any pleasure."

"Why should I have pleasure, when you cannot?"

"Remember when I came to your bed the first time? When I was so sore? Would I have to be recovered to have pleasure?"

Jole's breathing was harsh in his own ears. His erection, lessening in her, surged to readiness again. Susan sank around him with a moan. Her head rocked back and her eyes closed. Jole watched her reactions in growing arousal. She was so very responsive to every touch.

His forward thrust was slow. He felt her inner muscles shudder as his length slid home. His pull back had him teetering on the edges of release. Jole cupped Susan's head forward, possessing her mouth as he slid deep again.

"Look at me," he rasped.

Susan opened her eyes, shimmering circles of lizor purple surrounding the deep pools of her dilated pupils.

"Will you scream for me again?"

She shook her head. "No cheating," she whispered.

"No cheating," he agreed. Jole pulled back and slid deep within her again.

Susan closed her eyes, shivering in pleasure.

"Look at me. Look in my eyes."

Her eyes opened, and Jole started moving again. Susan's hands gripped at the braid on the shoulders of his uniform jacket. Jole smiled as he changed position, lifting her under her knees and opening Susan more fully to his thrusts. A breathless, little cry of pleasure escaped her lips, as he pushed deeper, twisting to stroke her inner muscles as he moved.

"Let me tell you what your screams do to me," he whispered.

Susan's eyes widened. She bit back another cry, as Jole stilled inside her and moved his thumb in a circle around her clit. She threw her head back and her breasts heaved as she drew in spasming breaths.

"Look at me."

She nodded and met his eyes. Her thigh muscles tightened in his palms. Susan dropped her hands to the top of the vanity and pressed down, levering herself up to move back and forth on his length.

Jole moved with her. "All I ever wanted was your love and happiness, Susan. Hearing you scream out your enjoyment and feeling your body respond to my lovemaking affect me in ways you cannot imagine. It makes me proud that I can give you pleasure that cannot be contained. It makes me happy."

He kissed her, speeding his possession of her. "And it makes me want you again—immediately."

Susan shattered, her cry hoarse and formless. Jole joined her, nipping at her jaw line. Their breathing came in short gasps.

"Thank you for that gift," he groaned.

"I couldn't disappoint you," she teased.

A brisk knocking intruded on the moment.

Susan chuckled. "Oh no. What now?"

Jole smiled at her, then roared his answer at the door. "Go away."

Pyter's muffled voice reached them. "It's time, Jole."

"Soon," he yelled in irritation.

Susan's chuckle turned into an outright

laugh. "This is a first, I'll wager."

Jole's laughter echoed off the walls. "We're not going anywhere for a few minutes."

They used the time wisely. Jole tied the bodice flaps shut and smoothed her dress over her chest. Susan straightened his crumpled uniform jacket. When his erection released her, Jole lowered her to the floor and smoothed her gown. Susan buttoned his trousers over him, and Jole willed his body to still as he hardened under her fingers again.

Susan rushed to the chest of drawers, pulling out underwear that Jole plucked from her fingers. Susan looked at him in confusion.

Jole tucked them into his jacket pocket like a handkerchief and shot her a heated look. "For me?"

She blushed. "It means that much to you?"

"I will know. I will want you all day."

Susan grinned. "On one condition."

"Name it. I'd give anything for this."

She ran a hand over his stiffening member. "I'll ask for anything when I wear a day dress for you this way."

Jole growled, remembering his excitement the first few days, before the clothier had created underclothes for her, knowing Susan was bare beneath those dresses. She hadn't worn them that way since she had the underwear delivered to her. He had reined in his excitement with reminders that he couldn't have her then. Now it would be torture for him, knowing that what was carefully hidden but available was his to take whenever he wished to take it.

He kissed her, his arousal growing. "I'll have to wear my cloak tied shut."

"For today—"

"Yes?"

"You'll agree to learn more of my Earth seduction techniques."

Susan turned and walked away, leaving Jole straining for breath as she opened the door and accepted Jenneane from Syl's hand. She thought that was a payment? A penalty? Jole prayed to Fion every night that there were more techniques Susan could teach him.

When Susan took him to completion in her mouth the first time, Jole thought he might never recover. When she'd introduced him to water play, it seemed the bathroom became the place of choice to take her as often as she would allow. And when she'd introduced him to taking her like a hottel in rutt, Jole reveled in the barbarism for the waves of pleasure it gave them both.

Jole moved forward, lost in shock and knowing how much he enjoyed Susan's Earth-style seductions. He nodded as Barri placed Joseph, his son and heir apparent, in his arms.

Barri turned to help Syl manage Susan's skirts. She furrowed her brow as she smoothed wrinkles from the layers of lace and looked to Jole with a smile on her face. "Couldn't you have undressed her first?"

CHAPTER TWELVE

Pri 18ᵗʰ, Ri 25-2989

Jole pulled Susan to the shelter of his chest, listening to two-year-old Joseph and Jenneane chattering in the nursery. They would descend on their parents soon, ready for the celebration of Christmas Susan had planned for them. But for now, they were busy with Pyter.

Susan had introduced seasonal traditions to their household, wanting her children to experience the joys of her Earth roots. The twins loved Christmas best. The decorations and trees, shiny wrapped presents and stories of Santa, his reindeer, and the Christmas King's star seemed designed to capture a child's imagination.

Though Jole enjoyed the festivities, it wasn't his favorite Earth celebration. That didn't stop him from insisting on a sprig of gola plant, which Susan proclaimed '*mistletoe*' on sight, being hung over their bed.

He enjoyed watching the children hunt for bright colored boiled eggs and candies with Syl and Pyter on Easter. He enjoyed the fireworks and picnics that accompanied Independence Day. But, Jole's favorite was Halloween.

Jole loved Halloween, with its face paint and costumes, bobbing for autumn fruits in vats of water, spiced fruit cider, masked balls, and tables of candies, pies, and cakes. Human traditions were like human genes. They had life and energy that Keen traditions lacked. They weren't stagnant.

Susan chuckled. "They're so excited. I remember asking those same questions. Has Santa come? Did he eat the cookies we left for him?"

"The entire household is excited. Earth celebrations always excite."

She glanced to the gola sprig. "And Earth seductions? Do they excite, too?"

Jole groaned, remembering her seduction lesson of the evening before. He'd never dreamed there could be so many ways to make love, and it seemed Susan had an endless supply of ideas for his torture. Maybe if Keen lovemaking had the inventiveness of Earth lovemaking, their reproduction wouldn't have grown stale in other ways.

He kissed her shoulder. "Mik contacted me yesterday."

"And how are Danellan and Gibby?" she asked.

It was good that she no longer feared Mik. His brother was still banned from their home and probably would be for a good many years, but his mate and child made him more stable.

"Danellan is recovering well, and Gibby is eating constantly. Of course, Mik claims temporary victory."

"How does he figure that?"

"Once Kell's son— He had a girl without a boy." Jole scowled at the narrow-minded view.

Susan shivered.

"Cold?"

"Just a chill. Could you get another quilt for

the bed?"

Jole nodded and headed for the cabinet. "My answer was that he wasn't man enough to produce twins of any sort." He laughed lightly. Mik was as competitive as ever, but it was a good-natured competition now.

Susan rolled her eyes, a smile pulling at her lips. "Maybe we could outdo him with twin girls this time," she suggested.

He sighed. Susan didn't start releasing eggs for almost two years. Barri and Dr. Peri had speculated a longer recovery time due to the twins or the breech birth. Still, they had been trying for another child for five months with no luck so far. Susan wanted another so badly, and Jole was in perfect agreement.

Jole forced a smile back on his face and turned with the quilt. "Do I need to lock the door and let Barri know that we'll be making use of the gola sprig?"

Susan blushed and feigned a remorseful look. "I don't know, Joel. I may have need of your healing magic. I seem to have a splitting headache."

He stilled, looking to the quilt in his hands and stringing her hints together into a cohesive whole. "You're—"

"Merry Christmas, Daddy."

Section Two:
Mik

Second Son

CHAPTER THIRTEEN

Iric 24ᵗʰ, Ri 25-2986

Mik Hi ducked his head, biting back a smile as he rubbed his wrists against the shackles Pyter put on him before he left the ruins outside Lind. His brother's chief of security thought this was a punishment, an embarrassment. That was what Mik found most amusing about the situation.

It was liberating, this freedom that came with not caring if you lived or died. It was ironic that, when hope was handed to him on a golden platter, Mik no longer cared to grasp it. At twenty-three, he'd hit the lowest point a man could hit. He laughed aloud, earning him a worried glance from Rill, his own chief of security.

"Are you all right, Prince Mik?" he whispered, leaning across the transport's wide seat to pull Mik's cloak shut over his chest to keep him warm—or to hide his bound hands. "I can remove those shackles now."

"Don't. I'd prefer my father to see me in chains."

Rill's eyes widened.

"He will be furious. Won't he?"

"I imagine so, Highness." Rill lowered his gaze.

"Good."

Mik's days of living to please Kell Ri had come to a crashing halt when he realized what a fool his father was. All those lessons in conquering a mate— Mik barked in laughter again.

"Highness?" Rill asked, confused by his mad behavior.

Mik smiled. Yes. He was mad, but happily insane was preferable to desperation. "She's lucky," he mused.

"Princess Susan?" Rill whispered, aghast.

He sobered, biting back a sob. "No." Mik hadn't meant to hurt Susan. He wished he could give her back the last five days of her life, take away the pain he'd caused her in his bid to make her his, in his attempts to force Susan to accept him. Force was what Kell espoused. It was all Mik was taught, all he knew.

It should have been obvious to Mik that his father wouldn't know how to teach him the way to tame a mate. Kell had failed with Mik's mother, but even his father hadn't come so close to killing the woman he desired. No, desire wasn't part of it for Kell. Conquering a mate was a challenge, a battle. No wonder he'd failed with Jenneane.

"Then who?" Rill asked.

"My cross-mate." Mik didn't even know the girl's name. She was dead—raped and murdered before she reached her full maturity at twenty, before she left Earth and came to him. "She's lucky. She died quickly. It's probably a kinder fate Fion granted her than being delivered to me." He did sob at that. When he'd first learned she was dead, all Mik thought about was his loss. *Pitiful!*

"You don't mean that," Rill protested.

Mik hit the door of the transport, not even wincing as the metal edge of the shackles bit into his wrists. "Of course, I mean it," he growled. Why would anyone in his right mind not see that now? Mik had almost killed Susan in his attempt to control her. What would he have done to his own cross-mate, to one that he knew he wasn't stealing from another? One that he viewed as his own?

"You won't need an Earth-born," Rill said in a calming voice. "If this new plan works—"

"What woman would have me now?" Could he trust himself again? Probably not. Mik knew what he was capable of now.

"Highness?"

"I'm not stupid, Rill." He laid his head back on the seat, closing his eyes to the passing strides. "It's probably better that they won't want me."

Rill humored him. He marched Mik before Kell Ri, unwashed and unshaven, in shackles. Kell scowled at him.

Mik bit back a smile. *I am a complete fuck-up who has no prospects and no expectations in life. I cannot go downhill from here.* There was something life affirming in those thoughts.

"I'm disappointed in you, Mik," Kell growled.

Call the news services. "So am I, Father." *In both of us.*

"Do you know what it took to convince your brother not to kill you?"

Mik scowled. "You should have let him." Was that accurate? He didn't care if he died, but was

Mik seeking death? *You were. You wanted Jole to kill you. What do you want now, Mik?* He shook his head. He couldn't say what he wanted. Certainly, he didn't want what he did a week ago—or even two days ago. Did he want anything?

"What?" Kell snapped.

Mik pasted on a cocky smile. "What's it going to be? A prison cell? Execution? An estate in the polar region?" Mik smirked. Did it matter?

"You can't be trusted."

"I know. I revel in it."

"I'm going to keep you here where I can keep an eye on you."

"A fate worse than death," Mik muttered.

"It might be by the time I'm done with you. One way or the other, you'll do the duty you were born to. If this mad scheme of Jole's works—"

"Susan's plan," Mik corrected him.

Kell shot him a scowl, a warning couched in his glare. "If this mad scheme works, you will marry a Keen woman." Even now, Kell couldn't admit that the humans were their salvation.

"And if it fails?"

"You will have fifteen years to figure out how you failed so miserably."

By listening to you. Mik held his tongue.

Kell motioned to Rill. "Get these damned shackles off of him."

Mik smiled. "Too bad. I was starting to enjoy shackles and iron bars."

"Good. Then you won't mind them on your windows," Kell warned.

Mik shrugged as Rill removed the shackles.

"You will not leave the palace without guards. Until Jole's children are born, you will travel no further than Fint."

It hardly mattered. Where would Mik go if he did leave? To one of his estates? What was there that was any different than here?

"You will not be permitted to attend state functions until you are deemed safe."

Mik laughed harshly. "Then my schedule will remain quite open. I am not a safe man."

He turned and left his father's office without waiting to be dismissed. After all, what could Kell do but put him in a cell? Or kill him?

No. Mik wasn't seeking death. He was seeking an identity of his own. His whole life, Mik had been a vessel Kell had filled with misinformation and hate. Mik wasn't that man anymore. He couldn't be.

But who could he be? Mik pondered that as he waved the servants away and started drawing a bath. He took oaths once, in his early military training, oaths that he had abandoned in the intervening years. Those vows were the good pieces of him, the honorable man he could become.

It wasn't much, but it was a start. Every new beginning had to start somewhere. Mik stared at his reflection in the mirror, searching for the vows he'd broken in his scattered memories.

His voice was rough. "I vow to aid all who need my help. I vow to protect women and children, with my life if necessary. I vow to serve my people well. I vow to live as an honorable man. I vow to heal, as I possess the gift and it is a sacred pact with the gods that I do. I vow to live in peace while I might and fight when called upon."

Yes. That was the man Mik would be, but who was that man? Only time would tell.

CHAPTER FOURTEEN

Abrin 37th, Ri 25-2988

Danellan, daughter of General Cro, shivered in the darkness. She wasn't chilled because of the temperature of the night. It was a mild night for the end of the first month of autumn. It was terror that made her quake. It had taken her two days to escape Tranol. If this Len-be-damned driver would hurry, she might yet be free.

She bit back tears at what she'd become. Danellan was cowering in the back of a cargo transport, hiding, stealing what she needed to make good her escape. Her father would be shamed.

No. Her father taught her to survive and overcome. Sometimes, a judicious retreat was a warrior's only option. She would lead Tranol on a merry chase worthy of General Tolerin himself.

Danellan sobered. Unlike the great Tolerin, she wouldn't stop running until she reached safety. There would be no ambush for Tranol at the end of the chase. This wasn't a retreat to a better fighting stance. She couldn't pretend that it was.

The metal of the transport was cold under her fingers. Danellan sent up a prayer to Fion to deliver her from her brother's hands. Surely, Fion would not condone this travesty. She'd like to believe that Mag would not either, but Mag was the king of the gods, and kings were not to be trusted.

No. Kings and officers of the royal guard were at the bottom of her list. Danellan had always trusted those classes and the vows they took to protect those who needed them. Danellan needed them, but there would be no protection for her.

At twenty-one, she was barely an adult. Had her father lived, she would be under his care until the day she contracted a marriage, but Cro hadn't lived. He had died and left her at the mercy of kings and officers who had no honor and no respect for the vows they took. It was up to Danellan to protect herself, because no one else on Kegin would.

The transport started to move, and Danellan held her breath. She buried herself under the bundles of uniforms, as they approached the gate. The guard shined a lantern inside the back to search for stowaways, to search for her. She saw the light filtering through the cracks in the bundles that covered her. Danellan knew her brother ordered this. That was why she hid so well.

She fisted a hand around the hilt of her father's dagger, biting back tears. There was no option left for her. She'd fight her way out if she could. If that failed—

Mag, forgive me. Fion, convince him to show mercy and keep me from Len's Underworld.

Danellan breathed a sigh of relief as the guard waved them on. She remained undiscovered.

The transport bumped along the pitted roads. It would travel all the way to Bure that night. Danellan wasn't going that far. Though it would put her much closer to her ultimate goal, Tranol would catch her much too easily that way. There might even be soldiers waiting when the transport arrived, waiting to drag her back to her fate.

She pulled a blanket and some food from the packs around her and loaded her deep pockets with the things she would need to survive the first few weeks. She moved slowly and disturbed as little as possible to minimize the already-remote chance that the driver or his guard would hear her movements. The Garesh Mountains were upon her all too fast. If she was to survive, the mountains were her only hope.

Danellan dropped out of the back of the transport with the choc blanket wrapped around her form to hide the lighter beige of the travel coat she'd stolen from Tranol. She rolled away into the shadows silently and watched for pursuit. The transport didn't slow.

She ran for the foothills, using the moonlight to guide her. She'd sleep late tomorrow. By daybreak, Danellan intended to be deep in the mountains. Once there, it would be nearly impossible for her brother to find her.

It would be an easier task with a hottel, but it had been impossible for her to escape with one. For that matter, it had been all but impossible to escape without one.

Danellan paused to tie the blanket like a sling around her hip, gathering late berries as she walked. It wouldn't do to pass up what Fion offered while it was still available to her. Without a hottel or public transport, it would take her months to cross the continent to Stril's home. Those would be long, cold, hungry months, once her food supply gave out.

When she reached Stril's home in Caran, Tranol could join Kell Ri on the winds to Len's Dungeons for all she cared. As long as she was free, the two men meant not a thing to her.

* * * *

Veril 15th, Ri 25-2988

Mik rubbed the ache in the base of his skull. *A quarter of an hour. Paste on the smile for the last time.* The crowd waited patiently, while Kell gave his speech, some casting nervous glances at Mik.

The celebration was late this year, the alignment of the moon and the Great Star occurring in the last month of autumn. If he waited until next year, he'd have half the season before winter set in. But, Mik couldn't wait that long, and so his quest would be more difficult.

Kell shot him an irritated look that let Mik know he had missed his cue again.

Oh well. If I were that attentive to my duties, I would raise suspicion, and now is not the time to raise suspicion. Mik offered the crowd a dazzling smile and waved.

A cheer went up for him, and Mik forced the smile to steady when he wanted to cringe. *Cheer for me. Come see the second son, the prime piece of kit on the auction block.*

Mik turned abruptly and left the stage. He had to leave the stage. Mik wasn't permitted to stay while the heirs were presented. *As if I'd harm them.*

He sighed. No matter what assurances he gave, it was a chance they wouldn't take. Mik was mad, volatile, unpredictable, not to be trusted, especially not near Susan and her children.

His mouth went dry as he came face to face with Susan. Her smile disappeared, and she edged closer to Jole, clutching Jenneane to her chest. Out of the corner of his eye, he noted that Jole shifted Joseph on his hip to wrap an arm around his bride.

He stood for a moment, undecided. "Susan," he whispered, bowing his head reverently. Mik wanted to say more, but what could he say? 'I'm sorry' was insufficient. 'I still have nightmares about those dark times' would be scoffed at, an insult to her, though it was true. If anyone had a right to be tortured by nightmares, it would be Susan.

Mik smiled as Joseph reached a pudgy hand toward him. He raised his hand, letting the toddler grasp his finger. How he longed to hold his niece and nephew, but he would likely never be trusted that much. Mik swallowed a bitter lump at that thought.

"Highness," Pyter rumbled in warning. The telltale scrape of him testing his blade on its sheath announced his readiness to act.

Mik nodded, his smile replaced by a stony

look that would hide his pain. He dropped his gaze. "I'm sorry," he mumbled as he turned away. Mik all but bolted away from the stage, leaving his brother and Jole's family far behind.

The crowd erupted in thunderous applause and cheers. Mik clapped his hands over his ears, dropping them with a sharp in-drawn breath as he slipped into the brightly-lit palace. The crowd loved Jole. They had always loved Jole.

Mik made his way to his room, nodding to soldiers along the way and trying to ignore the ones that shadowed his every move. He was followed. Mik was always followed, especially when Susan was near. In addition to his father's guards, Pyter would have men watching him. Mik sighed. With any luck, he would give them nothing to watch tonight.

His uniform jacket was half off before he shut himself into his childhood rooms. Mik didn't waste time. He peeled off his uniform and boots and headed to the hidden corridor, where he pulled out the clothing piled on top of his travel pack in the darkness. The outfit was that of a common man, a hottel-hair travel coat and pants, a simple woven shirt, and scuffed boots.

There was no silin, no fur, and nothing in the trademark red and gold of the royal family. He removed his crest ring, tied it on a thong, and hid it deep beneath his clothes. It was the only thing clearly defining who he was he'd keep on his person, the only proof he'd need, the only safe haven he'd accept.

The brown woven cap pulled low over his eyes, Mik shouldered his pack and shut himself into the forgotten corridor. He moved quickly, following the passage past the walled-off entrance to Kell's rooms, past Jole's suite, down the stone staircase, and out into the war room.

Mik slid out onto the terrace and scaled the two stories down the iri vines to the ground below. The hard part behind him, he rounded the near-deserted courtyard and blended into the crowd pouring out onto the grounds.

He paused a moment, gazing at Jole and Susan holding their one and a half year-old twins before an adoring crowd. The twins' stunning blue-green eyes were a sign of hope, a sign of the future Jole had won for their world.

"Story of my life," Mik whispered through clenched teeth.

Pyter scanned his eyes over the crowd, and Mik turned away before his brother's chief of security could spot him and ruin his well-laid plans. The crowd fell away behind him. No one glanced his way. No one had reason to look at him. Without the trappings and guards that announced who he was, there was no reason for anyone to look twice.

The wide lawn was coming to an end, and the tents pitched for the nobles sat on the border of the orchard he would have to cross.

Mik tipped his cap further down, shading the taut lines of his face as he passed Minn. When his escape was discovered, Minn might be the one person on Kegin who would care. Not that Minn cared about Mik. Her upset would be purely self-centered.

"I can't believe you're actually doing this,"

one of Minn's sisters whispered.

He stopped in the deep shadows behind an Eir tree in full bloom, his heart pounding.

Minn chuckled. "Relax, Sari. The contract favors me."

He swallowed a sound of disgust. *I know. I've seen early drafts of the contract. The fact that she still argues it is reason enough not to trust her.*

"You'll contract and mate with a kidnapper, a half-mad re-bred—" Sari began.

Mik felt his stomach clench. That was what they thought of him. That was what they all thought of him. He deserved no better, but he still wished he could convince them that he wasn't that same desperate man.

Aren't you? You could be in a warm bed with a willing schente. Why are you here, Mik?

"Prince, Sari. He's a prince. It's the longest contract in recorded history. Aside from the production of children and official duties, I won't have to lay eyes on him."

That's why I'm here. Minn, Kell, the stresses of being notorious...

Sari shivered. "But to produce children—"

Minn shrugged and examined her manicured nails, gilded in the style of the current hopefuls. "Three children. It shouldn't take long, and if once a week for six months pass with no child, I collect my penalty. In the meantime, my contract allows me schaen."

Mik shook his head in disbelief. They actually approved schaen for her. What a nightmare! He'd have his schente, and she'd have her schaen. Once a week, he'd be called out

207

to stud like a bull kit. That wasn't Mik's idea of a marriage.

"Six months?" Sari squeaked. "It will never happen, Minn."

She smiled a cold, empty smile. "If it is intolerable, there is always Walla tea."

Mik fisted his hand and eased away toward the forest two stride from the cliff side. He'd heard enough to last him a lifetime.

"Walla tea," he cursed. The herb was used to prevent pregnancy. She planned to take the tea to win her penalty if he didn't perform to her liking? Minn picked the wrong man to play games with.

"Thank Mag I won't be tied to that jaglin." He thanked Mag for his justice in letting him hear her true thoughts. Mik knew Minn didn't love him, but he wouldn't stand for a woman actively plotting against him.

He thanked Mag, but he wouldn't thank Fion. As far as Mik could tell, the goddess of love and mercy had no interest in him past endless torture, and he had no time for a deity who so openly opposed him. From the death of his Earth-born cross-mate to Susan— No. Susan wasn't Fion's fault. That one, he would blame on Len driving him to madness.

The hottel Mik stashed in the forest was waiting for him as he'd hoped. It wasn't his war-buck. Only nobility would have a beauty like his steed. No. This hottel was a nondescript mare, white with a brown face and thick waves of long fur, much like the one his soldier shot from under Susan.

Chidan was that mare's name. "Beloved," he noted. Jole had named the mare for Susan, as a sign of how much Susan loved her...or perhaps as a sign of how much Jole loved Susan.

He pushed the unwanted memory of his brother's bride sailing over the beast's head from his mind and mounted the mare. Mik tucked his knees up, scowling at the fact that his feet all but dragged the ground as he rode, unless he drew up his knees as he would on his war-buck. The mare was not a dignified beast, but she was young and strong. Most of all, she was common.

Mik laughed. "My dear, your name is Frelang," he informed her, patting her neck. *Freedom* was a fine name for the mare he would ride to freedom.

He urged Frelang on with a cluck of his tongue and a squeeze of his knees. Common— His freedom would come in being the things he had been taught to avoid, the things that were supposedly beneath him.

CHAPTER FIFTEEN

Veril 16th, Ri 25-2988

Mik smiled at the clear blue sky, lacing his fingers behind his head and crossing his legs at the ankles. The late autumn grass was cool and crisp against his back, not brown yet but not the vibrant green of summer.

A day's growth of beard made his chin itch, but it would be worth it in the long run. He'd never been permitted to grow a beard like some common men did. Mik had always wanted to.

He sighed. He'd have to leave soon, but he intended to visit another of his dreams. This morning, there would be no servants and guards, no Kell making demands of him. There was only Mik and the splendor of a perfect, crisp autumn breeze stirring his hair.

Years ago, when Mik was a boy of five or six, he'd often snuck into Jole's room at night. He'd asked questions, endless questions about their mother and Jole's life with her. Mik had been starved for knowledge of her.

Kell didn't permit anyone to speak about her. The one time Mik dared ask—

He cringed. *Why must I always remember such things when I want to escape them?*

* * * *

He was three. Mik knew Jole would come to

210

live with him soon, the older brother he'd seen only on ceremony days.

"Who was Tolerin?" Kell quizzed him. Kell always quizzed him. There were never quiet moments between them.

"A general under Ro Ti, the great conqueror. He was a favored son of the king for saving Ro's life in battle. Tolerin took a blow intended to kill the king and slay the other man while he lay pouring his lifeblood on the ground." The little details were important to Kell. Mik tried to remember every detail of every story, but it seemed an impossible task.

"And?" Kell barked, raising a glass for a sip of brandy.

Mik searched his memory. "He led the final three campaigns in Ro's stead," he offered, proud of his recollection. "The final battle was in Pri Ti 10-476."

Kell's jaw tightened. "And?"

Mik searched for more frantically, but he had exhausted his knowledge of Tolerin. He shrugged, knowing what was coming.

His father made a sound of disgust. "He took Ro Ti's daughter, Riella, as mate and became the first king of the first Ri era. He fathered Deliya the fair and Benir the peace-bringer."

He nodded, his face burning in defeat. He'd failed again. He always failed. As if Mik didn't know his disgrace well enough, Kell gave him the look that announced his disappointment in his second son.

"You can do better, Mik. At your age, Jole knew the histories of two worlds by rote. He

211

spoke two languages. You are smarter than he is. You were raised in the Keen manner with the finest tutors. You must apply yourself."

But, Mik *was* applying himself. Was it his fault that Mag had blessed Jole with an almost Vid-like memory? "Will I learn my mother's language?" he asked, hoping to find a safer subject.

"Why, when you can barely handle Keen?" Kell growled.

"Will Jole teach me when he comes to live here?"

"No."

"But..." He faltered. How was Mik supposed to talk to his mother if he didn't speak her language...or an Earth-born bride? Surely not through translators!

"I'll not have you tainted by her inferior barbarian teachings," he decided.

"When will I get to meet my mother?" he asked innocently.

Mik realized his mistake when Kell turned his cold, black eyes on him.

"You won't," he promised.

"When I am grown—" Mik began, desperate to know that he would someday meet her. When he was grown, Kell couldn't order him not to.

The world went momentarily black then painfully bright. Balance deserted him. When Mik's vision cleared, Kell stood over him. Realization came slowly. His father had struck him. Mik ran a shaking hand over his cheek.

"Never ask me about the woman again. She is a selfish, proud woman. She denies Kegin *daughters. She locks herself away from me and from you. What kind of mother does that?"*

* * * *

Mik hadn't asked Kell again. Lessons like that were quickly learned.

He had asked Jole often and lived his mother's love vicariously through his brother's words. Jole had lived in love and freedom. Their mother had held him upright on his first mare. Jole hadn't broken his arm falling from a war-buck or been scowled at for crying out as the bone was set.

Jole had been permitted to lie in a field of lizors and contemplate cloud formations without a history tutor at his elbow. Jole had been told often that he was loved. Jole had been taught *how* to love. The only love Mik had known was Jole's, but there had been nothing Jole could do to improve Mik's lot in life.

Mik never knew if his mother loved him. She'd died when he was seven. Jole had hypothesized that she never talked about her second son, because it was too painful for her to think about losing him at birth. Mik chose to believe that. It was better than the alternative that no one had loved him but Jole. After Susan, even Jole had distanced himself.

Mik had lived for the day when he would turn twenty and be free of Kell's rule, free to seek out the mother he'd been denied knowing. He'd dreamed of one day being embraced by Jenneane as Jole had described her embracing her older son. Mik might have forgiven her for dying before he could have that wish fulfilled were it not for what he'd learned two years after she passed.

He'd found the hidden corridors that allowed him to sneak to Jole's rooms early in life. At the time, there were only three exits he utilized—his room, Jole's room, and the one near the kitchen. That night, Mik had been headed to the kitchen.

* * * *

Mik paused as he passed a bank of soldier's quarters, stunned by someone uttering his mother's name. There wasn't a doorway, but the stone had crumbled, making it easy for him to hear the voices in the room beyond. He stilled, placing his ear against the stone to hear better.

"Jenneane," he whispered, wary even in his solitude to speak it aloud.

"Lovely. A beautiful woman," one soldier attested.

"You looked at her?" another asked in disbelief.

The first barked a laugh. "Yes. I looked. I was all but ordered to bed her, if she were willing."

"Was she?"

Mik held his breath and waited for the answer. Please, not that. Please, Mag.

"No." His voice was petulant, as if he considered her refusal a personal affront.

Mik sighed in relief.

"Not for me," he continued. "But for someone."

His hand fisted on the rock, leaving cuts that Jole would heal before Kell could see them the next morning.

"Who?" the other man asked.

"I don't know, but I do know how she died."

"An accident, wasn't it?"

The soldier laughed harshly.

Mik felt weak. He slumped against the wall, the air thick in his lungs.

"That was the official release."

"Then what really happened?" the other demanded.

Mik imagined the first soldier puffing up, proud at possessing knowledge that the other didn't. He hated the man, but he wanted to know more.

"She poisoned herself."

There was more. Mik could hear the implied hanging knowledge in his conspiratorial tone.

"Losing her sons was finally too much for her?"

"No. She used gola berry tea and olum." He sounded gleeful.

Mik shook his head. At nine, pharmacology had not been one of his subjects yet. He didn't know what that combination signified.

The second soldier sucked in a breath, audible even through the stone. "Who was the father?" he asked solemnly.

"If Kell Ri knew that, I imagine the man's blood would have stained a blade by now. The king doesn't take being cuckolded lightly. Or maybe it was another man ordered to take her, and the bitch simply found a way to escape his *trap. I'm sure Kell isn't happy that she found a way to best him again."*

"They're certain?"

"Why else does a woman choose gola berry but to kill a bastard?"

* * * *

Mik had no memory of the trip back to his rooms. He was numb from the shock of what he'd heard. He'd drawn a bath and sat in it until he was shivering, the water chilled to the temperature of his soul.

Had Jole ever known the true woman, or had she lied to him, shown him a false face? Mik had wanted to gut the soldier for his lies, but he couldn't be sure that the man was lying. Was his mother truly a wanton and a traitor? Had her death been an accident, or had she left him by her own hand? Had she ever considered Mik when she chose her path?

There was no way to learn the answers to those questions. Mik wasn't permitted to ask his father or the guards. Jole wouldn't know for certain, and Pyter—

Mik had tried to ask Pyter how his mother really died. He'd trusted the man for one reason; Jole trusted him, and that spoke volumes to Mik. That misconception hadn't lasted long. Mik couldn't trust Pyter any more than he could trust Kell.

Pyter's cold look had put his father's to shame, as if the mention of his mother was a personal affront to Jole's mentor. Worse, Pyter had asserted that, by contract, Mik was never his mother's son. Legally, Pyter was constrained from telling Mik anything. All of it was delivered with undisguised hatred.

Mik never understood why Pyter hated him. He only understood one thing. Jole had Pyter to watch over him and care for him. Mik still had no one. Now that his mother was dead, he would never have anyone to fill that void.

He was ten before Mik understood that Kell didn't favor Jole, despite his brother's many strengths. In some strange way, Kell seemed to loathe Jole, even as he held him up as a shining example of success to his younger son. Mik had hoped he could win a place in their father's heart by simply besting Jole at something...anything.

Saying that was easier than doing it. Jole had been faster, stronger, and more knowledgeable. The fact that Jole was five years his senior rarely occurred to Mik. Since it made no difference to Kell, it had been immaterial to Mik.

In retrospect, it should have made a difference. Maybe that was the beginning of his madness, beating himself black and blue for something he could never hope to attain, under those circumstances.

In the end, Mik had excelled in only one area, before Jole set up his own household at the age of twenty-two. Mik was the better sneak, cutthroat, and all around bastard. Of the two of them, he had truly grown to be Kell's son. It was no wonder that Susan had spurned him.

Mik sighed and pushed to his feet. He had ridden half the night. He was far from the palace but not far enough. He should have kept riding. Mik should have been through Fint early that morning and within the southern hills of the Garesh Mountains by now. He had to move quickly.

He would purchase supplies in Fint and hide in the forests between the villages to make his way to the foothills. If Kell did try to find him, Mik would not be an easy man to find. This was one game he could win against his father. When it came down to it, Mik was a world-class sneak.

* * * *

Mik ducked through the marketplace, backtracking to the stable and Frelang. What in Len's Unholy Underworld were all of these soldiers doing in a small village like Fint? Well, there was only one possible answer to that question.

He berated himself. Mik had lingered too long, enjoyed his freedom too much. Now his enjoyment could cost him that hard-won freedom. His father had outflanked him. Mik hadn't expected pursuit to come so quickly and be so intensive.

Mik kept his eyes down and his shoulders hunched, making himself as inconspicuous as possible. He bowed to a passing general, thankful that it wasn't one he knew personally. Mik cringed at the meek exterior he was affecting. He would have died rather than do this two years ago, but there were worse things than death. If freedom meant presenting as if he was the lowest drifter, he would do it.

I am not a desperate man.

"Right," he quipped, fighting back a laugh at that thought. If anything, he was even more desperate than he had been in those dark times.

The stable was just ahead, and Mik hurried toward it.

His eyes passed over a woman, and he stopped, looking at her in dismay. "Susan," he breathed. Mik shook his head, sure that she was a hallucination of some sort. He prayed to Mag that his mind had snapped and supplied this torture for him, but Mag wasn't in the business of granting Mik's wishes that day.

Susan locked on his eyes and mouthed his name. She scanned her eyes up and down the alley.

Mik followed the movement, a stark terror making his stomach rebel. If she screamed, he would never make it from the town. He turned and ran for the stable. If she screamed when he was already mounted, he had a chance. Thankfully, the alley was deserted. He was on Frelang when she appeared in the doorway of the stable.

"Mik. Don't do this. Please." Her grasp of the Keen language had improved in the last two years, but the voice that spoke it was the same.

He didn't look at her. Susan wasn't his. Mik should never have looked at her in the first place. He should never have touched her. "I'm not hurting anyone, Susan. I don't intend to. You have— My vow isn't worth much, but you have it."

"Just talk to Joel. Don't leave this way."

He winced at her pronunciation of his brother's name. The Earth inflection was beautiful. Even when he was sure she was cursing him in her native language, her words were beautiful, elegant. Mik wished that Jole had taught him the language, but it was a risk his brother wasn't willing to take.

"What is my name, Susan?" he pleaded quietly. Mik had to know. What would his name sound like in the language he was denied.

"I don't understand." Her voice was closer.

Mik pushed down the urge to move away from that voice. She wasn't his to touch, but he wouldn't run from her either. "How would my mother have pronounced my name? Tell me. Please."

"Mik was a baby name, an endearment. She might have called you that."

"A baby name for what? What is my name?" Who was he really? Mik was the child. Who was the man?

"Till tells me that her brother's name was Michael. Jenneane named you to honor her brother."

Mik closed his eyes. He never knew that. He'd never known how she chose his name. It was a name dear to her. She must have loved him. "Michael," he repeated, committing it to memory. "Thank you, Susan."

She touched his knee, a tentative touch of a

shaking hand. Susan still feared him. "Talk to Joel. He's worried about you."

Mik hazarded a glance at her. Her eyes were bright with unshed tears. Was she frightened, or was it concern for her husband? Mik found it hard to form a response. He had never wanted to see Susan cry again.

"I want my eight years. Tell Jole— He had his time. I just want mine. Promise me you'll tell him."

Susan's hand eased away. "I promise."

Mik nodded and steered Frelang toward the door.

"Go South, Michael. There aren't many troops that direction."

He nodded and swallowed a bitter lump. "I am sorry, Susan." Mik didn't ask for forgiveness. Even if he deserved it, it was unlikely that Susan would ever offer it.

"I know."

He wound his way toward the mountains, smiling when the village fell away behind him with no sign of chase. Michael laughed. "Michael," he mused. "A new man deserves a new name. Perhaps Michael is who I would be if my mother had raised me." In any case, he couldn't use the name Mik and hope to hide long.

* * * *

Susan stood in the semi-darkness of the stable, biting back tears. She'd suspected how brittle Mik had become when he touched Joseph

221

the night before. She was sure that he was broken when he fled the stage. Now she had her proof.

She should call the soldiers, but she couldn't do that. Mik wasn't dangerous. He was lost, sad. He needed what he was doing.

And, if he hurts himself in this bid to find what is missing in his life?

Susan wouldn't think about that. Mik was a man, and he needed this journey. She wasn't his mother or his nurse.

She retrieved an implin fruit from a bin near the door and went to the stall that held Jole's war-buck. The male hottel nuzzled her face and ate the offered treat. She stiffened at the sound of Pyter's voice.

"He had to have come this way," he growled. "The merchant saw him not a quarter of an hour ago."

A shadow fell over Susan. She ignored it. Pyter would be furious with her. He worried too much.

"Princess Susan." His voice was edged in concern. "Where is Bell?"

"With Barri and the babies."

She felt Jole's presence before he wrapped his arms around her and pulled her to his chest.

His voice caressed her ear. "This isn't safe, Susan. These soldiers are with us for your protection. Mik—"

"Is searching for something. He doesn't intend to harm me or anyone else. He needs this, Joel."

Jole turned her toward him. His face was

tense. "You've seen him."

Susan nodded slowly, raising her chin a notch. She met his eyes fully. Jole could read her well. He'd know she had nothing to fear from his brother.

Pyter strode to her, trying to mask his anger. "He could have—"

"He won't," she assured him.

"You can't know that."

"I know," she whispered.

Jole took a calming breath. "What did he say to you?"

"He's searching for something. Please, let him do this."

"What is he searching for?"

"Home. Family. Someplace meant for him."

"I don't understand. He has a family."

"Does he?" she asked pointedly.

Jole grimaced, averting his gaze. She knew he'd distanced himself from Mik for her comfort, but Mik was left with no one.

"He wants his eight years, Joel. Mik wants what you had."

"He's insane," Pyter decided.

"No," Susan assured him. "I think this is the first sign that he's finally sane."

CHAPTER SIXTEEN

Veril 24ᵗʰ, Ri 25-2988

Michael slowed Frelang, taking in the figure walking along the mountain ridge in curiosity. He couldn't see much of the man between the long travel coat that reached his knees, the knit cap, and the high boots. Michael smiled. The mysterious traveler seemed to be as determined to hide as Michael was.

He'd slipped easily into thinking of himself as Michael. Mik was someone loathsome to his peers, his people, and himself. Michael was someone new, someone who could be the man he'd always wanted to be. He'd have to hide the winter, ride it out in whatever manner he could. After that, he would blend in to the populace and make his way. He had skills. Michael could work as a teacher or advisor. If it meant his freedom, he'd work in manual labor. At least it would be honest work.

Michael sighed. He had to show himself to people eventually. The merchant in Fint had recognized him, but only because Michael had been clean and barely unshaven. He was road-traveled now, unwashed and covered in a fine layer of dirt. There was soil under his fingernails and charcoal from the fire staining his hands.

The traveler would see him soon. It was time to learn if a week's worth of a beard and his disguise were enough to hide his identity. At least the man was small, hardly a challenge in a fight.

"Greetings, sir," Michael called out jovially.

The other man turned, weapon drawn. The dagger was sharp, showing tender care in maintenance. It had the look of an officer's dagger, like the one Michael had left behind because it bore the royal seal in its hilt. Michael wished he could see it clearer, but that would be foolhardy until he diffused the situation.

Michael looked at the man's face and gasped. It was a woman. She wore a travel coat like his and a man's tunic. Her hair was hidden beneath the laborer's knit cap. She didn't wear trousers, but with her coat closed, no one would be able to tell she wore a trouskit, a female's split riding skirt.

She looked around warily, as if she expected an ambush, then eyed him in distrust so thick he could nearly taste it on the air. She offered no comment and asked no questions.

Michael felt his anger spike. "Where is your guard?" he demanded.

She snorted and rolled her eyes. "I have no need of a man to protect me from the likes of you."

He smiled. She had fire. "It is not safe for a woman to travel alone," he reminded her.

"I do well enough."

Michael sighed. Her stubbornness would get her killed one day. "Come along," he ordered.

She shook her head and motioned with her blade. "Move on, sir. I have no need or want of your company."

"I cannot leave you to travel alone." He could.

Mik would have. She was a common woman. But, protecting women was deeply engrained in Michael, and Michael was who this woman would deal with. Michael remembered the oaths he took. Michael lived by them, *damn it!*

"You owe me nothing," she growled. "I would prefer not to find myself in your debt."

"You are right, but you would owe me nothing. I owe the gods that much." And, perhaps they would be kind to him in the long winter months if he showed this kindness.

She scanned her eyes over him slowly. "You don't look like a cleric," she decided.

Michael laughed heartily, patting Frelang with his hand when she shied at the sound. "I'm not," he assured her.

She nodded. "Then you owe them nothing for my sake."

"I do. Now come. This is growing tedious."

She held her ground, glaring at him across the clearing. "You don't even know where I'm going."

"Since I had no destination in mind but where the winds of chance would take me, perhaps I should look on this as a sign."

"I don't believe in chance or signs."

A most unusual woman. Most women of Michael's acquaintance were tirelessly involved in portents and signs, except Susan, but Susan had been born on Earth.

"And I made a vow once to protect those who need me," he countered.

Her eyes widened. "You're an officer in royal service?" she whispered. That seemed to frighten her when it should have given her comfort.

Michael was intrigued. He bowed his head. "I was. I am no longer."

"You're awfully young to retire."

"I didn't retire. I left service." Considering his training had started with dagger at five, he was permitted to order troops at ten, and he was granted command above all but his father and brother at adulthood; Michael had served almost twenty years in service. That was enough for any decent man to retire.

"Why?"

"I didn't like taking orders." That was true enough.

Her mouth twitched, as if she was trying to hide a smile. She took a step back. "I don't believe you."

Michael growled a curse on stubborn women and slid off his hottel. He stalked toward her, reaching beneath his coat to draw his sword. The laser-edged blade was proof of what he claimed.

Her eyes widened, and she launched at him with a battle cry. Michael released his weapon. He hadn't expected her to attack, but perhaps he should have. Women never did precisely what you thought they would.

He blocked her blow with his forearm, deflecting the blade that would have taken his throat, determined to handle this without resorting to his own weapon. She spun, changing her attack like an expert soldier. Had Michael not been as well trained as he was, he might have lain dead after that move.

Instead, Michael captured her wrist in his

left hand and wrenched her dagger free with his right, tossing it a short distance away. She didn't hesitate. Her leg came up toward his groin.

He smiled as he swept her support ankle and sidestepped her blow. Mik could have done this to Susan when first they met if he'd realized that women would have training and fight as dirty as a man. Not having sisters had worked to his disadvantage with Susan. Michael had no disadvantage. This poor girl would be treated gently, but no blow would be unanticipated. She fought like a man. He cushioned her fall then straddled her thighs.

She tried to butt him in the face, but Michael dodged and pushed her back. She landed with a light grunt and went for his eyes, her fingers like claws. Michael captured her hands and transferred both wrists to his left hand. The girl cried out in frustration, trying to wrench her hands free.

Michael pulled his sword and flicked the switch to activate it. She stilled, eyeing the laser-edged blade in fear. The blue glow reflected in her black eyes. She shook her head, and her cap fell away. Dark curls spilled out from beneath it, cascading over her shoulder.

He locked his eyes on her face, trying to ignore the breasts heaving with every ragged breath she took. This was no girl. She was a woman, and she was definitely a woman he shouldn't tempt himself with.

Tears tracked down her cheeks. He cursed himself for scaring her. Michael released her hands, wary of attack. After a moment of peace, he turned the laser cauter off.

She looked at him, swallowing hard. "It appears you are what you say, sir. Men who steal blades like that do not care for them well. I apologize for calling you a liar."

Michael sheathed his sword, reeling at the sincerity in that apology. This woman wasn't seeking just to convince him to release her. She meant what she said, and that was priceless to him.

He nodded. "I meant only to show you my blade. You should never assume you know your opponent's mind. You should never attack prematurely, no matter how skilled you are." Michael met her eyes. "And you are skilled."

She darkened at the compliment. Surely, she wasn't ignorant of how rare a woman of her fighting skill was.

"Who trained you?"

She shook her head. "No one...formally. I— watched the soldiers train. My father thought it best if I practiced what I saw."

"Your father was in royal service?" He had to look at the blade he threw. It would tell him the man's rank and award.

"He's dead now." The bitterness in her voice stunned him.

"You are traveling to family?"

"No. To a childhood friend who will allow me to earn my keep."

"Where is this friend?"

She hesitated. "Caran."

Michael startled. It would take her until the end of winter to get there on foot.

"So, you see. I am sure you are headed nowhere near my destination. If you would set me free, I will trouble you no more."

He shook his head. "I will take you there." If he didn't, she'd freeze or starve before the month was gone.

"You owe me nothing."

"I owe your father. Out of respect for him, I will do this."

"You don't even know who my father is," she replied weakly.

"I know all I need to know. He served."

* * * *

Danellan stared at the strange man over her in shock. He was unwashed and unshaven, dressed in a laborer's clothing. But, he carried the sword of a high-ranking officer and he was highly trained.

His movements were graceful and strong. He never faltered in attack or defense. It took years to develop reflexes like those. His body was all lean muscle and angles. He was beautiful in some way an artist might capture in a fantasy scene, as if he were apart from the natural world.

There was an uncertainty in his eyes that belied his outward calm. The black depths were shadowed. He kept his gaze locked on hers. Aside from his initial examination of her, he hadn't looked at her body. He'd made no move to molest her. He was a most unusual man.

"What is your name, sir?" she requested.

He eased off of her and offered Danellan a hand to her feet, lifting her seemingly without effort. He turned from her and retrieved her father's dagger from the ground. "A general," he whispered. "So many years in service and highly decorated."

He stroked the hilt fondly. Was he recalling his own dagger? Danellan wondered what rank and honors his would have listed.

He turned and placed the blade in her hand with a bow of his head. "I am sorry for your loss," he told her. The sincerity in him surprised her.

Danellan sheathed the dagger. "What is your name, sir?" she repeated.

"Michael." He darkened, as if saying his name was somehow an embarrassment.

She furrowed her brow. "A most unusual name but pleasing."

"A family name of my mother's clan," he dismissed her question. "And your name, fair lady?"

She took a deep breath. He'd not listed a family relation for her. She owed him no more. "Danellan."

"Come, Danellan. We have a long way to travel."

Danellan nodded and headed for Michael's hottel. She ran a hand through the mare's silky locks. "She's beautiful."

Michael placed his hands around her waist, and she startled. He pulled her back to his chest slowly.

"Shhh," he soothed her. "I won't hurt you." Michael lifted her to the hottel's back.

She felt her cheeks heat. "I can't ask this of you. It's not right." She couldn't ride his beast while Michael walked. It was bad enough that he'd lifted her to the mare's back as if she were a child when Danellan had exercised her father's war-buck on a regular basis.

He smiled a devastating smile. "We're riding double, Danellan." He motioned her to move back onto the rear hump to give him room to mount.

"But—" She shifted back hurriedly as he moved.

Michael swung his leg over and pulled her arms around his waist, sliding her back into the natural indentation that kept her pressed to his body. "Frelang is strong, and it is the fastest mode of travel we have."

Danellan sank her cheek to his back, as the hottel started moving. *Frelang? How appropriate a name for the beast.*

She yawned and closed her eyes. Danellan was tired, more tired than she'd ever been in her life. She'd been running for three weeks. Tranol hadn't found her. Danellan thanked Fion every night in her cold blanket that she was still free.

"Danellan?" Michael asked quietly.

"Hmm?" She yawned against his shoulder again. He was warm. She thanked the Merciful Mother that she could share in that heat.

"Why didn't you use a portion of the benefits to travel by public transport?"

Tranol....

No. Michael won't understand. "I had no benefits. I wasn't Father's heir."

"A portion should have been yours by law."

"No. Not in this case."

A portion of it should have been hers. That was true, but Tranol had other plans for her. Danellan would rather die at the hands of bandits than submit to Tranol's plans for her.

CHAPTER SEVENTEEN

Veril 32nd, Ri 25-2988

Michael stared at Danellan across the fire, still stung by her outburst as they left the village and her silence during their long ride into the heavily forested foothills above, still unsure what had angered her. She was such a mystery to him. Michael didn't understand her drive. He didn't understand her anger. He wished he understood her.

"Why did the woman in the village upset you?" he asked carefully. That was the only thing he did understand. Danellan had bitten back tears at the sight of the pregnant woman leading her children through the marketplace. She couldn't drag Michael away fast enough.

Danellan gazed into the fire as if she could read futures in the flames, as Sivrah sometimes did. "She's being made old before her time.

"How? I don't understand."

"Of course you don't," she snapped. "You're a male of a noble family."

"I don't see what that—"

"When you return to your life, you'll make an advantageous contract and build your perfect little world. If you're lucky enough to love your bride, you might decide to have more than your required heirs, but you'll have servants to care for them."

"Is that what this is about? The fact that the woman had five children?"

"And no decent way to prevent it," Danellan shouted. "A husband without the healing magic and not decent food enough to keep her from feeling the pains of pregnancy almost every day."

Michael shot her a look of disbelief. "There are clinics. One is not far from here. There are sterilization procedures and Walla teas. We're not uncivilized. The procedures are free, Danellan."

She looked at him in stunned horror. "You really don't know the laws. Do you?"

"What laws?"

"The law works differently for the poor, Michael. The procedures and Walla teas are only free if one or both parties in a contract show a high enough level of genetic decay. Unlike the rich, they have not the luxury of hiring servants to care for the children they are forced by situation to bear. They have not the means to pay for the medical procedures or drugs to prevent it that the rich take for granted." Tears glistened in her eyes.

Michael viewed her reaction in concern. "Was that why you took this journey? So you wouldn't become like that woman?"

She paled. "No. I was offered a position. It was simply a position I could not bear. Scrubbing floors surrounded by children in a hovel would be preferable."

"What position?"

Danellan squared her shoulders and granted him a hard look. "I fear I would offend your naïveté."

Michael felt his temper rise. "Offend me

then."

She flicked an uncertain look at him. "You are an honorable man, Michael. Not all nobles are. Not all soldiers are, even officers."

"Then there should be punishment when they are not. No one is exempt from the laws, or they mean nothing."

"Then they mean nothing. I would not argue that point. Do you think royals follow the laws? I'm sure some of them are as forthright as you are, but others—"

His blood ran cold. "Like Prince Mik?" he spat.

Her eyes widened. "I do not know the man. I would not cast stones when I have no knowledge of what drives him."

Michael paused, furrowing his brow at her proclamation. "Then you are a better soul than most."

She shook her head. "His actions— The prince seems—" She took a slow, deep breath. "You know him?"

Michael nodded. He knew himself better than most men dared. He knew what he would do when he was desperate enough. He hoped he never knew that side of himself again.

"People judge him too harshly, don't they?"

"In what way?"

"He seems simply a man who gave in to desperation. Who hasn't?"

He looked at her in surprise. "You know the prince well."

Danellan laughed harshly. "I know him not at all. I know desperation."

"If not Prince Mik, what royal were you speaking of? Surely not Prince Jole." Michael couldn't imagine anyone casting stones at the image of perfection his older brother presented.

She smiled. "No. I've only seen him once, but he seems a good man. I know him not a whit better than his brother."

"That leaves only Kell Ri," he noted. Not that it would surprise Michael to learn that his father was dishonorable; he knew for a fact that Kell was not honorable. It would merely surprise him to know that it was public knowledge.

Danellan shifted nervously. "I do not seek to add treason to my reasons to hide."

"How has the king injured you?" However it was, Michael would find a way to make it right. No person deserved to be hunted as she was. He had no doubts that she ran from someone or something. No woman would choose this course unless she had to.

She scowled and poked at the fire with a stick. "He hasn't."

"But he would? Or you fear he would?"

She didn't answer. Her hand fisted on the stick.

"Danellan?"

"I do not choose to be injured. I choose to create options for myself, to make myself an honorable servant of no family rather than live by unjust laws, in the station I was born to. It is that simple."

"What laws?" he asked, desperate for insight into her plight.

She threw her stick into the fire, her eyes

hard. "The king's law. What other law is there? No other law binds against his whims."

Michael startled at the venom in her voice. "You've seen this? You've seen Kell Ri step around the laws?"

Danellan sighed. "Mag's justice. Yes, I've seen it."

"You know what drives him? It is not like you to judge without knowing."

A tear wound down her cheek. "I know what drives him. It is treason to say that our king is not an honorable man." She met Michael's eyes. "But he is not, Michael. Do not cross him, or Kell Ri will have no mercy on you."

A chill breeze ran in Michael's heart. She knew Kell Ri far better than she should. His father was ruthless.

* * * *

Veril 36th, Ri 25-2988

Her skin was softer than silin. The fragrance of the iri soap she used to wash and heavy musk filled the air around her. Mik was drunk on her scent.

It's fear. She fears you.

No. It's not fear. *She wasn't trembling in fear. She wanted him.*

She moaned as his hands caressed her back. It was arousal. His cock hardened painfully in the knowledge that she would accept him.

The clothing was in his way. He had to get rid

of it. *What fool allowed this precious blossom to wear a man's clothes? A woman shouldn't wear trousers and tunics. She should wear silin day dresses that would bare her to his thrusts with a single pull.*

He kissed her, and she shook under his mouth. It was new, their first time. Mik had no patience. He pulled his dagger and sliced her tunic, ripping it from her body. She covered her breasts as if she were virginal. She was wonderful.

Mik pushed her back onto the bed, pulling off her trousers, rougher than he should be for a first time. Her body was slick and waiting. He plunged into her to the hilt, groaning at the sensation of her body pulsing around him, his hands in her hair.

"No. Please."

Her voice chilled him. Mik looked into her face. "Danellan?" *He breathed the question, uncertain of her complaint.*

"No. Mik, please."

The eyes. It was Danellan's face and voice, but the eyes were—

"Susan."

Michael shot upright, venting his howl of horror at the uncaring stars. His heart battered at his ribs.

I didn't. I never did. Thank Mag, I never went that far.

Barely. He groaned in the realization of how true it was.

Danellan jumped back from the fire, shaking like a limb in a high wind. She stared at him warily.

"A dream," he rasped, scrubbing his hands over his face. Michael wished he could wash away the dream as easily. "Forgive me."

Michael wrapped the blanket tighter around his shoulders as a freezing wind whipped over the rocky plateau they'd chosen for the night. It was below the snow line, but it was still high enough that there was only sparse tree cover to break the high winds.

She nodded, somber. "What was it?" she whispered. "What do you fear?" Danellan looked haunted, as if dreams of that type plagued her nights as often as they did his.

"Ghosts. Just ghosts." *Ghosts of a man better left dead.*

Danellan raised a hand, and metal glinted in the firelight.

Michael looked at her in confusion. "What are you doing?"

"Cutting my hair."

"No," he protested. "Why?"

"It leaves a lump under my cap. It's showing. I can't have that. I was trying not to— I have to cut it much shorter." She shivered in the evening chill and bent to warm her hands over the flames.

He scowled. Danellan should have long hair. He cursed whatever ghosts drove her to this life. "Was it long?"

She stared at him, her brow furrowed. "Was what long?"

"Your hair. Was it long before?"

Danellan nodded sadly. "Very long. My father

liked it that way."

"And you?"

"Yes. I liked it that way. I'll grow it again—in Caran." She raised the dagger to him. "Will you help me? I'll need it short, above my shoulders."

Michael paused, heartsick at helping her embrace this horrid life. "Yes. I'll help you." It would keep her safe. Michael had sworn to keep her safe.

He crossed the clearing to her and crouched to her back. Michael tried to ignore the ache in his gut as he sliced her hair off as she wished, throwing handfuls of the thick black curls toward the fire beside them.

Satisfied that he'd done as she wished, Michael placed his hand on her shoulder. A flash of a memory assaulted him, nearly knocking him off balance.

Let's see if you can work with that, love. Had Mik laughed when he said that to Susan? Michael couldn't recall. He hoped he hadn't laughed.

Michael sheathed her dagger with shaking hands and retreated to his pallet. He wouldn't do that to Danellan. She could trust him. He hoped she could trust him.

"Thank you, Michael."

He nodded, pulling his blanket around him, shivering but not from the cold. *I'm not that man anymore. If I'm ever a danger to Danellan, I'll walk away. Mag, give me the strength to walk away.*

* * * *

Iric 1ˢᵗ, Ri 25-2988

Michael reached his hand toward Danellan, stopping half a finger width from the dirt smudge on her cheek. He shook himself mentally and pulled his hand back. He was mad to consider touching her.

The dream had only been the start for him. His gaze followed her constantly. He hardened every time she straddled Frelang behind him. Her scent taunted him, and he longed to clasp his fingers in her hair, to ease her mouth to his.

Even before the dreams, he'd wanted her. The last two days had been pure torture. He couldn't seem to get her out of his lust-choked mind.

Michael growled, crossing his arms and lying back on his blanket. He'd been too long without schente. He needed release. That was all.

He closed his eyes. Danellan was waiting for him behind his eyelids, as she always was. She was dressed in a presentation gown.

Fion! Why do you persist in this madness? Or is it Len trying to seal my fate?

He pulled his blanket over himself fully. Release was all he needed.

Under the blanket, Michael unfastened his trousers and took his cock in hand. In his mind, it was Danellan who held him. He shuddered at the thought of it.

She stroked him, her short nails raking up his length and teasing at the bundle of nerves beneath the head. Danellan leaned over him, her curls teasing his cheeks as her mouth brushed his.

Michael held her face between his hands, drawing at her mouth with his. Still, her hand played at his cock. Her tongue sparred with his, passionate, increasing speed in time with her hand.

"I want you, Michael."

He groaned. She'd call him Michael. He wanted Danellan to call him that.

"Come on top of me."

Danellan slid her leg over, mounting him as she would a hottel for a ride.

Michael tightened his fist on his cock, his breathing ragged. She'd be tight, gripping him in her heat.

Her eyes closed on a moan as Danellan took his full length. She rode him. Faster. Harder. Little mewling cries escaped her.

Michael ground his teeth to hold in his cry at release. He lay in the aftermath, come still warm on his hand and stomach, his cock thickened but not properly wedged in a woman as it should be. Still, Danellan taunted him in his mind.

He cleaned himself with a grumbled curse on Fion, grabbing a handful of soft Eir leaves from the branches that made up his sleeping pallet, branches that would feed the morning fire with fragrant green sucre wood. All his life, Michael had heard stories of men satisfying themselves when they didn't have schente. As far as he could tell, it didn't work.

CHAPTER EIGHTEEN

Iric 3ʳᵈ, Ri 25-2988

Danellan realized that danger was lurking an instant before the man struck. The nuglin cut off her air and bruised her throat as he yanked her into the shadows behind the stable. The packages of food Michael had sent her to buy fell from her hands, and she reached for the rope.

She pushed back panic. She couldn't panic, or she would die. She had to think.

It was no use. Danellan was wasting precious moments when she should be regaining her air. She would never be able to force the loop loose of the locking mecha. The nuglin was a hunter's tool, used by poachers who took jaglin and other large carnivores for pelts and menageries.

She pulled the dagger from beneath her travel coat and sliced the rope between her neck and the locking mecha. Danellan spun as the man fell back, slicing his throat and taking the large artery in his hip. Cro had insisted on the basics in defense training for her, so slaying the man was a simple task.

Danellan stared at the blood on her hand in shock. She'd never had to use her skills in battle before, except for Michael, and she hadn't drawn Michael's blood. She wiped her blade on the man's tunic and then her hand. Danellan turned to collect her packages and stopped in dismay.

Six more men crowded into the small

passage. They were big men, armed men, and they blocked her only way out. Danellan swallowed hard. If she screamed, she'd bring Michael, but she'd also bring the soldiers at the inn. Even if the soldiers ignored her, she'd be drawing Michael into a trap.

One of the men reached down and picked up a package of meat from the stores she'd dropped. Her mouth watered as he peeled back the steri-wrap.

Danellan blinked back tears. She and Michael had been without decent meat for more than a day, but she didn't dare balk this whole band. She couldn't win. Danellan raised her chin a notch as he bit into the meat, ignoring the twisting in her gut.

"Good," he commented, handing it off to one of his fellows.

Of course it's good. I bartered well for that meat.

Danellan nodded, giving her grudging consent to their ownership of the stores. If it got her out of the passage, she'd willingly starve a week.

Another of the men advanced on her, and she retreated, putting the dead man between them, then raising her dagger in warning. He scowled at her and knelt to the man she'd killed, examining his wounds. This one frightened her for some reason. If he were alone, Danellan was sure he would still frighten her.

"This is how you fight? Throat to cut sound and cause panic. The hip wound to kill more quickly, before he can hurt you in return."

Danellan met his cold eyes without flinching. "I know other ways. The three silent killers. The six bleeders. The five quick deaths. I wish only to leave here. The man attacked me. Let me leave in peace, and the food and his belongings are yours."

He sighed, pushing his shoulder length hair from his eyes. "Strom was stupid. He was supposed to wait for us. You wouldn't leave without your man. Would you?" He stood slowly, every muscle tense in preparation to fight her.

She backed off another step, searching for a way out of this trap. They set it well. There was nothing but walls three times her height on all sides and six men blocking the exit.

The man loosened the ties on his tunic. "You can scream. In this village, only your man would answer."

Danellan waited for him to draw a blade, but he didn't. That made her distinctly nervous. This man was sure in his training if he felt himself above needing a blade to best her when she was armed. She'd killed his companion. He knew she was trained, but he saw no need to arm himself.

He pounced. Danellan moved quickly. She landed a wound on his ribs, her hand knocked off course by his blow. It was a flesh wound, nothing that would still his fight.

She spun away, and he followed, ducking her blade as it came at him. His hand caught her wrist in a crushing grip that made her eyes water and the air burn in her throat. Danellan threw a series of kicks and punches at him, but he deflected them easily with his free hand. He was well trained, definitely a soldier.

Danellan cried out in frustration as one of the other men immobilized her other arm, stretching her back uncomfortably in the process. The soldier passed the arm he held to a third man, and the two new arrivals pinned her forearms to the wall behind her.

The soldier pried her father's dagger from her aching fingers. She pulled at the hold they had on her, desperate to save the blade. It was all she had left of Cro. Two more men grasped her legs and pushed her back again. He examined the dagger, smiling a feral smile that made her sick to her stomach.

"A general's blade? A commendation from Kol Ri, no less. Are you his daughter or his mistress?"

Danellan raised her head proudly. "He's dead."

The dagger cut into the skin of her throat, releasing a thin trickle of blood. She ground her teeth. She wouldn't lead Michael into this trap. This heathen wanted her to scream, but she was Danellan, daughter of General Cro, granddaughter of General Brai. This son of Len— This vow breaker would have a long way to go if he wanted to break her.

"You care for his blade well." He brought the blade beneath her chin, the point denting the soft flesh behind the bone. "Daughter or mistress?" he demanded.

"Daughter."

He pulled the cap from her head and let her curls fall to her shoulders. His smile widened.

"Danellan, daughter of Cro," he growled. "Your brother is looking for you."

The air went thick and heavy. Her head spun. They'd do their worst. She'd been prepared for that from the night she escaped. But they would also turn her over to Tranol's wrath and Kell Ri's lust. That was too much. She'd rather die.

"You'll have to kill me," Danellan promised.

The soldier raised Cro's dagger and cut the ties at the neck of her tunic one by one, his eyes bright in excitement. "You underestimate me."

"I think you underestimate me."

His fellows laughed heartily at her cheeky reply, and he scowled them down.

He played the blade over her stomach. "Call to your man," he crooned.

Her mouth went dry. Danellan clenched her jaw. They couldn't kill her. If they wanted the money Tranol offered, she would have to arrive alive and without serious injuries.

The blade bit into her ribs lightly, and Danellan closed her eyes against the pain. *No serious injuries, but they can cause me quite a bit of pain.* She pushed that thought away, panting through the burning in her chest.

"Call your man to you," he ordered.

Danellan pulled against the arms holding her ineffectually. She'd never harm Michael while she lived. Tranol sent these beasts for her. They were her difficulty, not his. If it killed her, she'd keep it between herself and Tranol.

The soldier grasped the back of her hair and crushed her mouth beneath his. Danellan bit back the bile rising in her throat. He released her, challenging her with his battle-face.

She stared him down, fighting for an unwavering voice. "You don't intimidate me. You won't be the first man I've known." *Though Fion knows, I've known precious little.* "The worst you can do is kill me."

He laughed. "We both know I can do worse. You will call for him, even if you do it while I breach your body."

The man at her right arm spun away, and Danellan made a grab for her father's dagger. The soldier spun to face something behind him, using the hilt to strike her along the back of her skull as he turned. She slumped against the arms that held her, and her eyes slid closed.

* * * *

Michael bit back a scream of rage as Danellan fell. He stepped over their lookout, the man he'd killed first, silently as the bandit watched his master force that bruising kiss on her lips. The man to her right went next, the only clear shot he had with his dagger. Now the odds were four to one, a much more even match.

The master held back, sending his men out to finish Michael for him. It was an uninspired move. The three men were poorly trained and carrying daggers against his sword. Seeing the blood on Danellan's throat and side, seeing her tunic cut to deep between her breasts set off a bloodlust such as Michael had never felt before.

The three lay dead in as many minutes.

The master smiled. "A trained man. Good. It has been quite a while since I've had a challenge."

Michael nodded, noting the wound Danellan gave him with a rush of pride. "Your underlings certainly couldn't offer much," he noted.

He sighed. "Unfortunately, I would have to agree. But...with them out of the game, the bounty will be mine alone."

Michael felt his stomach rebel. He glanced to Danellan's battered form. *Call your man to you.* They did all this for a bounty? They harmed Danellan to make her call him into a trap, but it wasn't a random robbery.

So, Kell set a price on my head. He looked back to his opponent, his fury rising. "It is a bounty you will never collect," Michael promised.

The bandit came at him, Danellan's blade in his left hand and a battered guard dagger in his right. They were well matched. Michael's extended reach was countered by the bandit's ability to attack from two sides at once. The man was highly trained, making Michael wonder if the battered dagger might be his own.

"Have you had her yet?" the bandit asked abruptly.

Michael startled, his concentration faltering. There was a reason for that question. Did he still think to take Danellan by force after their battle, or was he envisioning some greater prize for delivering a woman carrying his child to his father?

He snapped his blade up to deflect the

bandit's blow. *Maybe either or both, but he is using the threat to put me off my game.*

And it worked. Danellan's blade cut into his forehead, and Michael ground his teeth as blood streamed down his face.

The bandit locked on his eyes. His smile disappeared, and his face drained of color. "Prince Mik," he breathed, as if Michael's identity surprised him.

Michael took advantage of the opening, riding the rush of adrenaline and the battle skills drilled into him from toddlerhood. It wasn't until the bandit lay dead at his feet that Michael thought to wonder at the man's horror.

Had he been ordered to capture Michael unharmed and knew the injury meant his death? Or had he truly not realized who he faced? If that were the case, what bounty could he mean?

He focused his attention on Danellan. Michael cleaned her dagger on the bandit's trousers then his own, sheathing them both. He gathered her into his arms.

She was a fighter. Danellan had stood against seven men, killing one and wounding a highly trained soldier.

But what reason would someone have to place a bounty on Danellan? She was an innocent in many ways. Her father had been respected and trusted. His name was legendary in the guard. Michael had never seen a hint of anything less than pride and honor in the young woman, but she had run from something.

No. The bounty was meant for Michael. He had given his vow to protect her, but Danellan was safer without him if the bounty was high enough to make desperate men resort to these lengths.

Michael took her into the stable and set about healing her wounds. Using the magic sent a thrill through him, but skating his lips over her body, while the skin knit and damage disappeared, was torture on his under-used libido. Michael closed his eyes, pushing back visions of using his mouth in much more sexual ways and concentrating on the positive energies that fed the healing. He banished the thought that sex was a positive energy.

He healed the cut in her side first. It was the deepest and bled the worst. Still, it was minor enough for Michael to knit it to a pale pink discoloration on her ivory skin. He grimaced, wishing he could leave her without a mark, but the healing magic could only do so much. He healed her throat next, the cut and the deep bruising from the nuglin that lay beneath the slain man. He winced in the acknowledgement of what a cut even half a finger width deeper would have done to her. The cut on her neck was shallow enough that it left no mark.

Michael sighed as he started healing the lump on her head. Danellan shifted in his arms, groaning as the damage disappeared beneath the brush of his lips and the magic he sent into her. He closed his eyes, drinking in the musk and Eir tree scent of her hair.

Visions of Danellan asleep next to their fire on a pallet of Eir branches danced in his mind. How many times had he wanted to bury his hands in her lush curls? How many times had he breathed in her scent while Danellan rode with him? Enough to drive Michael near mad with wanting her.

She stiffened in his hands, pushing Michael away and grasping her dagger reflexively. Michael gripped her wrist to stop her from using her weapon blindly. Her eyes snapped open, and she looked at him without immediate comprehension.

Michael caressed her hand. "Shhh. I'm not your enemy," he whispered.

Danellan nodded, and he released her wrist. She sheathed her dagger and pulled at her tunic, running her fingers over the now-healed wound in her ribs. She looked to him in confusion.

He touched her throat. "I healed your wounds," he explained. *It was the least I could do. It was my fault that you were in danger.* Michael couldn't force those words past his lips.

She nodded and lowered her gaze. "It's a rare gift. I'm honored that you'd use it to comfort me."

"Those who have it are bound to serve," he dismissed her praise.

Danellan touched his forehead. "Let me help you."

She pushed up, and he locked on the length of her chest visible through the severed ties. Her breasts were full and capped by deep choc aureole. Her nipples were pebbled in the cold air of the stable. Michael swallowed hard, his hands itching to feel the silin ivory of her body.

Danellan glanced toward her feet and froze, looking to Michael with a rising blush and wild eyes. He snapped his gaze away and snatched up his pack. Michael tossed his spare tunic at her, glancing back as she held it to her chest. He turned away, regretful for his actions.

Michael ran a shaking hand through his hair. "I'm sorry. I'll collect the food while you change and prepare the medical supplies." He started away.

"Thank you, Michael," she called after him.

He nodded, stifling a sigh of relief. They hadn't told her who he really was. That would make leaving her easier.

No. I know it won't be easy, but it will be possible.

CHAPTER NINETEEN

Danellan winced as she cleaned the gash over Michael's eyebrow. Two fingers lower, and he would have lost the eye.

He sat rigid, staring at the wall across from him. Michael didn't acknowledge the pain. He kept it locked inside as he kept everything of importance locked inside. She saw him sometimes, hiding his shaking and his uncertainty behind an unyielding mask. The royal guard hadn't done that to him. It had another source, but she didn't know what it was. Danellan wondered what it would take to make Michael lose his precious control.

"You shouldn't have taken that chance," she whispered, cutting a steri-band to help the wound knit. *It will scar. He might have lost his eye, and it was my fault that he was in danger.*

"You would rather I let them violate you?" he asked in a detached voice.

Danellan darkened. "How should I answer that? Of course, I am grateful that you stopped them."

She was, but he didn't realize the danger. He was a fine protector. Michael had given his word to protect her, and she wasn't sure she could get him to break that vow if she tried. Worse, she wasn't sure she wanted to.

I have no honor. I would let him take that risk and not tell him what I'm asking of him. Danellan tried to find the words to admit her guilt in the

255

matter.

He closed his eyes, as she held the gash together and pasted the band along the ridge.

"Good," he growled, as if the discussion was closed.

"You could have been killed, and that would have been worse," she pointed out testily.

Michael laughed harshly, his eyes opening. "By those— Why would it be worse? You owe me nothing, not even regret if I died."

Danellan shrugged. "Now I do."

He sobered, a wary look shadowing his features. Michael stood and brushed past her, pulling on his coat and cap. "You owe me nothing," he repeated.

"You saved me," she protested.

"I gave my vow to protect you. It was my duty to protect you." His jaw tightened. "And you tended my wound."

"You healed mine."

"One with the power is required to render aid when he can. It is a sacred trust."

"It is not an equitable trade."

Michael didn't look at her as he shouldered his pack. "It is, if I say it is. I hold a kindness shown a stranger in high regard."

"You're not a stranger, Michael. We've traveled together for more than two weeks."

Isn't he? All I know about him is that he fled a high born family and served time in the guard. I don't even know what family claims him. She followed him to the stall, laying a hand on his arm.

His muscles bunched. He pulled away, then

stashed the pack on Frelang and sword under his coat. "I traveled with you, because I had use of a companion. It is too dangerous for you to remain with me now."

Danellan shook her head. She should let him leave. She owed him that much. "You promised," she breathed, stunned that he would abandon his vow so easily. Michael was an honorable man. She'd expected to argue with him to reach this point. On some level, she'd expected to fail to convince him to leave her...even wanted to fail at it.

"I don't want to endanger you any more than I already have." Michael led Frelang toward the stable doors.

She surged after him, confused by his words as much as she was desperate to have his company. The weeks she'd spent alone in the mountain had been torture. "From what I saw today, I'm safer with you than alone."

Michael turned to her, his face all harsh lines and his eyes pure black. Danellan sucked in her breath in surprise. She couldn't tell where his pupils ended and his irises began. It was frightening, on some base level.

He opened his mouth to rebuff her, but his eyes widened at a movement over her shoulder. Before Danellan could turn toward it, she found herself dragged to Michael's chest.

His lips covered hers, possessing her, seeking entry. She refused him, amazed by his sudden reversal. Was he trying to scare her off? If he was, Michael picked the wrong way. Danellan had wondered at the type of lover he'd be for days. She sighed and eased against him.

Michael cupped her buttocks, his fingers tracing the globe of her cheek to the line of her thigh. Danellan shivered as he massaged the line of her hip, opening for him.

His kiss was heated, intense. He swept his tongue into her and pulled her to the hard lines of his body. The ridge of his cock pressed to her stomach. She ran her hands up his chest. He could have whatever he wished of her. Michael could lay claim to her right here in the stable without argument.

His movements became more fevered, as if he heard that thought and intended to make it a reality. Michael groaned into her mouth, his hand pressing in at her lower back and holding her to the ridge that was getting impossibly thicker.

"Move on," a gruff voice ordered.

Danellan stiffened, but Michael held her to him, his hand wrapped around the hilt of her father's dagger beneath her coat. He met her eyes, looking tortured. She suddenly understood. He was using her to hide in plain sight. The ones who pursued him expected Michael to be alone. His hand was on her dagger, not in warning but to use it against these men if he was forced to.

"How long have you known this man?" a second voice asked.

Michael brushed her lips with his. "Please," he whispered. His muscles shook lightly beneath her hand. He was terrified that she would betray him.

"He's my husband," she lied. "We've been

married a full season, in Bure."

"Where are you going?" the first man demanded.

"Lind."

"Move on then."

"Yes, Captain," Michael rasped in a voice she wouldn't recognize as his. He bowed deeply, mounting Frelang and pulling her up ahead of him.

Michael all but buried his face in her shoulder. He laid a series of kisses on her neck that had her shivering in her arousal. Danellan never thought she'd like a man with a beard, but the whiskers marking her flesh sent tongues of flame through her.

The soldiers gave each other knowing looks and moved aside to let them pass.

Danellan closed her eyes and sank into Michael's embrace as he urged Frelang out of town. He didn't relent in his torture of her, until they were far away from civilization. Michael's hands cupped her breasts beneath her coat, strumming his long fingers over her nipples until she arched into his touch and groaned her approval. She gasped, as he rubbed slow circles at the seam in the crotch of her trouskit.

"You are so wet," he growled. "Are you so warm for me?" His mouth returned to her neck, nipping at her. Michael edged the tunic and coat off her shoulder, laying teasing kisses on more of her body.

"Yes." She was. No man had ever affected her this way, made her so desperate to have him. Danellan's body throbbed in need, and Michael's erection pressing against her back wasn't helping matters.

Michael nipped at her earlobe. His breath teased her cheekbone and stirred a tendril of her hair that escaped the cap. "I am in your debt, Danellan. Name your price."

Her body was making urgent demands. She could enjoy his lovemaking. After that, if Michael wished his freedom from his vow, she'd consider the trade an equitable one and let him go his own way. She squirmed against him. "Finish it. Please, Michael."

He groaned, making it sound as if she'd wounded him with her request. "That is the only thing I cannot give you."

"Why?"

"If you conceive—"

"It would be my problem," she insisted. "It's only a one in fifty chance that I would, and—"

Michael cupped her face, turning it toward his and seeking her mouth in a kiss that left her gasping for breath and hoping that it marked his agreement.

He stroked her jaw line with his fingertips. "No. It would be mine, and I would never take that chance with you. Don't tempt me," he pleaded with her.

"Michael," she breathed. Danellan ran her hand between their bodies and cupped his cock, teasing him with her fingers. He had to give in. She wanted Michael to be the first to take her to completion. She wanted to feel his cock locked in her female band.

He urged Frelang onto a wooded trail with a

growl. Far out of view of the main road, he swung Danellan to the dead grass and captured her mouth in a searing kiss. Michael dragged her trouskit down her legs like a man starved for a woman's body.

Danellan bowed up to the stroke of his fingers. "Yes," she cried out. "Now, Michael. Please."

He buried his fingers in her aching core with a groan that announced his need clearly. He twisted his wrist, finding her inner pleasure spot and centering his thrusts over it. Michael pulled the cap from her head and buried his hand in her hair, muting Danellan's cries with hot, drugging kisses as he drove her on.

She pulled at his shoulders, trying to entice Michael into her body. He shifted his weight to trap his cock against her inner thigh. Danellan squirmed against him, feeling him lengthen to her touch.

"Please, Michael." Her body was in a riot. She had to feel his length in her, filling her.

He shook his head. "It is the one thing I cannot give you." His hand stilled within her, his fingers making tiny circles over the pleasure spot while his thumb caressed her hood in time with that movement. Michael covered her mouth to take in her cry. When he pulled back, his eyes were half-lidded and his breathing ragged. "Come for me, Danellan," he growled.

His voice cut through her. Danellan bit her lip as her body soared. She rocked to his hand, forcing him to resume his earlier path past the sensitive spot he wanted to torture. Danellan

261

groaned, digging her nails into the rough weave of his coat.

Michael started to move his hips restlessly, the head of his cock sliding against the soft skin of her thigh through his trousers. "Yes, Danellan. By the goddess, please come for me."

She shattered. Michael didn't mute her cry as she screamed his name. Danellan shuddered as his fingers continued to stroke her, drawing out her pleasure.

"Dear Mag, give me strength," he muttered. Michael pulled his hand away as if she burned him. He tensed, turning to press his erection to her core.

Danellan grasped his hips, pulling him closer and riding the ridge. *Mother Fion, please let him take me. I would give anything in return for that gift.*

Michael managed a strangled cry. He gripped her hips to him, his fingers biting into her skin as a fierce emotion took hold of his features. Danellan gasped as he thickened; the heat and moisture of his seed soaked his trousers, teasing her stomach just above her curls.

Danellan licked her lips, glancing between their bodies. She hadn't realized how thick he would grow at climax, when his body should have been locked inside hers. A fierce hunger assaulted her. She wanted to feel him thicken within her.

Michael looked away in embarrassment, his face dark red. "I'm sorry. I've never done that before."

Danellan chuckled. "Don't be," she assured

him. "I've never met a man with your talent at love play."

His face hardened and Michael pushed away, pulling her trouskit up gently.

"What is it?" she asked.

"I do not hold well with false flattery." He stalked to the stream that lay across the clearing and cleaned her juices from his hand.

Danellan followed him, her fists on her hips. "You think I'd lie about that?" she demanded.

Michael shrugged. "Others have."

She growled in disbelief and turned on her heel, heading for the main road. If that was what he thought of her, she was better off without him. It was several glorious moments before she heard him following her.

"Danellan?" he called uncertainly.

"Go away, Michael."

"I've truly offended you, haven't I?" he asked in surprise. His voice was closer.

Danellan walked faster, crossing her arms over her chest when he sought to take her hand in his.

His voice came from just over her shoulder. "I had no right to compare you to them. I apologize."

"You're right. Now go away."

Michael spun her by the shoulders and scooped her over his shoulder as her balance deserted her. He marched down the slope toward Frelang.

"What are you doing?" she thundered. "Let me down, or I will kick."

He clasped her ankles in silent warning, and

Danellan punched his shoulder, wincing in the pain that started in her fist and raced up her arm to her elbow. *Dear Mag!* There was nothing soft about this man. She struck him again, heedless of the damage she was doing herself in the process.

Michael's voice was tense. "You don't lay your punches correctly," he noted. "You're only hurting yourself."

"You have the brains of kit, the sensitivity of jaglin, and the personality of a male geela," she cursed him, fighting his hold on her ankles.

To her surprise, Michael started laughing. "I do believe you are the first woman who has ever dared insult me to my face." He sighed. "No. But you are the second."

"You must not know many women," she shot back.

Michael set her on the hottel and dragged her face to his for another drugging kiss. His talented fingers played at her aching core. Her nipples tightened into peaks, as his other hand traced her ribs toward them.

Danellan tore her mouth away, cursing her reaction to him. It was so easy to lose herself when he touched her. She was running from men who wanted to own her. Did she want to give any man power over her if she could avoid it? No, but could she avoid it with Michael?

He crowded her, nipping at her jaw line. "I know many women," Michael informed her.

"Stupid women, to put up with you." She bit her lip, reining the urge to encourage what he was doing to her.

"Not stupid. Two-faced. They insult me. They simply do it where they think I cannot hear them." He nuzzled her neck. "Say it again, Danellan. Am I the best you've known?"

"No. Never. The words will never pass my lips again," she vowed.

Michael cupped her breast. "That sounds like a challenge. We have weeks before we reach Caran."

"And if I refuse your company?" she asked, arching her eyebrow in acceptance of his challenge.

He favored her with a look akin to his battle-face. "I can be very persuasive."

* * * *

Michael grinned at the feeling of Danellan pressed to his back. Convincing her that she would accompany him hadn't been difficult. After he put her back on Frelang twice and kissed her, grinding himself against her gathering heat until she all but ripped his tunic from his body, she came.

Then she gave him an embarrassed nod and accompanied him.

This was insanity. Michael knew that, but there was something in Danellan that he couldn't let escape him. Her brutal honesty and spirit drew him, but her sensuality held him fast. The memory of her face as she climaxed to his hand stirred his half-dormant cock.

No woman, not even the few uneducated

schente he'd requested when he wished to experience taking a woman's barrier and training her to his touch, had ever had that look of rapture before. Michael wanted to see that look many more times in the weeks they had together.

He would see it. For all her bravado, Danellan was affected by him. She wanted him. Convincing her to come for him would be the easy part. Michael sobered. The hard part would be convincing his body that she was off limits.

There were too many reasons not to take release in her. Aside from the danger of her being handed over to his father carrying his child, Danellan had no idea what she would be accepting. She would need extensive medical aid to carry his child, Hugam given at the right points in pregnancy and the best doctors. All of that would be provided for her without cost if she carried his child, but Danellan didn't know to ask for it. She thought he was a normal Keen male.

She would know what she faced if he told her who he was. She would know then *what* he was, but it was a risk he couldn't take, not even with Danellan.

CHAPTER TWENTY

Iric 4ᵗʰ, Ri 25-2988

Danellan stilled, the voices from her father's office catching her off-guard. It was the middle of the night. Who would visit at this late hour? Why would they?

"I don't think this will be overly difficult," Tranol commented.

She pressed an eye to the missing slat in the door and took in the scene. Tranol sat at their father's desk. A general she didn't recognize sat across from him. She could see them both clearly in the light from the desk lamp, each of them in profile due to the angle of the interior door. Tranol poured a glass of lizor berry wine for the general and placed it in his outstretched hand.

This wasn't military business. If it were, another captain or a colonel would have come to speak to Tranol. This was a personal visit. Why would a general visit their home? Was this man a friend of her father's? Was there something he wished? Some memento of service they'd shared?

"I don't need to tell you, Captain Tranol, that your father's decision has made him most unpopular with Kell Ri these last five years. His majesty does not like to be denied."

Danellan shook her head. That sounded like a warning. She knew there had been problems, that her father was unpopular with his superiors. This post was beneath him, but Cro had always served with honor. How had he

267

alienated his king? Her father had always been loyal, always followed orders.

Tranol chuckled. "My father used his heart too much."

The general cocked an eyebrow at him and took a sip of the drink in his hand, savoring her father's finest vintage. "And you do not?"

"I have no heart, where Danellan is concerned." His voice went cold.

Not as cold as her heart. Danellan gripped the rough wood of the door, digging her fingertips into it. Tranol had always been indifferent, but Danellan hadn't realized her brother hated her. Still the question remained. What deal was he making that concerned her?

"She is your sister," the general noted, as if he was examining a strange insect.

"No. She is a bastard born of my father's lust and her slut mother."

Danellan felt her fury spike. It was no secret that Cro had been miserable with Tranol's mother. Admittedly, he'd dissolved their contract with penalty, relinquishing Tranol to his mother and a substantial property exchange, to contract with Danellan's mother, but she was hardly a bastard. Danellan hadn't even been conceived until after the contract was sealed.

The general laughed outright. "Then this is a fitting place for her. She will please Kell Ri."

Her blood ran cold. *Please him? How am I supposed to please him?*

Tranol scowled. "I can promise to deliver her. I cannot promise that she will comply."

The general waved his hand in dismissal.

"His Majesty enjoys training the wild ones. Her spirit, more than her beauty, caught his attention." He leaned toward Tranol with a sly smile. "I could not swear that Kell Ri would remember her face. It's not their looks he wants his wild ones for, though Danellan's looks would not turn any sane man aside."

Danellan pressed a hand to her aching stomach as his meaning became clear.

"Well, the king is welcome to her. I have no use for her."

The general passed him a draft. "Your father's benefits." A piece of paper came next. "The writ you will need."

"And when I deliver her for sterilization?"

She bit back a sour wave in her throat. *He can't. A woman cannot be forced to become schente.*

"As agreed. Four times that much upon delivery. Do not fail, Tranol. His Majesty will have her in his bed. You can benefit from this or be as unpopular as your father."

"My father was a fool."

Danellan fisted her hand. Her brother was traitor to her and to their father.

Tranol smiled a cold, calculating smile. "And when Kell is done with her?" he asked.

"Second thoughts?"

"Not at all. I was just considering—"

"Yes?"

"When Kell Ri tires of her, perhaps the young prince might like a new face."

The general laughed heartily. "When she is trained, she will still have her beauty," he agreed.

"I imagine Prince Mik would prefer a gentle, pliant lady after his experience with Princess Susan."

"Is it true that he still bears a scar?"

Danellan didn't wait for his answer. She made it to her rooms on quaking legs. Her father had suffered Kell Ri's displeasure to keep her from becoming schente? Tranol was charged with forcing her into service?

She shuddered. The king took his pleasure in breaking a woman's spirit? Was that why he sought to force women in? Willing schente were too tame and compliant for his tastes?

"No," she breathed. Stril would take her in and give her a position. Danellan wasn't above work as a cook or nurse. Considering the alternative, mucking stalls and scrubbing floors would be an improvement.

Danellan snatched up a pack and started throwing in woven travel gowns and necessities. She added a bag of coin she'd earned teaching music to the little ones on the base. It wasn't much, but it was enough to buy passage on a public transport to Caran. If she took a bit of dried meat and fruit from the kitchen and slept on the transport, it would be enough to see her to Stril. She startled as the door to her room opened and Tranol stepped in.

He lounged against her cabinet, looking disgustingly smug. "I thought I heard you. Good. Then I need not explain this to you."

Danellan raised her chin in challenge. "My share of the benefits," she demanded.

His smile disappeared. "You have no share,"

he informed her.

"Of course I do. A quarter is my share by law."

"Not if Father's second contract was deemed made under duress."

"What duress?"

"A bastard child threatening his career."

"I was not conceived—" she stormed.

"You were born eight months after contract."

"And five weeks premature."

"Can you prove that? Your early medical records are sadly—misplaced."

"Keep it. I will survive without the benefits." She hadn't planned to wait for the benefits. It was no loss to her. Danellan headed for the door, heedless of her silin robe. She'd change in the stable to the riding outfit she kept there. That was suitable for travel.

Tranol swept her up and threw her to the bed. Her pack was ripped from her hand.

She tried to snatch it back. "Those things are mine," she shouted. "You have no right to my personal earnings."

"You owe me for your keeping this past month. I owed you nothing, but I didn't toss you to the winds of chance. You are in my debt. You own nothing. It is all mine in payment for your keep. Everything." His smile spread. "Even the clothes on your back."

Danellan launched away from him with a cry of fear. Her pack hit the floor a heartbeat before his hands were on her. The sound of silin ripping drowned out her choked scream, the only silin she owned.

* * * *

Michael startled awake, drawing his dagger blindly and throwing himself toward Danellan's screams. He could see her thrashing, but there wasn't another person in their camp. Was an animal troubling her? He hesitated for a moment, kneeling over her, at a loss for an explanation. There was no enemy he could see. What threatened her?

He sheathed his blade and grasped her arms. Danellan let out a piercing scream and beat at him. He blocked her legs as she kicked, her eyes squeezed shut.

"A dream," he whispered. "Mother Fion! What haunts her?"

"Don't do this," she pleaded through her tears. "Don't let him take me."

Was it the band of men they killed? But, Danellan was calm with them.

Perhaps she was too calm. Should a woman be so calm in the face of what they threatened? A chill ran down his spine. If she ran from that, the man would know no mercy.

Michael pulled her to his chest, wincing as she screamed in terror.

"Danellan. It's Michael. You're safe," he soothed her.

"Don't do—" She broke off on a wail.

He rocked Danellan, crooning to her over and over that she was safe with Michael, until she was crying silent tears in his arms. Her

272

hands were fisted in his tunic, and she shook uncontrollably.

"Danellan? What is it?" he whispered.

"Don't let him take me," she managed in a thick voice.

"Who? Who hunts you?"

Whatever answer she made was lost in a yawn.

Michael kissed her forehead and cushioned her to the ground in his arms, pulling first her blanket and then his over them to conserve heat. The weather was getting harsher. He prayed that they would find a wooded place to make camp the next night. It would be too cold to sleep without a mat of branches soon.

He ran a hand through her hair, as much to comfort himself as Danellan. That was no simple dream. It was terror at its most basic. Someone hunted Danellan in life and through her dreams. When Michael learned who that someone was, he would pay dearly.

* * * *

Danellan pressed her cheek to the hard wall of muscle. She smiled. Somehow, she'd ended up back in Michael's arms. She hadn't slept this soundly since she was a child cradled in her father's arms. She was warm, though the sun was barely over the furthest peaks. She hadn't woken warm in over a month. Better, she was safe. Danellan didn't know how she knew she was safe, but she was certain that she was.

Fingers caressed her back. Danellan moved, pressing her body to Michael in invitation. His cock pressed into her stomach, making her body warm even more for him.

"Michael." She lifted her face, seeking his lips with her own.

He obliged her. His mouth covered hers, and his cock lengthened. Danellan pulled at the clasp on his trousers and wrapped a hand around him. His weight felt soothing in her palm.

Michael groaned. "I can't," he rasped.

Danellan brushed his hand away, as he reached for her. "Come for me," she invited, mirroring his words of the afternoon before. She moved her hand, massaging him, exploring him.

He rolled to his back, giving her free rein over his pleasure. Danellan watched in amazement as his breathing quickened. Michael watched her movements avidly, fisting his hands and grinding his teeth, his expression fierce.

Droplets of his readiness pooled on the head of his cock, and Danellan licked through the cleft to collect them onto her tongue. He cried out softly, sweat breaking out on his upper lip as she savored the flavor. He was salty and wild like fresh game, and she wanted more.

Michael rocked his hips, teaching her how to please him. "Danellan." Her name was like a prayer on his lips. His muscles clenched, and he started to tremble. "So close. Please don't stop."

The first surge of his semen came faster than Danellan anticipated. She clasped the head in her mouth. Michael's body spasmed, and his eyes widened. He cried out harshly, and his body bowed up, driving him nearly full in.

His hand fisted in her hair, and his seed poured from him. Michael thickened with a strangled moan. Danellan swallowed slowly, and his hand tightened in her hair reflexively.

"Mother Fion," he gasped. "What are you doing to me?"

Encouraged, Danellan moved his length in and out, pressing her tongue to the thick veins as she had when she'd swallowed his essence. Michael's breathing became more ragged. He shook, tipping his hips in jerky counterpoint to her movements. She pushed her head down, feeling the crown tickle at the back of her throat.

"Danellan," he growled. "Stop now."

She released him slowly and smiled as he pulled her up and clasped her to his chest. "Well, I know how to get even with you for your torture," she teased.

"When I recover, I will kill the man who taught you that."

"I don't suggest it."

"Why not?"

Danellan ran a fingertip up his length, smiling at his groan. "I've never tasted a man before, and Fion didn't create a specimen like you to be wasted in suicide."

* * * *

It was a quarter of an hour before Michael recovered from Danellan's love play. He watched her moving around their camp, his cock

275

demanding to taste other depths. He couldn't leave her, but being near her was likely to drive him to madness again.

She plopped down beside him, blushing as she handed him cracker tack and dried meat. It was meager fare, not a quarter of his usual meal size. Michael sobered that he could find it as sweet as a banquet.

Danellan scanned her eyes over their surroundings. "Do you think we came far enough yesterday? Will anyone track us?" she asked.

Michael sighed. "I think we're safe, but I understand that you don't."

She shot him a look of confusion. "What do you mean?"

"Do you remember last night? Do you remember how you found your way to my arms?" he questioned.

Danellan dropped her gaze. "No. I don't, but I did feel safe there."

"You had a nightmare. A very vivid and terrifying nightmare."

She stared at the food in her hand, shaking her head. "I'm sorry I disturbed you, Michael."

"Do you remember it?"

Danellan set her food on the rocks at the edge of the fire ring. She gazed into the flames, her eyes sad. "No."

Michael startled. It was a lie. She knew very well what she'd dreamed. "Who hunts you, Danellan? Who do you fear? Who do you plead with in your dreams?"

"It was only a dream," she insisted.

"I don't believe that."

She didn't answer his accusation.

"Whoever it is, I promise I can protect you." It wasn't a lie. There was no one Michael couldn't protect her from. He wouldn't even have to give himself up to do it. If he delivered her to Jole with a letter written in his hand, his brother would put the power of the royal seal behind her.

Danellan shot him a look that was equal measures stunned disbelief and terror. "There is no one for you to defend against," she whispered.

"Then why do you take forest trails that have seen nothing but jaglin in years?"

"Bandits," she dismissed his query.

"And shade your face when you near soldiers?"

"Why do *you* fear soldiers?" she demanded. "I've seen it in your eyes."

Michael sighed. "I didn't have permission to leave. They'll take me back."

"You deserted your post?" she asked in undisguised horror.

"No. The guard has no hold on me. I left my duties behind."

"Why? My father was dead. Why would you leave your family?"

He shrugged. "I was the second son. There was nothing for me but grasping noblewomen hoping for an advantageous contract and dissolution. So, I left."

Danellan nodded.

"My family— I won't lie to you. My family is important. I can shield you from any enemy."

Hope burned in her eyes. It disappeared like ash in a cold rain. She looked into the flames.

Michael moved to her side and took her hand. "Why does he hunt you? I know you're not a criminal."

Danellan shook her head. "I just need to reach a job, Michael." Her eyes were over bright with tears. "If you wish to leave before they come to stop me again, I will understand. I have no wish to get you injured."

"I don't understand." He didn't. Who would stop her? Why?

"The men yesterday were charged with returning me." She smiled weakly. "I didn't have permission to leave, either."

He shook his head slowly. "They wanted me."

Her jaw tightened. "Only to keep you from interfering in their business. They were clear enough."

Michael clenched his jaw. The bounty was on Danellan? She took the brunt of their fury to keep him out of her problems, when he had already sworn a vow to protect her.

"Once I am established in Caran, there is nothing they can do. I will be safe."

"From who?" he pleaded.

Danellan didn't answer.

Michael sighed. "One day you will trust me. I ache for that day." He ached to end the man who dared put a bounty on Danellan.

CHAPTER TWENTY-⊕NE

Iric 19th, Ri 25-2988

Danellan pulled Michael closer to her, groaning as his mouth closed on her nipple. He drew at her like a man who hadn't experienced lovemaking in months or years. He hadn't been inside a woman in the four weeks they'd traveled together. She knew that much.

She shifted beneath him restlessly, the rock floor of the cave an unwelcome change from the Eir branches they'd used for the last few days. Still, they had shelter, and the heat from their fire warmed the air in the cave a hundredfold more than it had the open air when they slept around it outside. She almost wished they had a cave every night.

Michael's erect cock pressed to her leg as he suckled at her, and she bit back a cry of pleasure. Danellan wanted Michael inside her. Some days, she felt she'd go mad if he refused her again. This was one of those days.

Danellan unclasped his trousers and took his length in her hand, smiling as he shuddered. She guided him to her core. Michael pulled his head up, releasing her nipple and looking between their bodies in stunned silence.

She played the head in the honey coating her core and creating a slick down her thighs to the blanket beneath them. Danellan shifted and captured him inside her nether lips.

Michael sucked in his breath, closing his

eyes in intense pleasure. Then he pushed away with a grumbled curse. "No. I— Please don't tempt me. I want it too badly."

She choked back a sob. "Please, Michael. I have to feel you."

"I can't take that chance. I won't leave you with my child."

Tears stung her eyes. "There has to be a way."

"How?" he growled. "We can't afford Walla tea, and we can't risk walking into a clinic to get it, even if we could."

"What if—" She bit her lip. It was a risk.

He met her eyes, something dangerous and hopeful warring in him. "What? If you know a way to end this madness, tell me. I won't survive much more."

"If I don't release an egg, there can be no child," she reasoned carefully.

"We can't afford—"

"If I'm not stimulated," she spoke over him.

Michael's eyes widened. "If I'm not seated fully, I could cause you damage."

She nodded. "If you pulled out while you spilled—"

"Every instinct tells a man to push deep," he interrupted her.

Danellan sighed. "I'm sorry. I ask too much. Forget I—"

His mouth closed on hers, demanding her participation, heating her blood again. "You want this?" he panted, pressing his forehead to hers. "You'd trust me enough to take this risk?"

"I trust you, Michael. Please let me feel you."

She trusted him not to hurt her.

Theoretically, this was foolproof. He would do one of two things. Either he'd pull out to keep from hurting her, and there would be no risk of a child; or he would push deep and give her what she craved most, the bliss of stimulating her egg despite the risk of pregnancy.

He nodded, pressing the head back to her. Michael hissed out his breath as he slid in, finger width by delicious finger width. "So tight," he gasped. "Please tell me you've known a man before."

She managed a shaky nod, crying out at the sensation of his length sliding home. Danellan had known a man, one man and one time. She desperately wanted to know Michael. She wanted him to be the first to give her the bliss at true completion.

"It's been a long time for you?" His fingers caressed her cheek as he stilled, allowing her body to adjust to his size.

"Almost a year," she admitted.

His eyes narrowed. "Why?"

"The men feared my father." After that first one, none of them dared touch her. They didn't dare look at her.....as if she was a noble daughter and not the daughter of an unpopular general.

Michael slid back then in again. He took her slowly. "Calm," he soothed her. "I won't hurt you."

Danellan threw her head back as Michael moved faster and touched deeper. She moaned and ran her hands to cup his buttocks, urging him deeper. He wasn't brushing the ring at her apex yet. He wasn't fully seated. "Oh, Michael."

He slid deeper, and her eyes opened in surprise. Michael flashed her Len's own grin as he brushed at the gates of her womb, again and again. She dug her nails into him reflexively, the pleasure almost more than she could bear.

Michael moaned. "Yes, Danellan. Pull me in. Tell me how much you want."

"More. All of you, Michael. Let me feel all of you," she pleaded.

"All of me?"

"All of you. Please." She screamed in pleasure as he lodged hard against her gates and held his position.

"Come for me, Danellan."

She did. Her body pulsed around his length, and she cried out his name wildly. The sound echoed off the rock, filling the space with the music of her climax.

Michael trembled. His cock erupted, sending a wave of his heat inside her.

She tightened in preparation for the stimulus. *Yes, Michael. Please press deep.*

He pulled back with a vicious curse, pumping two more times before he left her. Michael cried out as if he was in bitter pain, sending round after round of heat against her outer lips. He pressed his hips hard against hers as he thickened, sating his body's command to drive into her the only way he could. Danellan grasped the still-pulsing head, applying pressure to simulate the grip of her band.

Michael roared, sweat breaking out on his

forehead. Danellan started to loosen her fist, sure that she'd hurt him; but he wrapped his hand around hers and forced her to tighten her grip again. He shivered, then captured her mouth in a searing kiss.

She released him as he lessened, and Michael gentled his kiss, cradling her to him. When he pulled back, he met her gaze.

"Do you trust me?" he whispered.

"With my life."

"And your body?"

"Completely," she assured him.

Michael kissed her, slow and sweet.

* * * *

Iric 23rd, Ri 25-2988

Michael sifted through the coins left in his pocket in mounting dismay. When he'd started this journey, he hadn't counted on supporting two people on what he had. He had planned carefully for the amount of money he would have to sneak away over the months to support himself until spring.

Danellan had to flee her home with nothing but the clothing on her back, a blanket, a few pocketfuls of food, and prayers that Fion would be merciful and see her through until she reached Caran.

Neither situation helped when Fion was not merciful and there were two of them to feed.

If it were any other season, they could

survive. There would be roots and fruit, plentiful game meat, and grain. They were trapped in a frozen wasteland. The animals were burrowed or hibernating. The plants were dead.

Worse, the weather was changing. They had lost two days of travel time, hiding from freezing rains in caves. Tonight they were outside with no caves within a day's ride. He prayed to each of the gods to grant them a clear night. They could survive the freezing wind with body heat, Eir branches and both blankets. They wouldn't survive if they were drenched to the bone.

He poked at the stew of redgrass roots and the last of their meat that Danellan had prepared. She had been overjoyed when she discovered the redgrass. Michael had almost cried that she could find glee in anything with their prospects as dim as they were.

She came to the fire and offered him a genuine smile. Michael stayed her hand as Danellan tried to spoon some of the stew up for him. There was enough for one.

Her smile dimmed. "You have to eat, Michael. You've barely touched food in three days."

"I had some cracker tack a little while ago," he lied.

She nodded with a strained smile and ate a mouthful of the stew. It probably tasted like paste, unspiced and thick, but Danellan didn't complain. She managed a few bites, then looked at him miserably.

"Eat, Danellan." She had to eat. She was too thin for his comfort.

"Please eat with me," she whispered.

Michael moved closer to her and took the spoon. He ladled up some of the stew and brought it to her mouth. "I ate," he assured her.

"Not meat," she protested.

He fed her the spoonful of stew, ignoring the growling in his stomach. "You need it more."

Tears filled her eyes, but she swallowed.

Michael wiped away the first track as it wound down her face. "For me," he pleaded.

"I'd be dead if it weren't for you." Her voice cracked.

"I'd be mad if it weren't for you," he countered, raising another spoonful to her mouth. "It's a fair exchange."

She ate it without comment. Michael scanned his eyes over her, wishing he could do better by her. Danellan's hands were blackened from digging roots, and her thumb wore a new scar from a thorn she'd caught while pulling up the stubborn stalks. There was dirt ground under her fingernails. Her hair was tangled, and her face was thin and pale.

The stew was nearly gone before Danellan refused more. She wasn't nearly full, though she swore she was. Michael obliged her whim, eating the last two spoonfuls of the stew without letting his disgust show. He would never let her think he didn't truly appreciate her gift. Danellan had provided better for them than he had that day, and he told her so several times. If redgrass roots stood between the two of them and starvation, he would eat it for weeks without complaint.

Danellan curled to his chest, sharing what little heat they each had to offer. Michael soothed her, rocking her as he would a child, as he would his niece and nephew...if he were allowed to hold them.

"We reach Bure tomorrow. It will be better then," he promised. Yes, it would be better. They would have food—for a day or two. The coin he had left wouldn't buy more than that.

That much would see them to Lind. He shivered. Trapped in Lind with no way out but contacting Jole or resorting to stealing. Could life be worse than that?

Michael kissed Danellan's hair, blinking back tears. Life could be worse. If he lost Danellan, his life was meaningless. If it came down to that choice, he would do whatever he had to do to protect Danellan.

* * * *

Iric 26th, Ri 25-2988

Michael held back, concentrating on the intense pleasure on Danellan's face. He had to hold back until her pleasure was complete. If she didn't climax before him, it would mean a long, agonizing wait for her until he was recovered and finished her another way. So far, he had only made her suffer that once. He had no intention of doing it again.

He could push her over easily if he pushed deep at his climax and let his cock taste her waiting band. Michael closed his eyes and imagined that joy. He wanted it with every cell in his body.

Michael pulled himself back to reality. He couldn't risk that. This wasn't a child that could be hidden away and delivered by a village woman healer. Any child he fathered would require doctors and Hugam. There would be no way to continue hiding.

Worse, they were each hunted. The time they did run would be full of danger. The cold and hunger they suffered alone would make her pregnancy unbearable, even with his healing magic.

He couldn't take that chance without a concrete plan to keep her safe. If Danellan agreed to a contract— Michael grimaced. She'd never contract with him. No sane woman would, but her animosity and fear of Kell Ri would guarantee it.

She wouldn't have to know until the contract was sealed.

No. That was a truly dishonorable thought. He'd have to tell her who he was.

Would I?

Yes. That much was a given, but when would he have to tell her?

Michael gazed at Danellan in longing. Would she contract with him? He would have to try. He opened his mouth to talk to her, to tell her who he was and ask her to trust him with her tale so he knew what enemy he had to protect her from. Michael ground his teeth. He couldn't do it.

Danellan bowed up beneath him, screaming for him as she gripped his length. Michael felt the first spasm grip him. It would be so easy to

287

push in, so glorious to take what he craved. Danellan grasped his hips, holding him, pulling him deeper. Her eyes were glazed in pleasure.

He came to his senses and pulled out, gritting back a string of curses as his body rebelled at the loss of his full completion. He couldn't do this.

She wants it. I want it.

Not without a contract.

She sobbed at the loss of him, and Michael cradled her to his body. He shook. Part of him, some animal inside wanted to punch something. *Fion! You torture me. We both want this.* Michael brushed Danellan's hair from her face, crooning to her.

Danellan nestled her cheek to his chest. "I'm sorry, Michael. I just need—"

He nodded. "I need it, too. If there was a way, would you do it?"

"Yes. You know I would. Any risk you ask."

"It is not a small thing I'll be asking," he warned her.

"Nothing worthwhile ever is."

Michael smiled. Danellan was wise beyond her years. He had a plan, but he didn't yet have the means to make it happen. For that, he needed more time, and their food wouldn't last more than another day.

CHAPTER TWENTY-TWO

Iric 27th, Ri 25-2988

"Len's Underworld," Michael cursed. His breath curled before him then disappeared, washed away in the mixed snow and rain.

Danellan pressed her face into his shoulder, shivering as the wind cut through her drenched clothing. "We need shelter."

He sighed. "I know." But there were no mountains, no caves in this area. It was too wet to make a fire without chemicals or petrols that he didn't have. They were too far from Bure, a full two days or more in this weather.

"Is there a town near here?" Her teeth were chattering.

"Yes, but it is a garrison town," he explained. Lind was the last place Michael wanted to show his face in this condition.

Danellan shivered again. Michael hoped it was in fear rather than the cold, but that was hoping for a lot.

"We may have to risk it," she decided weakly.

"No. Not that." *Anything but that.*

"We'll die of exposure."

"No. I know a place." His stomach clenched.

Mother Fion and Father Mag! Is this my punishment? You strand me where I must face my past to secure a future for myself and Danellan? It will be Len's Dungeon's on Kegin.

* * * *

289

Michael shuddered as he crossed the entry hall to the ruins. He wiped a layer of dust from the ancient control board on the far wall and fired up the electricity. Lights blazed around them. He checked the other controls. Comfort controls and water purification systems showed no warning lights.

He sighed in relief. "We have heat, light, and heated water."

Danellan nodded, beyond shivering. She was weaving on her feet in her sopping clothing. "How did you know about this place?"

"I've used it before, from time to time." *But I won't think about that. That time doesn't exist anymore.* He wrapped an arm around her and led her up the stone staircase, scanning his eyes down the row of rooms on the second floor.

Not the room I shared with Gilan. The memories of taking out his frustrations in sex with the servant were bitter enough. Danellan wouldn't sleep there.

Not the room where I kept Susan prisoner. Michael couldn't bear to look at it again. He pushed away the memories that came unbidden of the things that went on in that room. He had been mad, and the room would drive him to madness, if he laid eyes on it again.

Maybe when they left, he'd burn this ruin to ashes. It would be a kindness. Too many horrible memories lived in these walls.

Michael led her to the room Rill, his chief of security, had used. It was the most spacious room beside the one Mik had chosen for himself.

It was the most comfortable beside Susan's and his own.

He dragged the sheets and quilts off the bed and settled Danellan on the bare mattress. Michael dragged the top quilt from the stack in the cabinet and threw it at the pile of dusty linens. He returned to the bed with two more and started undressing Danellan.

He wrapped her in the quilts and settled her on the thick pillows. "Stay here. I'll see if I can find food."

Danellan nodded weakly and closed her eyes. Michael sighed. There was little chance of finding food here. If he didn't, he would have to chance a trip to Lind and exercise one of his options.

Michael didn't like the idea of visiting a town so close to Jole, but he couldn't let Danellan go another night without decent food. It had been two days since she'd eaten a filling meal. He clenched his teeth against the gnawing in his stomach. It had been longer for himself.

The kitchen opened before him. Michael sighed and pulled open the deep pantry, prepared for the worst. He dropped to his knees with a cry of thanks. Box upon box of food and other supplies filled the room, enough for ten days—or more, if they rationed. He would start rationing himself tomorrow, but Danellan would have her fill at every meal, and they would feast tonight.

Michael emptied a box of bottled goods onto a shelf and started choosing their fare for the evening. A kit and vegetable stew, dried bread, a jar of implin fruit slices in sucre syrup, and a bottle of lizor berry wine. If there were cheese and milk, he would have everything he needed to support Danellan through a pregnancy in the pantry.

He stilled with his hand on the bottle of wine, plucking the missive from between the bottles. It was in Jole's hand. Michael read it, swallowing a lump borne of gratitude.

Mik,

Susan explained your motives. Home is waiting when you are ready to find it. Until then, if your lot sinks low enough that you seek shelter in this dungeon, may Fion grant you comfort.

I checked the systems myself. The chimneys are not worthy of a fire; but this close to Lind, it would not be prudent, in any case. The comfort systems should keep you well enough.

I am waiting for your call. When you are ready, I will smooth your way however I can.

Your brother,
Jole

Michael finished loading food and utensils into the box. He snatched the field stove Jole left for him. It would truly be a feast.

* * * *

Danellan shifted, thankful for the warmth, drinking in a myriad of scents. Was that food? Surely, this old ruin wasn't stocked. Warm metal teased her cracked lips.

"Danellan," Michael crooned to her. "It's time to eat."

She opened her eyes, taking the spoon into her mouth. "Stew," she whispered in surprise. "Where— How did you do this?"

He raised the spoon, full again, to her lips. "My stores were undisturbed. No one comes here."

Danellan ate slowly, savoring the finest meal she'd had in almost eight weeks. After the stew and bread, there was implin in sweet sap and wine.

Michael kissed her forehead and left her with yet another glass of the wine in her hand while he ate the remainder of their food, savoring each bite. When he finished, he filled a tankard with wine for himself.

"Ready for a bath?" he asked her.

Danellan chuckled and eyed the muscles straining against his tunic appreciatively. "And will I end up naked in your bed, Michael?"

He sobered and took several deep swallows of the wine. "Do you wish to?" he asked in a husky voice.

"In bed, yes."

"And when we're not in bed?"

She smiled. "Silin and lace."

He furrowed his brow. "Really? That is your wish?"

"A dream," she assured him. "I wasn't meant for silin. I know that."

His eyes darkened, and he brushed the hair from her neck. "What makes you think that?"

Danellan blushed. "My father was not a favorite of the king, and now I am without position," she reasoned.

Michael laid a teasing kiss on her throat. "I would dress you in silin." He parted her lips and kissed her slowly, thoroughly.

Danellan sighed and ran a fingertip down his chest. "You are in hiding," she reminded him.

He peeled the quilts off of her and panned his eyes over her body. "So are you, but we don't need to be. I could take my place with my family—with you."

Michael suckled on her nipples, savoring them as he had the meal, as if he was starved for her body, though he'd had her only the night before. Danellan clenched her hands in his hair, pulling his mouth tight over her breast.

He traveled down her body, the heat of his mouth making her nerves buzz and her core slick for him. Danellan closed her eyes, dizzy in a combination of her warmth and arousal, the food and wine. She groaned as he parted her thighs and buried his tongue in her. His soft beard tickled her thighs.

"Michael," she whispered. "Come inside. Please, come inside."

Danellan sighed as he guided her hands to her thighs. She shivered in anticipation at the sounds of clothing and boots hitting the floor. Michael's mouth left her, and the rasp of his tunic over his shoulders announced his readiness. She opened her eyes, drinking in the sight of him, fully naked and aroused, for the first time.

She licked her lips, and his eyes darkened. She was right all those weeks before. There was nothing soft about his body. His muscles were chiseled into broad shoulders and a warrior's torso and arms. Michael's legs were molded by years of riding hottel—more probably war-buck. His cock was tall and broad, reminiscent of the rest of him.

Michael didn't move toward her. He stood motionless, until she finished her perusal and met his gaze. "Tell me," he growled, tense as a jaglin ready to pounce.

Danellan reached her hands out to him. "I've never known love like yours, Michael."

"Tell me what you wish," he stated the ritual words.

"Make love to me, Michael. Please, make love to me."

He nodded, crawling between her spread thighs like the jaglin she'd compared him to moments earlier. Michael looked between their bodies, seating the head of his cock inside her. He grasped her hips and met her eyes then filled her in a single thrust. Danellan's cry merged with his. Michael moved slowly, withdrawing and filling her, again and again.

Danellan wrapped her legs around him, urging Michael closer as her climax neared.

"Michael," she begged. "Please don't leave me this time." She'd give anything to feel him stimulate her, to feel the hot wash of all of his seed inside her.

He captured her mouth, his kiss urgent. Michael brushed his beard over the sensitive skin under her jaw, enticing her to give him more of her throat.

"Contract with me," Michael whispered against her body. "Be my bride."

Her eyes flew open. "What?"

His body didn't stop or even falter in his tireless pistoning of hers. Her surprise laid her further open to the sensations washing over her. She bowed up to his thrusts.

"Become my bride. Be my full mate," he repeated. "Say yes, and I will finish inside you." He nipped at her chin. "Will you scream for me, Danellan? When you release an egg for me, will you scream?"

The throbbing in her womb intensified. Her legs tightened, and the play of his muscles radiated through her thighs and calves, stealing her ability to reason why she wouldn't want exactly what he was offering.

She gripped his arms, feeling the interplay of muscles beneath her palms. He was making love to her with his entire body.

"Yes, Michael," she cried out. "Please, yes."

He captured her head between his hands, meeting her eyes. "Be my bride. Tell me, Danellan. Do you want to be my bride?"

"Yes. I'll be your bride."

Michael captured her mouth, his hands

sliding down her body and pulling her core deep around him. He was buried to his hilt, the soft fur of his sac teasing the bottom curve of her buttocks and the head lodging at the gates to her womb with every thrust.

He released her mouth as Danellan screamed his name, a sexy smile curving his lips. Michael drove into her, his length pulsing as she gripped him.

"Now, Danellan." His voice was rough. Michael's eyes closed, and his fingers bit into the swell of her buttocks. His cry of release was ragged, tortured. His climax went on and on, wave after wave of heat massaging the gates of her womb.

He thickened, and his cock bit into the natural notch her body afforded him then thickened further until he stretched her tight. A flood of his come seemed to radiate through her womb as he breached the gates.

Her breathing hitched as the answering shocks from her body warred with the heat of his seed. Danellan pressed up, a scream of ecstasy ripped from her throat as her egg sought a mate.

Michael cried out and forced still more of his heat into her. His mouth was on hers, leaving to make torturous trails over her cheeks, ears, throat, and shoulders, returning to capture her, again and again. His voice sent sweet tendrils of hazy pleasure through her, while he continued his exploration.

"I've wanted you so long, Danellan. You're mine now. Never leave me."

There was a desperation in his plea that

made her ache. Danellan pulled his head to her, her tongue tangling with his.

Michael lessened in her. He met her gaze uncertainly, probably embarrassed at his moment of vulnerability.

Danellan stroked a finger along his lower lip. "I will never leave you," she assured him.

The sexy smile returned to his lips. "Am I still the best you've known?" he teased.

She blushed and dropped her gaze.

"Danellan?"

She met his eyes and smiled weakly. "I've never—" Her blush deepened.

Michael's smile returned. "You've never dropped an egg?"

Danellan shook her head.

"Walla tea? Or did they withdraw as I have?"

"There was only one who got so far," she admitted.

"And?" he prodded. "I cannot believe a man's prowess would fail with you."

"My father dragged the soldier off of me and threatened to make him schaen without the typical surgery. After that, no man dared touch me."

"How old were you?" he asked in confusion.

"Twenty." She sighed. "I thought— I was legally an adult."

"Your father was a good man. He meant well, and I like that I was your first."

Danellan managed a strained smile and a nod. Her father was trying to protect her, but not from that soldier or from the chance of an unplanned child. She knew that when she heard

Tranol's plan for her. Cro feared his failure. He knew she'd mourn the loss of what Kell would steal from her if she'd had the experience. She sobered. He was right. She would miss it.

CHAPTER TWENTY-THREE

Iric 30th, Ri 25-2988

Michael opened his eyes a slit, then gasped in surprise. Danellan stood in the doorway, dressed in one of the silin day gowns he had for Susan. The dress was deep purple and reached only a hand width down her thigh on the taller woman. His cock hardened, and she blushed in response. Danellan was born for silin and lace, but that dress—

"What are you doing?" he growled. He couldn't seem to banish the gravel from his voice despite his best effort.

Danellan brushed her hand down the skirt, smoothing it over her thighs. "Our clothes are washing. I found these. Is there something wrong?"

Something wrong? With that dress, everything is wrong. He pasted on a smile. "I'd rather have you naked in my bed." *As if that statement hadn't nearly stolen my sanity when she said it the first time. Still, Danellan wasn't Susan. Susan never wanted to be naked in my bed.*

She inched the skirt up, revealing her ivory thighs to him. "You don't like silin?" Her voice was low and inviting.

Oh Fion, how I want to feel her nipples harden through the silin. "I like silin. I'd like to remove it."

Danellan sauntered to him, her hips swinging in silent invitation. She stopped at the foot of the bed. Michael took a deep breath, feasting on the knowledge that her nipples were hard beneath the thin material.

She hooked the hem with her fingers and eased the skirt up her thighs. Michael fisted his hands, resisting the urge to pull her over him. The dark curls that covered her mound appeared, and he bit back a groan.

Susan never wore the gowns. They aren't Susan's gowns. Danellan can wear the gowns whenever she wishes.

"Touch yourself, Danellan."

She hesitated, meeting his eyes uncertainly.

"Come to me and show me how you bring yourself to climax," he instructed her.

Danellan circled the bed until she stood beside his chest. Michael reached out and spread her thighs so that he was looking up at her glistening sex.

Her hand dropped down. She picked up her juices, leaving her slit and stroking her clit. She hissed out her breath slowly, her fingers coating the small nub with every caress.

"That's right," he crooned. "Show me how to touch you." Michael reached up and circled her distended nipples, smiling as she bit her lip.

She met his eyes, hers half closed in pleasure. "How do you pleasure yourself, Michael?"

His cock surged as what she suggested became clear to him. "Would you like to watch?"

"Yes."

Danellan licked her lips as he fingered his girth, wrapping his hand at the base and squeezing. He worked his way up his length slowly. Michael repeated the motion, growing rougher and faster with each repetition but resisting the urge to drive himself over.

She watched him breathlessly. Michael moved his attention from her rapt expression to her self-pleasure, over and over. What would she do if he came for her? Would she follow him over in empathetic reaction? Someday, he would find out, but he had no intentions of finishing anywhere but in her depths today.

"I've heard you do this," she whispered. "In your blanket in the dead of night."

"Always dreaming of sliding into your willing body," he assured her.

Danellan let out a low cry of longing as a trail of his precome slid down the head. Michael scooped it off on the thumb of his free hand and raised it to her mouth. She took it into her mouth and skated her tongue over him, drinking in every drop. Her moan of pleasure vibrated through his body. Her fingers moved faster, coating her hood with more of her honey.

Michael lowered his hand, dipping his fingers in her. Danellan looked at his hand, her color high. He worked his fingers in and out slowly, his body aching for more. Her eyes followed the route his fingers took from her core to his mouth. Her body trembled as he sampled her honey.

Michael wrapped his hands around her waist and pulled her to the bed. He removed her hand from her core and pulled it into his mouth, cleaning each finger slowly, much as he had with a cloth when he'd bathed her their first day at the ruin.

He eased Danellan to her back and knelt beside her, cupping her full breast in his hand as he lowered his mouth to her core. "I want to taste you, Danellan." Michael licked a path around her hood and inside her seam.

She spread her thighs for him, and he drank from her deeply. Danellan tipped her hips to push him deeper, urging him on with pleas punctuated by breathless little cries. Michael stilled, as Danellan wrapped her hand around his cock and shifted to encase the head in her mouth. Her tongue teased at the thick veins under the head, but the position was awkward for her.

Michael dropped his hip to the bed and straightened his legs, guiding her body so that she was laid over his chest. Danellan took him deep in her mouth.

"Yes," he hissed. For a moment, he lay back and let her play on his arousal. Then he reminded himself of his original plan. Michael lifted her hips and spread her knees around his face.

Danellan pressed toward him, seeking his mouth. Michael thrust his tongue deep, swirling inside her and finding the sweet spot. She cried out against his length, moving him relentlessly toward the abyss.

Michael increased his efforts, massaging the spot with the flat of his tongue and probing it with the tip. He wouldn't complete in her mouth. His plan required that she carry his child before they left the safety of anonymity, before they left this ruin and returned to the world they'd fled.

She released his length and screamed his name, her inner muscles contracting. Michael lifted her, settling her over his hips, facing away. Danellan pushed up on her knees, and he guided his cock into her. She settled over him. Her body still spasmed, and her fluid coated his length. Michael bucked his hips, losing himself in pleasure.

"Lay back," he ordered gently. "I want your breasts."

Danellan lay back until her hair fanned over his chest. She pushed further onto his length as Michael increased his pace. He cupped her breasts, flicking his thumbs over the silin-encased peaks. Danellan squirmed against him.

"I'm going to come in you again, Danellan. I'm going to stimulate your egg for me. Only for me."

She groaned. "Yes, Michael. Never leave my body again."

"You'll carry my child," he breathed. "You'll contract with me."

"Yes. A son. Please, Michael."

"No. A daughter as beautiful as her mother. Promise me."

"One of each," she gasped.

"Just one?" he teased, holding off his climax.

"As many as you wish."

Michael roared out his possession of her. His seed filled her, and his cock locked him to her. Danellan whimpered, her hands fisting in the sheets as her body responded to him. He teased her nipples, and she cried out harshly.

He smiled. "You are my bride."

She nodded weakly. "Will you still dress me in silin? We may never leave the bed."

"You may wear silin whenever and wherever you wish," he promised. Susan had never worn the gowns. She hadn't wanted the gowns. They were Danellan's. And at the moment Danellan told him she was expecting—

But that day had not arrived yet.

Danellan sighed as he lessened in her. "I did want to taste you," she said wistfully.

Michael chuckled and lifted her onto the mattress, a wicked idea taking hold. He rolled to his knees between her ankles and grasped her knees lightly. Her eyes widened as he pushed her legs wide and knees up.

"What are you doing?" she asked, her voice husky.

He growled at the sight of his come trickling from between the lips of her swollen sex. "I love seeing my seed in you." He smiled. "Don't move," he ordered as he released her knees.

Michael cupped his fingers under the trail winding down her perineum. She gasped as he ran his hand up, collecting a small amount of his essence on his fingers. Danellan's muscles tightened, spilling a little more into his hand. He hardened at the sight of it.

"Michael? What are you doing?" she groaned.

He leaned over her, seating his cock inside her again. He brought his hand to her mouth carefully and met her eyes. "You want to taste me?" he offered.

"Yes." Her tongue darted out and sampled the fluid collected in his hand.

Michael started moving in her. "Slowly, Danellan. I want to watch you enjoy my essence while I take you."

She obliged him, her tongue painting hot trails as his seed disappeared. When she sucked in his fingers, Michael nearly lost control and climaxed without her. He captured her mouth, tasting the faint musk of their mixed climax.

"We taste good together," he mused.

Danellan smiled. "Do you think that means we'll make good babies together?"

"Absolutely."

Her fingers tangled in the curls on his chest. "How long will we stay here?"

"Do you want to leave?"

"Never," she assured him. "But, we can't stay that long. Can we?"

"No, we can't. Unless you have a reason to leave, I believe we'll stay until you tell me you're pregnant."

"And then?" she asked nervously.

"We sign our contract." Michael felt his control shatter.

Danellan pulled him deep, and he spent in her again. "Promise me," she begged.

"You have my vow."

* * * *

Iric 35th, Ri 25-2988

Danellan giggled as the sila-bubbles danced over her breasts. Michael nuzzled her neck with his soft beard, making her nipples harden in anticipation.

"Do you ever tire?" she teased him.

"Of you? Never."

She snuggled her back to his chest, and he pulled her closer. The evidence of his arousal pressed against her spine.

Danellan smiled. "I see that. Will we break our record today, Michael?"

He growled and nipped at her ear. "Do you wish to?"

"Oh, Fion. Yes."

It had been more than a week since they came to the manor, a week of warmth, food, and love games. Danellan had experienced one moment of terror, when she found the royal chamber on the third floor. This was no abandoned manor of Michael's family as she'd first assumed. This place was owned by Kell Ri, the lair of the enemy.

Michael had soothed her, assuring Danellan that the manor had been abandoned generations earlier, that they were safe. As he'd promised, no one ventured near. The snow mounted outside while she and Michael enjoyed each other's bodies.

Danellan had reasoned her way out of her fears, as the days passed. If she was contracted to another man, Kell Ri couldn't force her to his bed. Even if Michael's family rejected her or he refused to contract, it was against the law to terminate a pregnancy for the express purpose of sterilizing her.

Michael was a rare male, a male still possessing of the healing magic. The blood tests would show that, and even if she begged them to, the doctors would not mechanically take the baby, unless her life depended on it.

Surely, Kell Ri wouldn't want her after Danellan's body had known childbirth. Even if he did, in the absence of a contract, the child could not legally be taken from her. Having a genetically strong baby granted her aid. She would be gifted a place in service...as a teacher or staff in a government facility so that her child would want for nothing. No matter what was to come, carrying Michael's child would improve her lot.

Danellan sighed as his hands trailed over her body, slick from the fragrant sila-soap in the water. Michael was an attentive and talented lover, tireless in his pursuit of her.

Every time he took her, Michael asked her to be his. Danellan had to admit that the only casualty she'd suffer if Michael turned from her would be her broken heart. So every time he asked, she assured him that she would sign the contract he offered.

Michael groaned into her throat as his fingers slid deep in her and found her ready. Danellan rocked against his hand. He lifted her from the water and tossed a quilted silin robe on the floor. He lay down on his back, pulling her over his length. Danellan's eyes widened in surprise as Michael locked her hips to his.

"Don't move," he rasped.

He raised his knees, planting his feet flat on the floor. Danellan gasped at the change in angle. His thighs cradled her and supported most of her weight.

Michael balanced her with his hands on her hips and started moving. The position allowed him to take her faster and harder, deeper than when she normally rode him. He filled her, his cock teasing at the muscle that stimulated her at the pinnacle of each stroke.

He came quickly, more quickly than usual. Danellan screamed his name as he locked into her body. Tears of joy tracked down her cheeks as she shattered, his roar echoing in her ears. There were no shocks, no egg released. They had succeeded in producing a child, and that child was implanted in her womb and making changes in her body, as her mate lay locked inside her.

"Will you," he began.

Danellan silenced him with a passionate kiss, her tongue caressing his as he cradled her head in surprise. She laid kisses down his throat to his pulse point and back to his lips, nipping at him. "Make love to me, Michael. Never stop making love to me." Was this the schen? The plea for him was out before she could wonder at it, but she did want him again...desperately.

Michael's eyes locked on her face, and his smile disappeared. He brushed at her tears. "What have I done?" he asked in dismay.

She shook her head and pulled one of the hands from her cheek to her womb. "You've given me a baby. Do it again, Michael."

He looked at the hand between them in

shock, rubbing a circle over her silin curls. "My daughter," he breathed.

"It could be a son," she reminded him.

"Then I will train him on war-buck, with dagger and bow." His smile returned. Michael stared at his hand with that same smile until he lessened in her.

Danellan shivered as he released her body.

Michael startled, taking to his feet with her cradled to his chest. He vaulted to the bed in three leaps, settling her on the pillows and covering her with the quilt. He pulled two more quilts from the cabinet and added them.

She watched him in confusion. "Michael? What are you doing?"

"I let you chill," he berated himself. "It won't happen again. I'll turn up the temperature for you and get food." Michael turned to her with wild eyes. "Healing. Do you need my healing or massage?" he asked urgently.

"Michael, calm down. I am warm. I'm well. My pregnancy signs aren't noticeable."

"Yet." He knelt next to her and kissed the hand she'd moved from beneath the quilts. "You carry my child. Anything you require, I will provide. Anything you desire is yours for the asking."

Danellan raised an eyebrow. "I desire you." She smiled a coy smile. "I think my schen will keep you very busy."

Michael's eyes darkened, and his cock surged, ready for another round. "I would ask a favor of you."

"Anything," she promised him.

"Wait here." He sprinted away without dressing, coming back with a purple silin bundle in his hands. Michael knelt beside her and pressed it into her hands.

She looked at it in confusion. "What is this?"

Michael darkened. "Will you wear this for me? Will you honor me?"

Danellan unwrapped the bundle, setting the silin cloak aside carefully. The dress unfurled in her lap. She bit back tears. It was a presentation dress. Royalty wore such dresses, brides of kings and the highest-born nobles. Michael was honoring her by giving her this.

Or would he have had his bride presented to him? The gown was new, as the food, sheets, quilts, and silin day gowns were new. None of it had been here for generations, abandoned by Kell's father. How high born was he?

"What is your family, Michael?" she asked quietly.

His eyes shifted away. "Will it matter to you?"

She shook her head. "I love you. Your family is immaterial."

A smile lit his face, making his eyes bright. "You love me?"

"You doubted that?"

"I'm glad you said it. I love you, too."

Danellan laughed heartily. "I know." No man could suffer for her and show her such regard and not love her. "I love you, Michael. I will love you, no matter who your family is."

"Even if I was the son of Kell Ri, himself?" he teased.

Her stomach sent one warning swirl at that

311

chilling thought. She pushed it away. She trusted Michael above all else. "Even then," she assured him. "You are an honorable man."

"Then we travel to Lind tomorrow to contact my family."

"So soon?"

He kissed her again. "The weather is clear, and we have no milk for you here."

Michael would be practical at a moment when her heart pounded in terror of what his noble family would think of her, the disavowed daughter of a general.

"But first," he growled playfully, "I'd like to see you in that gown."

Danellan nodded. Michael was perfect. Even the family he fled couldn't be enough to make her think twice.

CHAPTER TWENTY - FOUR

Iric 36th, Ri 25-2988

Danellan looked around the common room in dismay as Michael whispered an order to the matron. He cradled Danellan's elbow when she would have bolted and removed the quilt from around her shoulders, handing it off to the matron with a nod. He led her to a curtained table in the rear and settled her in the semi-darkness. The matron came to set a mulled berry drink for her and lizor berry wine for Michael.

She leaned close to him. "The soldiers, Michael," she pleaded quietly.

He nodded and sipped the wine. "I know. It is a soldier I need to contact my family."

"Then do it, please. Before—"

"I need an officer, not one of these bits of war fodder."

Danellan nodded and took a hearty swallow of the warm liquid, her hand shaking. Not in a century had she pictured herself in this position. She was trusting Michael to place her within a hand's width of capture.

I trust him. I have to trust him.

"That's more like it," he breathed.

She looked at the three officers walking in, two lieutenants and— Her heart stuttered. Danellan grasped Michael's arm as he started to stand. He looked at her in surprise and cupped her cheek, questioning her without speaking the words.

Danellan shook her head. "No, Michael. Not that captain. Please, not that one. Wait for someone else."

"What is it?" He stared at Tranol, and his jaw tightened. Michael turned back to her, his expression ordering an explanation.

"He cannot see me. Please, Michael."

"Has that captain injured you?"

She gasped at the fury in his eyes. Danellan didn't want to answer that question. She didn't want to lie to Michael, but the truth was more than she could bear to spill to him in the common room of an inn. She had hoped he would never have to know why she feared Tranol and why he hunted her.

"Has he?" Michael demanded through clenched teeth.

Tranol had hurt her but not in any way she could describe simply to Michael. "He is—my brother, my father's son with his first mate." The last left her lips on a rush.

"But you fear him. You're shaking at the sight of him."

Danellan dropped her gaze, unequal to giving him the answers he deserved, at least for the moment. "Please choose another."

Michael cupped her face up, wiping an errant tear from her cheek with a gentle expression. "He will not see you. You have my word. Not here and now."

Before she could protest, Michael stood and pulled the curtain to shade her. She could barely see the table Tranol and his friends took through the gap. She held her breath as Michael

314

approached them. Danellan wished she could hear their conversation.

* * * *

Michael strode across the common room, pushing back the haze of fury clouding his reason. Danellan's words coursed through his mind.

Not all soldiers are honorable men, even officers.

I wasn't Father's heir.

He is my brother, my father's son with his first mate.

Danellan was frightened of him, this pompous cur that Michael wanted to snap in two. Whatever her older brother's crimes were, she felt she couldn't tell Michael the tale. He had no doubts that this was the man who'd put a bounty on her, the man who haunted her dreams.

Don't let him take me.

Michael ground his teeth in fury. If her brother was the one she pleaded with in her dreams, his suffering would be endless.

He stood over the trio for a moment, scanning his eyes down the polished young officer a few years older than himself. At first, the captain didn't react to his presence. When he did, he shot Michael a cold look; taking in the muddy boots, worn clothing, and thick beard that marked his assumed station in undisguised disdain.

The captain's hand went to the hilt of his dagger. His eyes narrowed. "What is your business, sir?" He affected a tone of smug superiority that turned Michael's stomach.

Michael leaned closer. "We have business, Captain. Send your friends away."

He roared in laughter. His friends joined in.

One of them clapped the captain on the shoulder. "You have business with this ragged drifter, Tranol?" he taunted.

Michael suspected that the lieutenant was taunting him rather than his captain.

"Certainly not," Tranol insisted, ruffled by the implication. "Move on."

Michael reached into his tunic pocket and pulled out his crest ring. He set it on the table and pushed it to Tranol with his index finger, tensing as Tranol tensed. "We have business to settle, Captain Tranol," he assured the older man.

The cocky officer picked up the ring as Michael pulled his hand back. His smile disappeared, and he paled. Tranol met Michael's eyes and swallowed hard. He fisted the crest ring reflexively.

Michael nodded. "Send your friends away."

Tranol waved his empty hand. "Go," he requested faintly.

"Tranol?" His friends surveyed Michael warily.

"Go," he ordered in a stronger voice. "Go back to the base. Now."

The lieutenants rose slowly and went to the door, looking back at Michael in confusion several times.

Tranol eased the ring to the tips of his fingers to examine it more closely. His hands shook. He winced as Michael settled into one of the newly vacated seats at the table and favored Tranol with a dark look, one he used when someone was in serious danger of pushing him too far.

"What business have we, Prin—"

Michael motioned him for silence. "You will deliver a message to my brother. Is he residing at his retreat home?" Susan liked that house, so they spent most of their time there rather than Jole's manor near the palace.

Tranol nodded.

"Good." He pulled the missive he'd prepared from his coat pocket. Michael plucked his ring from Tranol's fingers and pressed the missive to them. "You will bring my brother here."

"What if—"

"He will come. You will accompany him. Our business is unfinished, Captain."

"What have I done to offend you?" he pleaded in a hoarse whisper.

"Now is not the time. This is not the place." He ground his teeth at the idea of waiting, but Danellan would have the chance to see her brother's fall. "There will be a time and a place very soon."

The captain shuddered, and the last of the color drained from his face.

Michael nodded. That was good. Tranol was afraid of him. He should feel fear. He should feel hunted, even if only for a few hours. Danellan deserved that much.

Instilling fear was a simple task for Michael. His reputation as a half-mad re-bred bastard with royal blood in his veins worked in his favor. Even if he weren't perceived as mad, a personal offense against him could mean a ritual death.

The matron came to set Tranol's drink down, and Michael picked it up, downing half the iri cordial in a single gulp. He arched a brow at Tranol.

The captain looked away, fumbling out the coin to pay the matron. He pulled out far more than was needed. "Anything His—"

Michael gifted him another hard look.

Tranol gulped. "Anything my friend requires, Rienna. If this is not enough, use my account."

Michael smiled. "A suite, Matron. The best you have."

The captain nodded his agreement. The matron smiled and hurried away to make the preparations. Tranol pocketed the missive and pushed to his feet, looking unsteady.

Michael rolled the glass between his fingertips. "Remember to come back with my brother, Captain."

He nodded, his face an unhealthy shade of gray.

"Captain Tranol? Would you be the son of General Cro?" he mused.

"Yes, H— Yes, I am."

"It's been years since I've seen your father." That was no lie. The last time Michael had laid eyes on the general was at least a decade earlier.

Tranol managed a weak smile. Did he believe

himself safe, based on that fictitious friendship?

"I know Cro's second mate died years ago. Have you any family left?"

He stilled, searching Michael's face as if trying to decide on the answer he should give. "A—a sister," he whispered.

Michael nodded and downed the rest of the cordial. "Family is very important, Captain Tranol. It is a grave responsibility."

"Yes, it is." Tranol all but fled to the door.

Rienna returned and placed a key in Michael's hand. "Room ten, sir. You and your bride have the top floor. The bath is stocked with all necessary toiletries."

His smile widened. He pulled a second missive from his pocket, and placed it in Rienna's hand. "This is a list of the things I require, Matron. We'll need the food and lounging wear immediately, the rest as soon as possible."

"On Captain Tranol's account?" she asked.

I wasn't Father's heir.

How did he steal her inheritance?

"Yes, Matron. The captain's account will bear up nicely." Michael doubted Tranol would need money much longer, and Danellan's portion of her father's benefits would more than cover what he'd asked for on the list.

She bowed and left him.

Michael rose and returned to Danellan, pushing back the drape. She met his gaze, running a shaking hand over her mouth. Danellan was pale. She looked decidedly ill. Had she really worried so much about what her brother was capable of?

He lifted her hand and kissed her palm. "Our room and bath is waiting. Food and clothing will be delivered shortly," he soothed her.

Her eyes went wide. "An inn?" she squeaked.

"We are not hiding any longer, Danellan. Promise me you'll take me as full mate."

She had to. Danellan wasn't a cross-mate bred for him. Short of a contract, the child she carried was hers alone. If she walked away from him, he would have no rights to his own child and no means to convince her to stay. Michael wouldn't survive that.

Danellan nodded. "You know I will."

"Then let us prepare to meet my family."

She nodded and stood. Danellan looked around the common room as if she expected her brother to be lying in wait for her. Michael kissed her cheek. He wanted to know why she feared Tranol, but this stress wasn't healthy for her or their child. Michael would have to learn his answers another way.

"He cannot touch you," Michael promised. "You have my vow that he will never harm you again."

* * * *

Jole looked at Pyter in confusion. "He says he can't deliver it to you?"

Pyter shook his head. "Captain Tranol claims the message is for your eyes alone."

"He's from my father's guard?"

"He is."

"Send him in."

The captain was about Jole's age. He was pale and shaking, his bow so unsteady that Jole wondered if Tranol was intoxicated.

"You have a message for me?" Jole prodded him.

He scrambled to remove it from his jacket pocket and offered it to Jole with a stiff bow of his head.

"Who gave you this?" Jole asked in surprise as he broke the royal seal on the back. It wasn't the seal his father typically used. This was an older seal, one from Kol Ri's time.

"Your brother, Highness."

Jole fumbled the missive to the desktop, his heart hammering. "You've seen Mik?" he asked hopefully. After all these weeks, had his brother finally contacted someone?

"Yes, Highness."

"Where and when?"

"Three quarters of an hour ago in Lind."

Only three quarters of an hour? Captain Tranol must have risked death to travel that fast. Jole smiled. "The Leaping Lamor?"

"Yes, Highness. He waits us there."

"Us?"

The captain shuddered. "He said— His Highness said we had unfinished business together, but I can't imagine—" He swallowed hard, looking even more peaked at the thought of facing Mik again.

Jole pulled the missive from its envelope slowly. It was in Mik's hand.

Jole,

I have little right to ask for favors. The kindness you have shown me so far is more than I ever expected.

The ruins. He sank to returning there.

But, in this case, I find I must ask more from you.
I have found my peace and seek my home. If you can see past my mistakes and remember the boy you loved, the man I send to you will tell you where to find me.

Your brother,
Michael

Jole closed his eyes. *Michael. Susan was right.*

He stood and pulled his uniform jacket over his tunic. Jole looked back to Tranol as he headed for the door. "Let's go."

Pyter cleared his throat. "How many men will you be taking, Jole?"

"None. I don't believe this is a trick, but in case— You are responsible for Susan and my babies. I'll be back shortly."

* * * *

Danellan smiled at the sound of Michael in the bathroom. He assured her that he'd let his beard grow in again for her, but he needed to make the appropriate impression with his family. She wasn't sure precisely what he meant by that, but she assumed it meant that he would have to show a willingness to embrace the life he'd left behind.

He had been attentive in his lovemaking and in his patience. Michael hadn't asked her about Tranol. Rather, he'd said that he wanted her to relax completely and that their problems would be solved when the time came. She didn't wonder at it. Whoever Michael was, his family name was enough to frighten Tranol, and that made her more than willing to put worry aside.

She ran a hand over the silin lounging robe she wore and plucked a bit of lamor off of the tray beside the bed, washing it down with warmed milk. Michael had thought of every comfort.

A brisk knock came at the door, and she crossed the room to answer it. "What else has the man thought of?" she mused. Already, they'd bathed and made love, eaten and been clothed in finery.

Danellan startled as she swung the door wide, taking in the royal uniform breathlessly, a scream of fear lodging in her throat. She relaxed slightly as she met Prince Jole's piercing green eyes.

She'd met the prince once, on a troop inspection. He was a decent man. He wasn't Kell

Ri. She broke contact with his eyes, remembering her station, and bowed her head to him.

He stepped into the room without a word, scanning his eyes around as if he'd expected something different.

A second man entered and closed the door behind them. She recognized the silver braid and insignia of a guard captain on his cuff and looked up in sick certainty of who'd accompanied the prince to their rooms.

Danellan backed off a pace in fear, her hand grasping at the bedpost to steady her. Tranol's face erupted in a vicious smile. She pulled the robe tight around her chest, raising her chin and fighting back tears.

Her brother advanced on her. "The errant sister returns," he drawled. "I can call my men in from Caran. Do you have any concept how much trouble you've caused me, little thief?"

"What you stole from me doesn't begin to compare to what little I took with me," she managed in a low voice.

He scowled. "An interesting situation you've created here," he mused. "Will the prince decide to return you to me, or will he claim the destiny you ran from, without my prize? Either way, I can rest assured that you will be delivered. The worst you have done is stolen my reward, but I can live without that if I know your fate."

She darkened. "I told you before I ran that I would never submit to that. I will die first."

Tranol laughed harshly. He flicked the neckline of her robe. "I find you here in his rooms, half dressed and looking decidedly tousled. Yet, you have the gall to claim you're not his bed maid?"

Danellan flinched, and her stomach fought to bring her mid-day meal back.

Michael has offered a contract. I am not a bed maid. I was once, but that ceased to be. And, what has Prince Jole to do with this? Has Tranol betrayed both Michael and myself by bringing him instead of Michael's family?

She shook her head, shrinking back as Tranol reached for her again.

"Take your hands off of her," Michael demanded.

Tranol backed off, his smile wavering as Michael slipped around Prince Jole's shoulder and shoved Tranol toward the door. Michael placed himself between Danellan and her brother with his hand on Cro's blade, currently pushed into the waist of his lounging pants.

The prince watched the interaction in surprise, his eyes narrowing.

Michael drew her to his chest; his freshly-shaven chin locked in warning as he glared Tranol down. "This is what he did to you?" he asked. "Your own brother tried to force you into palace service?"

Danellan took a shuddering breath, then nodded.

"Schente?" he persisted.

She glanced at Prince Jole and closed her eyes at his look of concern. "For Kell Ri," she whispered. "Then for..... I imagine for anyone who'd have me, based on what he—he said." She shuddered at the memory.

"Have you any love for him?"

Danellan looked up at him in confusion. "I don't understand." *Did she care for Kell Ri? Michael knew the answer to that.*

Michael cracked a smile. "Will you miss your brother if I kill him?"

She laughed in relief and considered Tranol's faint appearance. "Death is too easy," she decided.

Michael nodded. "Service for service. After he spends— How long did you run?"

"Nine weeks." Danellan scowled at those long weeks. She was always cold, almost always hungry.

He nodded and kissed her forehead. "Twelve weeks in a cold cell...twenty remen or so will do...and by Len's name, I should have them douse you with icy water once a week, but that is a punishment I wouldn't wish even on you. Quarter rations should hold you to life well enough. I trust you'll handle that for my bride, Jole."

"Bride?" Tranol croaked.

Michael chuckled. "You're lucky I don't kill you for daring to touch her. And calling her a bed maid—"

But Danellan found it hard to concentrate on what he was saying. *Who was Michael that he addressed the prince so casually?*

CHAPTER TWENTY-FIVE

Jole watched the interaction between Mik and his bride's brother in amazement. He hadn't seen Mik so relaxed in years, so at peace despite his anger with the captain. It was truly like watching him when he was a boy, before he'd become so competitive and angry.

The woman brushed her cheek against Mik's bare chest. She was a beauty, though she was a bit on the thin side. Her hair was surprisingly short, shockingly so. Susan came from Earth. Her hair had been cut in the style of many Earth women of her culture, but it was unusual for a Keen female to have hair above the shoulder.

Mik finished his browbeating of the terrified soldier and returned his attention to the woman in his arms.

Jole had seen only a single moment of murderous rage, when his brother had left his place in the bathroom doorway and headed for the soldier who'd dared touch his bride, who'd dared threaten her. Jole had backed away to let him pass, certain that Mik was beyond control, but he'd kept his bearings better than Jole could have ever anticipated.

The moments before Mik moved had surprised Jole more than what Mik did when he did move. When his brother had appeared in the doorway, Mik's eyes had narrowed at the scene before him. Jole had been so stunned at the look of undisguised menace on Mik's face that he'd barely heard the short argument between Captain Tranol and his sister. It had been over in moments, with Mik making it clear that any further moves of Tranol toward his mate would end in the usual fashion.

The captain was so stunned that he forgot himself. He still stared at the woman, inviting a ritual death at Mik's hands.

Jole motioned to the dumbfounded captain. "You will wait for me downstairs. Do not attempt to escape punishment. I assure you, there is nowhere you can hide from my wrath." *Or Mik's.*

The captain paled. He left the room as if he faced Mik with a ceremonial blade within the hour.

The woman sighed in relief. Jole took a moment to study her. Her road had been a long one, nine weeks of cold and hunger to escape her brother and—

He glanced at Mik, busily calming her, his voice low and soothing.

Their father was at the root of this? It wouldn't surprise Jole to learn that Kell desired the young woman, but forcing her into service was deplorable. Why would Kell do that when he was never without women willing to fill his bed?

Jole shuddered at an unwelcome thought he would have to discuss with Mik at a private moment, when he would not upset the woman. If Kell wanted her unwilling— If he wanted her to fight him, to resist— He blanched at that thought. It wasn't the Keen way.

Still, Kell had never shown honor in dealing with their mother. Jenneane had contracted for two mechanical implantations to keep him from touching her ever again. What treatment must a woman suffer to go to those lengths? In the time before Jenneane won freedom from his touch, perhaps Kell found he liked forcing women to his hand. It didn't bear considering, when this woman was his brother's bride.

He moved toward them slowly. "Mik?" he called out.

His brother kissed his bride and left her to clasp Jole to his chest, missing the look of shock on her face as he did so. "Thank you, Jole. Thank you for everything you've done, brother."

The woman sank to the bed, swallowing hard. "He really is—" she whispered. "I thought Tranol meant..."

Jole ignored her for a moment, needing to feel the solid reality of Mik in his arms. It had been a long seven weeks. At times, Jole feared his brother must be dead. No one could hide that well.

Mik stiffened, and Jole saw the stark terror in his eyes. "Does it matter?" Mik asked quietly.

She took a calming breath. "No. I told you it didn't. I love you."

Realization came slowly. She really hadn't known who Mik was until just that moment. This woman had taken Mik as her husband without the slightest knowledge that she was embracing her enemy's son.

Mik's expression eased, a sigh of relief rushing from him. "Thank you."

She nodded slowly.

Jole clapped him on the back, laughing

nervously, still in stunned disbelief. "We've all been worried sick," he exclaimed. "I can't believe you did this."

Mik pushed back, meeting his eyes sadly. "I doubt that, but thank you."

He cringed inwardly at the pain in Mik's voice. "We were. I scoured every corner for word of you, and Susan has been restless."

Mik backed off, shaking his head, a sullen expression making him look more like the Mik of recent years. "In fear, perhaps. That man is gone. He has been for a long time."

"I know. Mik..... You asked if I could forgive the past. You are the only one who cannot forgive."

"Susan—"

"Worries when she sees that longing in you, sometimes. Susan spoke to you when you ran. Did she fear you then?"

Mik shook his head, pushing his hands in the pockets of his silin lounging pants.

Jole surveyed him. Mik was lean, more muscular than he had been months ago. His bare stomach was packed tight. There seemed to be no fat left on him.

"You haven't eaten well," Jole noted.

Mik shrugged. "Commoners on the run don't have comforts. Sometimes dried meat and redgrass root or cracker tack were the best life offered."

Jole grimaced. That had to be horrible, but Mik talked about it as if it were a matter of pleasant conversation. "You could have called for me sooner."

He crossed to the window and stared out over the snow-covered land. Mik furrowed his brow.

Jole locked on the movement. "You're scarred." He crossed the room and touched the scar that started within the inner corner of Mik's eyebrow and angled slightly to a point half a finger width above the apex of his brow.

Mik cracked a smile. "It was a fair fight," he quipped.

He fought back a laugh. "How many?"

"Six armed men. One highly trained. The rest... The usual rabble."

Jole laughed heartily. "What did they do to deserve you in a rage?"

His smile disappeared. "They tried to take my mate unwilling. They took a dagger to her body."

Jole sucked in his breath in shock. After what happened to Mik's intended Earth-born cross-mate, it was a fatal error to cross Mik that way. Even when he had been near mad in his loss, it was a line Mik hadn't crossed himself, the only reason Jole hadn't killed him when he finally got Susan back.

The woman grimaced, pressing a hand to her ribs in what could only be the spot they'd cut her. "I wasn't your mate," she protested weakly.

Mik went to her, his face tortured. He settled to the mattress and drew her onto his lap. "I wanted you to be," he assured her. "Even if I hadn't wanted it—"

Jole continued for him. "That is not a fate my brother would consign any woman to. The fact that he wanted more from you only made him

331

more determined."

Mik nodded and kissed his mate's forehead. Jole cleared his throat and waited for his brother to meet his gaze. He motioned to the woman and shrugged, suggesting a formal introduction.

Mik darkened. "This is my bride, Danellan, daughter of General Cro. Danellan—"

She smiled. "I've seen Prince Jole, Michael," she chided him gently. Danellan sobered. "I'm sorry. What should I call you?"

"Michael. I'd like it if you'd call me Michael."

"But why?"

Jole sighed. "It's his name, Danellan. Mik was a baby name our mother used. His given name was Michael."

Mik smiled, his eyes glittering in amusement. "I don't suppose you'll remember it," he noted.

"I'll try," Jole promised. "Now. Tell me what you need from me."

He nodded. "What magistrate do you trust?"

He didn't need to be more specific. Jole understood Mik's plan. He intended to be contracted and moved into his manor before Kell had a chance to object to the match.

"Por wrote my contract with Susan. I trust him. What provisions will there be?"

Mik nodded. "Fidelity from each of us. Full mates. Much like your contract."

"Danellan?"

She took a deep breath. "If Michael tires of me—"

"I won't," he promised.

"If you do, our children are mine."

Mik nodded. "And my retreat home, servants,

and half of my personal wealth."

Danellan's eyes widened. "You don't owe me—"

Mik kissed her passionately. "I never intend to let you collect it. If you tire of me—"

She dropped her gaze. "You owe me nothing."

"The same split," he whispered.

Jole smiled at her amazement. "You're sure?" he asked.

Mik stroked her cheek. "Absolutely."

"What else do you need?"

"Loan of some clothing until we reach my home and a doctor that you trust."

"Doctor?" Jole asked in concern.

Mik arched an eyebrow. "How early should Hugam be given?"

* * * *

Pri 2nd, Ri 25-2988

Michael raised Danellan's hand to his mouth and laid a kiss on her knuckles. She offered a strained smile, smoothing the ankle-length lavender gown self-consciously. She was terrified, though she hid it well.

"You're beautiful," he assured her. The backdrop of his retreat home was a perfect complement to the radiance of her presence. The wood and marble accented her innate warmth.

"He won't approve. I know he won't."

"My father doesn't have to approve. He's never approved of his sons or our mates. I don't care if he does. Jole approves of you."

"That matters to you," she noted.

"No. It wouldn't have, but I'm glad he likes you."

Her blush was beautiful. Danellan gifted him a look of invitation that had Michael aching to take her again. Her schen was fierce, and he loved it. He had spent the last three days reveling in it, assuaging her body's pregnancy demands whether it was healing her pregnancy signs, feeding her, or satisfying her formidable urge to mate.

But now was not the time. His father had contacted them three hours earlier, announcing his visit. From the voices rising in the entry hall, it was clear that the battle was about to begin. Michael had orchestrated this meeting perfectly. At every turn, Kell would be turned back. It was a battle Michael would not risk losing.

Danellan took a shuddering breath. Michael led her to a place near the fire. It was most likely her fear of Kell that made her shake, but he wouldn't chance that it was her pregnancy signs.

"Where is he?" Kell growled.

"In his office, Majesty." That was Captain Rill, perhaps the only man beside Jole that he trusted to keep his back in a fight.

Kell stormed into the room. Michael bit back a smile. It was rare to see his father so out of control of a situation, and Michael had barely begun.

He noted with satisfaction that Rill slipped around his father and took a place at Danellan's side as he was ordered to. Rill had one purpose in today's events, keeping Danellan safe from harm.

More people crowded into the room, and Michael scowled. He had hoped to keep this a private affair between himself and Kell, but it seemed that was not to be. Minn and her father, General Gree, were followed by one of Kell's personal magistrates.

"Mik," Kell began coldly.

"Michael," he countered. "If you hadn't taken me from my mother so quickly, you might have learned that Mik was a baby name Jenneane used for me. I am a man, and my true name was Michael."

Kell's eyes widened. "Very well. You have put off your duty long enough. It has not been easy to salvage this contract for you."

"Send them away. I'll never sign that contract."

Minn's surprise melted into a feigned look of adoration that turned Michael's stomach. She glided toward him, placing her gilded nails on his chest and running circles designed to drive a man to distraction.

Michael took stock of her. Her hair was in a complicated mass of pins and curls. Her nails were too long to be of any use. Minn was undoubtedly waited on night and day by servants. Her face was heavily painted: pale powder on her cheeks, blood red on her lips, and deep blue to draw out her eyes.

He compared that to Danellan. His bride's hair fell loose in curls with only two gold combs as decoration, hair that welcomed Michael's hands. Her face was bare save a protective balm on her lips, her sun-kissed cheeks, and her pure Fion-given beauty. She had short nails with a gloss of lavender that matched her dress, hands made for dressing children and undressing a mate.

Michael pushed Minn's hand away. "I never agreed to the contract, and I never will. Your agreement was with my father, not with me."

A flush of anger showed through the powder on her face. "I'll forgive you deserting me and worrying me, Michael, but—"

Michael scowled at her. "I won't forgive you, Minn. And you will address me as Highness. You do not have leave to be familiar with me."

"Forgive me?" she bristled. "Whatever for? I only—"

"I won't have to lay eyes on him," he mimicked her bracing tone. "The longest contract in recorded history. My contract allows me schaen. If it is intolerable, there is always Walla tea." He laughed harshly at her shock. "You should have been more mindful of your surroundings, Minn."

Danellan gasped softly. No one else seemed to notice. His father and all his guests were locked on Michael to the exclusion of all else.

Kell sent General Gree a sour look. "Be that as it may be, Michael. You have a duty. If not Minn, then—"

Michael laughed deeply, anticipating his father's reaction. "I've done my duty. I contracted two days ago."

Minn's eyes locked on Danellan. Minn surged

toward her with a scream of rage. Michael wrapped an arm around her waist and hoisted her none too gently, carrying her back to her father and pushing her into the general's hands.

He placed himself between his bride and the howling shrew and addressed Minn coldly. "While I would love to watch my bride tear you limb from limb, I swore to protect her with my life. If you seek to harm her, you take your life in your hands. I suggest you remember it."

Michael tipped his head to the general, then went to Danellan's side. He took her hand and met his father's gaze. "May I present my bride. This is Danellan, daughter of General Cro."

Kell darkened and flicked a pained look at Danellan.

Michael tapped down his fury. Danellan was right. He really didn't know her from any other woman on Kegin. "Yes. I know why you didn't consider Danellan," he growled at his father. "Your loss is my gain."

"Where is this contract?" he demanded.

Michael motioned to the desk.

Kell tramped to it and snatched the single sheet from the desktop. He waved it at Michael in disbelief.

Michael kissed Danellan's hand and arched an eyebrow at his father. "The magistrate assures me it is the shortest contract he's ever written, perhaps the shortest in history."

His father scanned his eyes over the paper. He crumpled it. "Unacceptable. I use my right of non-allowance. This contract is void."

Danellan stifled what sounded like a sob.

Michael squeezed her hand. "You can't."

Kell pitched the paper into the fire. "I can and I will. That contract offers you no protection."

"It offers more protection than the one you allowed General Gree's daughter. And legally, you cannot dissolve our contract."

His father's eyes narrowed. "Why?"

"Danellan carries my child. You cannot dissolve a contract that has borne children, unless one of us asks it."

Danellan laughed nervously, his push for a child before their return clear to her. "We don't," she stated for them both.

CHAPTER TWENTY-SIX

Caj 27th, Ri 25-2989

Michael looked up at the mother of the boy sitting on the table. "He should recover well now." He smiled at his patient. "No more climbing iri vines?"

The child laughed. "On Mag's honor," he promised solemnly.

"Good boy." He scooped the child up and handed him to his mother. "There should be no scar," Michael assured her. "If you need anything, let the assistant at the desk know."

The woman bowed her head, her cheeks bright red in embarrassment. "Thank you, Prince Michael."

She'd need food and Walla tea at the least, he knew. He pasted on a smile, hoping that she'd ask for what she needed. If not, he would have to have it sent to her. He would not let his people suffer for fear of asking.

"Those who have the gift should serve," he reminded her.

Tears shone in her eyes. "You are good to us."

"It is my pleasure, as it should be. Caring for my people will never be simply a duty."

She left, and Michael sank into a chair in the corner. He laid his head back and closed his eyes, rubbing a hand over the close-cut beard he'd grown for Danellan.

"Hello, brother."

Michael smiled at Jole's voice. "Still can't remember, can you?" he teased.

"No, but I am trying."

Michael crossed the room to hug Jole. "It's good to see you."

His brother nodded grimly. "Summer festival will be held at the palace next week. Will you be there?"

He grimaced. "So, Father has you running his messages now?"

Jole sighed. "You know that's not what I meant. I'm sure Father would like to see you there, but he knows better than to use me to convince you."

"I don't know. It's hours away, and Danellan—"

"Has a month to go."

"Susan went early, and during a celebration."

"With twins," Jole pointed out.

"Danellan was early." His arguments were getting thin, and I knew it.

Jole sighed. "There is more to your position than addressing the council for reforms and healing children. The people look to us, even to you. You are a prince of Kegin, and you have found reasons to skip every major celebration since the one you fled."

Michael pushed a hand through his hair. "Kell is still unhappy. Danellan does not need to be harassed."

"He's happier now that he has a young bride," Jole noted slyly.

They both laughed heartily.

Michael wiped away a tear of mirth at the

thought of his father's marriage. "I wonder how long the contract is? Minn has a history."

"Probably the longest ever written, but I'd wager that it doesn't favor her nearly as well as the one she intended." He sobered. "Will you promise to come? The people need hope. Your mating with a Keen woman gives them hope for their implanted cross-bred sons."

Michael nodded. "As long as Danellan can—" He faltered, looking past Jole to Danellan standing in the doorway. He glanced to the clock and back to her face. She should be resting after her morning class.

She was pale, her eyes wide. Captain Rill stood at her elbow, looking tense.

"Michael," she gasped.

He pushed past Jole and touched her sweat-beaded forehead in concern. "What is it?"

Danellan pulled his hand to the swell of their baby. Her muscles spasmed under his hand, and she groaned in response.

"How far?" he asked calmly.

"She still has her cap," Rill informed him. "I brought her to you as quickly as I could."

"Michael, please," she groaned, another ripple cascading through her abdomen.

He nodded and swept her into his arms. "Rill, have them ready her room and summon her doctors." He started out the door. Michael turned to Jole with a wide grin. "Tell Kell I will expect him here in a month's time. It seems we will be throwing a celebration."

Jole nodded, swallowing a laugh. "Take care of her. I'll take care of Kell."

* * * *

Wend 27th, Ri 25-2989

Danellan smiled at Michael as the crown settled on her head and Sayd, one of the church councilmen, gave his blessing to the newest princess of Kegin. The crowd roared their approval. Michael stepped forward with their daughter in his arms and his own crown tipped back jauntily on his head.

Sayd draped the sky blue silin cloth that represented Fion's goodness over their child's chest. He bowed his head and kissed her brow tenderly. "May you rule with Mag's justice and Fion's tender mercies. May you serve your people well, as has your father before you." He met Danellan's gaze. "Name your husband's child."

"She is Gibril Hir, daughter of Michael Hi, named for my mother, bride of General Cro."

The old man smiled. "So, she is. May Fion bless you with many more."

Michael shot her a heated look.

Oh yes. As soon as the reception was in full sway, she and Michael would disappear to end the fast, to resume their sexual relationship.

Danellan turned into a hug blindly and smiled shyly at Susan. Jenneane pulled at her mother's skirt, and Joseph weaved through the crowd toward the stairs with Jole in pursuit. He snatched his son up and tickled the young prince, then tossed him over his broad shoulder.

She glanced at Kell, standing at the edge of the dais with Minn at his elbow. Kell looked as if he wanted nothing more than to escape the chaos of his children and grandchildren. Minn looked smug and secure. Her contract must favor her greatly, Danellan decided.

Danellan looked back to Michael, smiling openly at the sight of Gibby holding his finger in her tiny fist. Even Kell couldn't ruin her mood today.

Michael leaned close, laying a kiss under her ear. "Soon," he promised.

Danellan purred in response. "I can't wait to get out of this dress." The coronation dress was six layers of lace, silin and satil that made Danellan wish she'd never asked to wear any of it.

"My pleasure. I will ask one favor of you."

"Which is?" she whispered.

"Wear the crown." His eyes sparkled in mischief, and his voice held a tone of invitation.

"And a presentation dress," she offered hopefully.

Michael growled his approval.

SECTION THREE:
Alex

Aliens Among Us

CHAPTER TWENTY-SEVEN

September 21st, 2006

Alex Braeden lay on the hard bed in his prison cell. He had given up asking why he was here more than a year earlier. The reason they gave was too insane to contemplate.

In an hour, Patterson would come in and the questions would start again.

"How did you get here, Alex?"

"Why are you here, Alex?"

"Which one of the endless stars is your home world, Alex?"

"Where is Susan?"

Alex sighed. Susan had been gone for more than four years. He had no more idea where she was than they did, and maybe that was a good thing for Susan. There were times that Alex might have cracked if he had known what to tell them.

That was how this whole thing started. Susan's neighbors had called the police to report screams in her apartment, but when the police arrived, Susan was gone. Large portions of her belongings were gone, but curiously, her clothing seemed untouched.

There were signs of a struggle. The items on top of her nightstand were swept off onto the floor and crushed under the heel of a boot with a strange tread that the police couldn't seem to match. A lamp was knocked over. A bloodstain marred the sheets of her mussed bed.

346

It would have been a simple missing persons' case if it weren't for two things. First, how could Susan and her belongings have disappeared from a fifth-floor apartment, when three witnesses stated that no one had come out? Neither Susan nor her attacker came out the hall door or the fire escape. The second reason was the blood.

Alex pushed to his feet and walked to the small bathroom. He splashed water on his face and considered the shower. No, he always preferred to take his shower *after* an interview with Patterson. Alex felt strangely dirty after spending time with that particular agent.

Behind him, someone keyed the lock, and a tray of food settled onto the edge of the dresser. Alex pulled a worn copy of *Stranger In A Strange Land* from the shelf of books they allowed him and scooped the tray up, setting it on the nightstand. The food was good enough and plentiful enough here. It was the only decent thing about the place.

Alex tried to concentrate on his book while he ate, but he was still playing the events over in his mind.

He didn't like to think about that single bloodstain. One little bloodstain had destroyed his life. He swallowed a mouthful of coffee and stared into the black depths inside the cup, as black as the space outside the atmosphere these people seemed convinced he came from. Four years ago, Alex had been in his last year of college. Four years ago, he'd had a life and a future.

He should have realized something was

seriously wrong when the guys in dark suits with no senses of humor started showing up instead of the police. At the time, Alex had hoped the feds were hanging around to find Susan. They wanted Susan, but not as a public service to find a missing person. They wanted her because of that blood.

The questions the feds asked had grown more and more bizarre. Had anyone in the family ever been abducted by aliens? Had any of them ever disappeared unaccountably for a few days? Alex had thought they were cracked. He still believed they belonged in rubber rooms, Patterson most of all.

A year after the feds took over the investigation of Susan's disappearance, things got ugly. The feds acquired a warrant for blood samples from family members. Alex got a lawyer, and it went to court. With an airtight alibi for the night of Susan's disappearance, Alex had been let off the hook. Some of the other family members hadn't been so lucky.

The feds took their samples, and the questioning went on. It had been another nine months before they got their blood sample from Alex. He had no doubts about how it happened. He had been mugged, beaten. A decent smear was all they needed. His attacker went away with more than that on his clothing.

Two days after the attack, Patterson and two of his goons dragged Alex from his home in handcuffs. He hadn't seen his family since then. Alex had no idea if he was still in Pittsburgh, no idea if his family thought he was alive or dead.

He was tortured by the idea that they were all here somewhere, even Susan.

Alex set his coffee cup down, his appetite gone, as it always was when he let himself dwell on being held captive in this room. He was let out for the endless lab tests, some of the almost endless questioning, for daily visits to a small gym in the complex, and for occasional treats of fresh air and sunshine in an enclosed courtyard. Other than that, Alex hadn't seen the outside of his room in over two years.

They allowed him books and movies to break up the boredom. They allowed Alex to keep a journal that he was sure they read when he was out of the room. He hadn't seen a news broadcast, magazine, or newspaper in his entire captivity. Alex had no idea who was president, what new stars there were in Hollywood, or what the current fashions were.

The last was almost laughable. His wardrobe never varied. The drawers were stocked with navy blue sweatpants with a broad white stripe down the outside of the legs and, when he cared to wear them, long-sleeve white t-shirts with the word 'prisoner' in navy blue on the front and back. Alex typically passed on the shirt, and he'd go stark naked in protest if the pants were stenciled in a similar manner.

The hollow sound of leather shoes on the tile floors reached Alex long before Patterson keyed his way in the door. Alex sat back on the bed and laid his head against the wall. Every day was more of the same. He could almost mouth the questions with Patterson.

Patterson took a seat across from him and eyed the tray. "Not hungry this morning, Alex?"

"Not really. I don't need any lab tests. I'm sure I'm fine." It never hurt to tell Patterson that he wasn't sick, though it might not save him from a stick in the arm to check.

"Feel like talking to me yet?"

"Sure. Breaks up the boredom."

"How did you get here, Alex?"

Alex cracked a smile. "You arrested me, remember?"

Patterson didn't smile. He never smiled. "How did you get to this planet?"

Alex rolled his eyes. "You have a birth certificate for me. I was born here...Mercy Hospital. No illegal aliens in this room, unless it's you." It was a stale joke, but there were only so many jokes he could come up with for the same questions.

"Why are you here?"

"Because you and your cracked buddies won't let me leave."

"Where would you go if I let you leave?"

Alex blinked, his smile disappearing. That was a new one. After more than two years, he didn't think there was such a thing. "Home." He forced the word out and tried not to let longing make his voice rough. He failed.

"Where is home?"

"Thirteen Sterling Street." He paused. "Unless Mom has moved while I've been in here." Alex met Patterson's cold blue eyes. "Why won't you tell me anything about my family?"

"You wouldn't want to know."

"I do." *Anything.....any news would be better than this.*

Patterson cocked his head as if he were examining a strange phenomenon. "She's dead. Your mother is dead."

Alex found it hard to breathe. "How? When?"

"A year and a half ago. Car accident. Your Uncle Joseph was with her. Both of them were D.O.A."

His pain solidified into anger. "How convenient for you. Susan's father and my mother are dead. Her mother was already dead. No one is left to fight for us."

"I won't deny that."

"I bet you won't." For a split second, Alex considered beating Patterson to a pulp. He rubbed the four-inch scar on his forearm and reminded himself why he wouldn't try that again.

"Where is Susan, Alex?"

"I should ask you that question. You probably have her locked up in another cell here. After all, you're the masters of making people disappear."

"I assure you that we don't."

"Why is she so important to you?"

"Come now. A purebred female of your kind is priceless to us."

Alex groaned. He knew better than to ask that question. Patterson's delusions were grand. They wanted Alex and Susan because, of every trace of alien blood the feds had found in the last decade, theirs was 'pure.' No one else, even in their own families, was as pure as the two of them.

Tests had been run. Alex was incapable of reproducing with 'humans.' He could have sex easily enough, if his partner didn't mind his abnormality. It was a rare disorder but harmless. His doctor had assured Alex that his body simply became overexcited at climax and dumped excess blood to his cock, making it thicken another twenty-five percent. For most women, that meant he was locked inside them until the swelling subsided, but sex was still possible. Fertilizing an egg wasn't.

The scientists had tried every trick in their arsenal. Alex's sperm wouldn't form a cohesive zygote, even with women who had a 'taint of alien blood.'

The idea of them finding Susan made him ill. Using his sperm to impregnate his first cousin smacked a little too close to inbreeding and incest for Alex's tastes.

"Do you miss it, Alex?"

"I'm too tired for games, Patterson. Miss what?"

"Sex."

"Don't start that again. Whatever the reason I was put on this Earth, I am sure it's not for your peep show. Let's see how Alex fucks. You know how Alex fucks, the same as you do, but you can have children, and I can't."

"The same except for that little expand-o-matic bit," he noted.

Alex closed his eyes and bit back a half dozen smartass comments that would get him put on punishment again.

"How does it feel?" Patterson asked.

"What?" he snapped.

"Being locked in a woman?"

Memories of hot, mindless sex had Alex rock hard in ten seconds flat. "It feels good, Patterson. Being in a woman feels really good." Despite his determination not to create a beat-off tape for Patterson, Alex missed sex more than he could bear.

"Up for a walk, Alex? I could use to stretch my legs."

"Sure. Why not?"

* * * *

Annalyssa Carpenter sat curled on the bed, her short legs pulled as tight to her chest as she could hold them. She had cried herself out days ago and screamed herself hoarse sometime not long after that. The only blessings were that she was unbound, dressed, and alone now. Anything was better than what they'd subjected her to for the first two days.

She still had no clue why she was here. Lyssa simply came home from class and found herself arrested. No one had read her the Miranda act. There was no phone call. She had simply been locked up.

Then came the worst. They'd started with blood tests. Lyssa had asked if she had some disease. No one had answered her, but no one was wearing bio-suits, so contagion was unlikely. The poking and prodding came next. They were standard examinations, and they'd allowed her a female doctor, so Lyssa went along.

When the doctor hooked up monitoring equipment and produced something that looked like a jelly vibrator, Lyssa had balked. That was when they tied her down, spread eagle, on a wide exam table. The doctor had talked her through the procedure while Lyssa pleaded with her not to do whatever she was intending to do. Lyssa hadn't bothered pleading with the grim man in the corner. She could tell instinctively that he would be no help, but the doctor had seemed like a reasonable woman...until she went on despite Lyssa's crying and protests.

Inserting the machine in a roomful of strangers was bad enough, but the results had been worse. The machine had stretched her, setting off a series of shocks in her system. Lyssa had screamed in pleasure, pulling against her bonds as she bowed up. When it was over, she'd lay shaking and crying, confused by what happened to her. It wasn't an orgasm but it was intense and as pleasurable if not more so.

The doctor had used the machine twice more, taking different tests each time. She'd recognized the ultrasound machine Dr. Bradley used with a strap over Lyssa's hips to keep her from bucking. She'd recognized the monitors used to measure uterine contractions.

Machines had taken her blood pressure, body temperature, and pulse at every stage of her reactions. A pulse oxymeter had monitored her lung function. More blood tests had been taken during and after the procedures.

Finally, Lyssa had been taken to this room

and given food. She'd fallen into an exhausted sleep before the plate was empty. They'd left her in peace for the night.

The questioning had started the next morning, crazy questions about Lyssa being an alien. She wasn't an alien, and she told them so. Her mother was Pilar Esperanza Varga, and her father was Andrew Evan Carpenter. She had a birth certificate. She had a social security card. She paid taxes.

The testing had started again. Just when Lyssa thought it couldn't get any worse; they'd added straps to her chest and hips while they used the damned machine on her. The first time they'd used the needle had been the worst. After half a dozen times, Lyssa had been numb to it. She'd made the mistake of asking what they were doing, and Bradley had replied that she was harvesting Lyssa's eggs.

Lyssa raised her head at the sound of footsteps. She knew those shoes. Bradley wore running shoes, and Patterson wore dress shoes. No one else came to her room. She cringed at the thought of another session with the cold, untouchable agent. *Not again. Dios mio, por favor. Not again.* The door opened, and she looked up fearfully.

A man stopped inside the door. He wasn't one of them. He wore the same prison pants she had on, though he was barefoot and bare-chested. If she wasn't in the situation she was, Lyssa might have come on to him, especially after seeing that chest.

His blonde hair was shaved to stubble, but

he looked like a man who would feel at home with longer hair, maybe brushing his neck. His blue eyes widened. For a heart-stopping moment, they simply stared at each other.

He turned on the suit behind him. As Lyssa guessed, it was Patterson.

"What the hell is this?" the blond man roared. "What possible reason could you have for this? I can't have children. Your eggheads told you that."

Patterson laughed. "What? You people can't recognize each other? She's one of you, a pureblood."

He took a step back, glancing at her and shaking his head. Lyssa hunched further into a ball, trying to make sense of what was going on.

"I'm not in the mood for games, Patterson."

"No games, Alex. She's a perfect match for you. Your sperm even works with this one."

His name is Alex? The name suits him.

Alex turned red in fury. His muscles bunched as if he planned to punch Patterson. "You inseminated her? Tell me you didn't inseminate her, you worthless bastard." His voice was tight and dangerous.

"Just a little Petrie dish experimentation. You have a few sons and daughters in cold storage, Daddy. I believe the count was ten out of twelve successfully fertilized."

He paled and ran a shaking hand over the stubble on his head. "What's your game, Patterson?"

"Getting sperm from you is a hell of a lot easier than getting eggs from her, even when you're not willing." His smile widened, a feral sort of smile. "I promise you, she'll enjoy your brand of sex."

Lyssa shivered. Not that she would mind getting to know Alex a whole lot better, but this wasn't her first choice for the where and how part.

Alex fisted his hand. "You want me to—" He flicked an uneasy glance at her.

"She's not ready for that. The extraction and testing procedures were rough on her. Your bodies aren't exactly made for easy study. We thought you might like to take a few days to get to know each other, some family time. The behavioral sciences department would love to see how the two of you interact."

"And if I refuse?"

God, no! Please, don't refuse. Even if you don't want to have sex with me, don't leave me with Patterson. He'll do something worse to me. I know it.

"We'll get less data, but we don't really need you. We can do in vitro on her any time we like, now that we know how her body works."

"No," Lyssa sobbed. *Not the machine.*

Patterson laughed. "Dr. Bradley thought you'd feel that way. The choice is yours, precious. You could have company, sex, all the best in life; or we could strap you down again and use the machine to inseminate you."

Alex took a menacing step toward Patterson. "Machine? What damned machine?"

"A girl's best friend, Alex. It simulates your little sexual aftereffects. Know what that reaction is for? It makes her release eggs for you, and damned if it doesn't make her feel as good as you do at that moment, even when it's artificial."

Alex searched her face for something she couldn't name. Lyssa averted her gaze. She didn't want to remember that she enjoyed it. She didn't want to admit that she had.

A hand touched her cheek, and Lyssa recoiled to the painted cinderblock wall behind her. She met Alex's eyes and sank into the concern in them, easing away from the cold stone.

"Shhh. I won't hurt you," he whispered.

Lyssa nodded.

He pushed one of her sleeves up a few inches and looked at the bruises on her wrist with a grimace. She couldn't seem to stop herself from bowing up when the pseudo-orgasms hit, and the bruises were deep and painful. He checked her ankles.

Alex stared at her, pained, swallowing some riotous emotion. "I can't decide this for you."

Lyssa looked at Patterson then grasped Alex's hand. "Don't leave me alone with him," she pleaded.

Alex nodded. "I'll try my best."

CHAPTER TWENTY-EIGHT

Alex shook in rage. "Get the hell out of here, Patterson. If I get close enough to strangle you right now, I will."

Patterson laughed. The sound turned Alex's stomach. He'd never seen Patterson smile until this morning. He wished to God that he'd never seen it.

"Glad you've seen reason, Alex."

"I haven't agreed to anything."

"Yet."

Patterson was right. He might be forced into a choice between having sex with this woman or letting them strap her down and torture her again. "Get out," he shouted, rallying the last of his shattered control.

The door closed behind Patterson, and his heels clicked down the hall.

Alex sighed as he looked at the girl. She was young. That struck him first. Her brown eyes were wide in shock and fear. Her long, dark curls were tangled around her flushed face.

"I won't hurt you," he reminded her.

She managed a shaky nod.

"What's your name?"

"Annalyssa Esperanza Carpenter." Her voice was scratchy.

"Screaming?" he asked.

She darkened. "They—"

Alex put up a hand to stop her explanation. What they did to her wasn't pretty. In some ways, it was probably much worse than the things they'd done to him. "I can guess. What do your friends call you?"

Annalyssa looked at him in confusion.

"Annalyssa? Anna?" he prodded.

"Lyssa."

He smiled. "Well Lyssa, my name is Alexander Joseph Braeden. Most people call me Alex."

She managed a weak smile.

"How old are you?" He had a hundred questions. It had been ages since he'd had anyone to talk to.

"Nineteen. You?"

"Twenty-five. How long have you been here?"

She paled.

Not long.

"Umm... I'm not really sure. Three days, I think. What about you?"

Alex hesitated. He didn't want to scare her. "Too long."

Lyssa wiped away a tear. "How long? A month? Six months?"

"Two years."

Her face lost the last of its color. "No, Alex. Please— You're joking, right?"

He took her hand. "I wish I was."

"There's no hope, is there?"

Alex kissed her hand, fighting the urge to touch her. If he kept touching her, he wasn't sure he'd ever be able to stop. "You have me." *As much of me as you want.* Alex closed his eyes. Had he just forgotten how good women smelled? How soft they were? "We'll figure something out."

He knew that part was a lie. There was no way out but in a body bag, unless Patterson opened the door for them. In other words, they'd be here or someplace like it until they died.

Alex looked at the bruises on Lyssa's wrist. He met her gaze and kissed a bruise. Visions of Lyssa tied down raced through his mind. Alex wanted to put Patterson through a wall for doing this to her.

He wished he could erase the memories from her mind. Alex kissed the bruise again, feeling her pulse race under his lips, drinking in her musk. It was becoming more potent. He was sure it was.

Lyssa cried out and stiffened, pulling her arm away from him. Her eyes were wide and wild. She rubbed at the spot he'd kissed, examining it as if searching for more damage...or leery of any touch after putting up with that of Patterson's goons.

Alex tucked his hands under his arms miserably. He'd pushed too hard, moved too fast. He was starved for companionship, and she wasn't ready for more than talking. Who could blame her for that? If getting eggs from her was harder than getting sperm from him, he shuddered to think about what it had been like for her.

"I'm sorry. I won't—"

Lyssa scrambled to her feet and dragged him with her to the bathroom. Alex stumbled after her, his confusion growing as she slammed the door behind them.

"I'm sorry," he repeated. "It's been so long. I

won't—"

"What did you do?"

"I kissed—"

Lyssa shook her head and extended her wrist toward him. "What did you do?"

Alex touched the perfect skin over her pulse point. It was marred only moments ago. There wasn't a break in the bruising then. "I don't know."

"You healed it. Do it again."

His heart pounded in his ears. She wanted him to touch her...to kiss her again? "Lyssa—"

"Please, Alex." Her eyes pleaded with him for a simple touch.

He nodded and turned her wrist, pressing his lips to the marred flesh.

Lyssa furrowed her brow. "Nothing's happening."

Something was happening. Her sweet smell was getting to him. Alex kissed her bruised wrist again.

She whimpered. "Yes. Alex, please."

Alex circled her wrist, brushing his lips over her, tasting her pulse with the tip of his tongue. He met her eyes. Lyssa pushed back the sleeve on her other arm and offered her wrist to him slowly, her eyes begging for more of his touch.

He took her hand, raising it to his mouth. Lyssa locked on the movement, her breathing irregular. Alex twirled his tongue on her skin, and Lyssa started to shake. His touch healed her, excited her, excited him. He wanted to run his fingers in the vee of her legs. She would be hot and wet, he knew.

Lyssa looked up at him again, needing more than his healing. Alex lifted her to the edge of the sink and raised one ankle. He hardened at the sight of her spread open before him with that look of longing on her face. Lyssa dropped her head back as his lips touched her.

He healed her, his eyes straying to the dampness gathering in the crotch of her sweatpants, aching to make use of the position he'd put her in.

She didn't react when Alex lowered her ankle and switched to the other. He was shaking by the time he lowered the second ankle. There was a fire in his blood for her, a desire to strip her and take her on the countertop.

"Where else?" he asked.

Lyssa raised her shirt to just below her breasts. Alex saw the two bruises extending below the waistline of her sweats. He knelt between her knees, peeling her pants down to uncover the bruises and fighting the urge to peel them further. Her arousal teased his nose. Alex wanted to bury his tongue in her, to taste the musk he knew was seeping from her for him.

Alex moved his attention back to the bruises and sucked in his breath at the sight of the damage. *This was an egg harvest. This is where they took her eggs. I have children with this woman, children Patterson is holding hostage in cold storage.* Why did that thought make him feel possessive of her, protective?

Lyssa stifled a cry as he started healing her. Her musk tantalized his senses. Alex touched her, feeling her thigh muscles bunching under his fingers as his tongue completed its slow dance over her stomach. She jolted lightly to his touch, and her smell changed to a more fragrant, enticing scent. He didn't need to ask if she'd come for him. She had.

Alex pushed to his feet, gathering her to his chest. He shook in his need to take her, to taste her climax and plunge into the depths of her and drive her over again. Lyssa wasn't ready for that. When she was— If she was—

Oh, God. I'm going insane.

Lyssa kissed his bare chest. "Alex?"

"Hmm..."

"You won't let them inseminate me, will you?"

He hardened further. "What are you asking me?" Alex had to ask. He had to understand exactly what her intentions were.

"If— I want you, not some machine and straps and—" She shuddered.

"And what, Lyssa?"

"Patterson watching," she whispered.

Alex nodded. "Tell me you're willing, and you'll have me when you're ready. You have my word." He lifted her to her feet. "We should go back out."

Lyssa nodded and followed him toward the door. Alex stopped in the doorway, staring at Patterson and willing himself not to do anything stupid. He moved to block the agent's view of Lyssa, suddenly wary.

How lost had Alex been that he hadn't heard Patterson key back in? He had Lyssa now. He couldn't let his guard down.

"What do you want, Patterson?"

"Just curious. I was wondering..."

His smile disappeared as Lyssa wrapped her arms around Alex. Patterson took a step toward them but stopped when Alex shot him a menacing look.

"How the hell did you do that?" Patterson demanded. "The bruises—"

Alex laced his fingers through Lyssa's. "She's mine, Patterson. You'll have to kill me to take her. You can't separate mates in our race," he bluffed.

"I thought you didn't know anything about your race," he challenged.

Alex shrugged. "I know that. Call it instinct. Call it species memory. I know we won't thrive alone now that we have each other." *I won't thrive alone. He can't take her from me now.*

* * * *

Lyssa snuggled to Alex's chest. So far, what he'd told Patterson had worked. The fact that Alex was still here, curled in bed with her in his arms, was proof of that.

The bed in her room was a full-size, but it was better than the twin Alex said he spent the last two years on. Alex suggested that it was by design, that the room they now shared was intended for an alien couple. His clothing, books, and videos had been moved to the room for them.

For the last two days, they'd cuddled on the

bed, watching movies and joking that they needed a bowl of buttered popcorn, reading, and talking. Alex had devoured news of the outside world. Lyssa shuddered to consider two years with nothing outside of these walls.

Alex hadn't pressed her for more than her company, but he spent much of their time together touching her face, holding her hand, kissing her forehead, and trying to hide his almost constant state of arousal from her. Alex hadn't had sex since he got here. When they'd tried to convince him, he'd refused.

His arms tightened around her in his sleep, as if he had to assure himself that she was still there, even in an unconscious state. And maybe he did; Lyssa found herself searching him out, every time he left her line of sight, even pacing or trembling when he was closed behind the bathroom door.

Alex shifted, and the hard ridge of his cock brushed her thigh. She sucked in a breath, the unique scent that was Alex filling her lungs and making her dizzy. Lyssa's mouth went dry, and warm tendrils snaked over her body, knotting tight in her womb. Just that quickly, one innocent touch, and she wanted him. Her skin flushed with heat. She was wet and aching for him.

Lyssa feathered a kiss over his lips. "Alex," she whispered.

Alex sighed in his sleep.

She reached for him under the blankets, slipping her hand in the elastic waist of his sweats and circling him. Alex rocked his hips, sliding between her fingers with a moan.

"Oh, Lyssa." His voice caressed her lips, as he cupped her face with one large hand and brought his mouth down on hers. Alex was ravenous, his tongue plunging into her, his lips hard and his breathing ragged.

Lyssa stroked him in invitation.

Alex trailed his hands down her throat and chest, cupping the weight of her breasts in his hands and testing the sensitivity of her aching nipples. One hand slid lower, his fingers nudging her thighs apart and easing inside her panties to glide through the cream her body seemed unable to stop producing for him.

Lyssa gasped against his still-questing tongue, tipping her hips to capture his fingers inside her. She shuddered, rocking against his hand.

His lips trailed to her ear, the position gifting her the stronger scent at his throat. She'd always loved a man's musk, but this was more potent. She wanted to leave a love bite, just to taste him.

"You know Patterson wants this," he reminded her in a whisper.

"I don't care. *I* want this." She wasn't exaggerating. If Alex shut her down, she'd go insane. Lyssa pulled at the waistband of his sweats, running her fingertips through the soft curls at the base of his cock.

Alex pulled back and met her eyes. "Be sure. If I go much further—"

Lyssa fisted the hem of her t-shirt and started to drag it up.

He slid the hand from her breast down to

stop her. "Not yet. Give me a few minutes."

She released the shirt and nodded, wondering why he was so adamant that she not get undressed yet.

Alex pulled his hands away, licking her cream from his fingertips and favoring her with a hungry look that made her go weak and feverish. He straightened his sweats and rose slowly.

Alex wedged the chair under the doorknob and kicked it tight. Lyssa furrowed her brow at that. What was he doing? Why now?

He dragged shirts from the drawer and knotted them over the two security cameras. Lyssa blushed in understanding. If she had pulled off her shirt, the free show for their captors would have begun.

They weren't going to like losing video. She glanced at the chair. *But they'll have a hell of a time getting in with the door wedged shut.*

His eyes glittered in the dim light that was on all night. Alex stripped off his sweats, baring muscular thighs and an incredibly aroused cock. He was a fantasy come true. Alex was six feet two and eyes of blue embodied, broad and muscular and all hers.

He headed for the bed. "I promised," he explained as he slid in next to her. "I promised he wouldn't watch."

"Thank you. I forgot that—"

She forgot what she wanted to say as his fingers returned to her panties. He peeled them off while he nuzzled her throat. Lyssa dropped her head back, baring her neck to him as Alex explored from one jaw line to the other.

"I have to see you, Lyssa."

She nodded, dragging her t-shirt off and dropping it off the edge of the bed. Alex pulled the blankets back and tossed her panties over his shoulder. He moved his gaze over her as if he couldn't decide what to do first. Alex spread her thighs, his eyes questioning. Lyssa moved closer to his hand, closing her eyes as his fingers sank through her folds again.

Lyssa bowed up as Alex's tongue circled her clit. He started off tentative. Every move Alex made was careful. Every touch was like a firestorm across her nerves. Lyssa wasn't aware of his increasing fervor as much as the pressure building in her.

She moaned as her sex swelled, not just her outer sex but her womb felt full and heavy. Her nipples peaked. Tremors started deep in her stomach and radiated out, up to her breasts and lips, down to where his tongue swirled in and out, his fingertips spreading her for his invasion. Lyssa screamed, her body tensing, on the edges of a shattering release.

Alex settled over her, his mouth pulling at her nipples, suckling her. The tremors increased. Lyssa took his cock in her trembling fingers and started to push him back to take him in her mouth. Alex pushed back, guiding her hand away and brushing his cock over her spasming core.

"I can't wait," he breathed. "I'm sorry. I can't be slow this time."

Lyssa nodded.

Alex slid into her, grumbling comments

through gritted teeth. "So hot. Too tight. I can't, Lyssa. I'll hurt you."

She wrapped her legs around him before Alex could withdraw. "You won't. Please. I know what will happen. I want you, not that machine. Please, Alex."

He kissed her gently, sliding deeper in her. Alex moaned into her mouth, his muscles rippling under her hands. His movements became more fevered, his mouth more insistent as he took her deeper and harder. She knew he was close when his body started to tremble.

Alex bucked deep, arching his back and driving her hips into the mattress. His shout echoed off the painted cinderblock walls as his cock started to spasm and hot come invaded every corner of her. He swelled, stilling when he was locked inside her.

Lyssa cried out as the pressure set off the shocks and pushed her over the edge again. She contracted around his length, his body pressed into hers and his breath tickling her lips. They stared at each other, stunned into silence.

"How long...?" Lyssa whispered. They'd tried varying times with the machine, some long enough to make her heart stutter in exhaustion.

Alex shook his head. "It varies. A few minutes, at least. The stronger the orgasm, the longer it lasts."

She blushed. "It was good for you?"

He managed a strangled laugh. "I wouldn't be surprised if it lasted an hour. I have never come that hard and fast before."

"Thank you, Alex."

He sobered. "For saving you from insemination?"

"No. For making love to me. For being so attentive."

Alex lowered his lips to hers. "I'll take my time next time. You have my word."

They blinked in the sudden brightness as the lights were turned up.

Lyssa sighed. "After this message from our friendly neighborhood captors?"

* * * *

Alex smiled at the heavy-handed knock on the door. Since the cameras were still covered, they weren't sure that the chair had been moved. He squeezed Lyssa's hand in comfort, and she offered him a strained smile.

"Come in, Patterson," he called out.

Lyssa smoothed her t-shirt over her sweatpants and nestled to his side. Alex wrapped an arm around her as Patterson keyed in and the door swung wide.

Patterson sauntered in, his hair disheveled and his tie askew as if he had been roused from bed to come deal with them. He shot them a weary look and dropped into the chair. He motioned to the cameras. "That is unacceptable."

Alex's smile disappeared. "We'll uncover them during the day, but you're not watching us make love."

"Total monitoring. That's not possible. We have to know what you're doing."

"We're not making love like that. We're not lab animals."

Patterson darkened and sent a hard look at Lyssa. "You could be."

Lyssa's hand fisted in Alex's shirt.

He stroked her hand in response. "I promised," he whispered. "I know I promised."

Lyssa nodded. "Infrared," she suggested.

"What?"

"They can see us on infrared, basic outlines but no real definition."

Alex grinned, biting back a laugh. "Perfect. What do you say, Patterson?" He didn't bother to look at the other man.

"I'll run it past them. It'll probably fly. In the meantime, uncover those cameras."

Alex nodded. "Don't take too long. We're still covering them for the times we make love." He shot Patterson a quelling look before he could protest. "The sound effects will be sufficient."

Patterson sighed, stuck between his urge to follow the letter of the rules and his urge to have Alex and Lyssa agree to mating. The sight of Patterson so out of control of a situation made Alex smile.

The agent nodded. "Your food will be delivered in a few hours. Is there anything special we should be feeding you?"

Lyssa looked at him in confusion. "Like?" she prodded.

"What foods should your diet include once you're pregnant?"

She blanched and looked to Alex for assistance.

He nodded in understanding. "Wing it, Patterson. She'll crave anything extra she needs."

Patterson yawned. "If you're done disrupting my night, I think I'll get a few more hours in before I start the day."

Alex raised an eyebrow. "If you're done disrupting our night, I'll get back to my mate." He reveled in using the term, in making himself separate from Patterson and the whole human race. As long as Patterson thought they were separate, he would heed Alex's warning—he hoped.

Patterson scowled at them as he disappeared around the door.

When he was gone, Alex turned and drew Lyssa onto his lap, facing him so they could talk in whispers that the mics might miss. "I'm sorry. Pregnancy isn't something I can avoid, considering the circumstances."

She wrapped her arms around his shoulders. "It's not that. As long as it's with you, I can accept that."

He massaged her shoulders, growing hard for another round with her proximity...and the delightful scent of their mixed orgasm. "Then what?"

"What happens when I am, Alex? They can't separate us, can they? You said—" She swallowed a sob.

Alex cursed the lie. She thought he knew what he was doing. He had to give her hope. "No. They can't," he assured her. "We need each other."

"And the baby?"

"I don't know. I think that's part of the deal. I don't know."

CHAPTER TWENTY-NINE

November 23rd, 2006

Alex dragged Lyssa's t-shirt off over her head and suckled a nipple, his movements hungry and urgent. It seemed he couldn't get enough of her. They had been together for two months, and he still covered the cameras as often as she seemed receptive, and Lyssa was receptive more often than he'd ever dared hope.

Sometimes their lovemaking was slow and tender, but other times neither of them seemed to have any patience. This was one of the latter.

Lyssa stepped forward around his knees, as Alex sank to the edge of the bed, her hands pushing his sweats down his thighs with a curse that announced her drive. Her drive had been particularly strong the last two days. It seemed the cameras had been covered more than uncovered.

Patterson gave them a blissful reprieve from his presence, probably believing they were in the midst of some alien fertile cycle. He sobered. Alex couldn't be sure that Patterson was wrong about that one. Something was affecting Lyssa, though he didn't know what it was.

She pulled his hands to her hips. Alex lifted her slightly, and she spread her legs further for his first thrust, her toes brushing the floor as she settled into his lap around his length. Lyssa draped her hands over his shoulders to balance herself as she eased up and down by the strength of her thighs.

Lyssa was vocal; her cries of pleasure echoing off the walls of their room. She had developed a certain disregard for the monitors that Alex admired. He had years of practice ignoring them, but it was new to her.

Alex rode harder into her, his possession an opiate as always. "That's right, baby. Oh, I love you, Lyssa."

She shuddered and dropped to his chest with a choked cry of release. Alex followed her over, trembling uncontrollably as his cock linked them. Lyssa offered a weak cry then stifled a sob in his chest, and Alex tensed.

He nuzzled her face in comfort but also as a show for the infrared camera. "What is it?" he whispered, laying a kiss near her ear.

Lyssa stifled another sob. "I'm not releasing eggs."

Alex stilled, his heart pounding as he considered the possibilities. "Are you sure?"

"The sparks— That feeling isn't there anymore. Patterson and Bradley said— Are they right?"

He closed his eyes. Alex wished he knew for sure, but if Bradley's tests showed that was what happened, he'd be inclined to believe it. "Do you think—" He swallowed hard.

"When else do women stop releasing them?"

"Can you fake it?"

"I have been for three days. I'm scared Alex."

"I know. We'll hide it as long as we can."

* * * *

Lyssa huddled under the blanket, shivering in the room that Alex assured her was warm. It was getting worse, and she didn't know how to stop it. She was cold, always cold. Alex could heal the headaches and massage away the aches and pains, but he couldn't heal the bone-deep chill. They had been hiding the baby for more than a week, but they couldn't keep hiding it, if this kept up.

Alex crawled into the bed behind her and started massaging her shoulders and back. He laid healing kisses on her neck. "You could be sick," he reasoned against her skin.

"Does it matter? If I ask for more blankets or complain, they'll run tests—"

"They'll find out eventually. If you're sick, they can treat it. If it's part of your pregnancy, they'll give us heavier clothes and blankets without a fight."

The door opened without warning. Lyssa held her breath as Patterson strode in. He headed to the bed and reached for her.

Alex knocked his hand away from her, wrapping his arms around Lyssa before Patterson could protest the move. "You don't touch her," he growled.

"Territorial," Patterson noted. "I'm trying to help. You can see she's sick, Alex."

He didn't answer. Alex dropped his forehead to her shoulder, letting Lyssa make the decision of how to proceed.

"You have to let us help her," the agent argued.

Lyssa shrank closer to Alex's body. "I don't need help. I need heavier clothes and blankets."

Patterson's eyes widened. "You're fevering?" He placed his hand on her face and pulled back before Alex could land his blow. "Cold," he mused. "What is this?"

Lyssa closed her eyes. There was no way to hide it. Patterson thought she was sick. They'd do blood tests now. "I'm pregnant."

"How far?"

"About two weeks, I think." She didn't know. Could it be further? She only knew when the eggs stopped.

"Come with me," he ordered.

Lyssa hesitated and met his eyes. There was something empty in those eyes that frightened her. She laced her fingers through Alex's.

"Just you," Patterson qualified.

"No. It doesn't work that way."

Alex sat up, drawing her with him and tucking the blanket around her. "We can't be separated."

Patterson rubbed his forehead. "We need to run a few tests, Alex. You're obviously unstable. We can't have you attacking our medical team."

"Treat her right, and I won't. You have my word."

Patterson eyed them critically. "Not good enough." He slapped a breather over his face.

Alex tried to launch off the bed with her in his arms, but the mist was already settling around them. He fell back, his arms tightening around her as if he could fight off the inevitable with enough force of will.

Patterson pushed Alex off of her and hoisted Lyssa into his arms. She locked with Alex's blue eyes for an instant before the mist won.

* * * *

"Dammit, I want a sonogram on her," Patterson thundered.

Bradley huffed. "We can't. Whatever that block is, we can't scan through it."

"Cervical endoscopic?"

"We can't take the chance. If we damage the block, we could cause her to miscarry or bleed to death. I can't see what's inside it. If there are major blood vessels, I could kill her."

Something crashed. "You're telling me we can't do anything?" he demanded.

"Not a sonogram for three or four more months. We're stuck with blood tests, for the time being."

"Doctor," a new voice cut in.

"Thanks." Paper rustled.

Lyssa opened her eyes. The room spun around her. Everything was surrounded by halos of color, and sickening light trails accompanied her eye movements. She pulled at the straps weakly. She was naked and tied down, but blankets were piled on her to stabilize her temperature. Her head and neck ached. She needed Alex and his healing.

"God damn it," Bradley exclaimed.

"What is it?" Patterson asked, his voice strained.

Bradley ignored him, hovering over Lyssa. "Good. She's awake again."

Lyssa fought her dry mouth. She'd been awake before? She couldn't remember it if she had.

"Annalyssa, there is a toxin in your system we can't identify. What do we need to do?"

"Alex," she whispered. "I need Alex." Alex would heal her. He'd know what to do. They couldn't separate them.

"Annalyssa, listen to me. The toxin in your body has tripled in the last eight hours. I need to know how to stop this."

"Alex. Please, let Alex stop it."

"Maybe we should—"

Patterson snorted. "He's unstable."

"Maybe it's instinct to protect his mate. There may be a biological precedent we don't know about."

"Maybe. What else can we do?"

Bradley shrugged. Watching it hurt Lyssa's eyes.

"Food, water, keep everything natural, keep her warm, keep monitoring her— We can't treat this. If she doesn't pull out of it, you'll have to let Alex—"

"If, Bradley. If."

"Untie her. She can't fight you."

* * * *

"Eat, Annalyssa."

Lyssa opened her eyes. She'd lost track of

the days. Her waking moments had no real meaning to her. Thinking was difficult. At first, she didn't eat because she was so heartsick for Alex. Now, she couldn't eat. Everything made her sick.

A block of cheese touched her lips. She turned her head away, gagging.

"I can't," she forced out. Lyssa turned to the edge of the bed and heaved air. She fell back to the pillow weakly.

Dr. Bradley supported her head and brought a cup to her lips. "Drink some water."

Lyssa swallowed twice then brought it up onto the floor. She groaned. Her entire body hurt.

"What do you need? Tell me what to do."

"Thirsty," she croaked.

"More water?"

"No." Lyssa bit back a sob. Her eyes focused on the tray beside her. She grabbed the cup of milk, sloshing some over her hand as she brought it to her lips. She drank the milk and held the cup out to Dr. Bradley with shaking hands.

"More?" the gray-haired woman asked.

Lyssa nodded and collapsed to the bed.

* * * *

"I can't stop this. You have to let Alex try or she'll die. The toxin has taken over."

A hand touched her cheek, and Lyssa screamed in agony. Air moving over her skin hurt. That simple touch was like a punch.

"She's dying, Patterson. Her temperature is down to ninety-five degrees from ninety-nine. She's shivering and sweating. I can't identify the toxin, and I can't stabilize her."

"You said milk would do that," he growled.

"It temporarily forces a plateau, but she can't drink it anymore. I'm not even sure what she needs in it. Shots of vitamin A, D, and calcium have all failed to recreate the plateau. It could be the lactose or milk fat or one of the proteins. She'll die before I know for sure."

"Is there any other option?"

"Abort. That might stabilize her. It might not. I don't know enough about her physiology to know for sure."

"Unacceptable."

"Then there *is* no choice. Give her to Alex."

* * * *

Alex lay on his bed, staring at the walls. He had no urge to do anything else.

He had screamed himself hoarse and destroyed the room when he'd woken from the gas in his old cell. They weren't bringing her back to him. They'd gassed him again as he lay in the wreckage.

He hadn't bothered to destroy the room again. He hadn't bothered to scream obscenities at the mics for Patterson. Alex had curled on the bed and stared at the walls much as he was doing now. For the last four days, he'd left the bed only to use the bathroom. Alex hadn't managed more than a few bites of anything they tried to entice him to eat. The only thing that mattered to him was Lyssa and their baby.

Patterson had only come in twice. The first time, he'd stood inside the door with a taser in his hand.

Alex had looked at the weapon and closed his eyes. "How is she?" he'd croaked. They had taken her from him sometime the day before, and he was sure that Lyssa had been subjected to test after test after test in the interim.

"Sick. I told you she was sick."

"I need to see her. I won't cause trouble. I have to—" He'd choked off, realizing that he was repeating himself.

"Tell us what to do for her, Alex."

Alex had swallowed a sour wave. They didn't know what they were doing. "I don't know," he admitted.

"You mean you won't tell us."

"I need to see her."

"No." Patterson scrubbed his hand over his mouth. "By not telling us, you're hurting her."

He cursed telling them he knew what he was doing. They thought he had all the answers. "By keeping us apart, you're hurting us both."

Patterson had stormed away, furious that Alex wouldn't give them the information they needed, the information he didn't have.

The second time had been worse. Patterson had paced the room, looking harried and unshaven. He'd rounded on Alex with the promise of pain in his eyes. "Goddamn it, Alex.

Talk to me."

Alex had stared at him. There was nothing he could tell Patterson. For the first time, he'd wished there were.

"What is happening to her?" Patterson demanded.

"She's pregnant."

Patterson glared at him. "There's more to this. There has to be."

"You separated us."

"Convince me. What is happening to her?"

"She has a headache. She's in pain. Her muscles ache. She's cold, shivering."

"You can do something about that?"

Alex had nodded, praying that it was true.

"What? Tell me, and we'll do it for her."

He'd choked on a laugh, remembering Lyssa's shock when he'd healed her bruised wrist. "You can't. I have to touch her. There's no other way. You can't do it."

"Why not."

Alex had shot him a cynical smile. "You're *human*."

Patterson had taken a step back, stunned by his bald statement. "You're admitting what you are openly?"

"I don't know what I am, but people like you make me proud to say I'm not human."

Patterson had seemed to consider that, running a hand through his mussed hair and staring for a moment at the far wall. "You can reverse everything?"

Something in his tone had started a panic in Alex. "I don't know until I see her, do I?"

He'd stopped pacing, his face set in fury. "The toxin, Alex. Can you undo that?"

Alex hadn't been able catch his breath. They were killing her. "I need to see her."

Patterson had stormed away again. For two days, Alex hadn't seen him.

And now, he was coming back. Alex could hear Patterson's heels on the tile in the hall. The door swung open.

Patterson wasn't angry anymore. He looked haunted. His face was pale. He wore the same suit he had two days earlier, and Alex was fairly certain that he hadn't showered or slept much since then. That was fine with Alex. He hadn't either.

Alex stared at him, barely breathing. Patterson was at some impasse. Either Lyssa needed Alex badly enough that he'd relented, or she wasn't ever coming back. If they stabilized her without him, they wouldn't need Alex to help her. If she died in their care, they'd have to kill him next. He'd force them to kill him next, and he'd take Patterson with him if he could.

"I was surviving alone, Patterson. You brought Lyssa to me. If I lose her and my baby, I have nothing to live for. I can't go back to the way it was before her."

"Come with me."

Alex stared at him. *One word. I only need the word that she's alive.*

"She needs you, Alex."

He closed his eyes, thanking God for her life.

"Now, Braeden! I won't tell you again."

Alex pushed to his feet, weaving toward the

door. Patterson led him back to the room he'd shared with Lyssa.

The smell hit him first, the sour smell that set off a pure panic in him. He pushed Dr. Bradley away from her and knelt next to Lyssa, touching her face. "She's so cold."

Lyssa was wrapped in layers of blankets, but she was shivering. Her hair was plastered to her head with sweat, and her lips were cracked.

Dr. Bradley cleared her throat to get his attention. "Her temperature has dropped to ninety-three degrees, Alex. What can you do?"

"Get out."

"Alex, let me help."

"You can't. Don't you think I wish you could? Get out. Don't come back unless I ask you to. You can see and hear me." He met her earnest green eyes. "Go away. Please."

Bradley nodded and dragged Patterson with her. The door closed behind them.

Alex cradled Lyssa to his chest and stroked her cheek. "Lyssa? Baby, it's me. Talk to me."

She didn't respond. She didn't open her eyes. Her breathing was shallow and her skin unnaturally pale.

"Please, God. I don't ask for much. Let this work." He kissed her forehead, letting the memories of Lyssa in his arms fill his mind.

Lyssa groaned and shuddered.

"That's right. Come back for me, Lyssa. I can't do this alone." He kissed her again, running his lips over her face and back to her forehead. That would do her the most good, that and her spine. He didn't know how he knew that, but he did.

"Hurts," she whimpered.

"I'll make it better, Lyssa. I promise I will." He worked his hands under the blankets and started massaging her neck and shoulders.

Lyssa started to cry. "It *hurts*."

"I know, baby."

She was tense, her muscles in knots. Alex sighed as they started relaxing under his hands. He kissed her forehead again then looked at her in shock. A milky substance was coating her skin, leeching out of her pores, foul-smelling and oily slick.

Alex peeled the blankets off of her and swept her into the bathroom. He had to wash it off. Maybe it was simply his disgust with seeing that slime on her skin, but Alex doubted it. He knew, without a doubt, that he couldn't let it stay on her. It was poison of some sort, and it would kill Lyssa if he didn't cleanse it from her.

He filled the tub with hot water and peeled off Lyssa's clothes. Alex furrowed his brow as the water turned milky and more droplets appeared on her skin as he washed them away. The concept was right but the bath wasn't washing it away quickly enough.

Alex let out the water and pulled off his sweatpants, cradling Lyssa to his chest under the hot spray of the shower. When the slime stopped appearing, Alex started massaging and using his healing kisses on her again. The slime started seeping from her pores in response.

He sighed in understanding. Patterson said there was a toxin in her system. Alex was forcing it out of her, and he couldn't stop until it stopped appearing on her skin. Two rounds of washing later, Lyssa was aware of Alex and what he was saying. Four more rounds, and the toxin stopped leeching from her.

Lyssa was still pale and shaky, but she was on her feet. Alex dried her carefully and wrapped her in the heavy robe hung on the back of the bathroom door. He wrapped a towel around his waist. Lyssa shivered now that she was out of the hot spray.

Alex wrapped an arm around her. "We'll get you in clothes," he assured her.

Her stomach growled.

He laughed at her sheepish look. "And get food in you. You haven't been eating, have you?"

"No more than you have."

Alex nodded and pushed the door open. Patterson sat on the edge of the freshly made bed. His eyes narrowed as he locked on Lyssa. For a moment, none of them moved. Alex felt a spike of irritation that the agent could intrude on every happy moment this way.

"Come with me," Patterson ordered.

Alex tightened his grip on Lyssa. "Not without me. You can't separate us. Haven't you learned that yet?"

"We have to test to see if she's stabilized."

"Send Bradley here or take me with her."

"Alex—"

"She's stabilized," he argued. "The toxins are gone. All she needs now is food, sleep, and warm clothes."

"Warm clothes are covered. There are

sweatshirts and heavy socks in the drawers. The tests will only take half an hour. You have my word. If she's stable, she's coming back."

"She's coming back, either way. You can't help her. What if she needs me? I'm coming with her."

Patterson pulled a slim handgun from his pocket and turned it on them. "Not this time."

Alex pressed Lyssa to the wall and blocked her with his body. Was Patterson insane? He could kill her. The sound of compressed air behind him answered Alex's question. The dart struck him in the shoulder.

He locked eyes with Lyssa as his knees buckled. She screamed, trying to hold Alex as he crumpled to the floor.

Patterson pulled her back, brandishing the handgun at her. "Don't make me drug you, Annalyssa. I don't know what it will do to the baby, and it will slow down your blood tests. Half an hour, and you'll be back with Alex. You have my word."

Lyssa looked to Alex with tears in her eyes; her hand feathered over her abdomen. He understood before she turned away. Lyssa was afraid for the baby and was begging Alex to understand her reason for not fighting this. She didn't want to go with Patterson, but she couldn't take that chance. Alex wished he had some way to put her at ease.

He watched the door shut behind them, drawing painful breaths and fighting for consciousness. He seemed to lose several minutes, but he couldn't be sure of that. When he was able, Alex stumbled his way to the locked door. He punched it in frustration and sank to the floor.

"Patterson," he growled, knowing they'd replay the tape for him if he wasn't watching. "You listen to me, you unspeakable bastard. You don't know what you're screwing around with. You bring her back, and don't ever do this to us again. I promise you'll regret it, if you do."

Alex donned a pair of sweatpants and sat on the edge of the bed, his elbows on his knees. She was gone longer than half an hour but not by much. Lyssa crossed the room into his arms. Dr. Bradley stepped into the doorway, and Alex looked around her for Patterson. He was nowhere to be seen, and Alex relaxed.

Bradley nodded. "Her temp is back to ninety-eight. The toxin is just a trace in her blood stream. She's stable, Alex."

"I told Patterson she was," he noted.

"I'll have to take readings for the next few days to monitor her.....a few times a day."

Alex shot her a look of mistrust.

"Here. I'll come here."

He nodded.

"Promise me you'll be calm, and I'll talk Patterson into letting you accompany her for internals and sonograms. We've always been straight with each other, Alex."

"One condition. Just us and your staff. I know Patterson will watch via the cameras, but I don't want him in the room with us."

"That will take a little work."

"We've always been straight with each other.

You keep them away from my family, and you've got a calm alien Daddy."

Bradley cracked a smile. "I'll do my best."

CHAPTER THIRTY

Pri 26th, Ri 25-2991

Jole wrapped an arm around Susan as they followed Pyter into the meeting room at the medical center. They had no idea what this meeting was about, which made being summoned here this way worse. He took stock of the men assembled at the table. Dr. Peri was flanked by Till from the Breeding Office, Sayd from the Church Ethics Committee, and Daje from the Council of Worlds.

Susan sucked in her breath. "This doesn't bode well, Joel."

He squeezed her hand in reassurance, though being summoned before this board less than four months after Kell's death chilled him. "What is the meaning of this?" Jole demanded.

Till motioned to the two comfortable chairs across the table from the bureaucrats. "Sit please." His eyes scanned Susan, as she lowered herself into one of the chairs and Pyter took his place behind her. "You are well, Majesty?"

She nodded.

Jole stiffened. Susan was a month into her third pregnancy. If Till was worried about her health, it was a bad sign. Jole sent the man a quelling look, and Till darkened.

"Explain this summons," he demanded again.

Till cleared his throat. "There is a serious situation requiring discussion, Majesty."

Jole waved his hand for Till to continue.

"Pyter requested a search of records when the gateway realigned for scanning of electronic media. He wished us to search for news of Queen Susan's family to ease her mind."

Susan stiffened. "And?"

Till lowered his eyes. "I am sorry, Majesty. Your father was lost in an accident of an Earth conveyance almost two years ago."

Her hand gripped Jole's under the table. She took a calming breath, refusing to break down in this company. "Thank you, Till." Susan looked away, fighting to control her emotions.

Till seemed at a loss for words. "You— Your father had a sister, Janice Braeden?"

Susan nodded mutely.

"She was in the conveyance with him. She— did not survive."

She closed her eyes. "Alex?"

Till didn't answer.

"Please, Till. If he's dead, tell me."

"He's alive."

Susan stared at him, her eyes brimming with unshed tears.

"He's a prisoner of some sort, not a common criminal, I assure you. We're having difficulty discerning his crime from the file we have liberated from their database."

Jole nodded. "Why this meeting?"

Peri stepped in. "The one part of his file that's clear to us is the medical reports. Alex is a third-generation male, and they know it."

Susan shook her head. "But that would mean Aunt Janice was a second-generation

393

female."

Till shrugged. "It happens at times. We implanted your father, knowing his mother was receptive and sexually active. She wed her mate."

"And he was a first-generation male," she guessed. "Dad was a first-generation male and Aunt Janice was a second-generation female from the same mother."

"Yes."

"Alex's father was a first-generation?"

"Yes. Janice spent more than two years with him, but I suppose they had a limited contract to a child."

Susan blushed. "Something like that. If he is a third-generation male, why didn't you bring him through the gateway with me? He was over the age of adulthood."

Till cocked his head in confusion. "He was male."

She shot Jole a weary look that announced her feeling of exasperation with the old mindset from before she introduced Hugam. She groaned. "Give me his file."

Till nodded. "We knew you would ask. Actually, we could use your expertise in deciphering the logic of the file." He slid a thick stack of papers across to her and shook his head. "I left it in English for you. If you'd prefer Keen—"

"No. Your translator program is a little stiff. English will be faster for me." She scanned her eyes over the information, turning pages quickly in the silence of the room. "His crime is *being* a third-generation re-bred. They don't understand that lesser Keen cross-breds are breeding stronger stock with the dominance of many Keen genes. They think he's a pure-blood alien." She turned a page, and her eyes widened. "I need a scan gateway," she ordered.

Till motioned to the corner of the room behind the door. Susan gathered up the file and took it with her. As usual, Till had provided her with an English keyboard. She typed for several minutes in silence. A young woman's face filled a quarter of the screen. Susan glanced at it and started reading the file that accompanied it.

Jole looked over her shoulder. "Who is she?" he asked.

"His mate."

"An Earth woman," Peri decided.

"No. A third-generation re-bred female," Susan corrected him.

"That's impossible," Till decided. "They'd have to be mating him with a girl of nine years. Are they capable of gene manipulation and implantation."

Susan shook her head. "Oh, they're capable of a lot, but their attempts to splice his sperm with humans or second-generation females failed. *Oh, God!*"

Jole startled at her use of the English expression in this venue. It wasn't like Susan to slip out of Keen. *"What is it?"* he asked, inviting her to use English with him if she wanted to...or felt she needed to.

"They harvested her eggs and fertilized them, true fertilization not splicing, with Alex's sperm. They have ten fourth-generation zygotes in cryo."

"They intend to inseminate," Sayd growled.

"No. They got Alex to accept her as true mate. She's pregnant to him."

"That's not possible," Till repeated. "If there was a third-generation re-bred female, we'd know it."

"How?" Susan asked.

Till bristled. "What do you mean, how?"

"How do you track them?"

"By mates, of course."

"By mating or by mates?" she persisted.

"One mates with a mate."

Susan rolled her eyes in irritation. "No one gets pregnant accidentally on Kegin?" she asked sarcastically. "No one has sex and gets pregnant without meaning to?"

Till darkened. "On rare occasions, of course."

"Well, on Earth it happens quite a lot." She scrolled down the file on the screen. "I take it Pilar Esperanza Varga was one of your second-generation females?"

"Yes."

"Was Andrew Evan Carpenter a first-generation male?"

"Yes, but he is mated to a human female named Colette and has a daughter named Angela, a second-generation female." As usual, Till didn't need to check his files to offer any information of Kegin-seeded children on Earth.

"How long has he been mated to Colette?"

"Seventeen years." He scowled. "Andrew took her to mate when he was only nineteen."

"Well, when he was seventeen, he had a little mating practice with Pilar, successful mating practice, it would seem."

Till paled. "That's barbaric."

Susan didn't anger at the rude comment. She answered in calm dismissal before Jole had a chance to reprimand the stodgy old gentleman. "Oh, really? How old were you when you had sex for the first time?" she inquired.

Till's face darkened in outrage that she would ask so impertinent a question. Sayd bit back a blast of laughter at Till's reaction. Peri ignored the growing scene. Daje shot her a speculative look that had Jole itching to draw his dagger. Queen or no queen, it was occasionally necessary for Jole to remind his people that Susan was more than they took her for.

He placed a hand on her shoulder in a show of support and stared Till down. "My first schente group was presented to me on my fifteenth birthday. How old were you when you first took a man, love?"

"Just shy of eighteen," she answered.

Till cleared his throat. "Be that as it may be, precautions were taken."

"Hmm—" Susan was actively ignoring him. That much was obvious, even to Till. "You knew Pilar had a child?"

"Of course."

"Why didn't you check on the father?"

He blushed. "We don't know how. If the father isn't in evidence when the gateway reopens—"

Susan groaned. "*Oh, for pity's sake.* Did it ever occur to you that you have an expert in American Earth culture sitting here? Why didn't you ever ask?"

"We— We didn't realize humans kept such records of mating," he stammered.

"Give me another second-generation with a child you can't track," she ordered.

"What will you do?"

"Just give me the information. This isn't foolproof, but it will solve some of your cases for you."

"Elise Brown has a son named Jacob."

"City and age of child."

"Philliadelphia."

"Philadelphia," she corrected him. "Age?"

"Six years."

Susan worked diligently for several minutes. "The father's name is Peter Lorenzo."

"Not one of ours." Till sighed in relief.

"How many others aren't you sure about?"

"Fifty-two."

Susan rubbed her forehead roughly. Jole bent and healed her. She offered him a strained smile in thanks.

"Okay," Susan began. "We have to review all the extent Keen seeded on Earth. I'm guessing we only need to worry about third-generation for now." She pulled up another file, her own.

Jole looked at her in confusion, as she scrolled through the data in it. "What are you doing?"

She nodded sadly. "Checking a notation in Alex's file that confused me. I led them to Alex. We did."

"What do you mean?"

"My blood. It's not completely human on a

DNA scan. They'd seen taints of Keen blood in first and second-generation before, but from their point of view, I was pure, the strongest concentration of alien genes they'd found. They searched my family and found Alex."

"Where did they get your blood? Why would they do a *DNA* scan on it?"

"Bell. The night I was brought through the gateway, he hit me, remember?"

"The lump?"

Susan nodded. "It bled, just a little but enough for them to test it. They often test *DNA* in cases of criminal acts where there is blood or hair left behind." She turned her gaze to Jole. "We have to bring them through the gateway at the next opening."

"Alex?" he guessed.

"And his mate, Annalyssa. And as many of the other third-generations as we can convince in the few minutes we have. How many portal-style gateways can be set up at any one time?"

Daje motioned for her attention. "Twelve, Majesty. That is all we have available for use."

Till met her eyes. "We can't bring Annalyssa through," he said, red-faced.

"Why not?" she asked, horrified.

"She's not yet of age. She's only nineteen."

Jole shook his head. "We can't take her unwilling." He looked to Daje for a ruling. "If she agrees to come, we're not breaking the Council law. By human law, she has been an adult for more than a year."

Daje considered it for a few moments. "In theory, I agree with your assessment, but how can the envoy convince her in the few minutes he'll have?"

Susan laughed. "That's the easy part."

Till raised an eyebrow. "How so?"

"I'll hand bands to Alex, and he'll convince her for me."

Jole fisted his hand. "You're not going, Susan."

"For Alex, I am. Keen breeding measures got them into this mess. We have a moral obligation to get them out of it."

Sayd beamed, something Jole had never seen him do. "Well said, your Majesty. We do indeed. They are our children, and we must do everything in our power to protect them."

"Thank you, Sayd."

He bowed his head to her.

"No," Jole thundered. "You're pregnant."

"So is Annalyssa. Alex has been a prisoner for almost three years. Who else will he trust on sight?"

"Then I'm going, too."

Pyter's voice had a hint of an order in it, something Jole hadn't heard from him since he was sixteen. "No, Jole. You're not going, but I am."

Jole turned to stare at him in open-mouthed wonder. "What did you just say?"

"The Council will not let you pass through the gateway."

All four men at the table nodded. They didn't bother to disguise their determination. Jole had a sudden realization that they would lock him in a prison cell at the palace for his own safety for the period of alignment if they had no other way to stop him.

Pyter continued. "Queen Susan would trust no one beside yourself to protect her, save Bell and myself. I can't speak for Bell, but I can speak for myself. You know I will give my life to send her back to you if need be."

Jole groaned and looked to Susan. "You're determined to do this, aren't you?"

Her eyes pleaded with him for understanding. "Yes, I am. He is my family, Joel."

"If Pyter and Bell both agree to accompany you, you may go."

She smiled. "They will."

Jole nodded in resignation. They probably would. Pyter and Bell were unnaturally attached to Susan.

* * * *

Endl 32nd, Ri 25-2992

Susan laughed heartily. "You never know. It might just work."

Jole scowled at her from across the steaming tub. "Just walking up to these three men and announcing that there are women they can mate with waiting through the magic doorway?" He was trying not to scoff at her suggestion.

"Yes. These three men are not married. There's a very real possibility that they haven't married because they've been told they're sterile, that their malformed sperm can't do the job. Or they fear the reaction Earth women have to the swelling at orgasm." She rubbed the washcloth over her face and continued. "If that fails, we have to tell them the danger they're in if they stay on Earth."

Jole moved closer in the tub. "And if that fails?" He kissed her throat.

Susan sobered. "Sayd says we can't force them if they choose to stay, but we can let them know they'll have one more chance. We can ask again in five years."

Jole lifted her to the edge of the tub and kissed the softness of their baby. "Please reconsider."

She ran her fingers through his hair. "Just for Alex. The other gateways aren't my problem."

"I have to try, Susan. You're everything to me. I'm running out of time. I only have two more months to convince you."

"The last two months haven't worked. Another two won't. Another two years wouldn't, if you had that long."

"Think of Joseph and Jenneane. Think of Eve. Think of the baby you're carrying." He lowered his head, tracing the seam of her folds lazily.

Susan leaned back against the wall, her body in its usual fervor for him. "How could I face them if I abandoned Alex?"

Jole buried his tongue in her, and Susan found forming coherent thoughts impossible. She raised her knees, planting her heels on the edge of the tub and spreading wide for him.

He rose up in the tub, his body glistening

with water and the cleansing oils she'd chosen for their bath together. Jole leaned over her, drawing her legs around him. He planted his hands on the edge of the tub around her hips.

Susan shivered at the intensity in his eyes. Jole eased into her, his body radiating the heat of the bath and his arousal combined. She gasped at that heat moving in and out of her.

Jole kissed her neck close to her ear. "There are other ways, Susan. You could write a short letter to him. We could enclose a video likeness of you. Please consider it."

She shook her head, then raised it as Jole moved down her throat. "Humans have almost perfected simulated videos. It has to be me so there is no question. Alex has to believe instantly. He's like my brother, Joel. I can't leave him."

He kissed her, his movements tender. "Promise you'll come back to me."

"I promise."

* * * *

April 15ᵗʰ, 2007

Alex held Lyssa's hand, casting nervous glances at Dr. Bradley. Lyssa was five months pregnant, but she was larger than Bradley expected. Bradley wanted a sonogram; Patterson demanded one. The doctor furrowed her brow again.

"What is it?" Alex forced his voice to calm,

knowing Patterson would steal this moment from him if he could.

Bradley raised an eyebrow. "Your bodies seem designed to make testing more difficult.

"What now?" Alex inquired.

Patterson was frustrated by the block over the cervix and the inability to take fasting tests. A few hours without food meant an increase in the toxins in Lyssa's blood, so much so that a small fridge had been installed in their room for one or more nightly snacks. Her body required a steady flow nutritious food, and she craved foods almost constantly, though Alex suspected much of that was designed just to drive Patterson nuts.

"The amniot, I think. It seems that the viscosity is much thicker than human amniot."

"Which means?"

"The sounds waves don't propagate the same way. I'm getting images back, but they are muted, cloudy." She sighed. "Let me see if I can make sense of any of it."

Patterson's voice came over the speaker set in the ceiling. "We could sample the amniot," he suggested.

Lyssa's hand tightened on Alex's. "No." Her eyes pleaded with him not to allow it. After the egg harvest, the idea of needles in her abdomen terrified her.

Alex looked to Bradley for help. Only she could stop this. Alex would simply be knocked unconscious and taken away if he tried to stop them from running tests.

Bradley met his gaze, then Lyssa's. She looked back to the screen and bit her lower lip. "I wouldn't recommend it," she decided.

"Amniocentesis only has one chance in two hundred of loss," Patterson replied irritably.

"In humans. If their amniot is this different, I can't predict odds. Once the membrane is breached, it may not repair like ours does. The patch may not withstand the increased pressure of the heavier amniot. Worse... There are so many protective layers, the infant may be more susceptible to infection and injury than a human infant is. Any move we make that introduces outside matter, even sterile matter, may have catastrophic results."

Alex held his breath while he waited for Patterson's response.

"For now," Patterson replied grudgingly. "Give me answers, doctor."

Bradley nodded and moved the wand on Lyssa's abdomen.

Alex resisted the urge to thank her. It couldn't seem that Bradley was helping them in any way or life would get much worse. He leaned to kiss Lyssa's forehead. "How's it going?" he asked.

"I'm starving."

"No wonder that baby is huge," he teased.

She grimaced.

"Headache?"

"Yeah."

Alex healed her then stroked her cheek. "Dr. Bradley?"

"Uh huh?" she answered distractedly.

"Any chance of a snack for Lyssa while you work? Her stomach is talking to her again."

"Sure. It won't hurt anything."

The nurses took a tray from one of the guards at the door just a few minutes later.

Alex bit back a wide smile. Patterson was keeping his distance, thanks to Dr. Bradley. A little conniving in the form of easing off on the healing when it was appropriate and a little artful storytelling on Bradley's part had Patterson believing that the stress of his presence was detrimental to the pregnancy. Since the lab results showed an increase in toxin after his visits, Patterson had had to agree to stay away.

Luckily, the lab tests on Alex could find no reason that his touch was so healing. If they couldn't synthesize it, they couldn't separate them.

Alex started feeding morsels of the food to Lyssa. Most of the tray was gone when Bradley spoke again.

"I think I have your answers, Patterson," she called out.

Alex raised an eyebrow in surprise. It was unusual for Bradley to find answers to anything, and that was a source of major strife with Patterson.

Patterson answered for him. "What did you find?"

"Twins."

Lyssa groaned and looked at the juice in her hand in distaste. "Figures," she complained.

Alex stepped down the table next to Dr. Bradley, looking at the fuzzy round shapes on the screen without comprehension. "Show me."

Her fingers traced the darker lines. "This is a face. Eyes, mouth, nose. You can see it dead-on forward. See?"

"Yes." Excitement settled in the pit of his stomach at the sight of his son or daughter on the screen.

She shifted the wand a few inches to the left. "Another face in profile. Eye, mouth, cute little button nose." A smile lifted the corners of her mouth.

Alex laughed nervously and shifted his eyes back to Lyssa. She cracked a smile at him and rolled her eyes. He sobered. It was hard not to get too excited. They both knew there was no way they'd get to be a normal family and raise their children in a manner they'd like to raise them. Their children would be prisoners, lab experiments. The only reason they'd be allowed to keep their children would be as a study in alien family dynamics.

"Are there any problems we should know about with twins, Alex?" Dr. Bradley forced his attention back to the conversation at hand.

He looked at Bradley, at a loss for words. Lyssa rubbed her forehead, and he moved to heal her, trying to decide what to tell them, how to bluff his way through this one.

Lyssa met his gaze. "It means he has to purge the toxins constantly," she answered.

Alex nodded. It couldn't hurt to remind them that they had to be together.

"What about delivery? How different is that?"

Alex shrugged hopelessly. Not knowing was frightening. A delivery gone wrong could cost him

Lyssa and their babies.

Bradley favored him with a searching look.

"Instinct has guided us this far," he managed, needing to give some answer. "I wish to God I had an expert here, but I don't. I have to trust that we'll figure it out as well as we have so far. Since everything is based on our touch, I'd assume delivery will be the same."

"I'd have to agree. In the meantime, we'll continue the routine. Daily visits to the gym together, but no weights for Annalyssa."

Alex nodded. "I don't suppose— Fresh air and sunshine—"

"No," Patterson barked over the speaker.

Alex fisted his hand in frustration.

"Anything she needs inside the complex is fine. Anything within reason."

Lyssa laughed harshly and looked at the huge mound of her stomach. "I'm hardly scaling walls, Patterson."

"And you're not learning to on my watch."

CHAPTER THIRTY-⊕NE

Zor 36ᵗʰ, Ri 25-2992

Jole paused outside of his office. It was the middle of the night, and Susan had disappeared from their bed. She should be sleeping. With the missions through the gateway twelve hours away, she needed her rest. He didn't question where she'd gone when he found her missing. The scan gateway was the only possibility.

He froze as an ungodly howl rent the air around him. Jole launched through the door into his office. His eyes locked on the video likeness viewing on the screen.

"Patterson, you fucking bastard," the man on the view screen shouted.

"Alex," he breathed, recognizing the man's face from the photographs Susan had shown him.

Alex paced the small windowless room, stalking back and forth like a caged jaglin. He hooked his fingers behind a bookshelf and pulled it over with another howl. "Bring her back, damn you! She's my wife. You can't take her from me like this." He pounded on the door. "You can't separate us now."

This was Alex? Mag be merciful! This madman was the one Susan wanted to save?

The rage went on. Furniture was smashed. Books were thrown, bouncing off the equipment recording his actions until the camera was knocked slightly off center. Bed linens were torn from the bed. Finally, Alex collapsed in the midst of the wreckage, sobbing. He choked out his mate's name, Lyssa.

Susan paused the image. She shook in silent sobs with her splayed hand on the screen.

Jole put his hands on her shoulders, automatically soothing the knots in her back made worse by the stress she was under. He stared at Alex, remembering his pain and fury when Mik took Susan from him. Alex was a madman, but he had good reason to be.

"Joel, please don't ask me not to go," Susan whispered.

"I won't ask you not to go. I'd be ashamed of you if you left him there."

* * * *

May 31ˢᵗ, 2007

Alex opened his eyes in confusion and eased off the bed. Something wasn't right. He pulled on his sweatpants warily, casting his eyes about for some sign of Patterson, but there seemed to be no reason for this paranoia.

He headed for the bathroom with a sigh, suddenly wide-awake. Alex searched his faculties, afraid that Patterson was testing some new drug on him. He rubbed his eyes. He had to be drugged. Nothing else would account for the rippled look of the wall.

Two men stepped through, towering over his six feet one, at least six feet six or eight. Both of them were dark-haired, and neither of them looked particularly friendly.

Alex took a step back in fear and grabbed for the chair behind him, the only weapon in the room since his temper fit when Lyssa was taken from him at the beginning of her pregnancy caused Patterson to have all the furniture bolted down.

One of the men reached for what appeared to be a gun at his hip.

"Bell," a woman's voice shouted from behind them. "Gi, ni har Alex. Hol mae."

The man stilled, his hand still hovering over the weapon.

"Alex?" Lyssa's voice was edged with panic.

"Stay there," he ordered, for the first time actually welcoming the cameras and mics that would bring guards.

A woman ducked from behind the two men. The first man gripped his weapon at the movement.

The taller man grabbed her by the shoulders and pulled her to his chest. "*Ni*," he growled at her.

"Pyter, you're wasting time," she pleaded.

Alex fought for a decent breath. "Susan?"

"He's armed," Pyter argued, switching to deeply-accented English.

"It's a chair, Pyter. I order you to let me go."

Alex dropped the chair. It clattered to the tile floor. "Susan?"

Pyter released her, and Susan surged toward him. She pressed two black elastic bands with small boxes attached into his hand. "Please,

Alex. Don't question me. We have only a few minutes. Put these on, you and Lyssa."

He hesitated, touching her shoulder-length blond curls and scanning his gaze over her black-clad body to the swell of her pregnancy.

"I'm real, Alex. It's time to go."

Pyter shook his head. "Yellow, Susan."

"Now," she ordered, pushing Alex toward Lyssa.

Alex dragged his band on his arm like Susan wore hers. He started threading Lyssa's onto her arm, but she pulled away.

"Alex, please explain."

He sighed. What could he say? He didn't know what this meant, but he trusted Susan. "I told you about Susan, Lyssa." He started pushing the band on her again.

Lyssa didn't fight him. She looked past him fearfully, scanning her eyes over their visitors in the dim light. "Where will we go?"

"Somewhere better than here," he answered with conviction. Anywhere was better than this complex with Patterson.

Susan reached a hand out to Lyssa. "Freedom, Lyssa. You have my word that all of this will be a hateful memory."

Lyssa took her hand then looked at her long sweatshirt. "I'm half dressed," she whispered with a glance at Pyter and the other man.

"I went through in a nightshirt. Nothing will shock them."

Susan's smile was punctuated by a grunt from the shorter man and a hearty laugh from Pyter. She helped Lyssa to her feet and pulled

Alex with her toward the rippling doorway, guiding them in front of her.

"The bands will protect you from the gateway as you pass through it," Susan explained. "Go on. We'll be right—"

The door flew open, and they all turned back. Alex looked at Patterson in dismay. Why hadn't he jammed the door with the chair? He'd been stunned by Susan's appearance, but he knew they'd come.

Patterson locked eyes with Alex, then took in Lyssa and Susan. A calculating smile curved his lips. The entire exchange took less than a heartbeat, though it seemed to last hours. Time went from frame by frame to fast forward in a snap.

Patterson's gun came up. Alex moved toward Lyssa. Susan caught him mid-stride and shoved him through the gateway. The smaller man lunged for Patterson, and Pyter reached for the women. The sound of compressed air and a man's bellow of rage followed him through a swirl of color. Alex stumbled into a bright room.

Strong hands steadied him, and Alex blinked and squinted into the face of a dark-haired man about his own size. The man's green eyes were crinkled in amusement.

"Welcome to Kegin, Alex." His accent was crisp and clear, the drawl of a Pittsburgh native.

"Who—" Alex abandoned his question and turned back to the gateway in dismay as Lyssa screamed.

* * * *

Jole looked over Alex's shoulder, his muscles tensing. Bell's battle cry was to be expected, but the women should not have been endangered.

"Go," Pyter ordered in English.

"Don't hit the women," a strange man bellowed.

Jole felt the color drain from his face. They were in the midst of a battle with the human soldiers. One of his soldiers cast a wary look at him. Jole knew they were ordered to stop him if he moved toward either the gateway or Alex's band. He pushed Alex toward the throng of soldiers in frustration, waiting for a sign of Susan coming back through.

Lyssa launched through the gateway. He caught her and handed her off to Alex gently. Jole waved his hand toward the couple. "Stay back, Lyssa," he ordered.

Jole turned back to the gateway, but there was still no sign of Susan. He held his breath at the sound of laser weapons echoing through the gateway, distorted but recognizable. Why wasn't Susan out of there? Was she behind the shield of Pyter's body, unable to move closer to the gateway?

"Bell," Pyter thundered in Keen. "*Get back.*"

"*Take the Queen. Leave me.*"

"*I ordered you back.*"

"*My band is damaged. Time is short. Leave me. This is my duty. Go.*"

Jole motioned to the two soldiers at the control panel. They had turned to listen to Bell's plea in awe, but he needed their attention on the readouts. They nodded and turned back to their work.

Pyter's voice came through the gateway, cold and emotionless. Jole had never heard him sound that murderous before. *"Release Patterson when we are through."*

Bell choked in laughter.

Jole motioned to the small squad of soldiers, but their weapons were already raised. Pyter meant to let Patterson walk through the gateway with no protection, but the human might still have enough fight left in him to injure someone before the deterioration of his nervous system killed him.

Pyter stepped through the gateway with Susan in his arms. Jole roared in fury. She was as still as the night Bell brought her through. If she was injured, he would kill Patterson with his bare hands before the gateway shock could do the job.

"It was a dart," Lyssa tried to assure him.

Jole couldn't identify the word. His grasp of English seemed to desert him. He rushed to Susan and touched her pulse point, thanking Fion and Mag that she still had a pulse to check.

Pyter shouldered him back to the soldiers and looked at the gateway with a shrewd expression. Patterson stumbled through with Bell's broken band strapped to his arm and a small weapon in his opposite hand. Lyssa screamed, and Alex pulled her behind him, shielding her with his body. Patterson took one step toward them, then collapsed to his knees, his weapon falling from his hand. His entire body started to twitch as nerves misfired and nervous links started to dissolve.

Pyter smiled a cruel smile. "You should have stayed on Earth where you belonged. Now Kegin will be your grave."

Jole ignored the interaction, knowing the pain of Patterson's death would fit the crime of whatever he had done to Susan. He yelled for Peri, then turned to Lyssa. "What is a dart?" he demanded.

"A—a drug." Lyssa grimaced and flicked a look at Patterson. "It was meant for Alex. It was measured for his weight. He said— He doesn't know if it will hurt a baby, and in that dosage..." She stroked a nervous hand over her own babies.

"*One of their drugs,*" Jole barked at Peri, "*and too much of it.*"

Peri nodded, already at work taking a sample of her blood from her fingertip and inserting it in the spectro-analyzer that would tell them which antidote to use on her.

Jole flicked his gaze between Susan and their new arrivals, wary despite his bride's assurances that Alex was a stable man.

Alex swallowed hard, his arms wrapped around his young bride, blocking Lyssa's view of their common enemy with his chest. His gaze locked on Patterson as the man collapsed to the floor. Patterson's eyes rolled back in his head, and he started to seize uncontrollably.

Alex looked to Susan as Peri cut away her sleeve. The doctor's breathing was ragged and his hands shaking. Peri administered an injection, the hypocil hissing softly.

"What is he doing?" Alex asked in a shaky voice.

Pyter grimaced. "Susan supplied the doctors with the details of the drugs they used on you, taken from their files. A simple blood test identified the drug for the doctor. He is giving her the antidote to reverse its effects."

Lyssa wiped away a tear. "Will it hurt her baby?"

Pyter turned to Peri. "*Her Majesty's baby?*" he barked.

"*It won't hurt. The baby is safe.*"

Pyter relayed the information.

Alex sighed in relief. "Good."

Susan groaned, and Jole focused on her fully. There would be time to get to know her family later.

Jole touched her face. "Susan? Wake up for me, Susan," he crooned to her.

Her purple-blue eyes opened. A slow, lazy smile spread over her face. Susan touched his cheek. "I told you I was coming back," she whispered.

"You are never permitted through a gateway again," he replied gruffly. Jole took her from Pyter and kissed her passionately, relieved that she was back and unharmed.

Alex laughed heartily. "I'd guess you're Susan's husband."

Susan broke off the kiss, giggling into Jole's chest. "Alex, Lyssa, may I present my husband, Joel."

Alex sobered, his smile disappearing. "If you're her husband, why—" He motioned toward

417

the gateway.

Jole nodded. Alex didn't understand why he'd allowed her through, why he wasn't there to protect her himself.

Pyter laughed harshly. "Our queen is permitted to be a bit foolhardy.....when it comes to her family. Our king is not."

Alex took a deep, calming breath and nodded. He pulled Lyssa to his chest again. A thousand questions burned in his eyes, but he seemed at a loss to choose what to ask first.

Susan scanned her gaze over the room, and her smile disappeared. "Where is Bell?" she asked quietly.

Jole hugged her closer to him, anticipating the blow he was about to strike on her mind and heart. "He didn't make it."

She turned toward the gateway and stifled a sob at the sight of the green light. "We can't leave him there."

Pyter bowed his head to her. "It is too late. By now, the building has been destroyed. I assure you, his death was painless. He would not have felt the explosion."

Susan trembled in Jole's arms. "He said he would give his life for me, but I never wanted that."

Alex grimaced at her words. His expression mirrored her sadness, as if the two of them felt each other's pain. He cleared his throat. "Destroyed? Explosion? I didn't hear an explosion."

Pyter sighed. "It was Susan's idea. It was necessary. The records, their facilities, and your frozen babies had to be destroyed. I am sorry for your loss. We couldn't allow them to harm any more of our children."

Alex paled, and he weaved on his feet for a moment. "Then we really are aliens?"

Jole started to explain then stopped, weighing the enormity of what he had to impart. "We will explain everything if you will join us for the evening meal. For now, Susan needs to rest, and you need to rest. Coming through the gateway is physically taxing.

"Pyter will show you to your rooms, and Syl will come to care for you. You are free here." He looked at Lyssa's shirt in distaste. "You need never be a prisoner again."

* * * *

Lyssa pulled Pyter's cloak around her body. The palace was huge, but there were no other extraneous guests here beside themselves. Pyter said that the six other rescued 'Earth-born' were on smaller estates across the continent. Apparently, being the cousin of a queen had its perks.

People bowed as they passed, and men dropped their gaze or turned away at Pyter's approach. It seemed they refused to meet his eyes or the eyes of anyone with him.

Lyssa tapped Pyter on the shoulder. "Are you a noble? A prince or something?" she asked.

He chuckled. "Why do you ask that?"

"People— Well, they bow to you and avoid

looking at you."

"No, Lady Lyssa. You and your husband are the nobility here, and the men do not look at you, because you are not theirs to look upon. You are Lord Alex's mate. They will not look at you, unless you address them directly. Queen Susan has instructed me to treat you as if I was a human man, and so I break with our customs for your comfort, but no one else will dare do that."

"I don't understand."

"Jole will explain this evening. It is quite a long story." He turned to Alex, changing the subject. "I understand that you have learned to use your healing magic, Lord Alex?"

Alex hesitated. "Uh.....yeah, I have. Is that unusual?"

"Extraordinary. It is amazing that you learned without a Keen teacher. It is a work of Fion's mercy that you took the proper actions to keep your mate alive while she carries your children."

"Everything I did..... It felt right. At times, I had gut feelings that I had to do something specific to solve the problem. It never failed me. I thought it might be instinct of some sort."

"Amazing. Perhaps your human instincts guided your Keen side."

He pushed a door open and waved them into a luxurious room with a king-sized bed and thick carpet on the floor. A woman bowed deeply to them. Now that Pyter explained it, Lyssa noted that she met their eyes when she rose.

Pyter nodded. "This is Syl. She will see to

your needs and translate for you, if you require it. Food has been prepared for you. Carrying twins, I imagine you will be hungry shortly."

He smiled as Lyssa's stomach grumbled at the mention of food. Alex stifled a laugh, and she smacked his arm playfully, going red in the face in embarrassment.

"There are bathing facilities and clothes. Oh, and Syl is a...midwife. If you have need of her services, she would be happy to check on the babes for you." He glanced around as if searching for anything he might have forgotten to tell them. He bowed his head. "I have duties to attend to. Until dinner..."

Lyssa started to return his cloak.

Pyter put up a hand to stop her. "I would be honored if you would keep it."

Lyssa nodded. "Thank you, Pyter. It's lovely."

He left them with Syl.

The young woman smiled. "What would you have first? The bathroom is through here." She motioned to a door against the far wall. She turned and opened a deep closet full of clothes. "You could dress." She turned again and opened a glass door with a heavy drape. Beyond it, there was a sunlit terrace overlooking a field of golden flowers. "Or you could eat."

Lyssa walked through the door, drinking in the sunshine with tears in her eyes. Alex snuggled to her back and wrapped his arms around her.

"Lady Lyssa?" Syl asked worriedly.

"I haven't seen the sun in almost nine months, Syl. I didn't think I'd ever see it again," she whispered.

Syl paled. "Queen Susan's boots should be a close enough fit...until your own are made for you. If it pleases you, you can picnic and walk on the grounds. Once you are delivered and recovered, you can ride the hottels in the stable. Queen Susan says they are like your—ponies."

Lyssa sighed. She looked to Syl. "You're a midwife?"

She bowed. "As were my mother and grandmother before me, all midwives to the royal house. I helped deliver all three of Queen Susan's children." She beamed at the admission.

Alex coughed. "Three?"

"Yes, Lord Alex. Jenneane and Joseph are four. They are—twins. Eve is a year and a half. You will meet them at the evening meal."

Lyssa ran her hands over their children nervously. "What is delivery like, Syl?"

Her eyes widened then she smiled warmly. "Wonderful. I will begin your lessons as soon as you wish. The fact that Lord Alex has the healing magic means that it will be nearly painless for you."

"Will there— Will there be strange doctors there?"

Syl's smile faltered. "Do you wish for doctors? My mother and I are quite capable—"

Lyssa laughed. "Syl, I would be happy never to see another doctor in my life."

"Then unless you are ill or seriously injured, you never will."

Section Four:
Pyter

Son of My Heart

CHAPTER THIRTY-TWO

Wend 29th, Ri 25-2992

Jole looked up from his desk, as the women entered his office. There was bad news. He looked from Barri's ashen face to Susan's tear-streaked cheeks without voicing his question. Susan walked to him. Jole drew her onto his lap and wrapped her in his arms. He kissed her cheek and wiped away her fresh tears.

"Tell me please," he requested. Susan would give birth to their fourth child at any time. It wasn't good for her or the baby to be so upset.

She met his eyes. "It's Pyter. He died last night, Joel."

Jole brushed a hand through her pale hair. Despite their rocky beginnings, he knew Susan and Pyter cared deeply for each other. In fact, all the Earth-born who came through the gateway seemed to latch onto Pyter eventually. Lyssa would be distressed to hear that he was gone, and Jole was saddened that her twins, Alex The Younger and Andrew, would never know the man their parents had respected and held so dear.

"I will make arrangements for him. He will have a place of honor to show our love and respect for him."

"He made a request, Joel. He wants a very private, special place."

"Tell me. I would give Pyter anything he wishes."

Barri approached and placed a faded

notebook in Susan's hand. She didn't meet Jole's eyes as she backed away again.

"What is it?" he asked.

Susan held the book to her chest. "A diary. I've read it. I think you should too."

"Pyter's diary?"

She nodded.

He looked to Barri. "What is the matter, Barri?"

Barri cringed at the sound of his voice and bit back a sob.

Susan sighed. "She's afraid you'll punish her when you read the diary. I assured her that you wouldn't."

Jole took the book uncertainly. There was a folded sheet of paper in the front, a letter written in Pyter's hand.

> *Jole, son of my heart if not of my loins,*
>
> *If Barri has given this journal to you, I have passed from this life. I pray I pass to the gods' rest, though I fear such a reward is not for me. Fion may welcome me to eternity for the purity of my love, but I fear her husband Mag, king of the gods, will cast me out to Len in his underworld for my treachery.*
>
> *Many are my crimes, and sick am I for my deception and my trespasses. I have broken the laws of Kegin. I have broken trust with*

*my dearest friend, Kell, with whom I
was raised as brother since he was
five and I six. I have injured my love,
the one I should never have injured.
I am guilty of treason.*

*I lay my secrets bare before you.
I dare not ask your forgiveness. I do
not anticipate your understanding. I
ask only one small favor, a dying
wish, one pitiful boon that would
give my tortured soul paradise, even
if Mag cast my essence to the wind.*

*I ask a small, unmarked plot
near the grave of my love. You know
the place well. I would lie next to
She, the only woman I have ever
loved and will ever love, Jenneane.*

Jole took an unsteady breath. He knew his
hands shook, but he couldn't stop the shaking.
He looked to Barri, kneeling and waiting a
deathblow at his hand, and his heart broke.

"Leave us, Barri. I will call for you if I have
questions."

"As you wish, Highness."

"Never call me that, Barri. Please. You are all
I have left of my childhood. Don't steal that from
me."

Susan watched her leave. "Are you all right,
Joel?"

He nodded. "Let's go to our rooms. I'd rather
read this there."

Susan smiled as if she had a secret. "I have
to admit that I agree."

* * * *

I was the one assigned to bring Jenneane Boroughs to her home and husband. I walked through the gateway and onto an alien world.

The beauty of her rooms surprised me, but the beauty of the woman in the bed stole my breath. Her hair was rich as lizor berry wine and skin as pale as snow. She was innocent, most of all innocent of the fact that her life as she knew it was a lie.

I knelt next to her and placed my hand over her mouth. Her eyes opened and locked with mine, wide frightened eyes. That was the beginning of my fall. Her eyes were of a green that Fion herself would have begged to possess. Her skin was like silin under my hand.

Jenneane didn't fight me. She made not a sound. She simply looked at me with the questioning stare of a wild hottel under the hand of a trainer. That was Jenneane—wild, untapped potential. I saw it at once, and I was lost.

The warning light blinked amber, and I came to my senses. This was my princess, the bride of my prince and my dearest friend. I was honored to touch her this one time. She was not mine to touch, not mine to love, not mine to look upon.

But look I did. I leaned close to her and whispered calming words in Keen that she couldn't possibly understand. Like that wild hottel, the words were unimportant. It was the soothing she required.

I eased my hand from her mouth and pushed the band onto her arm. She had a moment's hesitation when I lifted her from the bed, covering her body with her hands pressed to the filmy nightgown that covered her. I wrapped Jenneane in my cloak, and she calmed under my hand again.

I gathered her into my arms and took her back through the gateway just before the light went green. A cheer went up from the soldiers, and my heart was sick, sick in longing for a woman who was not for me, sick in knowing that I delivered her to her fate so that I might see her face again, sick at her screaming as the shock wore off. And so I released her to Barri and walked away, hating myself for delivering her to another man.

Things did not improve for Jenneane or for me. After three days of ignoring his bride, Kell Hi ordered her prepared for him.

When she stepped from her rooms, I dared not look at her, though my heart pounded and her nearness teased my senses. I kept my gaze cast down. I could feel her confusion, though its cause was not readily apparent. Jenneane asked questions over and over again in her language, pleading questions I would have answered had I the knowledge of language to answer them.

Her tears, when I delivered her to Kell, made her meaning clear. Jenneane had allowed me to take her from her bed and her world, because she'd believed herself bound for me. I betrayed her by giving her to another, but that was only the first of my betrayals. Betrayal was to become a way of life for me.

Kell had no understanding of her spirit and intelligence. To Kell, Jenneane was a brood mare in heat to be mounted by her stud, a mare that bucks her stud in willful show though she longs for the mating. Her screams and tears will haunt me even to my grave.

He never forced his cock in her. Of that, I am both grateful and sure. He never beat her. But beyond those two things, she was spared little. Every night for months, Barri would prepare Jenneane to be touched and badgered until she broke emotionally. Still, she walked to her rooms with a tear-streaked face and mussed hair but with her head high and the bearing of a queen.

How Jenneane came across the knowledge of contracts was a mystery. I never asked Barri if it was her doing, and she never volunteered the information. I owe whoever told her a debt of thanks.

Over the months, I found myself watching Jenneane, heedless of my life for I felt I might die outside the radiance of her presence. That night, I knew something had changed in her. Jenneane was stunning. Her royal bearing was more pronounced, though her hands shook.

There was no crying that night, no screaming save Kell's screams of rage. Jenneane had learned a few precious words of Keen and used them wisely: "Don't touch me." and "I demand a contract." I bit back my laughter when I heard Kell's outrage.

Jenneane had made excellent use of her time with Barri. The servant had a crude understanding of English and played the part of advisor and translator during the negotiations.

Kell sent me to Jenneane's estate as his guardian of trust. My heart sung to be so near Jenneane and to know that Kell could not abuse her again. I became bolder in my illicit lust for her, using my duty to protect Kell's interests as justification for letting my eyes linger too long.

Things might have continued thus for all our years together were it not for Jenneane's fear. Again, I know not if Barri had a hand in the events of Jenneane's life. Surely, Jenneane asked Barri's help, though innocently enough it might have been given.

When Barri approached me, I was torn between a glimpse of paradise and belief that I had descended to the lowest dungeons of the dark underworld. It was a simple request, an innocent request. I was asked to massage the knots from Jenneane's back. She required a firmer hand than Barri could offer. I agreed, my need to touch her again so overpowering.

Jenneane wore a simple day dress, but I knew a little of the body beneath from the night I brought her through the gateway, and so my cock was hard when I had barely laid hands on her. She tossed her head back, her hair cascading over my hands as I stood beside her bed. She sat before me, her legs curled beneath her body.

I had no idea that Barri had been teaching her Keen, language that she had not admitted knowledge of with Kell, and so her first words caught me by surprise.

"Your hands feel wonderful."

My mind ceased to function as my body's demands screamed at me. The sound of our language on her lips caressed me, soft and lyrical. "Thank you, my princess."

"Am I?" Her voice turned sultry, reminding me of sucre sap warmed over cakes and placed on tables for lovers' repast.

"Are you what, Highness?" I couldn't seem to follow her logic.

"Your princess."

"Of course." And I reminded myself to remember that she was and stop my mind's wandering down paths where she was brought through the gateway for me instead of Kell.

Jenneane turned to face me, and I jerked my hands away to avoid capturing her breasts in my palms. She pulled my hands to her shoulders.

"I've seen you watch me, Pyter. Your eyes are hungry, as they were that first night. Do you deny it?"

I shook my head. I should have denied it, but what point would there be? She could see what I wanted clearly. "I should not— I will not—"

Her fingers traced my cock through my trousers. "Your body is hungry, Pyter."

I shuddered, sanity and duty warring with my need to possess her in every way a man can possess a woman. I reached for her hand, but she pulled it away before I could do it.

"Do you know why I came through the gateway? Why I didn't scream or fight?"

"Yes," I whispered. I knew, and it tortured me that I knew.

"Do you?"

"For me." It was presumptuous. It was treason. It was true.

Her fingers traced the head of my cock. "Because I wanted you to be my first."

My eyes widened in surprise.

Jenneane opened my trousers and eased my cock out. Fion only knows why I let her do it, but I did. She didn't speak. Jenneane teased at my cock with her tongue, stealing a drop of my arousal and driving me near mad for her. Her fingers stroked me, and her mouth caressed me shallow and deep over and over.

I watched her, my breathing ragged, my hands fisted at my side as she drove me on. I clenched my jaw, thrusting forward as if I might die if I didn't have more of her, and she moaned around me. I could stand no more. My seed filled her mouth, and she swallowed it, sending shards of pleasure up my spine.

She cleaned me with gentle licks and suckled me shallow and deep while I was swollen in her mouth, her lips a great red O around my increased girth. The feeling of her moving over me while I was swollen, of not being locked motionless in a woman, nearly sent me over again.

Jenneane released me, and I sank to my knees with my head in her lap, shaking not in fear but in restraint. Fion, how I wanted that woman!

Her hands stroked my hair and back, and I nuzzled my face into her like a kittle. Jenneane raised my face until I met those new leaf eyes.

She kissed my brow tenderly.

"I want you to be my first, Pyter." Her eyes pleaded with me.

And what a selfish, ungrateful cur I felt. The danger to us both was too great. "I cannot." After she gifted me with pleasure the likes of which I had never known, I was refusing her. I cursed myself for it, though I knew it was necessary.

She dropped her gaze, crushed by my refusal, my dismissal of her as a woman.

"Prin— Jenneane, I cannot. If you conceived, the doctors would know. Even if, gods willing, the cap did not form until after the procedure, if the child between us was female, we would both die without question." I touched her face. "We cannot—"

"They inseminate me tomorrow, Pyter. Don't let them take my barrier."

"Barri can—"

"No."

"It will be painless, a cauter bar."

Jenneane shook her head, tears streaming down her cheeks. "Taking a barrier... It should be memorable, Pyter. It shouldn't be with a cold, metal bar but with someone you care for."

I might have walked away if I cared nothing for her, but her tears affected me too much. I wanted to be that fond memory too much.

Jenneane gasped, as I pushed the skirt up her thighs. I kissed her, knowing that I could not do exactly what she'd requested but willing to go to any lengths to give her a memorable experience as she wished.

My fingers teased at her core, while the feel

of her mouth merged with mine fired wild imaginings of thrusting into her. Just a thrust to take her barrier, I reasoned. I could complete her with my tongue and hand and be content with her maiden's blood on my cock.

But, I would not be content. I knew myself that well. If I dared pierce her in that manner, I would not stop until I spilled my seed full in her and felt the warmth of her sheath locked around me, her muscles clenching me tight, my child in her womb instead of Kell's.

I met her eyes, then dropped my mouth to her core. Jenneane was ready for me, and I dared not take her. Her sweet nectar was like no woman I'd ever had. Perhaps it was her human genetics. Perhaps it was simply Jenneane. Her nectar was as wild as she, hidden within the most beautiful but proper packaging. I drank from her body while she trembled against me.

Jenneane bit her lip, stifling cries of pleasure. I could feel her body nearing completion, taste the spice of arousal in her fluid. I moved to her hood and teased while I eased my fingers into her. Her barrier under my fingertips, my body ached for her, ached for that one slide to take her barrier that would become many more and seal my fate to hers.

Her body rippled around my fingers, and I swept her mouth to mine as I rose, piercing her barrier with my fingers and massaging her, twisting to take every corner of it from her body. Her climax quickened, and her mouth came at mine urgently, her scream muted in me.

I pulled back, my hands still on her—in her

hair and in her sheath. Her eyes were wide and dilated. We both trembled. To this day, I know not if Jenneane trembled in ecstasy or fear, only that she lay her head against my chest and thanked me. She thanked me for granting her wishes. Her barrier was taken in the manner she'd hoped it would be, and it was taken by the man she'd wished for.

I sent her to wash. Jenneane left me kneeling by her bedside, unable to right myself in body or soul. Her blood stained my hand, a sure penalty of death for me.....but for her as well, if the truth were known. Perhaps not. She was a criminal but too important to kill. I was a traitor to my world and my brother.

Then why was my instinct calling me to spread her blood over the head of my cock? I complied, shuddering in the imagined feel of her barrier shattering to my cock rather than my fingers. However I took her barrier, Jenneane was mine in a way she would never be Kell's. She was mine not by virtue of her blood and her barrier but by virtue of her craving for me. She'd asked me to her bed, and she would never ask that of Kell.

By the time she emerged from her bath, I had returned to my duties, her blood on my cock a sweet reminder of my possession of a wild, pure fire. My hands and face cleaned of all evidence, it was a secret held close to my heart.

CHAPTER THIRTY-THREE

"Joel?" Susan's hand brushed over his.

Jole eased his grip on the book, forcing a deep breath into his burning lungs. "There could have been Kegin-born re-bred daughters. If she had a choice, there would have been."

"Do you understand why there was no choice?"

He nodded. "Kell couldn't mate with a Keen woman. He needed heirs. So, she was the sacrifice."

"Read more, Joel. Please read more."

* * * *

Jenneane was a woman of honor and courage. She'd contracted with Kell, and she was determined to complete that contract, to protect herself, and to protect me.

I was the coward in our relationship. In the early hours of the morning, I offered to sneak her from the house with me, to hide her from Kell for the rest of our lives if need be. Jenneane sobbed as she refused my offer. She would not risk my death...or the penalty of her contract, true mating with Kell to the production of a daughter.

Again, I felt the rush of my place in her heart. She would have carried for me as true mate had we the chance to exercise such a contract. Again, I felt the torture of knowing she could never be truly mine.

When the sun rose over the hillside, I escorted Jenneane and Barri to the medical center as she'd requested, giving her one of my cloaks to wear over her day dress, since Kell had not provided her with travel dresses and cloaks of her own. I was banned from the room while they harvested her eggs. For that, I thanked each of the gods in turn. I expected her screams, but she bore up in silence.

As Kell's guardian of trust, I was required to watch her implantation. I held one of her ankles and watched the wand go in. I forced my eyes open, forced myself not to show my dismay as Kell took the one thing from Jenneane I could never have. The wand stimulated her, and she bowed up, gritting her teeth against the cry building within her, refusing to vent the pleasure at conceiving Kell's child.

We stayed in the center for five days. As if the torture of Jenneane's implantation were not enough, we had to endure it a second time. When a cap had not formed after three days, the procedure was repeated.

When the cap formed on the fifth day, we both wept. Jenneane wept for the child she would have for so short a time. I cried in a combination of relief that we would not have to endure the implantation a third time and fury that the woman I loved carried the child of another man, a man she would never love.

For more than a week, I couldn't look at her. I feared my loathing and envy of Kell would be misinterpreted by Jenneane. When I allowed my eyes to return to her again, her uncertainty and pain stunned me. Kind looks from me were all she needed to bloom again. I had heard of women radiating warmth and beauty while they carried, but I had never seen it until Jenneane carried Jole.

We were like a family—Jenneane, Barri, and I. Kell's soldiers patrolled the lowest level and grounds, but the upper floors were off-limits to all but the three of us. It was our sanctuary.

Barri started to teach me the woman healers' arts I would need to aid in Jenneane's pregnancy and delivery. I massaged her daily, aware always of the outcome of that first massage. Would that I had the healing magic of the royal family, I would have taken every discomfort from her.

It was more than three months before our situation changed. That time, there was no question that Barri knew of the course we chose. She approached me after one of Jenneane's irritable outbursts, laying a hand on my shoulder in comfort as I stared out the window of my room. I was at a loss. There seemed no reason to Jenneane's fits of temper. I greeted Barri with a sigh.

"It is no fault of yours Pyter," she assured me.

"Then what is it?" I demanded, turning to her.

Barri blushed. "She is suffering schen, Pyter. She cannot help but be frustrated."

I stilled. The sexual needs of a pregnant Keen female are formidable. I flashed on the stories of the long-ago days...before the forced breeding began, the days of the schaen. The woman's sexual drive had always been the stronger, no time more than in pregnancy. The schaen were the female's version of schente, a group of sterile men kept to appease the hungers of the women they served. The schaen came first, before men *invented* the need for their own amusements.

"But, the other cross-mates....." I reasoned. It was thought that the human genes suppressed that urge. The former cross-mates had not exhibited any need for sexual gratification but self-gratification, even in pregnancy.

"Have never had a male they were sexually attracted to close to them while they carried."

I sucked in my breath. "Barri, I—"

"I am not blind. I see the way you look at each other. If it will make you both happy—"

"And break her contract," I countered in a fierce whisper.

Barri shook her head. "Her contract does not specify sexual fidelity by either party." She smiled. "Neane refused to be bound if Kell was not. Kell believed your presence and the mores would ensure her lack of a sexual partner."

I shook my head in denial.

"You have a copy of the contract as guardian of trust. Read it."

"Kell will still retaliate."

"Not on the princess. He cannot. Her contract only specifies that she give him his two sons and not bear for another man."

I sobered. "But he would retaliate on the man," I reasoned.

"She will not ask this of you. Neane knows

the danger to you. She will accept any discomfort to keep you safe. Such is her love for you." Barri arched an eyebrow and waited for my reply.

Jenneane was suffering in relative silence to protect my life. I could not allow it. I brushed Barri aside and stormed back to Jenneane's rooms, pushing through the door and slamming it behind me.

She sat huddled in a chair, her arms crossed over her abdomen. Her shaking was severe, and I cursed her stubborn streak. Jenneane turned her face to me as the door crashed shut. Her confusion melted into pure fury.

"Go away, Pyter," she demanded. "I told you I don't want you here."

I crossed the room without a word. If it surprised Jenneane, she gave no sign of it. She kept her eyes locked on mine, her fisted hand shaking as she fought back the fire in her blood. I took her arms in my hands and dragged her to her feet, capturing her mouth as she opened it to order me away again.

Jenneane's scream of outrage ended on a groan as her body responded to mine. Her shock at my kiss was short lived. Her mouth was urgent, and her hands fisted in my clothing. She was fire unleashed in my body and soul, untamed in her need for an end to the schen.

I pulled back, cupping her bottom and lifting her to fit to my cock. She gripped my shoulders, her cheeks flushed and eyes bright, her body trembling against mine.

"Pyter, you can't do this."

"You want me here, Jenneane. Can you

honestly say you don't?"

She muttered something in English that could only be a curse of some sort.

"Do you want me Jenneane?"

Her body temperature jumped at my invitation. "Pyter, if Kell—"

I kissed her again, seeking to drive her beyond reason.....further, to the release we both needed to stay sane. I dragged her dress up over her hips as I carried her to her bed. I pulled my trousers down and poised her over my rigid length. Jenneane strained down over me, releasing my mouth with a strangled cry. She stilled with my cock encased in her heat and looked into my eyes, her lip trembling.

"Tell me what you want," I whispered, unwilling to take any step she didn't truly want.

"You, Pyter. Only you."

I nodded. "Take off your dress."

She pulled her dress over her head and dropped it to the floor.

For a moment, I was incapable of thought. She was perfect, and yet she was unlike any other woman I had seen. Her nipples weren't the choc brown of a Keen woman but tan as a newborn hottel. The curls that covered her sex were the same vibrant color as the hair on her head. Her slim waist was just beginning to show the softness of her son, and her legs were long and muscled.

Jenneane covered her breasts, blushing in her virginal insecurity of her own worth as a woman.

My mind kicked in for a brief moment. I

cursed my haste. By Fion, this was her first time with a man, and I was handling it all wrong. I guided her hand from her breast and captured one of those silin tan nipples as I followed her down onto her bed.

She pulled up at my tunic, and I dragged it off for her. Jenneane's hands explored my chest, while I took her in long, slow strokes.

"Never hide from me, Jenneane. You are so beautiful."

Jenneane's touches became bolder. She urged me on in a mixture of Keen and English. "Only you, Pyter," she breathed into my chest.

I groaned. If only the situation were different, she would be mine forever, openly, and in every way possible. The only consolation was that she would keep to her contract and never be forced to accept Kell as mate. In that, she would be mine alone.

Jenneane climaxed, burying her scream in my chest, and I followed. Tears filled her eyes, as my cock swelled within her.

I wiped at them, horrified. "Have I hurt you?"

"No. Never."

"What is wrong?"

"He'll kill you," she whispered.

I managed a smile. "He will not if he doesn't know." I paused, not knowing what assurances she needed from me. "You are worth any cost."

She smiled weakly through her tears. "I will do anything I have to to save you."

Her meaning was clear, and my body and mind rioted at the thought. "No. You will not. You are mine, mine alone. Promise me you will let me go to my grave knowing you never made that sacrifice for me."

Jenneane nodded. "That is my only value to him." She sneered. "Children. He doesn't even want sex with me for the enjoyment. His schente take care of that." Her voice was bitter.

"I've seen his schente." I didn't add that I'd been gifted nights of pleasure with more than a few in the fifteen years that Kell had schente. As prized brother of the prince, it gave Kell a certain thrill to give his women to me. "They are chosen only for their physical beauty and willingness to be mounted. Kell is a fool to be impressed by them."

My erection lessened, but I lay in her for a long time, loath to leave her for fear that she'd refuse me again.

"Are they very beautiful?" she asked.

"The schente?"

She nodded.

"No. They are simply Keen, and Kell has always had a love for things Keen." And a hatred for things not Keen. "They are tall and dark-eyed."

She blushed, the innocent blush of a woman still not certain of her worth. It hurt to see.

"You like my eyes?" she asked.

"The goddess Fion is said to have eyes like yours." I kissed her nose playfully. "She is not said to be as beautiful as you are."

Jenneane laughed heartily, and I smiled at the joyous sound, glad that I could make her happy.

I traced my finger over her eyebrow. "It was

your eyes that first drew me. Your intelligence and spirit showed through—and your vulnerability and trust. I love your eyes."

She sobered. "Do you think— No. Kell has the Keen black eyes. My son will probably have them, too." She dropped her gaze.

"Maybe not. Kell doesn't like to admit it, but his mother was blue-eyed. He carries the genes for it. After all, in humans, blue eyes are a recessive, are they not?"

She nodded.

"Jenneane?"

"I'm sorry, Pyter."

"You have nothing to be sorry for."

She flicked me a nervous glance. "I have nothing to offer you but the risk of death."

"You have everything to offer," I protested.

"Not children."

I nodded in understanding and touched her softening womb. Jenneane stiffened and tried to push my hand away. I gathered her to my chest, my cock growing hard in her again. She closed her eyes in the returning need that the schen demanded of her. I rolled to my back and explored the mound of her child slowly.

Jenneane gasped. "What are you doing?" she asked.

"Taking back what is mine. You are mine. The child you carry—"

"The contract," she reminded me in a panicked whisper.

"Legally, this child belongs to Kell, but he is child of my heart. Will you give me that?"

"I cannot ask—"

I pulled her hard against my hips, and Jenneane leaned back in pleasure. I would see her like this as often as she would allow.

"You haven't. I am offering this. Give me a son, Jenneane. Let me think of him as my son."

"You have my word." She pulled my hand over the baby fully, shivering at the connection.

I took her tenderly, pushing the memory of the implantation from my mind. Her son was mine, and Kell could not take that from me, even when he took Jole by virtue of his contract.

Jenneane's pregnancy ended all too quickly. We passed long winter days in Jenneane's bed or in front of the fire in her rooms. We took walks in the fields with Barri that spring, flanked by a half-dozen of Kell's soldiers. We shared picnics for three in the summer, surrounded by the lizors that Jenneane loved so much.

We spoke softly and in English around the soldiers. Still, we said nothing someone capable of translating could use against us, in case Kell has spies in our midst. Since we spoke, the soldiers didn't question that I looked at her full in the face. I didn't touch her in their presence, save to lift her to her feet when she was large in her pregnancy.

I found little ways of showing my feelings that the soldiers would miss. I would take a basket from Jenneane's hand and pick lizors for her room. I had a cosmeticist mix her a perfume from their scent. Of everything on Kegin, Jenneane loved the sea of lizors at her home best of all. I was glad to see that Kell allowed Jenneane her wish to be buried there among them, when the time came.

The soldiers interpreted my looks of silent warning as reminders of their place, issued as Kell's guardian of trust. Little did they know that my warnings were not on Kell's behalf, at all. Jenneane was not theirs to look upon. She had given herself to me. Only Kell could take that liberty with her and live though—thank Fion!—he could not touch her.

When Jenneane's time came, I massaged her nerve bundles to ease her discomfort, heartily sick that I couldn't make the birth painless for her. She kissed me, as Barri eased Jole from her body. Jenneane had chosen our son's name months earlier, in the human tradition. Perhaps the kiss was another human tradition, or perhaps it was symbolic of her giving Jole to me. I never asked, for in the heartbeat after she pulled back again, Barri placed our son in my hands.

He was as beautiful as Jenneane...with blue eyes already ringed in green and a sea of black curls. This was my son, the son of my heart and of the body of the woman I loved. To this day, I love him unconditionally as I did in those first moments of his life outside of Jenneane.

I took great pleasure in traveling to give Kell the news in person, content in the secret I held in my heart. He smiled and clasped me as a brother when I entered his library.

"What news, Pyter?" he boomed out.

"Your son was born early this eve, Kell."

His smile faltered, and he turned away, sighing and pushing his hand through his hair.

"I assume he is well?"

"A fine, strong son. He will make you proud."

Kell nodded, distracted.

"His mother came through well. She is a strong woman," I assured him.

His laugh was harsh. "Breeding stock is typically strong, Pyter. If only they weren't so high-strung."

I fisted my hand behind my back, willing my face free of rage, as my friend and prince insulted my mate, the very woman who'd presented him with a child that night.

Kell turned to me. "You talk to her in her barbarian language. Tell me how to convince her. What will it take to make her my true mate?" His expression was earnest, tortured.

I was torn. Perhaps Kell was not as unaffected and cold as he seemed. I had known him since we were boys. I never understood how this man I respected could treat Jenneane so shamefully. Perhaps if Kell knew the beauty of Jenneane's mind and soul, he would be the man I knew with her.

An image of Jole in her arms settled in my mind. Jenneane chose me. She was my mate, in every way that mattered, and her heart had been bared to me in love and trust. I could not betray her again.

I met Kell's eyes and sealed my fate as traitor. "She will never come to you, Kell. I am sorry, but she will never be yours."

Chapter Thirty-Four

Jole threw the diary across the room with a roar of rage.

Susan touched his face. "Please finish it," she begged.

"Traitor," he shouted. "I could have had her for my lifetime if Kell convinced her. Pyter stole my mother from me." Jole's stomach clenched at what he had lost.

"No, Joel. Please—"

"How can you defend him? Because he wanted her, he stole Kell's only avenue of success, his hope, his last chance for love with his bride." *All this time, Kell has been wronged, and I never saw it. I hated him to his grave, when I should have pitied what he lost. He could have had what Susan and I have, if Pyter had only told him what it was Jenneane needed of him.*

She recoiled, tears in her eyes. "He wanted her. That much is true. He loved Jenneane. If he believed she could be happy with Kell—"

He silenced her with an angry glare.

Susan took a calming breath. "It is not what it seems, Joel." She turned away with a sob and headed for the door.

"No. Susan...wait. I'm sorry. Don't leave this way. I didn't mean to yell at you. This is not your doing."

"Read the rest," she whispered. "That's all I ask. Trust in me, even if you don't trust in Pyter."

Jole sighed. "Hand me the book. For you, I will read the rest."

* * * *

Kell snatched up a decanter of lizor berry wine and sent it crashing into the fire. "Damn the woman to the darkest levels of the underworld. She never backs off the slightest degree."

Something in Kell wasn't right. This was a side to him that I had never seen. "Why does she upset you so? Do you harbor love for her?"

And what would I do if he said that he did? What machinations of Len would I be enacting to thwart Fion's true course and Kegin's salvation for my whims? Could Fion have truly sent me this love, if Kell loved her too?

Kell laughed heartily. "I? Love a barbarian beast? I would sooner love a hottel or a jaglin." He scowled. "She has the claws of a jaglin. I know."

A spark of white-hot hate settled in my chest. "Then why do you want her?"

"She is mine, bred for me. I was raised and trained to succeed, to win daughters from one of her kind. Don't you understand, Pyter?"

"No, Kell. I don't." I hoped I didn't. When had the boy I loved become the man I despised?

His face darkened in fury. "She is a failure. I was not born to fail."

"That is true. You have never failed."

And that is where Kol Ri failed Kell. All his

life, Kell had been taught to persevere at any cost, but he was never taught the fine art of negotiation and compromise. Kell had been taught authority, but he was never taught compassion.

Kell sobered. "I disappoint my father, Pyter. I cannot fail."

I was at a loss. "Perhaps if you learned her language and negotiated—"

"With her?" Kell shook his head. "She is full of pride and plans, Pyter."

"Plans?"

"Why eight years?" he demanded. "What is the trickery in that number?"

I blushed, remembering my surprise when I asked the same of her.

Jenneane had whispered the explanation in the dead of night. "Give me a child until he's seven, and he's mine for life." Humans held that the lessons taught in a child's earliest years would remain dearest to his heart, despite all the lessons learned in the intervening years to adulthood.

"It is a human custom," I told him. "Eight years is the formative time in a child's life. If he spends those years with his mother, Jole will never forget her."

"Jole?" he thundered. "She gave my son a barbarian name?"

"It is our way to allow a woman—"

"Did you suggest Keen names?"

I nodded. "Of course I did." I had, but I hadn't pressed the issue.

Jenneane said there was only one Keen

name she would ever consider using, one that would cost me my life, and so she would never use it.

"It was her right to choose, Kell."

He nodded. "Unfortunately, you are correct," he growled. "What of my son, Pyter? Has he the look of a prince of Kegin?"

"He has your hair, Kell."

"And his eyes?"

I smiled. "A beautiful mix of blue and green that the gods alone could possess."

Kell snorted. "Or a filthy human. He is young. They may yet change to a respectable color."

That simply, any guilt I'd harbored was expunged. Not three hours earlier, I'd helped a woman with more heart and honor than Kell could ever hope to possess bring forth a child more beautiful than a god and strong and hearty as a jaglin, and the man who should have treasured them above all else saw fit to dismiss them so easily.

I could not regret my choice to keep Jenneane's confidence. I would never knowingly commit her and our son—our son!—to the care of this man. I only prayed his eight years with Jenneane would be enough to make Jole into a man worthy of her name.

"I do not trust her, Pyter. I will not have my son corrupted."

I looked at him in surprise. "Corrupted? In what way?"

"He will know our ways. It will be your duty to ensure that he is trained as a prince of Kegin should be trained."

I smiled. "As you wish, Kell." But, the idea had taken hold. I would train Jole in the way Kell should have been trained, in a manner that might someday win him his cross-mate bride as I had won mine.

Jole was inquisitive and adept at learning. By the time he was four, he could speak Keen and English. He was learning to read and write in both languages. He knew the histories and customs of both worlds.

When Jole was past his nursing year, Jenneane granted Kell Jole's presence at all of Kegin's public celebrations. I took him to the events and ducked through the crowds, playing a game of snatch and giggle with the toddler. Kell held Jole for formal speeches, then passed him to me. All of us seemed happiest with that arrangement. Unless he was giving a speech, Kell rarely held our son. Kell did take the opportunity of Jole's presence at the celebrations to test him on his knowledge of Keen traditions and history.

"Do you know who Ro Ti is, Jole?" Kell asked on that fateful night, when Jole was more than four.

Jole paused with Kell's ceremonial dagger in his hand. He nodded. "He was the great conqueror, son of Kor Ti, the law-bringer. His army took the Eastern continent in the fifth century of the tenth Ti era, four-seventy-four. He was the Keen version of Ghengis Kahn."

I bit my cheek to keep from laughing, but nothing could have prevented the smile that curved my lips.

Kell shot me a look of disbelief. "Who?"

Jole placed the dagger on Kell's desk carefully and climbed into Kell's chair. "Ghengis Kahn. He was a conqueror from Earth, from my mother's world."

"And how would you know that?"

Jole cocked his head, his pouting lips and lowered eyes announcing his confusion with the question.

Kell turned on me. "She's teaching my son about her world?"

I nodded. "She felt knowing about Earth would help Jole win his mate, when the time comes. It does seem to be a sound premise."

"What has she taught him about Earth?"

I shrugged. "Many things. Jole knows much of their history and traditions of the American continent, things that will help him understand his cross-mate."

"Does he speak that language?"

I looked to Jole. "Answer me in your mother's language, Jole." Since Jenneane made a habit of speaking English to Jole and nothing else unless he wasn't present, there would be no confusion.

He nodded.

"What on Earth would you most like to see?"

Jole's face lit up, as I knew it would. "The Grand Canyon. The beautiful red rock that falls almost forever and the sunrise over—" His smile disappeared as he looked at Kell. Jole slid off the chair and ran to me, reaching his chubby fists up to me.

I didn't hesitate. I pulled Jole onto my hip and let him bury his face in my uniform jacket.

"It's okay," I soothed him. "Your father isn't angry with you, Jole." I almost choked on the words, on the lie I was telling him.

Kell shot me an appraising look that made my stomach clench and my blood freeze.

"You love my son, Pyter," he breathed, stunned by the concept.

I felt my mouth go dry. I nodded mutely. Had I made a fatal error in caring so openly for Jole?

"Jole, go to the kitchen for a snack before Pyter takes you to your mother," Kell ordered.

Jole looked to me, and I nodded, setting him on his feet and sending him off to find Kell's cook. I faced Kell, praying that I would live long enough to take Jole to Jenneane again.

Kell watched him go, considering something carefully. He turned back to me. "He loves you like a father."

The air felt like fire in my lungs, but I forced myself to breathe, forced myself not to tremble.

"I don't know why I never saw it."

"Kell—"

"When the time comes, you'll come to the palace with Jole."

"You want me to—"

Kell cut me off with a look of warning. "The boy needs a sense of continuity. You will provide that. I would rather have his male keeper accompany him than his nurse."

"What about his mother?" I asked hopefully.

"That woman will never set foot in the palace unless she comes as my true mate."

My head spun at the implications. I would come to the palace. Jenneane would not. She would lose both her mate and son in the same day.

"Has there been any trouble, Pyter?"

"Trouble?" I couldn't follow the path his mind had taken.

"Has she shown her barbarian blood and seduced her guards to her bed?" His eyes were hard and his muscles clenched.

I shook my head. "Your soldiers do not dare meet her eyes, do not dare hope."

Kell sighed. "A pity. I have put the most likely men to fall for it there in hopes..." He scrubbed his hands over his face.

"Kell?" He wanted her to take other men?

"If she betrayed me, I could have her as true mate."

"But the contract clearly states—"

His laughter made my heart stutter.

"The Council decided long ago that such a bargain was ridiculous. She was bred for me. She is mine, Pyter. No other man may ever have her."

I shook my head. "Consider, for argument, that she would someday accept a man as true mate. You would have your heirs by her and your schente to warm your nights. Would you put your pride ahead of Kegin's salvation and hold her to that?" I clamped my mouth shut, afraid that I had gone too far.

Kell smiled and came to clap a hand on my shoulder. "Always brutally honest with me," he mused. "You are my truest friend, because you dare to challenge me."

I nodded. "And your answer?" I prodded him.

"I will have a daughter from her first. If she wishes another, I will have my claim first."

I rubbed my neck. "But that would make her refuse altogether. Wouldn't it be better to have a Kegin-born re-bred female of any man she chose than none at all?"

"I will not accept such disgrace. If she is willing to take another man, she will take me. If she has the capacity to accept a man fully, it will be me."

"But she has not the heart to accept you," I mused. "If you must fail, everyone must. If anyone succeeds, you will cross the line first."

Kell laughed. "You know me well, Pyter."

I knew him too well. A mutinous wish to strike his selfish hide dead took root. I pushed the treasonous urge away. I would be dead before I left the house, and Jenneane and Jole would be unprotected.

Kell sobered. "I will come for her in three months' time, Pyter."

"Come for her?"

"It is time for her to carry my second son." He smiled a cold smile. "Or to give me a daughter."

My mouth went dry. "I will inform her of your decision, but why will you come for her?"

"This child is mine from his conception. I will watch the insemination, and he will be placed in my hands at his birth."

I nodded, sick at how the news would be received by Jenneane. "As you wish, Kell."

"Approach her with my offer, Pyter."

"Offer?"

"A contract giving her the freedom to take any mate she chooses when Jole comes to me.....if she mates to a daughter with me instead of the insemination to a son. Assure her that the new contract would free her of her obligation to undergo that insemination, after she presents me with my daughter."

"And her children by you? She will ask."

"Those children are mine. I would give her my daughter for her nursing year but no more than that."

"I will present your case, Kell."

I tried to hide my upset from Jenneane as I handed Jole into her hands. It seemed to work.

She kissed our son's head and carried him to his bed. "I can see he enjoyed himself," she noted.

"He kept me busy."

"Chasing him, I'd bet."

"Is there any finer game for a four-year-old boy in a crowd?"

Jenneane chuckled. "I suppose not." She brushed Jole's dark curls from his beautiful eyes, the eyes that Kell considered his greatest failing. She looked to me, and her smile fled.

I turned away, fisting my hand in the tiny red uniform jacket I'd removed from Jole in the transport.

Her hand touched my shoulder. "What is it?" she whispered.

"Come. We have much to discuss."

I headed to her rooms without looking at her. Barri tried to scurry away at my approach, but I took her arm and guided her with us. Barri was instrumental in getting us to where we were that day, and much of what we had to discuss involved her, at least indirectly. I bolted the door behind us before turning to them.

Jenneane sank to the bed, looking shaken. "What is it?" she repeated.

"Things—are not good."

"Why?"

"Kell will arrive in three months' time to take you to your insemination."

Jenneane shook her head. "The contract—"

"He has arranged certain provisions with the Council that you did not agree to."

"For instance?"

"This child is his from conception."

"He is not living here," she shouted. "My contract specifically states that."

"No. He will not live here, but he will watch the insemination and he will attend the birth."

"There's more."

I nodded, pacing angrily. "If he learns you have ever taken a lover on Kegin, the Council has decreed that your penalty will be forfeit."

"But my contract—"

"Does not mention fidelity. It doesn't grant you sexual freedom, either."

Jenneane paled. "He can't do this," she whispered.

"He has. The Council has ruled that you are Kell's property, unless he chooses to free you."

"He'll never do that," she moaned.

"He would contract for that. He wants to contract for that, freeing you to contract with any mate you choose."

She met my eyes, and her surprise faded into dread. "What are his terms?"

"You know his terms."

"True mating to a daughter."

"And full loss of both children to Kell."

Tears made her eyes over bright. "As agreed in the previous contract?"

"Jole would be. Kell would give you the nursing year with his daughter, and her birth would free you from the obligation of a second insemination."

"What aren't you telling me?"

I took a deep breath. Jenneane was too attuned to me for me to hide anything from her. "He's ordered me to accompany Jole to the palace, when the time comes."

"Until he's settled?"

"No."

I didn't need to say more than that. We stared at each other miserably.

Jenneane nodded. "I could have you, but I'd have to accept Kell first. Either way, I lose my son. If I have you, Joel loses both of us when Kell takes him from us. If I don't accept Kell's offer, Joel has you, but I lose both of you."

I nodded, and she closed her eyes. She had the full situation firmly in mind.

"What should I do, Pyter?" she croaked. She was defeated. "How can I make a choice like this?"

"I cannot choose for you. I will accept whatever decision you make. I have no wish to see you submit to Kell. He has no regard for you, but it would allow us to have children of our own, to love openly.

"I will never hate you for what you choose, Jenneane. If your choice is to stand your stated course, I will admire you for the sacrifices of son and mate you make for your goddess of love and our son's future. If you choose to win your freedom from Kell, I will do my best to wipe his touch from your memory, when you are free to return to me."

"It will hurt you," she whispered.

"Either way, a piece of me dies. Either way, a piece of you dies. You must choose which pieces die and which grow stronger from the pruning."

She bit her lip and swallowed a sob, though her tears fell. "You made me promise once not to go to Kell to save you, to let you go to your grave knowing no man had touched me but you. Is that still your wish?"

"Jenneane—"

"Is it? Given the choice of the hidden love we've shared and having Joel as son of your heart or knowing Kell was free to use me at his whim—"

I fisted my hand and uttered a curse on Kell.

Jenneane nodded. "You know my choice."

Relief I hadn't realized I would feel coursed through me. I fell to my knees at her feet. I hadn't consciously made a choice, but my heart had. I raised my head and kissed her passionately. "Thank you, Jenneane."

She touched my cheek. "How long do we have until we have to stop using the Walla teas?"

Barri sighed. "Two months. The drug takes two weeks to leave the system, but we should double that for safety."

I felt my hands start to shake. We had to discontinue the tea that stopped her release of eggs, but the fact that Jenneane would want to put off that step as long as possible gave me hope. "You would still have me?" I whispered. "Knowing the penalty if we are caught, you still want me?"

"I suspected Kell would find a way to take that penalty long ago." She pulled my hand to the hem of her dress.

"And if he learns that we are lovers?" Fion, but I was already hard for her.

"He will never have me willing, and I will follow you as soon as I am able."

It was a soldier's choice, the bravest choice of a woman in love.

"Barri, leave us," I ordered gruffly, already pushing her skirt to her hips.

Jenneane gasped as she reached for the buttons on my uniform jacket. "Only you, Pyter." Her plea was lost in my mouth.

CHAPTER THIRTY-FIVE

Jole pulled Susan to his chest, kissing her forehead and adding a spike of healing that he was sure she needed, though she didn't ask. "I'm sorry," he breathed.

She nodded, running her hands over his chest. "It's all right," she assured him. "I know this can't be easy for you."

"It explains so many things."

"There is more, Joel. There is so much more to the story than you know yet."

* * * *

The months until her insemination passed too quickly. For a week after Jenneane stopped taking the Walla tea, we felt safe in sating ourselves. After that, we resorted to love play like we'd enjoyed when I took her barrier. After more than two weeks of our abstinence, Jenneane arranged something that proved to me the intelligence of humans.

She met me at the door to her rooms after I had Jole settled to sleep, with Barri in her adjoining room to keep an eye on him. I stared in wonder at the presentation cloak she wore. My cock's reaction was immediate and intense.

"What is this?" I growled.

"I am yours. Do you refuse me?"

"Refuse you? By the gods, Jenneane! I would

kill any other man who looked at you."

She fingered the tie at the neck of the cloak. "Then this is yours to remove."

I strode to her and pulled the ties free, whipping the cloak from her shoulders to reveal the presentation gown. I moved my eyes over her. I'd always wondered what she'd look like in one, but I'd never dared ask for this favor after her months with Kell.

Her lush breasts were outlined for me. I ran my lips over them and drank in the scent of the lizor perfume I'd had made for her. My fingers traced the slit to the soft curls, which were already damp for me.

I groaned. I wanted to flip the slit open and plunge into her against the wall. "What would you have me do?" I asked, unwilling to dredge up memories of Kell in my haste.

"I am presented to you. What do you wish of me?"

I ground my teeth in fury. "That is not what the presentation means," I managed in a harsh whisper.

Her lips caressed mine. "It is what I'm offering you. I present myself to you. You may take any pleasure you wish."

I stroked her wet folds, watching her green eyes widen and then flutter closed. "Not anything I wish. Promise me you'll wear this again when I can have anything."

She smiled. "Anything, Pyter. I fashioned an Earth device for us."

"A device that keeps eggs from dropping?" I asked in fascination.

She shook her head slowly and went to work on the buttons on my trousers. "Not quite. It stops your sperm from reaching an egg. Coupled with a bit of Walla paste, it should be foolproof." My trousers unbuttoned, she turned her sexiest stare on me. "What would you like, Pyter?" Her voice purred.

She eased my trousers over my thighs and urged me toward her with her fingers digging into the cheeks of my ass.

"I'm yours, Pyter. Tell me what you want."

"All night. You won't be getting rid of me until the sun rises."

"Good."

"You won't be getting rid of this gown, until the last time I take you." The thought of having Jenneane as if she had been prepared for me had me pulsing. It would be a long night with many encounters, I was sure.

She nodded, her eyes glittering at the proof of my loss of control.

"The first time won't be gentle," I warned, guiding her back to the wall.

Far from discouraging her, Jenneane started to pull up at my tunic. "Show me how much you want me."

I leaned to allow her to pull the tunic off and took her mouth hungrily as it cleared my head. Jenneane stilled with the tunic in her hands as I spread the slit wide and lifted her with my hands beneath her thighs. My first thrust went deep into her, and I smiled as I encountered the soft give of the ruv cap she'd fashioned.

Jenneane tried to wrap her legs around me,

464

but I held them spread wide for me, opening her fully to my thrusts. My possession of her was a fierce, animal drive. Thank Fion for Jenneane's sounds of pleasure. I took her deeper, took her higher. Her cries became more intense, and I became more fevered in a relentless cycle.

She pulled at my face and brought my mouth down on hers to mute her screams of release. Her body rippled and pulled around my ceaseless pounding. Fion, but I could never let this woman go. My cock started to swell before my seed poured from me. Jenneane threw her head back. Her body went taut as I locked inside her. She shivered in the release of her egg, the first time I had released an egg of her.

Like the first time I took her, we stared into each other's eyes, forming unspoken agreements in our hearts. There would never be another for either of us. There would never be another moment like this.

When the morning of her implantation came, Jenneane came down in a travel dress and cloak that Kell had brought with him. Apparently, if she traveled with Kell, Jenneane was worthy of the proper dress for the occasion.

Kell waved her toward his transport. Jenneane guided Barri with her, placing the servant between herself and Kell. Jenneane didn't bother with having Barri or myself translate an explanation. It wasn't necessary. Even Kell knew her mind.

At the medical center, Kell placed a hand on Jenneane's back.

She stiffened and sent him a look of cool

disdain. "Pyter, tell this bastard to take his hands off of me," she requested in her most imperious English.

I paled. "Kell, the contract," I urged. "She is threatening to dissolve with penalty."

Kell fisted his hand at his side and motioned her to precede him into the building.

I waited with Kell while they harvested fresh eggs from her. There was no reason for it but Kell's wish to punish Jenneane for refusing his offer. The zygotes saved from the last harvest were sufficient. Kell seemed annoyed that she didn't scream during the procedure. Thankfully, he didn't try to engage me in conversation while we waited.

Kell motioned me into the procedure room with him. I hesitated. If he watched the procedure, there was no reason for me to do so as guardian of trust.

"Come, Pyter," he ordered. "I need one friendly face in that room. Since my bride will not send me a kind look, my brother will have to be there."

I followed him, swallowing the foul proof of my disgust for the man and the act.

Jenneane lay on the table, her lower body raised by the six-inch wedge and covered shoulders to thighs with a heavy sheet. She panned her eyes over us and looked away.

"Are we prepared?" the doctor asked.

Barri repeated the question in her broken English, though it was unnecessary for anything but hiding Jenneane's knowledge of the Keen language from Kell. Jenneane nodded and pulled her heels to the grooves in the base of the wedge.

Kell moved to one side of her and I moved to the other. I grasped one ankle a split-second before Kell grasped the other. I looked away. My witness was not required this time. Surely Kell did not want me to look on 'his woman' if it was not required of me.

"Don't touch me," Jenneane shouted in Keen.

I looked at her in shock, but her eyes were locked on Kell. Just as Kell opened his mouth to retort, she looked to me.

"Don't touch me," she said only slightly less forcefully. For an instant, a deeper emotion flickered in her eyes...fear.

I moved my hand to the edge of the table and bowed to her. This was a show for Kell. If she demanded he remove his hands and didn't demand the same of me, Kell might become suspicious.

Jenneane looked back to Kell, cold hatred in her beautiful eyes.

"The contract, Kell," I reminded him on a sigh. "You could lose your sons to her, unless you heed."

For a moment, he didn't move. His jaw clenched with the torrent of words he was holding behind his teeth. Kell pushed her leg away with a look of disgust and muttered several curses while he gripped the edge of the table.

The doctor sighed and pulled out a set of hide straps from a drawer. "Tell her we will have to use these, if she will not be touched. Tell her it will hurt."

I nodded and met Jenneane's eyes. My voice

shook, as I switched to English. "Are you sure you want this? It won't be pleasant."

She nodded.

I extended my hand to the doctor, still holding her eyes until two straps were in my hands. I couldn't look at her as I bound the ankle and wrist on my side to the table. I hated myself for doing it to her, for not convincing her to allow Kell's hands rather than that. The only bright star on our horizon was that the doctor ordered Barri to handle the straps on Kell's side, not willing to risk the penalty with such a mundane act.

I looked to Kell, attempting to give him the encouraging nod he'd asked me for in the corridor. He jerked his head toward Jenneane. I didn't look in her eyes. I watched the wand slide in, willing myself not to scream, my stomach not to empty. I couldn't look at her face, and Kell wouldn't let me look away. It was the only place left for my eyes to settle.

She fought the straps when she was stimulated, a single whimper escaping her clenched teeth. Jenneane sank to the table, a trickle of blood winding down her foot from where the strap cut into her ankle. I removed the straps and accepted a bandage from the doctor, as he set about recording the proper documents of insemination.

Jenneane didn't fight it as Barri removed the straps on Kell's side, didn't fight my ministrations. She swiveled her foot in my grip and curled away from Kell, pressing her thighs together in discomfort...or the aftershocks of the pleasure she'd hidden from Kell.

"Come Pyter," Kell ordered.

I nodded to the doctor to tend to her and followed him to the door.

Kell paused. "I return to my home, doctor. Be sure to contact me if I need to return for a second attempt."

My stomach rebelled at the suggestion.

"Yes, Highness," the doctor replied.

There was no second insemination attempt. The cap formed within the day, and I took Jenneane to our home as soon as the pregnancy was confirmed. I wanted nothing more than to hold and comfort her, but as I'd found it difficult to look at her after Jole's insemination, Jenneane couldn't meet my eyes for three days after Mik's.

When Barri half-dragged me to her rooms, Jenneane was curled on the floor in her bathroom, weeping. I gathered her to me and rocked her until she quieted.

"How can you stand the sight of me?" she whispered.

"I love you."

"Even when I carry another man's child? Even when I....."

"What is it?"

"How could I enjoy it, Pyter? In a room full of people, Kell watching me, with a metal and ruv machine— The last time, I concentrated on you, but this time— How could I?"

"The nerve conductor has no understanding. If you are free to release an egg, the stimulation will be pleasurable. It is—the body's design."

"You mean if Kell—" Jenneane paled, her

eyes going wide in horror at the conclusion that she would feel pleasure from anything that Kell could do to her.

"Shhh." I kissed her, and she melted against me. "Did Kell ever kiss you?" I breathed against her lips.

She stiffened in my arms. "Pyter—"

I kissed her again. "Did he?"

"You know he did." She tasted my lips, the schen pushing her to me.

"What did you feel?"

"Hatred."

"Good." I pushed her robe away and stroked her nipple to a rigid peak while I caressed my lips over hers. "Did he touch your breasts?"

Jenneane groaned. "I hated it."

She lay over me as I sank back to the floor. I took the nipple in my mouth, suckling at her while her lubricant seeped over the ridge of my cock through my trousers. I moved to the other nipple while I unbuttoned my trousers and slid them down my legs.

Jenneane rocked over me, seeking the tip but not daring to move too far while I suckled her. My cock strained toward the heat and moisture it knew waited so close. She gasped, as I released her.

"You like that?" I asked.

"Yes, Pyter." Her voice was more pleading than a confirmation.

"You want more from me?"

"I want you."

I guided her down onto my length. Jenneane rode me until she shattered around me. I held her to me, while her body drew at my cock, fierce contractions of rippling warmth.

"Has Kell ever done that for you?" I asked patiently.

Her eyes were half-closed in pleasure. She didn't acknowledge my question.

I bucked up into her. "Jenneane," I ordered in a hoarse whisper. "Has Kell ever given you pleasure? Made you shatter in his hands?"

"No." She trembled as I quickened my pace.

"Has that damn stim wand ever made you feel this good?"

She shook her head, her contractions subsiding but still pulsing around me.

"This is real, Jenneane. This is love. This is pleasure. Who gives you this?"

"You," she moaned, laying a kiss on my chest as I pulled back to thrust into her again. She was close. Her inner muscles clenched around me in preparation to shatter again.

"Scream for me, Jenneane. When it comes to you, scream into me while I come." But, waiting for her was going to be difficult. Already, my sac was drawn up tight to my cock and my body in restless anticipation. She was so close. I had to wait for her. "Will you scream—"

I made it no further. Her mouth was on mine, her movements urgent as she climaxed again. Her scream teased my mouth. I lifted her and pulled my hips back, sliding from her body and spilling my seed between us.

Jenneane's eyes opened wide in surprise, panning from the slick of my come to my face. "Pyter, why—"

"Which is more important, Jenneane? The loving touch that brings you true release or that single faceless stimulation that makes your body release an egg? Anyone with equipment enough can give you the latter. You know who gives you the former. You know who you seek to fill your bed and body. Should I be jealous or envious of the biological crest you cannot help but feel or proud that I am the only man who can tease your body to bliss?"

She kissed my chest. "Thank you, Pyter."

"For explaining?" I asked.

"For explaining it and for believing it."

CHAPTER THIRTY-SIX

Jole set the book aside and pulled Susan to his body, needing to feel her in his arms. This was what Pyter and his mother shared. He ran his hand over their growing child. This was the closeness they should have been permitted, the knowledge that the child she carried was theirs alone, the knowledge that their love would not lead to death or violation.

"He would do anything for her, Joel," she whispered.

"I know. I'll grant his request, Susan. You have my vow. No matter what the rest says, I'll grant his request."

Susan didn't reply. She played her fingers in his tunic and didn't meet his eyes.

Jole cupped her face to his. "What is it?"

"Part of me knows you have to know the whole truth. Part of me wants to beg you to stop now. What you read will hurt you, I know."

He stilled, the warmth of his discoveries leeched away by her warning. "I must know," he whispered.

Susan nodded. "Yes, you must."

* * * *

That pregnancy was very different. This child was not our child but Kell's, a child who was not ours to love and raise, not ours to guide.

473

Jenneane called it 'surrogate.' I didn't ask Jenneane to let me claim Mik as child of my heart. Mik wasn't hers to give.

She didn't discuss names with me. Aside from her requests for me to massage away the worst of her pregnancy signs and the force of her schen, we didn't discuss the pregnancy. There were no long hours running my hands over a son I'd grow to love.

Life went on for us much as it always had. We picnicked in the lizors. I taught Jole to ride war-buck and spar with daggers, as it was the time for such things in his education. The seasons passed, and Jenneane became heavy with the child she carried.

There was tension near the end of her term, when word came to us from the Breeding Office. Jole's mate had been born. Jenneane was sick with worry. She spent weeks schooling Jole in the qualities of patience, negotiation, compromise, respect for others, empathy, and love. Jole was an avid student, excited at the concept of having a mate bred to be his partner in all things, for that was what Jenneane taught him his mate should be.

Then came the moment we'd dreaded but never discussed. When I pulled Jenneane to me, and she cried out in pain, my smile failed me. I looked to the swell of Kell's son as if seeing it for the first time. I hated the man I'd once called brother, and I hated that he would descend on our peace again.

When Kell entered the room where Jenneane labored, my vague sense of unease gelled into a certainty that his aim was to destroy her. His eyes narrowed, and he threw his cloak toward a waiting chair.

"What are you doing?" he snapped at me.

My hands stilled, resting on the silin of her gown where I had been massaging the nerve bundles in her back that would relieve most of her pain. I met his eyes, willing myself not to tremble in a mixture of fear and fury. "I was relieving her birth signs."

"That is my place."

I eased my hands to the edge of the mattress and nodded, knowing his game and knowing I had no way to stop him, short of the sacrifice of my death that Jenneane would not welcome.

I moved aside, and he knelt in my place. My place! His hand touched the bundle of nerves, and Jenneane recoiled, making it appear that she had only just gleaned his intent.

"Don't touch me," she panted.

Kell pushed away from the bed with a warning look at me. He ambled to the chair and dropped into it with a smile.

I chanced reasoning with him. "Kell, if it will ease your son—"

"If she wishes relief in birthing my son, she will ask for my help. Tell her. Tell her I'll use my healing magic to make this painless for her."

Jenneane groaned as the worst of her pain returned.

I cleared my throat and addressed her in English. "You heard him. I don't want to see you in pain, but I won't beg you to do this. It could be painless for you, but the choice is yours."

"Do you really want his hands and lips on me? I'd rather be in pain." There was a bite of bitterness in that, making her beautiful language sound like the guttural abomination Kell described it as most often.

I nodded. I'd expected that answer.

Kell misinterpreted my nod and started to stand.

"Don't touch me," she growled. "No one touch me."

Kell shot me a look of pure hate.

I shrugged. "You said it long ago. She has her pride."

"Leave the room."

"Kell?"

"She finds comfort in you, much as Jole finds comfort in you. She will not break if she feels your comfort."

"She labors with your son," I pleaded.

"Which means she will reach for me, when my son makes her uncomfortable enough."

I hesitated, the mind-altering fury stealing my sanity.

"Leave us," he warned.

I bowed to him, my prince, my brother, the man I would kill with my bare hands if I cared so little for Jenneane that I would leave her alone and unprotected. "As you wish, Highness."

Kell raised an eyebrow in surprise. "You call me Highness, brother?"

Jenneane mumbled an English curse that I vaguely recognized. "Pyter, please go. Don't let him kill you," she pleaded.

"What did she say?" Kell demanded.

"She thinks you mean to kill me, Highness."

Jenneane cried out, sweat plastering her hair to her head.

Kell nodded. "Leave us, brother."

I turned and left, pacing the corridor while Jenneane labored in pain.

She screamed, and I cringed. This wasn't a Keen birth. It wasn't the Keen way to allow a woman to suffer this way. I couldn't make her delivery painless, but I could make it bearable as I had with Jole. Helping Jenneane birth and raise Jole is one of the few things I am truly proud of in my life.

Jenneane screamed again. I looked into the room through the gap between the doors. She was shaking and bathed in sweat, throwing her head back and forth while Barri checked her progress.

I locked on Kell. He sat at the bedside watching her suffering with a look of smug satisfaction. The self-serving bastard was enjoying this. If Kell really thought Jenneane would give in to pain, he was a fool. More likely, he wanted to punish her for refusing him, and for that, I hated him all the more.

Barri spoke to her in low tones. "Please Lady. No tight. Hurt more."

Tears rolled down Jenneane's face. She glanced at the doors in longing. Jenneane knew I was there, that I would not desert her. She knew I could make this bearable, if Kell were so kind as to allow it.

But Kell was not kind! Had he been the least bit kind, she might have agreed to be his true mate.

Kell had always been impatient. From the first time he had Jenneane prepared and brought to him, he'd made unreasonable demands of her. He'd wanted her to act the part of a Keen woman, of a faceless schente to be mounted and used. No, he treated her worse. He wanted the outward appearance of a Keen woman but treated her like a breeding cow.

Jenneane wasn't a dumb beast, and she wasn't a woman of Kegin. After twenty-two years on Earth, ignorant of her true heritage, she would not relinquish the world she knew so easily.

She screamed again. I fisted my hand. I should have found a way to leave her on Earth. I'd subjected her to this fate by bringing her through the gateway, and I did it selfishly. The fact that a human male would be incapable of stimulating the release of her eggs, or fertilizing them if he was hung like their Earth beasts and could stimulate her, was immaterial. Jenneane would have been happier in a childless marriage on Earth than in this imposed torture and captivity.

I looked back to Jenneane. She stifled another cry behind barred teeth. I winced as a thin trail of blood came from her womb. I uttered a curse and braced my hand on the door. The boy was ripping her. This was not a Keen birth.

Barri bowed to Kell. "Highness, I could give her a potion of herbs to relax her muscles and make your son pass faster."

"She gets nothing."

"If irreparable damage is done—" It was her last recourse, giving Kell the hope of a daughter to rein him in.

"Any help will come from me. Am I understood, servant?"

"Yes, Highness. As you wish."

Kell leaned toward Jenneane. He didn't touch her. He had been warned off once that night. If he touched her again without her permission, he risked losing his sons, and Kell knew it. "I can take away your pain, woman." Kell said it slowly, knowing Jenneane had heard enough in her months with him to glean his offer.

"Woman," I spat under my breath.

Kell would never stoop to using Jenneane's Earth name. He had forbidden anyone to speak it in his presence, even Jole.

Kell reviled anything human. He would never learn even a single word of English. It was a dislike he'd learned from his years with Kol Ri. I prayed to Fion that Jole would benefit from his years with Jenneane, that he would not grow to be Kell's son.

Jenneane shook her head. She panted out a few of the words in Keen she admitted she knew, the same old lyrics she had been using with him for almost six years. "Don't touch me."

She could admit that she knew more, but she wouldn't give Kell the satisfaction of knowing it, and Jenneane enjoyed knowing what Kell said when he thought she couldn't understand his words. If Jenneane spoke Keen to a person, she was honoring them, and Kell was not worthy of that honor.

Kell's eyes were fierce. "It needn't pass this way. Let me touch you, and I will make this painless for you." He motioned to Barri.

Taking her cue from my ruse, Barri didn't waste her breath on translating what Jenneane clearly heard. "Relax. Kell Hi not take your fire. The babe well down in you now."

"I know. I feel it. How long?"

"Soon."

Kell leaned forward, his voice losing its calm composure. "Let me touch you," he barked. "I will make it bearable."

Jenneane turned her face away. She used the English she knew he wouldn't understand. "It could be bearable if anyone was allowed to help."

Kell shot Barri a look of irritation.

"She refuses, Highness."

"Damn the woman to Len's Dungeons," he growled.

"The baby is coming, Highness."

"Let him come. Maybe this one will not have the look of his filthy human mother."

I bit back a scream of pure fury, striding to the nearest column and punching it, feeling worse that it wasn't Kell I struck, that I lacked the strength of character to defend her as my mate.

"No," I breathed. It would serve Kell's purpose if I made the situation clear to him. Jenneane would be forced to Kell's bed by the damned Council and contract, if he had the slightest proof of the truth.

I returned to the doorway and peeked through the gap in time to see the boy slide into Barri's hands. Jenneane collapsed in relief.

Barri cut the cord and wrapped Mik in a blanket to warm him. She bowed as she presented the bundle to Kell. "Your son, Highness."

He took the boy, his smile widening. "He has the look of a true prince of Kegin."

Jenneane reached a hand out and laid it on her son's chest. "Mik."

Kell scowled at her hand and then at Barri. "What does that mean?" he demanded.

Jenneane dropped her hand in exhaustion and met Barri's eyes. "Mik," she repeated.

Barri nodded. "Your son's name, Highness. Her brother's name is Mik, and the princess names your son to honor him, in the way of her people."

Kell's face darkened. "My son will have a Keen name," he growled.

Jenneane affected a broken Keen not unlike Barri's broken English. "My contract. My choice. Name Mik," she reminded him forcefully.

"I will not accept this," he thundered.

Mik started to wail, and Jenneane reached for him automatically, the drive to mother even a child she couldn't keep strong enough to make her forget Kell's hold on his second son. So tender was her heart, and I loved that about her, the willingness to suckle the fruit of her enemy's loins without a thought to herself.

Kell backed from her, his expression murderous. "Keep your filthy human hands off of my son. You won't ruin this one. Servant, have Pyter inform the nursing maid that my son will have use of her before we leave this house."

Barri bowed, though her jaw was tight in anger. "I return soon, Lady. Stitch then."

Jenneane nodded. "Tell Kell to take his son and leave me. I cannot bear to look at them."

Barri shot Kell a wary look. "The princess begs you to take Prince Mik to his maid so she may recover, since you will not permit her to nurse him. Do not make him suffer for her, she asks."

Kell looked at Jenneane in surprise. He nodded slowly. "Tell her my son may keep the barbarian name."

Barri bowed and turned back to the bed.

Kell pushed through the doors with Mik in his arms. He pulled me along to the stairs. "There is some trickery here, Pyter."

I shook my head. "She is a strong woman, Kell. You said yourself that the Earth breeding stock—" My stomach clenched at what I was saying, but I had to dissuade Kell from further investigation.

"No. No woman is that strong. Be watchful, Pyter." Kell disappeared down the stairs, leaving me at the top.

I dared not go to her until Kell was long gone. There were no words between us. I am not certain that words exist in either language to describe the combination of loss, grief, and hate we both felt.

Her recovery was long, physically and emotionally. It was months before she pursued something beyond lying in my arms with her cheek pressed to my beating heart.

Kell's disdain for Jole wasn't lost on Jenneane.

Our teaching was modified. Over the next two years, our son's training intensified. Jenneane trained him to handle his mate. I trained him in the conventions he had to adhere to and respect to minimize Kell's animosity. To this day, I believe Jenneane was teaching him to be the better king.

Jole was athletic and adept at learning, much better than Kell was at any of his tasks in his childhood. Jole rode straight and proud as a general, and he was capable of holding his seat like his 'horsewoman' mother. He was a hunter the likes of which boys twice his age aspired to be. He played Nine Tails and Bell Ball as if born on the field. Still, Kell was unimpressed with his elder son.

The years until the end of our time with Jole, like all good times in life, were over too soon. Kell Ri's soldiers, for he was my king then, came without warning on the eve of his eighth birthday. I am sure Jole will remember that night to his grave, as will I.

It broke my heart to see Jenneane beg for my help. I would have given anything to stop her, to spare her that shame in front of our son.

Jole hated me that night. I couldn't blame him for it. I hated myself for taking him from a loving home to the father who dismissed him on his birthday with a sneer and an admonishment about the wrinkles in his uniform jacket after our five-hour drive.

I couldn't call Jole by his name anymore. I had betrayed him by bringing him here. Worse, using Jole's name engendered too many memories of a place I no longer had the right to claim. Son of my heart, I love him still and always will, but he hates and mistrusts me as traitor to our family. The son given to me by his mother was no longer hers to give. Jole belonged to Kell now, to a father who would never love and appreciate him as his mother and I would.

I walk a fine line. At times, I know Jole thinks I am unnecessarily harsh with him. At times, he resents that I serve his father as well as him. Little do they know that I serve Jole, when the choice must be made.

My way is often rocky. I remind Jole of Jenneane's teachings as often as I dare, in the privacy of his rooms.....always in the privacy of his rooms. It would be deemed treason to do so openly. I drill the traditions and expectations Kell demands of him. I'm continuing to train him, as I promised Jenneane I would our last time alone together.

"Why are you writing this?" the reader might ask. I ask myself that same question. Yes, even now, with my crimes laid out in my own hand, I question my motives for doing it. Am I hoping to be dealt Kell's deathblow, if this journal is ever discovered? Perhaps some corner of my heart wishes for death, but I promised to raise the son of my heart, and so I do not actively seek death.

I do hope my son will someday read this journal and know the parents he never really knew in life. Will Jole hate us for the choices we made or admire us? Will he think of me as traitor or father? I dare not ask.

I will hide this journal with Barri until Jole reaches maturity or I die, whichever is the latter. I leave his mother's necklace with her as well. If I die before Jole reaches maturity, I will trust that she will give it to him at the time I promised.

If this journal is discovered, I ask no mercy for myself nor even for Barri. I ask only that Jole, who was ignorant of our treason, be spared Kell's wrath.

I would seek death now were it not for my love for Jenneane and Jole. The news came to me today. I was unprepared. When Kell ordered me to tell Jole that his mother was dead, I felt the room begin to spin and the blood rushing in my ears.

"How?" I asked. "She was well, when I carried your offer to her two weeks ago."

Every year, on the day before Jole's birthday, Kell sent me with an offer for Jenneane. She could move to the palace and have her sons in time for Jole's birthday in exchange for her contract to a single daughter. She would take her place as queen or be freed.....if she chose. Kell would agree to turn to his schente rather than her for all but the production of his daughter.

By the third year, Jenneane started throwing the letters in the fire before my speech had begun, wrapping her arms around me as her answer. It was an answer that made my heart and body sing. Our hours together were few but passionate, a bitter reminder that our stolen moments were all we would have, until Kell died and we might petition Jole for our lives and love.

Kell scowled. "She stole medicinals from her servant's bag and poisoned herself. The servant attests that she confused the powders and meant only to make a strong lizor berry and olum tea to help her sleep. Is there any possibility that she knew the effects of the various herbs?"

I shook my head. "None," I lied. Barri had taught Jenneane the uses of the drugs long ago, but it was better for Jole and for us all if Kell didn't know that and thought this move an unfortunate accident. "Why do you ask?"

Kell waved his hand dismissively. "The poison was gola berry."

I nodded. "I will tell him after his lessons. No need to disturb him now," I managed.

"Wise idea," Kell decided, looking back to his vid screen.

I made it to my room without outward sign of my pain. This was no mistake. As Kell suspected, Jenneane chose gola berry for a reason, and she chose her dosage carefully. Barri had taught her well.

I never asked if Barri helped Jenneane in her task. I suspect that she knew what Jenneane intended, but I doubt that Barri would have had the heart to mix the tea herself.

In a smaller dose, gola berry would cause miscarriage but was treatable with pharmaceuticals Barri would not have access to. If Jenneane sought medical aid for gola poison, Kell would know her reason for taking it and force her to her contract penalty. Jenneane had only one choice to escape that.

Jenneane took an untreatable dose of the gola berry late at night...with a tea of olum to control the worst of her pain. She would have passed the babe early, perhaps into the toilet. After an hour or so of her bleeding, the doctors would be unable to identify the father, if they could prove that she carried at all.

There was only one reason for Jenneane to choose this course. The ruv cap and Walla paste failed us at last. Without my lovemaking, Jenneane might have denied the truth to herself, until her pregnancy signs became pronounced enough that Barri noticed the change in her. Barri's examination of her finding a cap, she would see only this one means of escape.

Jenneane would escape Kell as she swore she would while giving me my life. I knew the contract she proposed to me with this act. Jenneane gave me my life, so our son would continue to have my guidance. And so he shall, until Kell takes my life or Mag stands as my judge. May Fion move him to pity me when he does.

* * * *

Jole closed the diary and set it aside. "Pyter has his wish. He will be buried where he wishes with full military honors," he decided.

"No."

He looked to Susan in surprise. "Why? He deserves that much."

"No. He deserves better."

"What do you have in mind?"

"A small group. The two of us and Barri. And a small complement of soldiers who don't speak English."

Jole raised an eyebrow. "Why?"

"I intend to perform a human ceremony for him. He must be buried by Jenneane's side. Is that possible?"

"It is. What ceremony will you perform? The death rites?"

She shook her head and pulled his hands to the swell of their baby. "Do you see him as your father, Joel?"

"You know I do."

"Then if this is a boy, I want to name him Pyter."

"I'd be honored, but I still don't understand what you mean to do."

"I intend to give them the one thing they never had in life." She stilled his question with a passionate kiss. When Susan pulled back, she whispered to him in English. "*Dearly beloved, we are gathered here in the sight of Fion—*"

THE END

SECTION FIVE:
Jelise

In Her Ladyship's Service

CHAPTER ⊕NE

December 22ⁿᵈ, 2017

By the Keen calendar— Iric 26ᵗʰ, Ri 25-3001

Jelise Jackson grumbled a curse, kicking the bars covering the windows, wincing as the spike of pain raced up her leg in response. She limped a step before she felt confident enough to place her full weight on it again.

It was just a lark, her mind argued. She hadn't stolen a car and taken it across state lines or snatched a kid or anything stupid like that. *It was just a broken window, and that jerk deserved it!* So why were the feds after her, instead of the city cops?

She laid her head against the bars, gritting back a scream of frustration. It just wasn't fair.

Life isn't fair.

"Oh, shut up," she grumbled.

What did I do, pick some Senator's son to tangle with?

"Damn it! Story of my life."

Shouting and fighting echoed through the abandoned building, and Jelise stiffened, looking at the door in confusion. "What the hell?" she whispered.

Joey and the other guys had run for it. Why wouldn't they? The feds wanted *her*. No one else was of interest to them.

So...who would be fighting? She rolled her eyes at the idea of Joey taking on feds. "I'm not that good in bed," she quipped. The idea of Pete or Steve coming back for her was even more ridiculous. They'd had their asses kicked and their push for sex shut down far too many times to make that believable.

The sounds came closer. Then silence fell— an ominous absence of noise that had her heart pounding in near terror. Jelise shivered from a combination of unease and the winter wind streaming through the broken window at her back.

The doorknob rattled, and a man grumbled words she couldn't make out. Jelise grabbed the staff she'd set aside.

The door splintered around the lock, then swung in. A huge man ducked to enter the room, and she gasped in response. He towered over her five-feet-ten and was built like a dark-haired Greek statue, curls and all. He was a man who would have dwarfed even Joey, and he was certainly better looking than any man she'd ever met.

For a long moment, Jelise gaped at him, for once forgetting the survival skills that had kept her alive this long. She tightened her hold on the staff...then forced her grip to gentle. It was likely she'd need to use it in moments. Whoever this guy was, he didn't look particularly friendly.

His brown eyes narrowed as he panned his gaze over her body and settled his gaze on her staff. "Jelise Jackson?" he asked, his hand touching then leaving a wicked-looking dagger hung on his belt.

Great! For the second time in a night, some strange man was asking for her by name, but who was this one? She took in his black and silver uniform in confusion. She'd never seen anything like it. The markings at the shoulder and throat didn't look familiar, though she assumed he was some sort of soldier. "Who wants to know?"

He darkened, and his jaw tightened. "One who would save you from the government men surrounding us—if we move quickly and you wish to be free."

"What's in it for you?" No one gave anyone help like this for free. She'd learned that long before she ended up on the streets.

Maybe he wanted sex. Well, that wouldn't be a hardship, if he had any idea how to use that body.

"Knowing they won't torture you," he answered angrily. "Do you want to be free or not?"

"Well, that's a stupid question, isn't it?" she snapped. Okay, so he didn't intend to tell her his price up front. She'd cross that road when she wasn't in danger of a jail cell.

"Then come with me—now. There's little time."

She hesitated. "Right behind you," she decided. All right. Her survival instincts were still in her skull somewhere. *Never turn your back on an enemy.*

"As you wish." Conan turned and led the way down the dim hallway, either confident that he would win a fight with her or insanely stupid.

Jelise let out a whistle of surprise as they passed the feds—looking a little worse for wear and out for the count.

Her would-be rescuer snapped a look at her, one that fairly demanded an answer of her. "Yes?" he asked.

"Gotta learn how you managed that," she replied smoothly.

"It was not overly difficult," he dismissed her, turning back to the stairs without missing a beat.

Jelise raised an eyebrow at the boredom in his tone. *What a crock of shit! As if four armed feds aren't a challenge for Captain America here?*

Her disbelief melted into awe at the sight of the shimmering doorway in the workroom turned hangout. "Wow," she whispered, reaching out to touch it.

It looked like water shot through with opals and set up on its side. She couldn't help wondering what it felt like—and what kind of virtual projectors were needed to make that light effect. Whatever it was, it had to cost a fortune.

The man grasped her wrist and wrenched Jelise away from it. "No," he ordered.

She swung her staff, but he captured it in his open hand. Her protest stuck in her throat as she met his eyes. There was no anger in those eyes, no superiority. He was terrified. Jelise relaxed into his hold, certain that she'd nearly made a very big mistake.

He nodded. "My apologies, Lady Jelise. You cannot touch the gateway without a band."

"Band?" she managed. Her voice was strangely devoid of conviction, as if this Adonis had drained her of her will to fight him.

He released her staff and produced a black box on an arm band, much like the one she now noted he wore. She slid her gaze from his arm to her own, watching him thread it carefully over her hand.

Jelise sucked in her breath, abruptly aware of the brush of his fingers through the heavy shirt she wore. "Matches my look," she noted shakily.

A sharp tone originated from a second box at his hip, something akin to an old-fashioned beeper, and a yellow light flashed on its face. He glanced at it, then met her eyes.

"It is time. Are you ready?"

"Through there?" she asked in dismay. "I mean— What if these band things don't work or something?" This technology had to be new, whatever it was. She pushed away the thought that her odds of this succeeding might not be the greatest.

"They will."

"But—" Jelise forced her breathing to even, well aware that she was flirting with hyperventilating.

"The moment is almost past, Lady—"

"Here!" another man's voice shouted.

His head came up, his entire body tensing as if to pounce. Jelise turned, her staff up to fight...and found herself facing down a 9mm.

"Don't move," the agent ordered.

The soldier's arms closed around her waist, turning Jelise into the gateway and launching them through. She squeaked in pained surprise as colors danced around her, vivid colors that hurt her eyes after the dim light in the abandoned factory building. A shot reverberated, seeming to shake the air around them.

Then there was an even brighter light...white light. Stone was under her while her giant's body covered hers. Something shattered overhead, and someone screamed.

"*Loc en pret*," the soldier shouted.

Footsteps thundered over the stone, vibrating the floor beneath her cheek. Voices uttered words she couldn't understand. The man over her stroked her hair, whispering assurances that Jelise would be all right.

"Jace," a new voice demanded. "Is she injured, Jace?"

Her rescuer eased off of her, helping Jelise to sitting. His fingers brushed her cheek, probably dusting off dirt from the floor. "No, Hi. She is well."

The second man sighed in relief, offering his hand to help her to her feet. "Welcome to Kegin, Lady Jelise," he intoned in a heavy accent she couldn't place.

She eased further into Jace's chest, wary. All of the men were in uniforms like Jace's. Some were black like his. Some were blue. The one who spoke to her wore red and gold. "Where is Kegin?" she demanded, suddenly sure that the gateway took her further than she'd counted on.

The man in red—*Hi*, she reminded herself—shot a look of pure fury at them. "You didn't tell her?"

"There was no time," Jace defended himself sheepishly. "Between besting the human pursuers and—"

"Till will be furious," he shouted.

Jelise's head spun. Nothing made sense. The word 'human' circled in her mind. She had to have misheard him. The alternative was unthinkable. "Jace," she called weakly. "I think I need to lie down."

* * * *

Jace scooped Lady Jelise into his arms and vaulted for the door, barely noting that he brushed past Prince Michael in his haste. "Renel," he barked, calling the head of the local clinic to accompany them to the room prepared for the young lady.

Her cheek nestled to his pounding heart, and her green-flecked choc eyes slid shut. Jace cursed his delay in reaching her aloud. If Lady Jelise was seriously injured, he would never forgive himself for it.

The bed prepared for her was wide and lush—covered in the finest silin and heavy quilts as befit a noble of her status. Jace laid her in the center, then waved Renel to them.

Jelise's eyes fluttered open as the doctor touched her face. She shied in seeming panic, reaching frantically for Jace's hand.

"All is well," he soothed her. "This man is a healer." *Wrong term.* "Doctor."

"No," she breathed, pushing herself toward Jace. Her trembling body pressed to his, making him acutely aware of a primal need to protect her, to hold her closer to himself.

Renel readied a hypocil and injected her upper arm in one smooth movement, making Jace wonder if the doctor had foreseen a need to medicate her. Jelise startled, meeting his eyes, pleading silently with Jace for an explanation.

"*What was it?*" he asked calmly, knowing the doctor wouldn't understand English if he spoke it again.

"*Garigol and Brekel, to relax her ladyship and bring sleep.*"

"Jace?" Her voice was slow and measured, thick in the haze of Renel's drugs.

"Sleep, my lady. I will stand watch over you. You have my vow." Jace smoothed her deep choc hair, easing her to the bed.

"Stay," she requested, her eyes closing and her grip easing as sleep claimed her.

Jace smiled, running a finger along her Felgren-stalk skin. She was enchanting—and so different from any Earth born he'd yet met. Queen Susan had explained the races of Earth, how they went beyond even the hair and eye color differences of the ancient Keen races into a wide array of skin tones and facial features. The first time Jace saw a video likeness of Lady Jelise Jackson, he had known he had to win the right to bring her home.

He sobered, pulling his hand back and straightening. And now he'd done his duty. For a few precious moments, he'd held the woman who'd haunted his dreams for more than two years. He'd trained to win the right to bring her from Earth. He'd learned English for her, and now she'd leave him to begin her introductions to the Keen lords worthy of her attentions. Jace turned away—and stilled.

Prince Michael stared him down, his expression promising a ritual death.

* * * *

"Do you know who that woman is, Lieutenant Jace?" the Prince asked from the chair behind his desk.

Jace kept his eyes respectfully down. "Lady Jelise Jackson, Highness. A third generation Earth-born noble female and my better," he offered carefully, cursing himself silently for his stupidity in desiring her.

"She was the second-cross mate named by the breeding office as my mate," Michael informed him. "She was to be delivered into my hands this very night."

Jace winced at that. He hadn't known the Prince had some formal claim on Jelise. That made his crimes even worse.

"As it was, the breeding office and Church council were breaking laws to deliver her. She actually will not be an adult for two more months, but they could not ask me to wait another five years for that two month variance."

"I understand, Highness," Jace managed.

"Do you?" His voice went cold and deadly with that simple question.

He nodded, envisioning kneeling before the Prince and facing a ritual death, bathed in the blue glow of the laser-edged sword that now lay across the desk in silent warning, for the moment... thankfully... powered-down. "I believe so."

"Good, because you have a lot to answer for. Jelise trusts you. Why... I don't think I will ever understand why she does. You have taken her from her world without a full understanding of her choice. The explanation is yours to give."

Jace met Prince Michael's eyes, stunned into silence. He was trusted to see Jelise again? Despite his obvious attraction to her, he would be permitted to talk to her?

"Do you understand me, Lieutenant?" the Prince growled.

"I do." What had he been thinking? This suggestion was for no dalliance but rather for him to do what he should have done before he took her from Earth. "I will explain my actions to Lady Jelise."

"If she trusts you still, you will assist my bride and the tutors in acclimating her to Kegin."

Jace bit back a smile. His moment with Jelise wasn't ending anytime soon—if she accepted him once he admitted his crimes to her. "It would be an honor."

"And, Jace... One more thing."

"Yes, Highness?"

"I fully admit that Lady Jelise is too young to be my mate. Regardless, my bride holds my heart, but Jelise is mine by decree, and I feel a kinship and duty to her as I would any woman of my household. Consider her one of my daughters."

Jace's heart missed a beat, and his mouth went dry at the threat. He nodded. "I will, Highness."

"Ah, Doctor Renel," Michael rumbled. "Your findings?"

"Exhaustion and shock, with a few minor bruises and cuts. The lady will recover nicely."

Jace breathed a sigh of relief, wincing again at the Prince's look of warning.

CHAPTER TWO

Jelise burrowed under the thick blanket, reveling in the warmth. How long had it been since she'd been so warm? *Probably not since the first snowfall, a week before Halloween.*

She opened her eyes, disoriented at the feeling of silk against her skin and sweet smells she couldn't identify. Seeing her surroundings didn't help. In all her life, Jelise had never seen a room as decadent as this one was.

The drapes looked like silk brocade in gray and silver. The bed was at least a California King, and the brush on the dressing table looked like silver. Moreover, the carpet was a plush, pure white that matched the bed linens.

She rubbed her hand over her face, half-expecting the vision to disappear. It didn't.

Jelise grimaced, replaying the night before. *There was the jerk with the car*, she reminded herself. *As if I needed to run into him again!* She had a few beers with the guys. The feds showed up.

She sat upright in bed, her breathing harsh in her own ears. "Jace," she whispered. Where was she? What was that psychedelic doorway? Where or what was Kegin? Her memories after he dragged her through the doorway seemed scattered and incoherent. How did she get into this bed?

She launched from the bed, then stopped, fingering the purple silk gown that reached her knees in a mixture of anger and dismay. Who the hell had dressed her in this thing? Jelise scanned the room, but her clothes were nowhere in sight. She pulled open the two cabinets, but they were filled with nothing but colorful dresses in varying lengths.

Jelise stormed to the door. They couldn't keep her prisoner this way. A soldier dressed much as Jace had been looked up sharply as she approached, then turned his head away, darkening to crimson.

"Where are my clothes?" she shouted.

"Jelise Lay-ees. Wilm. Gan Michael Hi." He motioned to the room weakly.

She stared at him in confusion, her mind trying unsuccessfully to identify the language he spoke. He obviously had no grasp of English. What would he understand? "Jace," she requested.

He met her eyes and smiled in something resembling relief, motioning to the room again. "Wilm, Lay-ees. Gan Jace Lorn."

She nodded shakily, retreating to the bed and stiffening as he closed the door behind her. She prayed the soldier understood her. She sat and looked around the room in mounting unease, noting what appeared to be antique paintings and hand-laid tile designs, etched scrollwork on the chair and bed frame, and even how soft the carpet was.

The door eased open, and she jumped in response.

Jace looked to her, his strained smile freezing...then fading away. Stark male hunger settled on his face, making her shiver in sympathetic response. Sex had always been her weakness—sex with strong guys, and Jace was strong and capable.

He turned away, rubbing a hand over the back of his neck. "You should dress," he grumbled.

"Gladly! Where are my clothes?"

"The ones you wore earlier?"

"I don't seem to own any others," she snapped at him. Wherever the factory was, it was certainly far from here—and swamped by feds who wouldn't be likely to hand over her meager belongings, even if she did make it back there.

Jace motioned to the wall behind her. "In the cabinets. There are even—"

"I don't wear dresses."

He turned to her, furrowing his brow. "My pardon?"

"I don't wear dresses. You can't fight in a dress. Speaking of which, where is my staff?"

"Your weapon is—" He hesitated. "I'll find out for you."

"I'd appreciate that."

"Your clothing is probably being laundered. Until they return, will you—"

Jelise stood and crossed her arms under her breasts. "No way, Hulk-man. I am no one's little woman."

Jace seemed confused by that. Then his expression cleared in a look of understanding. "Trousers. If I get trousers and a tunic for you to wear, you'll dress?"

"I'd prefer my own things, but anything is better than this." She motioned to the nightgown distastefully.

He scanned her body slowly, drawing a deep breath into his lungs.

Jelise backed off a step, her body responding to the battle-ready expression and stance Jace adopted. *God, that man is hot!* She shook her head to dislodge that thought. This was not the time to jump the man. She needed answers—and clothes.

"Pants," she reminded him.

Jace turned to the door, striding away in a stiff, military manner. The door closed behind him, and he didn't look back.

Jelise sank to the bed, pressing her forearm to her aching nipples. What was wrong with her?

* * * *

"Trousers," Jace growled at the househead. "A pair of Prince Cro's should suffice. And a belt and tunic."

The woman scurried away, no doubt scandalized by Lady Jelise's request.

Jace ran a shaking hand through his hair, willing his errant body to cease its torture of him. He had to return to her and tell Jelise the truth, and doing so with his cock straining the seams on his trousers would not be conducive to his continued existence. Prince Michael had made that clear enough.

What did it matter? Once he revealed her situation to her, she'd send him away to dreams that didn't include her ready scent, that paled in comparison to the feel of her skin against his.

The clothing in hand, he returned to her rooms. Jace offered them to her on the plate of her worn boots. "I will wait in the hall," he decided, retreating before Jelise could speak.

It took her only a few moments to dress. She pulled open the door and faced him. "Now, where am I?"

"Will you walk with me?" he asked, grasping at the proof he'd need. Without it, she would surely think him mad.

"Sure."

He motioned her toward the stairs, clasping his hands behind his back to avoid breaking laws by laying them on her. Jace led her to the greenhouse behind the kitchen, playing the part of guard, making certain no man but himself looked at her.

He bit back a groan at that. Would that she was really his and not simply his duty.

Jelise touched a lizor re-blooming in the artificial heat. "Lovely," she murmured.

Jace raised an eyebrow in surprise. "Does the flower not answer your question?"

"I don't know anything about flowers except what looks and smells nice. These are pretty. What are they?"

He rubbed his neck, trying to ease the tension building, frustrated by her lack of understanding. "Lizor," he answered her.

"Why would this flower mean something to me? Does it only grow here?"

"Yes. It does."

"Oh." She sighed and moved on to a flowering Zura bush.

Now what? Who knew such a simple thing could be so difficult to prove? He glanced out the windows and across the grounds. "Come."

Jelise looked up in confusion. "Again?"

"Please."

She bit her lip in a look of confusion but followed him back to the kitchen without a fight. Jace settled a heavy hottel fur-lined cloak on her shoulders and fastened the front, then waved her toward the door.

"Shouldn't you?" Jelise motioned toward the other cloaks.

Jace shook his head, at a loss to explain why it would be wrong of him to borrow one of the Princes' cloaks while it was all right for her to. It was too complex. Jelise had to know where she was first. The finer points would follow.

He strode out into the snow with Jelise at his heels. The wind was frigid, but the slice of it through his uniform brought clarity, the sense of purpose he needed to complete his task.

The stable was before them all too quickly. Jace hesitated, then strode inside. He glared at the mountskeeper. "*Servant, leave us.*"

The man's eyes widened. Then he locked on Jelise. His mouth slackened in dumb wonder.

"*Leave us,*" Jace growled, his hand grasping the hilt of his dagger in warning. The laws the mountskeeper was breaking aside, he would kill the man where he stood for the unease Jelise fairly radiated at the unwanted attention.

The servant snapped a look at his weapon, bowed his head, then bolted away, mumbling apologies.

Jace put his hand out to Jelise, motioning her inside. She stepped over the bootstop, peering into the gloom of the deep recesses. He nodded. He'd expected the stables to be nearly empty. The older prince and princesses typically rode with their parents after midday meal. Still, a few mounts were guaranteed to be in their stalls.

"What language do you speak?" she asked quietly, as if the stillness unnerved her.

"Keen."

"I've never—"

"Come see our mounts." Jace walked to the rear of the huge stable to where his own buck was sheltered.

"My God. Is that a Clydesd—" Jelise squawked in surprise as she looked up toward the buck's shoulders.

"It's all right," he soothed her. "*Toribim* won't hurt you."

"Wh-What is that t-thing?" she stammered.

Jace took her hand and pressed it to Toribim's long, sleek black fur. "A male *hottel*. A *war-buck*. It is a common domesticated beast on planet Kegin."

Jelise shook her head.

"Yes. I should have explained this morning, but there was no time."

"No. This isn't a bad sci fi movie. Where am I, really?"

He guided her hand down the buck's shoulder until the slow thud of Toribim's heart resonated under their hands. "Does this animal exist on Earth?" he asked.

She turned to him, pale and uncertain, her face deep beige.

"It doesn't," he soothed her.

"If... If this is where you say it is, why did you come for me? You asked for me by name. Why me?"

"You are not like other Earth women," he began.

She nodded, tears shining in her eyes. "Because of the gang."

"Gang?" he repeated, wishing yet again that Queen Susan had taught him the entire English language, as daunting as learning the millions of words seemed. Jace had tried to study independently but abandoned that when he discovered there were many dialects of the English language. He had been studying what the Queen called "Queen's English"—useless in dealing with an American youth.

"The guys. My—brothers."

Jace scowled, his mind picking apart the file he'd memorized. "You have no brothers."

Jelise rolled her eyes. "Well, they might as well be. They hold my back."

"Like they did with the human authorities?" he challenged, irked by her insistence on supporting the cowards who'd left her to fight alone. "Worthless human scum."

She darkened, a deep red-brown touch high in her cheeks. "Watch it, Jace," Jelise warned. "You're insulting me, you know."

"No. I am not insulting you. You are Keen, Jelise. You are a re-bred daughter, not human."

"Me? No." She backed away, wrenching her hand from beneath his, her gaze roaming from Toribim to Jace, then toward the door. "You're nuts!"

Jace sighed, wondering what protein-rich seed snacks had to do with anything they were discussing...or how one could be such a thing. "You do not menses," he stated flatly, knowing she couldn't deny that.

She stilled, shaking her head slowly. "What does that—"

"You are not supposed to menses. Keen women do not."

"No," she gasped.

"You enjoy sex." Jace took a step toward her, caught up in visions of Jelise beneath him, experiencing Keen sex for the first time. "You enjoy everything about it: the smell and taste, the deep thrusts that touch your womb and the shallow ones that rub against your pleasure spot."

Her scent intensified, and she trembled.

"The smell of an aroused male makes you crazy." Her smell was driving *him* crazy. "Just smelling makes you want to taste and touch and—"

"No. I'm not. I can't be...what you say."

Jace reached a hand out to her, and Jelise struck it away. She turned to run, but he pulled her back to his chest.

"No," Jelise shouted, elbowing him in the ribs and diving away from him.

He threw himself down on the dry redgrass with her, pulling Jelise into the shelter of his body. She sobbed, pushing at his hold.

"Shhh. You are a Keen child," he soothed her.

"I can't be." Tears streamed down her face.

"You are." He eased her cheek to his chest. "And, I would have come for you in their darkest dungeons." He shook himself mentally. "To bring you home."

* * * *

Michael stilled, his fury rising at the scene in the stables. He had known something was wrong when Mountskeeper Kev took their bucks outside, but Michael hadn't expected this.

Jelise lay full out over Lieutenant Jace, a spare cloak fanned over them both. The lieutenant's hands stroked her hair, and he murmured words in English in a voice too low for Michael to hear them.

His tirade died on his lips as she sobbed. One small fist landed on Jace's shoulder, a half-hearted blow from a woman who'd entered their world bearing three deadly weapons.

"*I am not a child,*" she insisted, her voice hitching. "*I've been an adult for two years.*"

Michael winced. They'd known this would be a problem. Though Susan had argued Lady Lyssa as a precedent, the Church council and breeding office had decreed that Lyssa had only been permitted the status of "adult" by virtue of her Earth mating with Lord Alex, that her husband had acted the part of her guardian for the four months until she turned twenty. By Keen law, Jelise would not be treated the same.

He searched out the words to address her in his sketchy English. Denied the right to learn his mother's language as a child, Michael found the process of absorbing the complex sounds nothing short of torturous now.

"By Keen law, I am afraid you are—until your next day of birth," he offered quietly.

Jace shot him a pained look, no doubt anticipating a swift death for his seeming state of intimacy with Jelise.

"I will lend you trust this time. Do not abuse it."

The lieutenant nodded, sighing in relief.

Michael knelt beside them, trying to ease Jelise into his arms. Sleep would be best for her after a shock like this.

She wrenched from his hands with a word Michael recognized as a human curse, the same word Susan once used against him. Michael would have forced her to him had she not grasped onto Jace. He raised an eyebrow at the lieutenant.

Danellan's voice came from just behind him. *"Take Lady Jelise to her room, Lieutenant,"* she ordered. "*Perhaps she will feel up to joining us for evening meal.*"

"Yes, Danellan Hir." The young man stood, pulling Jelise up into his arms as if her weight were insubstantial.

Danellan took Michael's arm as he moved to follow them. "Leave them," she requested.

"Danellan—"

"She trusts him. Give her time to adjust to this change."

"And Jace free rein to touch her?" he demanded.

"Within reason. She's been raised in the human manner. Jelise is no untried maid. You know the decree is wrong."

"Then she can have schaen. My duty to her demands that I enforce the mores."

Danellan shook her head, offering a smile that announced her exasperation with him. "Perhaps, I should begin her training."

"Sooner rather than later," he agreed uneasily. What was Danellan up to that she changed course so abruptly?

* * * *

"Why the hell did you bring me here?" Jelise shouted.

Jace rubbed a hand over his aching neck. "Please, lie down, Jelise. This upset is not good for you."

"I am *not* a child!" She paced the room, her arms crossed under her chest again, forcing the lush globes up as if in presentation.

"I—believe that," he replied carefully. There was nothing about Jelise that made him think of her as a child—except the Prince's threat.

She stopped pacing, seemingly confused by his proclamation. "But?" she prompted him. Her mistrust was acute.

Jace considered his answer carefully. "The governing body will not permit me to treat you as an adult. It is only two months," he reasoned.

"Only? That's easy for you to say, buster. You're not the one in this mess, are you?"

He shook his head slowly. "No. I suppose not."

Jelise went to the window and swept the drape back, looking out over the snow. She touched the glass, and Jace wished fervently that he knew her mind.

"Can you not be happy here?" he asked quietly. "You won't be cold or hungry. You'll have money and a home. You'll have—"

"Freedom?" she interrupted him. "Will I have freedom?"

"In two months." Jace cursed the Church council silently for this heartache.

"Why did you bring me here?" she asked.

Jace sank into the chair at her ladies' dressing table, his elbows on his knees. "You know why the human government wanted you?" he asked.

Jelise rubbed a healing cut at the base of her thumb. She shrugged. "I assumed that jackass with the Beamer sicced them on me," she grumbled, her face darkening.

"You had an altercation with a human man and were injured," he guessed.

"Just a little cut when the window broke." Jelise came to him, offering her hand as proof that her injury wasn't severe.

Jace cradled it, stroking his fingertips over the cut. "Just a few drops of blood," he mused. "That was all they needed."

"What?" Her voice was weak.

He didn't meet her gaze; he traced the wound over and over, enjoying the feel of her skin. "Your blood contains Keen proteins. Their courts have decided testing for these proteins on the general populace is illegal, but—"

"But?" she echoed.

"If blood is collected in connection with commission of a crime—victim or guilty party—it may be tested fully, to the genetic level."

"So they came after me because I'm an alien?"

"Yes."

"What did they want with me, Jace?"

"There is a couple on Kegin, Lord Alex and Lady Lyssa Braeden. They were Earth-born, as you were. They were found out and abducted by the same Earth government that you curse. The—tests they ran were unspeakable, nothing short of torture. Lord Alex was a prisoner for almost four years, and Lady Lyssa for almost a year. I could never allow them to..."

Her hand curled in his.

"It *is* better here," Jace managed. "I am sorry I didn't prepare you, but given the choice of the two possible fates—"

She nodded. "I think I will lie down, Jace. I'm feeling..."

He released her hand, watching Jelise weave drunkenly toward her bed. Jace nodded and left her, though he ached to touch her again.

* * * *

Iric 27th, Ri 25-3001

Danellan smiled at the young woman before her. Jelise was a warrior. If her attitude wasn't proof enough, her manner of dress announced the fact clearly.

Jelise was in her black Earth-style clothing again: trousers, a thick shirt that reached her thighs, a waist-length pocketed vest that Danellan knew concealed two deadly blades, a pair of scuffed, military-style boots, and a strip of fabric tied around her forehead. She had left her staff at the doorway, a rare show of trust.

"Good afternoon, Jelise," Danellan greeted her calmly.

Though her Earth file spoke of a violent background and the young woman was armed, Danellan knew the guards outside the door wouldn't let her come to harm. Moreover, she didn't believe Jelise was stupid enough to attack in an unknown circumstance—or the type to attack unprovoked.

"And what should I call you?" Jelise inquired in a cool reserve.

"My name is Danellan."

"Okay, Danni. Tell me why I shouldn't turn around and leave right now."

"Are you uncomfortable here?"

Jelise raised an eyebrow at that. "Should I be comfortable with being stuck on another planet full of people who don't speak English? People who want me to wear frilly dresses and be some sort of princess?"

"I cannot change the fact that you have come here. We are no longer in alignment to send you back and will not be again for years.

"Some Keen do speak English—or *Español* or *Francais*. You could learn to speak Keen. Though it is not required of you, I recommend it.

"As for your clothing, many Earth-born ladies request unconventional clothing from the clothiers. Choose whatever you like.

"*And*, you are not a princess. You are a noble lady."

"I'm noble nothing," Jelise grumbled. "This is what I am. Deal with it."

"While a female warrior is unusual, I am proof that it isn't unheard of on Kegin."

Jelise panned her eyes over Danellan with a dubious expression on her face. "You? You're a— a soldier of some sort?"

"I've been trained. Yes. It's been years since I've had to use it, of course."

She considered that. "Were you born on Earth? Or was your husband?"

"Neither. Michael's mother was Earth-born, but he was born on Kegin."

"He doesn't speak English very well. Worse than you do, by far," she noted.

"Michael wasn't permitted to learn English when he was a child. His brother, Jole, and his Earth-born wife, Susan, speak it perfectly, as do all of the other Earth-born."

"Why wasn't Michael permitted to learn it if his brother was?"

"That is a story for another time. The reigning king was a different sort of man. Now...do you intend to leave the estate?"

"Why shouldn't I? I don't need a warm bed to survive."

Danellan smiled at that. "Until you reach Keen adulthood, you're ordered to stay here. After that, you will take up residence in your own home—or wherever, as you Earth-born say, you choose to hang your *chapeau*."

"Hang your hat," Jelise corrected her.

"Ah, yes. Your hat."

"And if I simply walk away?"

"There are guards, Jelise." Danellan raised a hand to still her. "Even if you made it off the grounds, you could not stay hidden long."

Jelise looked to her clothes, seemingly pained at the thought of giving them up.

"Even if you adopted our form of dress, you would be found. None of the Earth-born currently on Kegin are incapable of speaking Keen, and—"

"And?" she challenged.

Danellan sighed. "Your looks are unique on all of Kegin."

"Unique? I look just like—" She scowled. "I get it. You didn't count on a token nigga when you started this little breeding experiment, did you?"

"A what?" Danellan asked, perplexed.

"Black. You didn't count on me being black. That's why people stare at me like I have two heads."

"But...you're not black. Your skin is a beautiful shade of *choc*—brown. Susan said your coloring is quite common among humans. Is it not?"

Jelise furrowed her brow at that. "Why am I here?"

"On Kegin? Because, you are one of our children. Your home world is not safe for you, as you recently learned. If you choose to marry, it will be a blessing to Kegin. If you don't, at least you will be safe here."

"No. Why am I here? With you? Now?"

"To learn."

"Learn what?"

"Whatever you wish. The Keen language, our laws, our culture, your rights. What do you wish to learn?"

Jelise seemed to consider that carefully. "Whatever will get me out of here the fastest," she decided.

"Well then, you should learn our laws."

CHAPTER THREE

Iric 30th, Ri 25-3001

Jelise raised her head, squinting into the morning sunlight in confusion. "What the hell is going on?" she grumbled.

Feet pounded up and down the hallway, and children squealed and laughed. A knock came at the door.

"Jelise?" Jace called.

She pushed from the bed, pulling a robe around her body and stumbling to the door. It swung open on well-oiled hinges, and she scowled at his wide grin. "What is wrong with you people?" she complained. "I swear the nights are shorter here."

He flushed. "Actually, they are. My apologies. You will become used to it in time."

"Sure." She yawned. "I'll see you in a few hours."

"But... Do you not rise early for Yule? I thought it was customary—"

"Yule?" she asked, rubbing her eyes.

"Christmas? Or perhaps you call it—"

"You have Christmas on Kegin?" She stared past him at the young princess barreling down the hallway with a length of ribbon in her hand.

"Most of the Earth-born celebrate it, so Prince Michael thought you'd want to. Would you...like to see? The entire household has gone to such lengths to make Christmas for you."

"Yes," she whispered. "I'll come down."

His smile returned. "Good. Please, come."

Jelise followed him, half in a daze. How long had it been since she'd celebrated Christmas?

Five years. She hadn't had the chance since her mother died. With no other relatives, she'd been sent to the center. There was no Christmas her single year there. With kids who celebrated everything from Chanukah to Christmas and Solstice to Kwanzaa, it was easier to recognize no one's beliefs than everyone's.

Then came the Turners. She'd spent two years with them, the pit of her existence, and that was saying a lot, considering her time on the streets before she found her new family with the gang.

She supposed the Turners meant well, in their own twisted way. It was their aim to immerse Jelise in her "lost heritage," uncaring of the fact that she was more mutt than black. Her mother had only been half and half, and her father had been half-Sioux; his mother's roots had been some Heinz 57 European mix of Irish and German and something more that went unsaid. She'd been raised Roman Catholic, gone to Catholic schools, and even sung in the church choir. Christian traditions were in her roots.

It wasn't that Jelise had anything against what she considered her "Grandpa's culture." She'd just never been able to embrace it fully as her own. You can't take a kid with sixteen years of life experience and history and try to shove a new reality on her. In any case, if anything could give a person a bad taste for a new holiday, that was it.

After two years of cultural boot camp, life on the streets had seemed like a welcome relief to her. It had never been intended as a permanent move. Someday...someday soon based on her restlessness, she'd have resumed something resembling a normal life.

After all, she'd never been the dangerous sort. Sure, they were responsible for a few break-ins, but they only hurt people in self defense. The gang had been more of a survival group, a foster family that didn't judge her or try to change her.

"Lady Jelise?" Jace asked, seemingly concerned at her silence.

She managed a weak smile. "Just waking up," she lied.

He nodded. His smile returned, a childlike glee that seemed at odds with the soldier she knew him to be.

Jelise turned right through the ballroom doors, stopping cold in amazement. She raised her head, following the line of a huge tree that reached almost the full three stories of the centerpiece room, topped by a shimmering star of blue light. Mirrored balls in every conceivable color and twinkling white lights covered every square foot, accented with red bows, sweet-smelling cakes and candies, and sparkling garlands of what looked like fiber optic cable.

She stumbled, abruptly dizzy. Jace scooped her up amid a flurry of shouts and deposited her on a soft chair.

"Is she well, Jace?" Michael asked urgently.

"Fine," she breathed. Jelise shook her head at the sight of the tree and the mountain of bright-colored presents. None of it had been there the night before. It must have taken the servants all night to do this. "How did you arrange this?"

Danellan laughed, handing her a cream-filled pastry. "Michael never does anything half way."

"I see that."

"Do you like it?" Jace asked.

"I've never seen a Christmas like this," she admitted. "It's beautiful."

Cro brought her a gift, offering it with a smile. "Merry Christmas, Jelise," he exclaimed in smoother English than either of his parents spoke.

She laughed, feeling the sting of tears in her eyes. "And to you."

* * * *

Jace watched the proceedings from the far corner of the room. It was an amazing celebration, dwarfing even the Christmas celebrations held at the palace, in many ways.

But the lights and glitter couldn't compare with the brilliance of Jelise's smile. For her first few days on Kegin, he'd doubted she could ever be truly happy again—until today.

She'd taught the young princes and princesses the proper respect for the pretty wrapping paper. None! At one point, the room was an alarming cacophony of ripping paper and squeals of delight.

The morning meal had consisted of pastries and milk, but the midday meal would be served soon: a feast of roast kit and lamor, muklin and sucre-soaked baked implin, Earth-style tuber pies and sautéed vegetables.

Jelise looked away from Prince Cro, her gaze settling on Jace. She murmured something to the prince, then stood and ambled toward him.

Jace noted the young prince's wary look toward his father in unease. It was a bad omen when Prince Cro shot one a look like that; it was an occurrence that made generals shudder.

"Enjoying yourself?" she asked.

He smiled. "Yes," he admitted. He was, but he hadn't expected to. Jace had been ordered to the celebration to put Jelise at ease and translate if needed, though that hadn't proven necessary.

"You speak English very well. Better than Cro and much better than the other adults, even the Kegin-born re-breds I've met."

"You haven't met King Jole yet." The king was an amazing man. Though he admittedly learned the language from his mother and polished it with his bride, his grasp of the nuances, double meanings and accent was superior.

"How did you learn to speak English? Why did you?"

For you. But, it would be treason to say so. "Queen Susan taught me. She decreed long ago that any soldier who went through the gateway to contact a re-bred must be fluent—or as close to it as possible." Jace had studied much longer than most. He had to...for her.

Jelise nodded, shifting closer to him as Prince Gandl streaked past. "Do you know Earth customs?" she asked in what struck him as a conspiratorial tone.

"Not all, but many of them."

She pointed to the archway over his head. "Do you know what mistletoe means?"

Jace looked up in disbelief, noting the gola sprig he hadn't seen until that moment. He hadn't realized the decorations would include it. This was a family party, after all. Though Queen Susan considered it a necessary decoration, most Keen reserved its use for adult celebrations where the kissing game was more appropriate.

"Yes," he admitted. "I know the custom."

She pressed her body to his. "Good. Then you know what I want."

His mind argued Prince Michael's warning, but he silenced it. The Prince had obviously approved the hanging of gola. If Jace refused her custom, he'd offend Jelise. And he wanted this kiss. It would likely be the only kiss he would ever receive from her.

He lowered his face, tasting her mouth slowly. Her lips parted, and he nearly groaned in arousal. The taste of gelgrin was heavy in her mouth, mixing with her own flavors until his head spun in response.

He didn't embrace her; that would be going too far. Jelise was less restrained. Her hands pressed to his chest, and she tilted her head to his shoulder, giving him a cleaner angle.

The end came abruptly and without warning. Jelise was wrenched away, and a blade nestled to his throat.

"*I warned you,*" Prince Michael growled in Keen.

Jelise pushed at him, her eyes wild. "Stop! Are you crazy?"

"Michael!" Princess Danellan shouted. "*You're frightening her. Stop!*" She pulled Jelise from his grasp, hugging the young woman to her. "It's all right," she soothed her.

Jelise turned, not quite escaping the Princess's grasp, and gripped Michael's dagger arm, trying to wrestle it away from Jace. "Let him go!"

"Michael," Danellan warned.

He nodded, easing the dagger back. "Not in front of the children," he agreed.

"I am *not* a child," Jelise shouted.

Michael glared at her. "By Keen law, you are not an adult, either."

"I am sexually an adult, even by your laws."

Prince Michael shot his bride a look of dismay. "*You didn't explain?*"

"*Sometimes, we get led off topic by her questions. It is a possibility that we didn't finish this conversation.*"

He grumbled a Keen curse. "*Still, the Lieutenant knows better than this.*"

"What are you two talking about?" Jelise demanded.

Danellan took her hand. "Being sexually an adult does not mean you can choose your sexual partners, much as humans who menses are not permitted to—"

"You people are insane! I have been *choosing* my own sexual partners for the last three years. And, we weren't having sex! You're the ones who hung the mistletoe."

Prince Michael and his bride panned their gazes up the archway. The prince snapped a look of fury at Jace.

Jace felt his face heat. "It is her tradition," he reasoned, well aware that it might not save his head in the end.

"Of course it is," Danellan agreed. "Lieutenant Jace would have offended her if he didn't respect Jelise's culture after we went to these lengths to honor it."

Jelise pushed away from the Princess and turned on her heel, stalking away. "Offend," she grumbled. "Yeah, right."

Jace grimaced in the realization that he'd just offended her grievously, but he dared not go after her to admit the truth now. That kiss hadn't been a gift of friendship or pity, and she knew it as well as he did, but correcting the Princess would see him at the end of a laser-edged sword held by Prince Michael.

The Prince sheathed his blade. "*I don't believe we require your* assistance *with Lady Jelise any further, Lieutenant. Return to your normal duties.*"

He nodded, his heart sick. "*As you wish, Highness.*"

"Michael," Danellan ventured. "*Don't you think that's a little harsh?*"

"*No. I don't.*"

CHAPTER FOUR

Pri 7ᵗʰ, Ri 25-3001

"If you realize a woman is sexually an adult at fifteen, why isn't she allowed to have sex until she's twenty?"

Danellan looked up in surprise, but Jelise was staring out the window. It took only a moment for her to realize what the young woman was staring at. She smiled; her plan was working well. Jelise was finally asking the questions Danellan had hoped she'd ask.

"We don't disallow sex. We simply disallow pregnancy."

Jelise turned to her, her eyes wide. "You mean all I have to do is take the Pill, and I can have sex?"

"I will assume that 'the Pill' is some human form of birth control."

She nodded.

"While some young women illegally use *Walla* teas, they are not suggested for women less than twenty years old. In addition, it takes between three and four weeks to be effective in preventing pregnancy."

Jelise groaned, looking pained. "Four weeks? And I'm not even allowed to use it?"

"No. It is not permitted."

"I really don't understand you people. How do you have sex without risking pregnancy if

528

birth control is illegal? I mean, no offense Danni, but stroking it only goes so far."

Danellan bit back a laugh at her indelicate wording. "It's very simple. You take schaen to your bed."

"And what precisely are schaen?"

"Sterilized males."

Jelise furrowed her brow. "How do I know which ones are sterile? Do they wear a sign or something?"

She chuckled, anticipating her young student's reaction to the truth. "The servants dress to their position. If you wish me to request—"

"God, no!" Jelise's face was screwed up in disgust.

"Is there some problem?" she asked innocently.

"You expect me to let some... To screw someone's servant."

"They would be your servants and—"

"No! I'd rather go without."

"Do humans not have prostitutes? Or— perhaps mistresses or concubines would be a closer correlation? What is the human word for a male concubine?"

"I'm sure some people get off on screwing someone who's paid to do it. I prefer a more worthy partner. Thanks but no thanks."

"A worthy partner?" Danellan asked in genuine interest. "Is the male's social standing of concern to you then?" It would surprise her if it were. "Some schaen are of noble—"

"Look at me, Danni. Do you think I slept with nobles on Earth? I got caught by the feds, because I smashed some rich boy's car up." She rubbed the faint scar on her hand, her eyes sad.

"Why did you do that?"

Jelise shrugged again. "He was an asshole, like most rich guys are assholes."

Danellan winced at that. Jelise would never willingly take a noble to mate. "Then what men are worthy?" she asked. If she were to find a mate for the headstrong re-bred, that was of paramount importance.

Jelise darkened. "Those that can beat me."

"Beat you?" Her heart pounded at that. What barbaric mating ritual was this, and why had Susan not warned her about it?

"Win a fair fight with me."

"Sparring?" Danellan qualified.

"More or less. I mean, if it's an enemy, we're not ending up in bed together, whether he wins or not."

"Is this a typical human custom?"

Jelise smiled weakly. "Not really."

"But it *is* how you choose your sexual partners?" Danellan prodded.

She nodded. "I haven't had many," Jelise noted in a wry sort of amusement.

Danellan considered the possibilities carefully. Jelise was to be permitted whatever mate she wished. If any man within the compound besides Michael was her match in battle, it would be Lieutenant Jace. Jelise's attention had followed him sadly since Michael had sent him to his old duties. Even if Jace didn't best her, and there was little chance of that, Danellan would wager on a solid match between them.

"You miss it, don't you?" she asked the young woman.

Jelise shot her a look of confusion. "Sex or Earth?" she asked.

"Sparring. Testing yourself in battle."

"Yes. I do miss it."

"Very well." She pushed to her feet. "Collect your staff and come with me."

"Where are we going?"

"Women may be trained as soldiers, Jelise. Why should you be denied whatever training you wish?"

* * * *

Jace scowled at his opponent, sweeping Vul's feet from under him. "Pay attention, Vul. A child could best you."

The young soldier grumbled a complaint and pushed to his feet. He nodded to Jace and got in position again.

A woman's voice behind him broke Jace's concentration. It was a sultry voice he knew almost as well as his own, a voice that spoke only English. Noting his lieutenant's wandering mind, Vul landed an impressive punch to Jace's cheek.

Jace shot him a warning look, then turned to the laugh behind him. His heart nearly stopped in pleasure at the sight of Jelise. She was dressed in a tight pair of satil trousers and a flowing shirt, pushed to her elbows. She'd even traded her scuffed boots for a heavy pair of mountain-wear treads.

Her eyes glittered in amusement. *"I don't know how the feds kept from massacring you,"* she teased him in her lyrical English.

He bowed his head, fighting the tension in his jaw. This was his worst nightmare come true. Jelise had seen him at his most unguarded moment, in a mistake that would have proven fatal with a blade.

"Lieutenant Jace," the Princess greeted him in Keen. "Lady Jelise is to be trained in combat at a time convenient to you."

Jace looked to Jelise in amazement. He'd hardly caught a glimpse of her since the celebration of Christmas. Still, the dreams of her hadn't lessened, and now he was to train her? "Combat? Perhaps someone else—"

"It is her wish and my own that *you* conduct the training, Lieutenant." Her voice left no question that she would be obeyed.

Jace nodded, stifling the urge to inquire if Prince Michael knew of this decision. Perhaps he did. The Prince knew Jace had been adequately counseled in the penalty for laying hands on the noble lady. "As you wish, Highness." He looked to Jelise, watching her execute a smooth split to stretch her leg muscles. *"When you are ready,"* he told her.

"I am ready," Jelise assured him. *"There is no warm-up for a real fight."*

"Sensible and true. I will start you with one of my younger trainees."

Jelise rolled her eyes at that. *"If it makes you feel better."*

"Vul! Lady Jelise waits a sparring partner. Conduct yourself appropriately."

Vul snorted in disgust. "This child will not best me," he grumbled.

"We shall see." Jace looked to Jelise's staff. *"Can you fight bare-handed, or should I have Vul take up a training blade?"*

"Either. I can fight bare-handed, if it's called for. There isn't always room to swing a weapon."

"Good. Do that, then."

Jelise nodded and turned her staff over to Princess Danellan. She strode toward him, her chin up, a confident warrior on the field of battle. His men backed off to create a proper space for them.

Jace met each of their eyes in turn, nodding to their murmurs of readiness. He backed to the edge of the fight ring, watching Vul intently, ready to punish any inappropriate behavior harshly.

The first exchange passed almost too fast to track. Vul aimed a punch for her cheek, and Jelise ducked it. The young soldier scowled, looking to his fist in confusion as a titter of laughter raced through the crowd.

He came at her again. Jelise swung away around him and brought her foot up into the small of his back, missing Vul's nerve bundle by a hand width but sending him to his hands and knees on the floor with a grunt of pain. She backed off, anticipating his swing at her legs almost as well as Jace had.

Vul came back to his feet, grinding his teeth in fury at the outright chuckles rising from the other soldiers. Here and there, the other men were taking bets on how long Vul would last against the "warrior re-bred."

He stalked around her, trying to flank her, though she turned to keep him in her sights. Their muscles were tensed, their expressions fierce. He charged her, and Jelise stepped back, planting her forward leg solidly and bringing the rear one up in a near split that sent her tread into his chest and him to the floor again.

Vul grasped for her ankle, but she'd already moved, not back or to the side but straight up and into a tucked roll. She landed smoothly on the other side of his body then flipped herself backward, hands to feet, as he threw himself toward her.

Cheers went up from the crowd, and the Princess clapped heartily, her eyes alight at her charge's show of agility.

Jace studied her movements, admiring the dancer's grace with which she fought. With a light blade, Jelise could perform the Son Rel with ease, and few could do that.

It was obvious that Vul was no challenge for her. Jace had misjudged her prowess based on her failure against the humans, but in retrospect, it was probably their weaponry and not their hand-to-hand combat abilities that sent her running.

Vul vaulted to his feet, red faced, his eyes promising pain he wasn't capable of administering—or free to.

Jace shouted "stop" rather than his typical "hold," knowing it was a word in the Keen language Jelise knew from her training on hottel. She lowered her hands, unfisting them and looking to him for an explanation.

Vul struck; her head rocked back from the force of his punch, and Jace pulled his blade to kill the insolent brute—a heartbeat after she pulled hers. With a flick of her wrist and a blur of metal in motion, a short blade appeared and nestled to the artery in Vul's throat, drawing his blood in warning on the way up.

The silence in the room was absolute. Jelise looked half-crazed in anger, her hands steady and sure. She would kill Vul without question if he dared move against her again.

Jace eased to her side. In a little over a month, this would be her right. For now, it was Prince Michael's right to exact punishment and give his assurances that she had been avenged.

He wrapped his hand around her wrist, holding her fast when she tried to wrench out of his grip. "*No,*" he soothed her. "*He'll be punished by our laws. You have my word.*"

She scowled but nodded her understanding. Jelise looked at Vul, a look that seemed to mark him as her enemy. "I am not a child," she informed him in Keen. "*Release me. Please, Jace.*"

Jace bowed his head to her and released her arm, breathing a sigh of relief as she flicked the blade back into its metal casing and stowed it in a hidden pocket in her sleeve. Jelise turned on her heel and strode to Princess Danellan, collecting her staff with a murmur of thanks.

Her Highness winced at the rising bruise marring her face. "*Come. Michael will heal your injury.*" She shot a hard look at Vul. "*I trust you will deliver this soldier to my husband, Lieutenant Jace.*"

He bowed his head in acknowledgement of her orders, itching to offer assurances himself, though it wasn't his place to do so.

"*Perhaps it would be best if you handled Jelise's training from now on,*" she suggested.

"*Of course.*"

"*Personally,*" she stressed.

Jace's heart quickened. "Pardon?" he asked, forgetting to use English in his shock.

"*You will give Lady Jelise private instruction, so I may be assured of no more mishaps.*"

He hesitated, warily noting Jelise's blush and the sidelong glance she shot him. "*As you wish.*" *Anything you wish, Jelise.* He shook that thought away and turned to deal with his prisoner.

CHAPTER FIVE

Jelise stopped in the doorway, watching Jace practice, her breathing strangled. He seemed to be doing some sort of kata, a flowing demonstration of his fighting prowess. He performed it barefoot and without his typical tunic. Sweat coated the bronze skin that covered corded muscle and slicked his thick, black hair back.

He turned, stopping abruptly as he spied her. He lowered his blade and bowed to her.

"Don't stop," she requested. "It's beautiful, and I was enjoying watching it." *And enjoying watching you.*

"You won't be watching the Son Rel. You'll be learning it," he informed her.

She furrowed her brow. "I thought I was here for battle training not...dance practice."

Jace set his blade down on the mat reverently, then turned to her. In a heartbeat, her staff lay ten yards away, and she was pinned beneath him on the mat.

Jelise gasped, her body responding to the position and the tangy aroma of sweat and male musk. For some reason, Jace seemed even more alluring than any man she'd ever screwed.

He's Keen, she reminded herself. Danellan had taught her that the Keen musk contained pheromones missing in human musk, an aphrodisiac concoction that would prove hard to ignore.

Jace eased off of her and offered his hand. "You have nearly all the training I would suggest for you." He paused, lifting her to her feet as she took his hand. "My apologies for assigning Vul to you."

"I've taken worse," she dismissed him. "And obviously, there was no way you could have known he would ignore your order to stop."

His jaw tightened, and his eyes went hard in seeming fury. "No," he assured her. "I meant— You have my apologies for underestimating your training."

"Still, you have a lot to teach me. Look how easily you downed me."

He shook his head. "You have the skills, but you lack strength. You have agility, but your speed is only passing grade."

"And your kata will teach me strength and speed?"

"The Son Rel? Yes. It will."

"I'll be testing that," she warned him.

Jace chuckled. "Of course. I wouldn't dream of less. Now..." He left her and retrieved the dagger from the floor, presenting it to her with a deep bow.

Jelise took it, her mind protesting that such a fine weapon couldn't possibly be meant for her. The hilt was a shimmering gold alloy of some sort set with gems the color of emeralds and the consistency of amber. "It's beautiful," she gasped.

"An abinatine. The Son Rel is ancient. In its purest—and oldest form, it was performed by the High Priestess of Fion's Children. At some unknown time before the great unification, a newer form emerged within the Magden society—a two-person form. You, of course, will play the part of Mother Fion."

"And you?" she asked, not questioning that Jace would play the other role, nor that he would teach her the two-person style.

His eyes were hot in a sudden hunger. Before she could react to it...or question it, his face was studiously neutral again.

"I will play the part of Father Mag." He left her side, collecting a second blade, this one with bright red stones that looked like rubies set in the hilt.

"Mag," she whispered happily.

Mag and Fion were lovers. She furrowed her brow. Or were they married? Either way, the Son Rel was sure to reflect that. With the sexual nature of the Keen, it would likely reflect quite a bit of that nature.

* * * *

"Like this," Jace instructed. He stepped up behind her, placing his legs just outside of hers and his arms along the line of hers, his cupped hand beneath her weapon hand.

They swayed together smoothly, executing the steps of the second movement with him correcting her stance and thrust. It was a difficult exchange to master, even for a woman as agile as Jelise was.

"Again." His voice was rough in his rising arousal. Her body brushing against his played havoc with his concentration, and her scent was divine.

They executed the movement perfectly and flowed into the third. At the appropriate moment, he leaned back; her body laid over his, and visions of her over him in bed assaulted him. In this position, the scrap of fabric that covered her breasts did little to impede his view of her body.

"Hold," he whispered, though they wouldn't pause here normally.

Jelise panted and trembled, sweat rolling down her breasts. Her eyes closed, and a low moan escaped her lips.

"Feel the tension," he instructed. "Let it peak." The sexual tension between them was much more interesting than the burn in his muscles, and he longed to lay her down on the mat and capture a few of the beads of sweat from her body...

She cried out, breaking his train of thought—and what precious little concentration remained. They both crumpled to the mat. Jelise rolled away, rubbing at her calf muscle with a grimace of pain.

"Let me," he offered, kneading at the knot. "Cramps aren't unusual at first. You have much better stamina than most."

He looked up in surprise as she lay back on the mat. Her eyes closed, and she arched her back, licking her lips. Jace kept massaging her, inhaling her rising musk like a starving man presented with a tray of Gelgrin.

If only his life wasn't the price, Jace would trail his hands higher. He'd suck on the wells of musk at her pulse points, peel off those tight trousers, and introduce her to Keen lovemaking.

But his life *would* be the price for it.

He moved his hands to his knees reluctantly. "Better?" he asked.

"Yes."

He bit back a groan at her sex-charged voice. She wanted him, and by the gods, he'd go insane in that knowledge.

"I think that's enough for tonight," he managed, pushing to his feet and putting distance between them before he did something as stupid as kissing her. Jace shivered at the sound of her approach, praying she didn't intend to pursue him.

"Jace?"

He turned to her, looking at the abinatine in her hand in understanding. "You'll need it to practice with." He marched away again, breathing deeper when he left the radius of her scent. He removed the emi-beaded sheath from the cabinet and carried it to her, sliding it over the blade with the blessing and stepping away with another deep bow.

She hesitated, staring at the abinatine. "Will you..."

"Yes?" Yes to almost anything she asked, if he didn't remember to talk himself out of it.

"Will you teach me the prayer you just said?"

His heart sank. "Of course. Go, now."

"After dinner tomorrow?"

"Yes." But, would touching her this way be worse than never seeing her again?

* * * *

Pri 18th, Ri 25-3001

"Jelise?" Danellan asked, wondering at her uncharacteristic silence.

The young woman looked up, her cheeks darkening. "Sorry, Danni. My mind was somewhere else."

"If you'd rather not learn the laws—"

"How does a Keen woman tell a man... Well, how does she tell him she's interested in him?"

She smiled. "You do care for Lieutenant Jace. Don't you?"

Her eyes widened, and she started to protest. Jelise groaned. "Am I that obvious?"

"No. Not really. I doubt he expects you to act like a Keen woman. I think he'd find your honest approach more enticing—once you are legally an adult."

She grumbled several human curses.

"A month, Jelise. You're halfway there."

"It's not that. I mean...it's that too, but... You're saying I should just walk up to Jace, kiss him, and..." She motioned uncertainly, looking truly miserable.

"Is that what you usually do? Just kiss a man and offer yourself?"

Jelise winced. "Yes."

"I don't understand the problem. It would almost certainly work, and—"

"This is *Jace*," she complained. "He's not some loser on the streets, Danni."

She gasped in understanding. "You don't understand, do you?"

"What is there to understand? He's... I've never met anyone like him."

Danellan sighed. "This isn't Earth, Jelise. You are not the same person you were there. Perhaps on Earth, a man like Jace would have been seen as your better, but this is Kegin. I'm sure Jace feels he's unworthy of you."

"Because I inherited some bogus title?" she spat. "Do you really think I'm that shallow? I'm still me. I haven't changed."

"True. Perhaps you should consider that you were *always* worthy of a man like Jace, and the humans were the shallow ones."

She looked at her hands in confusion.

"You are strong and able, honest and sure."

She laughed harshly. "Sure? Me?"

"Yes. You are."

Jelise didn't protest it again.

"Are your lessons with Lieutenant Jace going well?" she asked.

A sudden smile lit her entire face. "Wonderful. Jace taught me the abinatine blessing, and we've reached the sixth movement."

"Abinatine? Movement? He's teaching you the Son Rel?" she asked. She hadn't realized how advanced Jelise was.

Her smile faded. "There's a problem," she guessed.

"Not at all. Few women are dedicated and skilled enough to learn it. In fact, it is almost always performed by two men."

"You said women trained."

"Yes, but few train as diligently as you have." An idea took shape. "I believe I would enjoy seeing the Son Rel performed as it is meant to be."

"We train every—"

"No. I meant a public performance."

"I don't know. I'm not—"

"Not today, of course. I was thinking about the middle of next month, so you have time to polish your performance. I'll have the traditional costumes made for you both, and we'll invite a few choice guests...just family, I promise."

Jelise seemed to consider it carefully. "You have something up your sleeve," she ventured.

"Yes. I do." Danellan leaned across the desk. "You do want Jace, don't you?"

"Oh, yes," she admitted.

"Then we have a lot of work to do in the next month." She started making a mental list of everything they'd need: clothiers, invitations, the house head, cooks...and a magetra.

CHAPTER SIX

Ite 18th, Ri 25-3001

Jelise stood behind the heavy curtain, fussing with the capi skirt. The "traditional costume" for the Son Rel made her feel like an idiot. The drasen was akin to a bikini, and the capi was really more of a cape attached to the back of the panties. Danellan said the costume was usually green, but in deference to her sense of style, the green of Jelise's was so dark as to appear black in the dim light.

The first strains of music pierced the curtain, and she strode through, head up and shoulders back, one hand on the abinatine hung in its sheath on a silin belt over her hips.

She held her breath, expelling it in a rush as Jace entered through the other curtain. The moment of stillness in the Son Rel suddenly made sense. It hardly seemed possible to move when faced with him in this context.

The music changed, and Jelise grasped the hilt of the abinatine in one hand and released the tie on the belt with the other so the sheath fell away. Across the hall, the red silin belt fell away from Jace's gold lounging pants.

Then they were in motion. Blades struck blades. They turned around each other, bodies touching bodies and moving on. Sweat coated them, sweet and sultry, making each slide a delight. Their eyes met for torturous moments, lost again as the music changed, signaling another volley.

Jace spun away, dropping to a defensive crouch, every muscle taut. She eased into the regal pose she'd practiced, the abinatine poised for a back swipe between them. Their eyes locked, and they held their positions, as still as stone.

The music soared to a thundering crescendo, and Jace pounced. Though they moved at a furious pace, their eyes rarely strayed from each other's.

His arm pushed her blade hand out and away, and his body pressed to hers. His fingers trailed back up her arm, cupping her cheek, his lips little more than an inch from her own, and the music stopped.

He didn't instruct her to hold the pose as he normally would. It hardly seemed necessary to. Jelise wouldn't have moved on a dare—unless it was closer to him.

"My lady," he breathed.

The applause was nearly deafening. Jace pulled away, his gaze lowered, bowing first to her...then to the assembled royals and nobles. He turned and strode to the curtains, scooping up the sheath for his man-style abinatine and sheathing it with the proper blessing.

Without missing a beat, Jelise did the same, and the applause stepped up another notch. Nobles flooded the stage, offering congratulations and accolades.

"A beautiful rendition," King Jole proclaimed. "The best I have ever seen. Would you consider performing at the palace for Spring festival?"

Jelise turned her head to share the moment, but Jace was gone, the curtains still swinging slowly in testament to his passing. She forced her smile to remain steady, though she wanted to cry in frustration.

"Lady Jelise?" he asked.

She met his green eyes steadily. "I'm sure we will." *If I have to order him! If Jace thinks he can escape me this easily, he doesn't know me very well.*

* * * *

Jace threw the sheathed weapon the length of the practice room, grimacing at the sacrilege inherent in that move. He grumbled a curse, retrieving it and saying a prayer begging forgiveness before the typical blessing, his heart aching as he said the words.

Nothing he believed in was good enough anymore. None of it would give him what he really wanted. Not the gods and not his training.

He paced the floor, images of Jelise in the drasen taunting him. The Son Rel seemed crafted for her. Performing it had never felt so right to him before. He'd been immersed in the movements until nothing existed but Jelise and himself.

Jace scowled. He'd nearly kissed her. What madness that would have been, with their Majesties in the audience...and Prince Michael.

He stared at the dagger in his hand miserably. Maybe if he practiced, he could clear his mind.

It didn't work. Minutes later, he realized that his body automatically followed the Son Rel, but now it was an empty endeavor. Jelise's eyes didn't meet his, her body and blade didn't touch his, and the faint scent of her on his skin only taunted him with what he couldn't have.

This was hopeless. The only thing left to do was change into his uniform and return to the barracks—where he wouldn't be able to sleep.

* * * *

Jace looked up at a sound from the doorway, drinking in the sight of Jelise in a fierce hunger that staggered his senses. His cock rose at the unexpected delight.

She was clothed in a purple day dress with a guard jacket over it, her legs bare save for a matching pair of silin house shoes. Her hips swayed as she glided toward him. Jace trailed his gaze up her body, reasoning all the while that he was courting death by allowing her to come to him.

His mind screamed that this was insanity. If Prince Michael saw him looking at Jelise this way, his head would soon part company with the rest of his traitorous hide. Still, he watched her come to him, praying she'd touch him. If she touched him, he wouldn't care what the penalty was for it.

Her hand brushed over the muscles of his lower abdomen, stealing his breath, then moved lower, examining his state of readiness. She smiled in triumph. "I knew it," she whispered.

"You shouldn't," Jace pleaded, the last vestige of his thinking mind demanding that he try to dissuade her. *Mother Fion, but I want her to.*

Her lips pressed to his chest through his tunic, her tongue tracing his nipple then prodding at the well of his musk, making his body throb for her. "I've learned a lot from Danellan and the tutors."

How to drive me mad. He bit back a groan as her tongue moved to the other nipple. The urge to cradle her head to him was immediate and intense, and he fisted his hands at his side to keep from giving in to it.

She teased him then nipped at the sensitive tip, and he jumped in response, his breathing labored. "I know customs and practices." Her fingers sought out the bundle of nerves at the back of his neck and massaged it.

Jace closed his eyes, his cock releasing a few drops of musk in response to the overtly-sexual stimulus she was providing. Jelise buried her face in his chest, inhaling deeply. He shivered in the realization that she was drawing the aphrodisiac into her lungs purposefully.

"I know the laws, Jace," she half-groaned. "A Keen female not of royal blood chooses her sexual partners at the age of twenty."

He nodded stiffly. Yes, that was the law, and that was the only reason she wasn't on the floor with his cock buried as deep as it would go already.

"Do you know the date?" she asked.

"It is—" He fought for clarity, something as simple as recalling the date suddenly tedious. "It is Ite the eighteenth."

"Mid-month in February is my birthday. I am legally an adult, Jace."

He snapped his eyes open, locking on her hopeful expression and drawing the proof of her arousal into his lungs.

Jelise started unbuttoning the jacket. "I am not of royal blood, and I want you."

Jace pulled her hands from the jacket, continuing to undress her, watching her dark skin appear in the opening. The dress was no common day dress but rather cut deep between her breasts...nearly as far as a presentation dress would have been. He pushed the jacket off of her shoulders and let it fall.

Her breathing was quick and uneven, her eyes locked on his. Jace captured her head between his hands and brought his mouth down on hers, not exploring as he did at Christmas but ravenous, needing to release two months...*no two years* of wanting into her. Jelise met him in a full frenzy, her body pressed to his in invitation.

He crushed her to him, finding the fit of her mound to his rigid length. Jelise pulled at his tunic, running her hands over his back beneath it, seemingly seeking to draw him closer, though the only way to be closer was to have him inside her.

He released her mouth, praying that she wanted more than a dalliance, needing to know she intended more before he would go further. "If I do this, you'll never be rid of me," he warned her.

"I can beat all of the other soldiers. Who else would I want?" she teased. Jelise nipped at the pulse point at his throat, urging Jace on.

He carried her to the training mat and knelt in the center, pushing her skirt up to the tops of her thighs, prepared to rip the ridiculous Earth-style panties from her body. Jace groaned aloud as his fingers trailed over smooth skin and through damp curls.

"You like my surprise?" she asked, a coy smile pulling her kiss-plumped lips up.

Jace pulled at the buttons on his trousers and pushed them away, taking just enough time to allow Jelise to drag off his tunic before he seated the head his cock just inside the canal. His mind protested his near slide into her. There were mores to be observed. No matter how much he wanted her, he couldn't ignore them.

"Tell me what you want," he ordered.

"Do you have to ask?" she moaned, attempting to rock further onto his length.

He held her still, aching to finish what he was starting. "Yes. I do. Tell me." Jace eased further out, stopping when the tip barely parted her seam, smiling at Jelise's cry of dismay. She would learn not to tease him.

"You, Jace. Please, I want you to make me a Keen mate."

He thrust into her, possessing her, marking Jelise as his own. She leaned back, stripping her dress down her shoulders and chest, baring her breasts to him. Jace took all of her at once, his body filling hers again and again while he feasted on her deep choc nipples and rich skin at every pass.

Her core heated around him, gripping Jace as she panted in a vain attempt to outlast him. Jelise cried out her surrender, her body pulling at his frantically, begging him for full completion.

Jace laid her back on the mat, lifting her hips with his hands and taking her deep. She squirmed as he nestled to the gates of her womb, and the realization that he would be the first to stimulate her nearly sent him over. Jelise bowed her back, begging him to finish her in desperate whispers.

"Now, I make you mine," he informed her. Jace pulled back slightly and impaled her with his full length, holding her hips tight to him while his seed warmed her body and his cock sealed the pact, locking into the stim band and making them one.

Jelise screamed in pleasure, her release quickening for him. Jace moved one hand from her hip to the base of her skull, lifting her with both hands to settle her in his lap and bringing his mouth down on hers again.

Her response was heated, a challenge he didn't need her words to interpret. Her hands sought out his pulse points and nerve bundles, massaging the erogenous zones and firing his body to life for another round.

"No," he growled, nipping at her chin.

"Jace," she begged.

"Not here."

Her beautiful eyes met his, pleading with him.

"In your bed," he informed her. "Now."

Another smile curved her lips.

CHAPTER SEVEN

Ite 19th, Ri 25-3001

Jace smiled at the feeling of Jelise's hair spread over his chest, her cheek pressed to his heart, and the perfume of their mating surrounding them. It was a moment he wanted to relive endlessly in the years to come.

There would be an altercation soon, but it was one Jace would win. Prince Michael's perceived claim or not, Jelise was correct about the laws. The Prince wasn't legally her guardian now. She was an adult, and by the very laws that had tortured them both for the last two months, it was her right to take any man to her bed she wished.

A rebellious spark ignited into a fierce desire for her. Jelise was his. She'd come to him and asked him to be her mate, and she would be his mate—now.

Jace smiled as he slipped his hand between her silin thighs, his thumb stimulating her hood while two fingers sought out her inner pleasure spot. Jelise moaned, her hips tipping against him and her nipples beading against his side.

"That's right," he urged her. "You are mine to touch."

Silently echoing his claim, her fingers circled his length and stroked him. She moved her hips back and forth, guiding his ministrations. "I need you, Jace," she pleaded.

"Come for me. Then we will have a riding lesson."

As if the promise of his cock was too much for her, Jelise's body gripped his fingers rhythmically, her sweet nectar coursing over his hand. She panted out an oath to her god, then one to Mag, arching against him.

Jace threw back the quilt and lifted her astride him. Jelise guided him to her body, closing her eyes as he thrust into her. He shivered at how perfect she felt, how her heat enveloped him, propelling him toward the soul's reward. He panted back his release, reveling in her sighs, her look of rapture, and her renewed musk.

The end came far too soon. Jace groaned at her cry of completion, his body relaxing at the stimulation of her stim band holding him snug inside her. This was where he belonged, the one place he had longed to be since long before he went to Earth for her.

A knock at the door interrupted the peace of the moment.

"*Leave us,*" Jace snapped in Keen, unwilling to relinquish the sense of purpose being joined with her instilled in him.

The door opened, and Jace scrambled to pull the quilts around Jelise's shoulders. He grumbled a curse. Who dared enter her rooms this way? But even before Prince Michael's fury-dark face appeared, Jace had reasoned himself to the obvious conclusion.

The Prince's hand fisted on the hilt of his dagger.

Jace didn't flinch at that. The law was on his side this time. "Jelise is an adult now," he offered in English. "She's made her choice."

Taking his lead, Michael used his rusty English. "You took advantage," he accused.

"Jelise came to me. I didn't pursue her."

She glared at Michael. "I am not a child, even by your laws. And I am not of royal blood. I have every right to choose a mate."

The Prince ran a hand through his hair, mussing it. He met Jelise's gaze, seemingly uncertain. "Have you any concept of the legal difficulties—"

"Yes. I do. Danellan took me to your *magetra* a week ago. If Jace will have me, I intend to offer him a contract."

Jace ground his teeth at that. "If? You think I would refuse to sign it?"

She laughed. "I hope not. If you try to ask for a *regit lus*, I will have to kill you where you stand... Um... Lay."

Michael nodded. "So would I. It would be a shame to kill my finest guard."

Jace looked at him in surprise. While he didn't intend to either refuse to contract or demand regit lus, it wasn't Prince Michael's right to take any action against him.

"I expect a signed contract delivered to me by midday meal."

"And if it is not?" Jace asked seriously.

"I will offer Jelise assurances and condolences by evening meal." He turned and left the room without giving Jace a chance to respond.

He watched the door close, then turned his face back to Jelise's with a smile and a raised eyebrow. "Well, then. I suppose you should tell me where this contract is."

"Commandeer the practice room," she suggested, her eyes glittering in mischief.

Jace stared at her. "What? Why would I do something like that?"

"We have to practice for our palace performance."

"Our... What in Len's name are you talking about?"

She ran her hands up his ribs. "I told King Jole we'd perform at the Spring festival. We don't want to disappoint him—and you *will* kiss me during the palace performance."

Jace chuckled, remembering how hard it had been not to kiss her the night before. "That is nothing compared to what I'll do to you today. You felt it, didn't you? The urge to strip off our costumes and mate?"

She purred like a nursing jaglin. "Why do you think I want to practice?"

"You're wearing the drasen," he ordered.

"Of course."

"Now will you tell me where the contract is?"

Jelise chuckled, shaking her head.

"We have only a few hours until midday meal," he reminded her.

"Then we should practice soon."

"Jelise," he warned.

"You'll have to convince me."

"I see. Perhaps the Son Rel will shake the location loose."

She smiled. "Hmmm... Perhaps it will at that."

THE END

SECTION SIX:
Graham

Training the
Earth-Born Lord

DEDICATED TO...

*Lisa, for suggesting I investigate my characters
more closely.*

*Debbie and the folks at the Mystic Moon, for giving
Graham his first test run.*

*My husband, for putting up with long nights and
short tempers.*

GRAHAM: TRAINING THE

EARTH-BORN LORD

May 31ˢᵗ, 2007

Pittsburgh, PA

Planet Earth

Am I sure about this? "Yes," Graham Miller breathed, pulling on the black band the soldier had handed off to him.

"Your pardon, Lord Graham?" the uniformed man asked in deeply-accented English. He was unbelievably tall, a full head taller than Graham's six feet one; and he blended into the shadows, his black uniform a perfect match for his dark hair and eyes, knee-high boots and deeply tanned skin.

"Nothing. I'm ready."

He motioned to the shimmering doorway. "We have little time. My men have taken the few things you requested. Do you require anything more?" He didn't add that there would be no coming back for anything he missed now. That went without saying.

Graham looked around his apartment with a sigh. "No. There's nothing here for me." There hadn't been anything there for Graham since Loraine left. In two years, that hadn't changed. That was why he was willing to take this foolish chance at a new life and a new identity.

He took a calming breath and stepped through the doorway without hesitation. *There is nothing for me on Earth,* he reminded himself as the swirling mass of the doorway seemed to swallow him whole. Maybe Kegin would be different.

Graham expected disorientation, flashing lights, discomfort—some jarring effect to crossing galaxies of space in an instant of time. There was none. One moment, he stood in a dark, dingy apartment over a bar on Pittsburgh's South Side. The next, he was standing in a brightly-lit room, being gently drawn away from the doorway by men in black tunics. The black box was removed from his arm, and everything seemed to happen at once. While he looked at the strange heavy wood and stone furnishings, garbled speech flew around him, the doorway seemed to disappear, and soldiers sped away with nods and bows to him.

A lord. They said he was a lord, a cross-bred son of their race and humans who was seeded on Earth and left there to adulthood. He was brought home for one reason, to have children with a Keen woman that would strengthen the failing genetic base of the Keen and save the world. He had stepped through the doorway in the hopes that a psychotic fantasy might be better than the sane reality of his life on Earth.

He looked at the strange room again. *If this is a psychotic break, rent me a rubber room anytime.*

An older man dressed in an ornate sky blue and silver jacket bowed to him. "Welcome to Kegin, Lord Graham," the man said with less of an accent than the soldier had.

Graham nodded slowly. "The soldier said I was... This isn't a joke, right?" He felt his cheeks heat. After the doorway proved real, asking about the rest seemed ridiculous.

He laughed heartily. "It is very real, my lord. I am Brid of the Church Council. Welcome to my home."

"Your..." Graham faltered. This place had to be the size of a small palace, judging by the size of this room. It wasn't clear what the purpose of it was, but if it were a ballroom, it would easily fit a hundred people.

"Yes. It will be your home, until you have learned a bit of our culture and language." Brid looked around with a grimace. "Unless my home is not to your liking," he amended.

"No," Graham replied hurriedly. "It is amazing."

It was amazing. Graham would have taken it for a museum of some sort. There was decorative tilework in the floor in shimmering colors of red, green, blue and white. The wood chairs and stone table were etched with scrolling swirls and curves that drew the eye and appeased some unnamed, unsettled feeling in him. Portraits of a woman with flowing white-blonde hair and green eyes and a red-haired man wielding a broadsword decorated the walls. The portraits showed the same couple in a variety of sexual and non-sexual poses together. A glance at Brid convinced Graham that the man in the portraits could not have been the priest, even several decades earlier in his life.

Brid smiled. "I am heartened that you think so. We will start your lessons as soon as you wish."

"Immediately," he gushed, blushing again. "I mean, as soon as..." Graham sighed. Kegin was new. Kegin held hope. It was difficult not to jump right in.

His host laughed again. "Tomorrow morning," he promised. "For now, you should rest. The exhaustion of passing through the gateway will tire you. A meal has been prepared in your rooms. You will probably sleep away the evening after that. Would you like servants to tend to your needs?"

"Servants?"

Brid nodded. "Queen Susan assures us that most American humans will turn down that offer initially, but it is good form to offer."

"The Earth-Born queen?" he guessed. The soldier told Graham that he would meet the queen when he was settled in.

The priest nodded again.

"Uh. No. I think I'll do this on my own."

"As you wish, Lord Graham."

* * * *

Carila watched Lord Graham enter the sanctuary. He was a beautiful male with deep choc hair streaked with gold and eyes the color of a stormy sky. When her father had asked Carila to tutor the Earth-Born lord, she'd been hesitant. Seeing him stride toward her, Carila was glad she'd reconsidered.

He dipped his chin to her in what she recognized as an Earth form of greeting, smoothing his tunic over his abdomen self-consciously. "Sorry I'm late," he offered in his language.

She was suddenly overjoyed that she'd learned to speak it to honor Queen Susan when she visited the palace. Though the queen spoke almost perfect Keen after five years on the planet, she was touched when a native went out of his or her way to make her feel more at home with her own language.

"It is quite all right. You have a lifetime to learn the culture, and we knew the gateway would tire you." Carila touched the front of his tunic, feeling his muscles tighten through the silin. "The clothing is to your liking?" she asked.

"Yes, they are. I... Is this the style?"

Carila smiled, glad for an excuse to touch him again. "May I?"

The lord nodded. "Please."

He sucked in his breath, as Carila bloused the tunic. She loosened the ties at the neck and bared a bit of his throat. Graham shifted, his lengthening cock brushing her hip. His scent intensified, and Carila resisted the urge to taste the skin at his throat.

"Miss?" he asked, his voice rough.

"Yes, my lord?" she answered, though she didn't understand what he was asking of her.

"Graham. Please, call me Graham. I'm afraid— I don't know how to be a lord," he admitted reluctantly.

Carila glanced at his erect length, stifling a chuckle. "You are more a Keen lord than you know." She moved away to the table, trying to calm her jangled nerves. Seeing his state of readiness and smelling his interest in her was making her forget her duty to train him.

Graham sank into the soft chair provided for him, looking like a child caught in some misdeed. "I apologize," he managed.

She raised an eyebrow in surprise. "For what are you apologizing?"

He motioned vaguely to his state of arousal. "I don't know what's wrong with me."

Carila planted her fists on her hips. "Wrong with you?" she demanded, reminding herself that it was probably a misunderstanding based on his human roots. "Am I so displeasing to you?"

His eyes widened. "No. Of course not. I just... Oh hell!"

"Pardon?" she asked, confused by what could only be an exclamation of anger or disgust.

"You are Carila. Right?"

She furrowed her brow, his logic escaping her. "I am."

Graham grimaced. "Brid is your father?"

"He is."

He buried his face in his hands, grumbling words foreign to her.

"Have I offended you somehow?" she asked curiously. "My studies have obviously not prepared me to deal with your cultural eccentricities."

Graham seemed at a loss for words. "You aren't offended by—" He glanced to his lap again.

Carila laughed heartily. "Why should I be offended? It is a compliment that you find me to your liking. I know my father would be pleased, if you took me to your bed—and the breeding office would cheer it."

He scowled, looking about as if he were uncertain.

"That confuses you."

"I'm accustomed to fathers who are a bit more protective. Brid doesn't even know me."

"He knows quite a bit about you." Carila crossed the room to him and traced the line of his jaw. "Keen women choose their own sexual partners. Is it not so on Earth?"

"It is, but that doesn't mean fathers don't offer their advice." He grimaced again. "Or their protests."

Carila shrugged and sauntered back to the table. "You will learn our traditions soon enough. What would you like to learn first?"

* * * *

Graham looked up at her, thankful for the reprieve from the memories of the beating Lorain's father had dealt him the week she left. She'd played her father against Graham most effectively.

He swallowed hard at the look of invitation in Carila's eyes. When Graham had learned that the Church Councilman's daughter would be his instructor, he hadn't expected Carila to be sex personified. From the dark waves of hair that cascaded around her thighs to the breasts, as good as uncovered in the skin-tight blue dress, to the length of her tan legs; she was beautiful. And, every move she made had him lusting for her all the more.

Carila raised an eyebrow, reminding him that she had asked a question.

Graham scanned his eyes over the room, the same room the doorway had brought him to. Again, the portraits caught his eye—and wrecked havoc on his libido. "Who are these people? They are obviously very important."

"Ah... A good place to start. The male is Mag, the king of the gods. He personifies laws, justice, vengeance, vows and duty. The female is Fion. She is the goddess of love, mercy, healing, and family. She is Mag's mate."

"Your..." Graham took a deep breath. "You display portraits of your gods..." He motioned to a portrait of Mag licking at Fion's clit. The enjoyment on both of their faces was captured with remarkable clarity.

Carila chuckled. "You will find that much of Keen culture stems from our intensely sexual natures. Why should we not embrace what our gods made us? Surely, you have a healthy sexual appetite."

He flushed, clearing his throat. "A little too much of an appetite, according to my wife," he grumbled. *My ex-wife*, he reminded himself sternly.

Graham rubbed the tension from his neck that thinking of Loraine always caused. She'd told her parents that she was leaving Graham because of his strange sexual habits. Funny how those same habits had always excited her—until he failed to give her the child she'd always wanted, the child David gave her before she ran to her parents to protect her from her "sex maniac" husband.

"You are contracted?" Carila asked in dismay.

"Contracted?"

"You have a bride?" she qualified for him.

"No. I *had* a wife," he spat, annoyed with himself for letting Loraine in again.

"She dissolved your contract, then?"

Graham sighed. "Dissolved is too pretty a name for what Loraine did."

Carila grimaced. "She was human. She could not properly appreciate the importance of your drives."

"Oh, Loraine appreciated it just fine, until it was a convenient excuse to leave me for a man who could—"

"Give her children," she finished for him, her eyes wide and sad.

Graham looked away from her pity. "Yes. Exactly."

"The females on Kegin," she began.

"Can they really have my children?"

"Yes. They can." Carila hesitated. "Many women will pursue you, Graham—for the purpose of a child and nothing more. You must be cautious."

Graham scrubbed a hand over his face. "Like Loraine," he decided. The baby she wanted had obviously been more important to her than Graham had been.

"I am afraid so, but you are an Earth-Born lord. In contract, the advantage is yours."

"Advantage?"

"In bargain. You can ask for things not typically granted a male. A woman who truly wishes to be your bride will grant you the assurances you require."

"For instance?"

"Any children would be yours in a split. The penalties for dissolution would favor you."

Graham snorted. "Well, that would be new and interesting."

Carila's face clouded in confusion. "Pardon?"

He waved the question off with a sigh. It wasn't Carila's fault that Loraine set out to publicly humiliate him or that the courts had taken him for what little he'd amassed in his life at her word.

"As you wish. Very well. Perhaps we should begin with the societal norms for sex and taking a mate."

Graham groaned. "Do we have to?"

"To safeguard yourself, you may want to," she cautioned.

He motioned for her to continue.

Carila eased herself up on the table and folded her legs under her. "Women will want the prestige of a child by you. They will wager on your ignorance of the law to help them get what they seek."

"In what way?"

"If a woman comes to your bed willingly and mates to completion, you have only the following day to demand the *regit lus*."

"Uh. What precisely is a regit loose?"

"A time of—test. *Ferdil Fion,*" she breathed then motioned for his patience. "*Regit lus* lasts one of our months. You need not mate with the woman again, though you may if you are willing. If she conceives during that month, the child is yours in a split. If you dissolve the union, you leave with your child but forfeit a substantial penalty. If she dissolves the contract, she receives a small stipend for gifting you an heir. The problem with demanding *regit lus* is... If at any time during the month she demands a contract, you are bound to contract with her."

"And?" he prodded.

Carila grimaced. "If she makes your life miserable enough and withholds intimacy—"

Graham groaned in understanding. "It would be worth the penalty to escape her."

"And she would have her penalty without producing a child for you. Of course, if she mates and slips away, eluding you until the time has passed for you to demand the *regit lus*, she has the best of both worlds. You have no rights to your child, and she receives government aid for the babe. As the offspring of one of the Earth-Born, her stipend would be astronomical."

"Why bother?" he groused.

"Pardon?" she asked again.

"With a world full of women like that, why would I bother mating?"

Her eyes widened. "Stopping may be harder than you realize."

"I've never had a problem controlling myself." *Despite what Loraine said about me.*

"With human women, you mean," she guessed sagely.

"Well, that goes without saying, doesn't it?" he commented sarcastically.

Carila chuckled, swinging her legs off the edge of the table. "Sex with a Keen woman is not the same," she assured him.

Graham swallowed past the lump in his throat, his erection fierce and insistent. His eyes locked on her slightly parted knees. He shook his head slowly, suddenly certain that he could smell her arousal from three yards away.

"Is that an offer?" he managed in a hoarse voice.

Carila cocked her head to one side, her hair fanning out over the stone tabletop. "Yes. It is." Her scent intensified.

* * * *

Carila smiled at Graham's shiver of anticipation. He shook his head again, apparently unprepared for the force of his arousal, much as Queen Susan had been unprepared for her reactions in King Jole's arms.

"Would you care to experience the true Keen drive?" she offered.

Graham's cock was hard and his scent heavy. Whether he was ready to admit it or not, he wanted what she offered. His eyes panned over the portraits of Mag and Fion, and his breathing quickened.

"Why?" he whispered. His eyes settled on the portrait to her left, and he swallowed again.

Carila smiled, knowing the portrait intimately. "I want you."

"You want me or you want a child?" he accused.

His mistrust does run deep. "Bargain with me. On Kegin, we are bound by our word. Mag demands that we keep to our vows."

"Bargain for what?" he snapped.

"I wave all rights. I have no claim on your estate."

"I have nothing to claim," he growled.

"Of course you do. You have two homes, dozens of troops and servants, a fortune and a title."

Graham seemed stunned by the revelation. Had no one told him what he inherited as an Earth-Born lord?

"I relinquish all claim." She raised a hand to still him before Graham could question her further. "I relinquish all claim on any child I might conceive by you."

"What do you get in return?" he asked suspiciously.

"Knowing that I am your first. The chance to educate you." She let her eyes wander over his body. "The chance to touch you as I have wanted to since you walked into this room."

"That's all?"

"Should there be something more?"

Graham closed his eyes, taking a deep breath. His fingertips skated over the length straining against his trousers.

Carila smiled at the move. "It is enticing," she teased.

"What is?" he asked in a dreamy voice, stroking himself again.

"The musk. It makes you crazy. The mating frenzy can be very intense."

His eyes opened slowly. Graham rose and came to her, a fine sweat on his brow. He planted his hands on either side of her hips and buried his face in her throat, drawing her scent deep into his lungs. He trembled in response.

"Oh God," he groaned. "It's true. I can smell you."

"Shall I be your teacher?"

Graham kissed her throat. "Where?"

"Here." A tingle of excitement coursed over her nerves. Yes, the sanctuary was the perfect place to teach one of the saviors of Kegin.

Carila expected Graham to balk at her suggestion, to demand a proper bed. He didn't. Graham captured her mouth, his movements frantic, lost in the frenzy.

"Is it always like this?" he breathed.

"Not always this strong," she admitted. *Fion, but he is a potent male!* "The musk is a powerful aphrodisiac."

Graham peeled the silin bodice from her shoulders and down her arms, uncovering her breasts. He sucked in the tip of one breast, his mouth hot, his movements insistent, a male lost in his drive, and it was wonderful.

"You taste of it," he groaned. "Your whole body tastes of it."

"The musk is much more powerful when taken orally," she instructed.

He nodded. "Yes. It is." Graham paid homage to her other breast, groaning at the feelings coursing through him.

"Did you enjoy tasting your human bride?" she asked.

* * * *

The force of that question shook him. He nodded numbly and glanced to the short skirt of her dress. Of everything about Loraine, Graham missed eating her to a screaming orgasm most. He pushed the skirt back, his eyes locked on the thighs appearing beneath his palms.

Carila slid toward the edge of the table, spreading her knees wide in invitation. Her tan skin darkened in a blush that seemed to release more of her scent.

Graham stared at the dark curls that covered her mound in confusion for a moment then met her eyes, seeking an explanation.

"Ah. Yes. Queen Susan requested Earth-style undergarments when she arrived on Kegin. You would expect to see them."

"No one here..." he managed.

"Were there useless undergarments in your rooms?" she countered.

He sank to his knees, shaking his head in confirmation, thankful that the Keen traditions seemed designed to facilitate unencumbered sex. Graham licked a long, slow path over her seam, circling her clit. The flavors went to his head, a dizzying mix of musk and spice that sent pleasure coursing over his nerves. He stroked his tongue over her again, addicted to the response of his body, a hundred times more powerful than his arousal with Loraine.

Carila wound her fingers in his hair, muttering something in her own language. "Anything," she pleaded. "Give me this, and I will give you anything you wish."

Graham looked to the portrait over her shoulder, knowing precisely what he wanted— after Carila came for him. He gave her his full attention, drinking in the dizzying flow of her musk as he stroked deep inside her.

She jerked, gasping in surprise as Graham discovered a slight ridge inside her. He investigated it further, groaning into her as Carila tightened her grip in his hair.

"Yes," she urged him. "It is the inner pleasure spot. Please, Graham."

He stroked his tongue over the ridge again and again, bracing her legs wide with his shoulders when she tried to clamp them shut, holding her hip in place when she tried to shift back onto the table. Graham stroked the pad of his thumb over her clit, smiling as she stiffened.

Carila cried out softly, a wash of her personal lubricant flooding his mouth, the rich, heady flavor making his head swim. Her inner muscles gripped him rhythmically, making the hunger for her surge.

Graham pushed to his feet, pulling at the buttons on his trousers. Carila dragged his mouth down to hers and kissed him passionately, her hands brushing his away and freeing him expertly.

She nipped at his lips, her breathing as harsh as his own. "I love tasting myself on you," she murmured.

"You do?" Loraine hadn't liked to taste herself. She wanted Graham to wash and brush his teeth before kissing her.

Carila nodded. She rubbed her thumb through the precome on the head of his cock and brought it to her mouth, licking it away with a look of ecstasy. She drew his face down again. "Taste yourself," she urged him. "Taste our mixed fluids."

Graham hesitated. One of Loraine's claims had been that his fervor for eating her after sex, his arousal that doing it caused—typically leading to a second round of sex, was unnatural. "I..."

"You like the taste," she stated with confidence.

He blushed, nodding his agreement.

Carila sealed her mouth to his, swirling a hint of his taste into him and firing his senses again. "You should," she whispered. "If I took you to climax in my mouth, as humans often do, the taste and the smell of my resulting arousal would make you ready for me again."

Graham nodded, taking in this new information. *Normal. Everything I do is normal.* Well, it might not be commonplace for humans, but Graham wasn't human, and he'd never been more glad of that fact.

"Would you like," she started to offer.

He looked at the portrait again. "No. I don't."

Carila scooted forward, playing the head in her welcoming body. "You want me." It wasn't a question. She didn't need to ask. Carila knew better than any woman ever did exactly what he liked.

Graham pulled back, shaking his head. "Not this way."

She nodded. "I promised anything."

He hesitated, looking toward the door. "Maybe we should—"

"Here. Trust me. It is appropriate that it be here."

"Why?" he asked, suddenly suspicious. "What is so special about this room?"

Carila smiled. "It is the sanctuary of our home."

"Sanctuary?" Graham groaned. She wanted him to have sex in a church?

"It is appropriate," she soothed him.

"Appropriate? Having sex in a church in a priest's home is appropriate?"

A frown of confusion turned her lips down. "I do not understand your words."

"Priest is... Oh hell."

Carila blanched.

"Your father is a holy man."

"Holy?" she inquired.

"A...man of your gods. Their go-between," he explained in exasperation.

She nodded. "Yes. Of course."

"And this is a holy place. A—"

"Yes." Her eyes widened. "This violates some human custom. You do not understand why this is appropriate."

"You're damn right I don't," he growled, cursing his aching body. Carila was right. Turning away from sex with a Keen woman was nearly impossible, even when it seemed so wrong to proceed.

Carila smoothed a hand down his chest. "In the days before unification, Fion's priestesses would shed their maiden's blood on the sanctuary stone. In the early days of the Ri era, kings often consummated contracts with their brides in the sanctuary, out of respect for that heritage."

Graham ranged his gaze over the portraits again. These were people who were biologically designed to be nymphomaniacs, who displayed portraits of their gods having sex in a sanctuary. Was anything taboo?

"What better place for the first mating of an Earth-Born lord?" she reasoned. "How appropriate to do it in the traditional way."

He nodded, turning her on the altar so that she supported her upper body on her forearms. Carila looked to the portrait she faced and spread her legs, pushing back toward his length for what she knew he needed.

Graham didn't stop to think about what he was doing. If he did that, he might argue it, and his sanity was strained nearly to brittle fracture, as it was. Anything that made him question what his body howled for was dangerous to him.

He filled her in a single thrust, shuddering at the feeling of being buried inside her heat. It had been too long. Graham hadn't picked up a woman since sometime during his divorce proceedings. "Two and a half years," he groaned.

Carila eased forward then back again, impaling herself on him. Graham found her rhythm, thrusting into her with increasing speed while she moved against him, matching his motions as if they were one being. That thought was too much for him. He thrust deep inside her, lodging to her cervix as his climax took over. His release seemed to go on forever, and then the swelling started.

Graham gasped as he locked in her, a tight band inside her squeezing hard around the head of his cock. He cried out harshly at the sensation, at the added stimulation that had been missing with Loraine. Carila screamed, her body milking his, intensifying the feeling of his climax.

He startled at the intensity of her reaction, afraid that he had done something incorrectly and hurt her. He ran his fingers along the column of her neck. "Are you—"

"Do not move," she gasped. "*Ferdil Fion.* The ova releases when you stimulate the band," she explained. "There is a one in fifty chance of conception."

Graham ran his lips over her shoulder, his body reacting to all of the knowledge she was imparting to him. "Every time?" he whispered. No waiting for the right time of month? A chance of a baby every time with a woman who could actually carry a baby for him? It sounded like heaven.

Carila nodded. "Multiple times in the same day increase the odds."

"How much?" And, would she let him try again?

"One in twenty-five for twice. One in fifteen for three times."

"Will you do this again?" he asked, steadying his voice so he wasn't pleading. He wanted her again. Graham didn't care if every woman on Kegin felt this good. Carila was the one he wanted.

"Yes," she assured him. "I would like that. I forfeit all claim."

The doors opened wide, and Brid strode in. His look of concern melted into pure red-faced fury. Graham groaned. He'd been set up again.

* * * *

Carila sighed. Her father wasn't angry with Graham, but the young lord wouldn't know that. This would have to be handled carefully.

"*You had no right to do this*," Brid stormed in their native tongue. "*It was not your place to test his readiness for mating.*"

"English, Father. Graham does not understand your anger."

Brid's color faded to a faint pale. "My apologies for that lapse, Lord Graham." He scowled at Carila. "And for my daughter's actions."

A slight tremor passed through Graham's body. He sighed in relief, pressing his cheek to her back and wrapping his arms around her waist.

Carila reached behind her to stroke his hair. The first mating would be shattering enough without his fear of her father. "It is fine," she soothed him. "I told you all would be well."

Brid shot her a stern look. "You took advantage," he accused. "Lord Graham has no concept of how to protect himself from the legal complications inherent in such a mating."

"He does," she assured her father.

"If he demands a Trial Moon, what will you do?"

Carila's pulse quickened at that. She hadn't set out to become Graham's mate, but the idea heated her blood.

"A what?" Graham mumbled into her shoulder, his arms tightening around her in an unconscious move as his cock lessened within her and released the band. It was a common thing for males new to mating, the urge to hold to that feeling, to stay buried in the women who brought them pleasure.

She shook her head and motioned her father for silence, halting his protest before he assaulted Graham's battered nerves further. "A *regit lus*," she crooned to him, running her fingers through his hair again in a calming gesture. "Graham does not wish a Trial Moon, Father. I have forfeited all my rights to his title and estate and agreed to bear him a child, if that is Fion's wish, with no legal hold on him or that child. He is legally protected with me."

Brid took a step back in surprise. "Why would you make that agreement?" he gasped.

Carila sighed. "*It was what he wanted, Father. He was frightened by the idea of the games Keen women would play with his love, the games that Earth women play.*"

Her father nodded.

"What did you say?" Graham asked.

Carila met her father's eyes. "I told him the truth. We were attracted to each other and wanted to experience each other. There was no need to add legal complications to that."

Brid sighed. "Very well. Lord Graham will have his heir. If he has waved his right to Trial Moon—"

"I haven't," Graham informed Brid. "I want one."

"One what?" Carila asked, dizzy in disbelief.

"The contract. The *regit lus.*"

Brid grimaced. "If he hasn't forfeit his right of demand, you must comply to the rules of *regit lus.* Have the forms been observed?"

Carila dropped her forehead to her hands, closing her eyes as Graham's cock pulsed inside her, abruptly ready to resume their lovemaking. "Yes," she admitted. "They have."

Graham shifted, teasing the head of his erection over her inner pleasure spot. "Then I want it."

"But even the penalty if I dissolve is formidable," she cautioned him. "There is no need for you to pay it. The forms allow for me to give you this, and there will be no stigma to your child."

"Do you plan to dissolve the contract?" he asked pointedly.

"No," she admitted. "I have no plans of it, but I do not want you to feel obligated—"

His hips rocked slightly back and forth, stimulating the ridge. "Are you going to refuse me and make me miserable?"

"I..."

"You have to keep your vows. Promise me you won't."

"I promised to share your bed."

"That wasn't what I asked," he replied patiently.

"I will not refuse you." *Oh, Fion. How could I refuse this? No man has ever made my body sing this way.* "You have my vow."

"Then don't fight this," he pleaded.

"She cannot fight it," Brid replied crisply. "If you call her to a Trial Moon, if you demand your rights, Carila must comply, but you are also bound. That is the law. Are you certain you want this?"

"Go away and let me discuss this with Carila," Graham decided in a voice rough in renewed need.

Brid's face went a deep crimson. "As you wish. You have until the sun rises tomorrow to revoke the call. If you do not, you are bound by Trial Moon."

"Understood."

Brid left, closing the doors behind him.

Graham left her body, turning Carila to her back and laying her out across the altar. He entered her again, rocking deep inside her, as she bowed up to his thrusts.

"I will not force you to *regit lus*, if you don't want me. Do you want me for more than this?" he asked, his eyes hopeful.

"Yes. I do want you."

"If you don't want a child..." He let the offer hang between them.

Carila shook her head in shock. He would give up the child he wanted for her?

Graham nodded, misjudging her silence. "I believed I was sterile anyway. What have I lost? How do you prevent—"

"No," she gasped. "I want a child. I want several children."

"But you—"

"You would really give up children for me?" she asked at the same time.

"If I wouldn't, I'd be no better than Loraine was. We have to want each other more than that. Otherwise, there is nothing to build on. You were willing to give up everything for a few days with me. I would give up everything for a lifetime with you—if you ask it." He swallowed some strong emotion. "The question is... Do you want it? Will you give me that?"

Carila nodded. "But not in *regit lus*," she decided.

"I don't want a mistress," he insisted. "I want a wife."

"You will have one. Contract with me. Make it clear that we are both willing, that I chose willingly to contract with you and that you were not demanding your rights simply to secure your heir from me."

Graham smiled widely. "I have your vow that you will sign the contract?"

"Of course."

"On one condition."

"Which is?" she asked suspiciously.

"We're trying out every pose in these portraits." He motioned to the wall to his right. "Including that one."

Carila glanced at it, laughing hysterically at the gods having sex while mounted on a war-buck. "Do you ride?" she asked.

"I'll learn."

"Then we will start with a mare," she assured him.

He smiled. "Agreed." Graham's gentle rocking became more insistent, his expression fierce in his barely controlled need.

Carila smiled. "There are more portraits," she informed him, nipping at the erogenous zone at the base of his throat.

"Are there?" he gasped.

"Yes. I felt it only fair to tell you that. Will we try those as well?"

"Absolutely."

He drove her over the edge of the abyss toward the soul's reward. If Fion were kind, she would conceive the first daughter of an Earth-Born lord on Kegin in the time-honored tradition of the Goddess herself.

THE END

SECTION SEVEN:

Justin

Earth-Born Lord

Earth-Born Lord

Justin Hayes sat at the table in the *magetra's* office, shifting nervously and pulling at the collar of his military uniform. The tutors provided for him assured Justin that it was the appropriate attire for a contract day, but he still felt like an imposter.

He wasn't a military man, but Justin held the rank of Captain in the royal guard. His rank was honorary. Justin could order troops. In fact, his estate was populated by two dozen soldiers that he ordered on a daily basis, but Justin had no idea how to hold the laser-edged sword belted to his hip let alone wield it. Any cadet in the Keen army would massacre him in battle, and the Earth-born queen's six-year-old son handled a dagger better than Justin did.

His title was no more noteworthy than his military rank. It was an accident of birth. *Well, aren't all noble titles?*

But, Justin's title was a bastardized version of a title, at best. *"What did I do to deserve it?"* he grumbled in the English he'd only had the opportunity to use with other Earth-born, the King, and a few servants educated in the language for his comfort.

Lord Justin hadn't earned his title—or even been born to it in the normal sense of the word. He didn't even know what noble line his Keen roots came from. He could know if he asked the Breeding Office, but what would be the point,

590

when the man who gave his genetic material had undoubtedly been dead for generations—perhaps for a century or more?

If most titles were an accident of birth, his was a cosmic joke—literally. Who knew when a six-and-a-half-foot-tall soldier stepped through a rippling doorway into the center of Justin's bedroom two years ago that the wholly unbelievable tale of his birth would prove true?

If the man hadn't known about Justin's condition, he would have dismissed the whole thing as a practical joke. *Well, maybe not. There was that doorway, and I couldn't dismiss that.*

The *magetra* smiled sympathetically. "Laes sint timetra."

Justin swallowed a laugh, his mind providing the translation almost effortlessly after two years of intensive study. Yes. Noblewomen were always late.

He sobered. He would marry Renna in a few moments, and he still didn't know for certain that this would work. Justin had only the word of alien doctors and a few Earth-born re-breds like himself that he could have children on Kegin.

The door opened, and Justin stood abruptly. Renna met his eyes and blushed deeply, just as she had every time he had seen her since the Breeding Office handled the introductions of young noblewomen interested in contracting with him. Justin had known the first time he met Renna's eyes that she would be the one he would accept.

Her father, Riel, stepped into the room beside her, offering Justin a smile and a nod. The tutors assured Justin that Lord Riel saw this as an advantageous match for his daughter, that he was pleased to have one of the new Keen lords as a close relation.

The queen herself sat as translator, though she was due to have her fifth child almost any day. She was a radiant woman, a third-generation Earth-born re-bred like himself, though she carried herself like a native after almost eight years on Kegin. Queen Susan was a shining example of what he'd been bred and brought to Kegin for, to produce the children he had wanted so desperately on Earth but couldn't have.

When the contract was sealed, the queen led Renna to him and placed his bride's hand in his. "*You may kiss the bride,*" she whispered in English.

Justin nodded his thanks and leaned toward Renna, expecting a chaste kiss. Her fervor surprised him, delighted him. His arousal was fierce and immediate. He pulled back, shaken by his reaction.

Queen Susan's smile was the widest in the room. "*Her barrier has been taken by her woman healer for you. The certificate is in the packet of paperwork.*" She left the room, trailed by her personal guard, before Justin could form a response.

His heart raced. Some men would be upset that they were denied taking their bride's hymen. Those men were largely human men with human wives. The complications of a Keen first mating were greatly reduced when the barrier had been taken painlessly by a cauter bar.

Justin grasped Riel's wrist in the traditional sign of agreement and led Renna to his private transport, his entire body humming. It would be a long drive back to his estate, but the only alternative would be taking Renna to a common inn. It would be an insult to take her to an inn, unless it was an emergency of some sort. His libido hardly rated as an emergency, no matter how overtaxed it was.

As the transport left the town and wound through the foothills, Renna slid to his side. She leaned her face up to his, nipping at Justin's lips. "Kiss me," she pleaded in Keen.

He obliged her, blindly pressing the button that would close the screen separating them from the driver and guards. Renna reached over his shoulder and pressed another button, closing thick blue drapes over the windows.

Her hands pulled at his jacket, opening the buttons in two tugs. Renna ran her hands over the silin tunic beneath.

"Renna," he cautioned her. He would finish what she was starting in the back of the transport, if she didn't slow down.

"Shhh. I know—Earth men wouldn't." She pushed his jacket off of his shoulders. "You are a Keen lord. I am your bride."

Justin untied her cloak, groaning as it slid away. She wore a presentation dress to the contract table. The ankle-length silin gown was slit neck to navel with her breasts pushed up and in, until the edges of her aerole peeked from beneath the material. A second slit reached from the hem to the crease of her left thigh.

Renna fingered the length of his cock as it rose behind his trousers. "You are a Keen lord," she whispered.

"The guards will hear."

She smiled. "And know you are what you were born to be."

Justin eyed the gown breathlessly. "I can do anything? Here?"

"You've waited two years and not taken a schente."

He blushed, shaking his head. No. He hadn't taken schente. At first, he'd equated the sterilized women with sex slaves. Justin found slavery abhorrent.

When the practice had been explained to him fully, he'd still resisted. Justin hadn't resorted to hookers on Earth, when finding a woman who wouldn't freak at his condition was difficult. He'd be damned before he'd resort to it when he lived on a world populated with women who reportedly lived for it.

Renna pulled up at his tunic, and Justin helped her remove it. She buried her face in the blonde curls sprinkled over his chest, tasting his skin with the tip of her tongue.

"Your scent is perfect—so strong."

Justin reached through the lower slit in the gown, fingering her weeping lips. He'd been told how sexual the Keen females were, but Justin hadn't expected such a heated response from a virginal bride.

Renna sucked at one of his male nipples. "Do I please you?"

"Very much," he admitted.

"The musk is more potent when taken internally," she told him.

Justin took what should have been a calming breath. Her musk settled in his lungs, a potent aphrodisiac as he was warned it would be. Yes. He had been educated in the uses of the musk in love play.

He raised his fingers to his mouth, sampling the fluid that coated them. Visions of Renna opened wide while he licked at her assaulted him. His cock surged at the thought.

"Yes," she urged him. "Take what you need."

Justin dropped to his knees in the wide expanse between the screen and the seat, thankful now that the transport seemed built for these antics. He pulled the dress back at the slit, baring her black curls to him.

Renna smiled as he spread her legs wide and eased her to the edge of the seat. "You've waited two years, Justin," she reminded him.

He groaned, dropping his head to the hearty musk calling to him. Two years? No. He'd waited thirty-two years for a woman he could call his own, for a female scent that made him ache and hunger, that scattered his thoughts.

Her flavor was intoxicating—the relaxation of shot after shot of hard Earth liquor without the bite in taste or the certain knowledge of after-effects to come. He lapped at her, sucked at her, massaged her inner walls. His head spun, full of visions of his cock traveling the channel his tongue did.

Renna twisted against him, her hands fisted in his hair. She didn't try to stifle her cries and pleas for him. Justin didn't stop until he tasted the change in her flavor, until she ground her spasming body around his tongue.

Justin pulled at the buttons on his trousers, pushing them down his thighs. She was high on her climax, as she would expect to be when he claimed her for the first time. *Anything.* He eased himself back onto the seat.

Renna didn't ask for direction. She settled astride him and guided Justin's cock to her entrance, throwing her head back as she settled an inch of him inside.

He grasped her hips. "Tell me what you want," he growled the traditional Keen phrase a male asked for first claming and every first claiming after a mother's fast.

She smiled. "*Make love to me, Justin.*"

He didn't question where she'd learned the English response for him. Justin bucked into her, drawing her hips down to seat her deep in his lap. Renna's eyes opened wide, her pupils dilated in her mating frenzy. She gripped his length, her walls hot and satiny, a feast of sensation for his starved body.

"More," she gasped. "Let your instincts guide you."

Justin drew back the silin bodice with his teeth, letting the full breasts beneath spill out to his mouth. He suckled her hard as he thrust into her again and again, shivering as she screamed his name.

Climax came quickly. As he was promised, his body guided him. He clamped her tight around him as his cum flooded her. Wave after wave of blinding pleasure drowned his senses. A strangled cry he hardly recognized as his own filled the air around them.

Justin held his breath as it happened, the moment he'd always dreaded with human women. His cock thickened another twenty-five percent. It wedged into the band of muscle at the os—the gates of her womb.

Renna screamed his name then panted out prayers to Fion, the Keen goddess of love and mercy. She kissed him, running her hands over his body, every movement frantic.

"Has it happened?" he asked as he lessened, hiding his terror that he hadn't stimulated her properly.

She reached between their bodies, bringing her fingers up with a sheen of their mixed fluids. Renna painted his lips then her own, kissing him. Justin bathed her lips with his tongue, and she did the same. His cock hardened within her again.

Renna smiled. "Yes. You know what you were born to do."

"More?" No woman had ever encouraged him to take her again.

"We have hours until we reach your estate. Love me three times before we reach the gates, and I will grant you any boon you wish."

He furrowed his brow, confused at her request. "What do you seek?"

"It took Prince Michael more than a week to impregnate his bride." Her fingers teased at the muscles of his chest.

Justin smiled. "You want to best that?"

"I want no one to ever surpass us. I want to conceive today."

His mind worked at that. With every mating within a day's time, they increased their odds of conceiving. They stood at one in fifty now. They'd be at one in fifteen if he took her three times today and one in ten if he took her a fourth. Of course, the numbers were largely theoretical. There were few Earth-born re-breds to base the numbers on so far.

"You'll increase your chance of conceiving more than one," he reminded her.

Renna pressed down hard on his length. "It took King Jole more than a month to conceive two at once and Lord Alex more than two months."

Justin lifted her to the carpeted floor, pulling her legs over his forearms. "Be sure."

She shot him a hungry look. "After I conceive, we will have the schen."

He thrust into her, reveling in Renna's scream of pleasure. Justin couldn't imagine the schen. His understanding was that the pregnant Keen female was insatiable. After thirty-two years of sexual famine, that would be reward enough in itself for three times before they reached his home.

* * * *

Justin laughed harshly as they passed the gates to the estate. His cock wouldn't lessen for several minutes.

"They'll wait for us," Renna assured him.

He nodded, pulling her cloak around her body and securing it at the neck and waist.

"You could ask anything of me," Renna whispered. "Is this truly what you want?"

Justin scanned his eyes down her body possessively. "I am a Keen lord. You are my bride. There will be no doubt of those two facts."

She blushed, pulling his jacket on over his bare back. He stilled her hands as she started to button it. Justin would enter his home looking his barbarian roots and revel in it.

He slid free of her body as his cock lessened, hiking his trousers up over his hips and buttoning them quickly. Renna brushed her fingertips over his length, and he hardened for her again. She nodded her approval.

I am a Keen lord.

Justin waited for Renna to straighten her cloak then stepped out of the transport, putting a hand out to assist his bride. Men looked away. Renna wasn't theirs to look upon. Women stared in wonder at Justin, with his bare chest visible through the open front of his uniform jacket, his tunic tucked into his beltline, a raging hard-on pressing to the buttons of his trousers, and his bride's presentation dress tossed casually over his shoulder.

There would be talk about this, the knowledge that Renna entered their home in only her boots, stockings and that cloak. Justin was half-barbarian, an Earth-born re-bred Keen lord. He was born for one purpose—to take a mate and produce the children that would make Kegin strong again.

"Send our evening meal to our rooms," he instructed the head of his household.

Justin led Renna to their rooms, gathering fluid from between her thighs as he kicked the door closed. She shuddered, her breathing ragged as he painted her lips and then his own.

"And now my reward for the fourth time in the transport," he growled. "Before the food arrives, our chances will be one in six."

THE END

ABOUT THE AUTHOR

Brenna Lyons wears many hats, sometimes all on the same day: former president of EPIC, author of more than 100 published works, owner of Fireborn Publishing, columnist, special needs teacher, wife, mother...and member in good standing of more than 60 writing advocacy groups.

In her first ten years published in novel-length, she's won 3 EPIC e-Book Awards (out of 15 finalists) and finaled for 3 PEARLS (including one Honorable Mention, second to NY Times Bestseller Angela Knight), 2 CAPAS, and a Dream Realm Award. She's also taken Spinetingler's Book of the Year for 2007.

Brenna writes in 26 established worlds plus stand-alones, poetry, articles and essays. She's a bestseller in indie/e fantasy and horror, straight genre and cross-genres thereof. Brenna has been termed "one of the most deviant erotic minds in the publishing world...not for the weak." (Rachelle for Fallen Angels Reviews) Milieu-heavy dark work is practically Brenna's calling card, with or without the erotic content.

She teaches classes in everything from POV studies to advanced editing, networking to marketing. Brenna enjoys hearing from people who read her work and can be reached by e-mail.

Website: http://www.brennalyons.com/

Facebook: http://www.facebook.com/brenna.lyons

Email: brennalyons4168@live.com

Also by this Author

Maher Men
The Blutjagdfrau Chronicles
Veriel's Tales I: Crossbearer Turned
Veriel's Tales II: Losing Regana

URBAN GRIMM
Catch Me, If You Can
Three Wishes
Temptation of Eve

WEREWOLF U
Werewolf U
Younger Daughter
Alpha Son
Never Alone
Her Christmas Wolves

ANGEL-WING SAGA
Sons of Heaven: Beldon
Sons of Heaven: Unexpected Mates
Daughters of Man: Prize Match
Daughters of Man: Claiming a Princess

COLOR OF LOVE
The Color of Love

KEGIN SERIES
Conquest
The Last of Fion's Daughters
Last Chance for Love
Rites of Mating
In Her Ladyship's Service
Matchmaker's Misery

KIELAN SERIES
The Lady's Lowborn Lover
Time Currents
Cubed

STAR MAGES
Written in the Stars

The Master's Lover

DAN AIDAN FAIRIES
Fairy Dreams
Monsters of Myth Anthology

XXAN WAR
Daahan Rising
Raashh Decisions

MYTHOS SERIES
The Punishment of Phoebus Apollo
Black Sail

IT'S ALL GREEK TO ME...
All's Fair...

SANCTUM
Dream Walk

GRELLAN WAR
With Great Power

BLOOD MAGES
Enslaved

CARSON COUSINS
All I Want for Christmas is You

FATES WAR
Fates Magic

Beyond the Veil
Mine for the Night
Once in a Blue Moon
Overtime Pay
Stay With Me
The Fire God's Woman
Nevermore
Bride Ball
Undead in Blue

Mama's Tales
Unexpected Daddy
We Shall Live Again
May the Best Man Win
Marked
And It Was Good
Monsters of Myth Anthology

Available from **Under The Moon**

Evil Overlords Union Issue #1 Anthology
Undead Embrace
"*Playing Games*" in *Forbidden Love: Bad Boys*
"*Marked*" in *Forbidden Love: Wicked Women*
"*The Master's Lover*" in *Forbidden Love: Sacred Bands*

Available from **Logical Lust**

"*Mine for the Night*" in *The Cougar Book* Anthology

Available from **Coming Together Charity Anthologies**

INSTINCT SERIES
"*Foundling*" in *Coming Together: Into the Light*
Anthology

"*Claim Mate*" (available separately and as part of the
Coming Together: Against the Odds Anthology)
"*The Fire God's Woman*" in *Coming Together: Under Fire*
Anthology

Available **self-published**

Snapshots from a Poet's Life

Award-Winning Books

EPPIE/EPIC eBOOK AWARDS WINNERS
Coming Together: Against the Odds- 2010
Time Currents- 2010
Coming Together: Into the Light- 2011

EPPIE/EPIC eBOOK AWARDS FINALISTS
Fion's Daughter- 2004
Collected Poems: Book One- 2005 (now titled *Snapshots of a Poet's Life*)
Renegade's Run- 2005
Rites of Mating- 2006
All I Want for Christmas- 2006
Phaze in Verse- 2008
"The Fire God's Woman" in Coming Together: Under Fire- 2009
Three Wishes- 2010
Matchmaker's Misery- 2010
The Cougar Book- 2011
The Master's Lover- 2011
Bride Ball- 2011

DREAM REALM AWARDS FINALIST
Last Chance for Love- 2003

PEARL HONORABLE MENTION
Night Warriors- 2004

PEARL FINALISTS
Schente Night- 2003 (now included in *The Last of Fion's Daughters*)
König Cursebreakers- 2004 (now titled *Will of the Stone*)

JOYFULLY REVIEWED BEST BOOKS OF 2010
Written in the Stars- 2010

SPINETINGLER'S BOOK OF THE YEAR 2007

NOBODY: An Anthology of Dark Fiction- 2007 (Brenna's pieces of the anthology can be found in *Beyond the Veil*)

TRS's CAPA FINALISTS
Ultimate Warriors- 2004 (Brenna's portion is now available as *With Great Power*)
Written in the Stars

LOVE ROMANCE AND MORE CAFÉ BOOK OF THE YEAR RUNNER UP
Last Chance for Love- 2008

ROAD TO ROMANCE REVIEWERS' CHOICE AWARD
Prophecy: Revelations- 2004

LOVE ROMANCES REVIEWERS' CHOICE AWARD
Black Sail- 2003

ROMANCE JUNKIES BOOK CLUB STAFF PICK
TYGERS- 2003

FALLEN ANGELS ROMANCE RECOMMENDED READ
Devon's Price-2005 (now available in *Bearing Armen*)

JOYFULLY RECOMMENDED READ
Fairy Dreams- 2008
The Last of Fion's Daughters- 2009

TREBLE HEART FINALIST
Prophecy: Revelations- 2003